EIGHT

A novel by

Dan Churach

Cover design and artwork by Dan Churach

Other novels by Dan Churach

PROOF!, 1990
BACK TO PARADISE, 2017
PROOF!, Second Edition 2019
FEVER, 2019
DREAMS, 2019

DEDICATION

For my friend, Janice Wentworth,
whose creativity knows no bounds.

CONTENTS

ACKNOWLEDGMENTS

Many thanks to Janice Wentworth, Martin Houchin, Leon Hallacher, Betty Bright, Paul Keenan, Val De Corte, Ray Kottke, Esther Kottke, Chloe Klaus, Barbara Speers, Iris Davis, Joe Cox and Graeme Thompson who have offered so much help in the past year or two. A portion of this novel evolved from an unpublished manuscript, *Journey to Mars*, which I wrote many years ago. For many of those ideas, I am grateful to my old Hawaiian mates Bruce Davis, Joe Halbig, Ernie Kho and Russ Schnell for their contribution to their scientific contribution via that work to *EIGHT*. To all of you, your knowledge, input and continued support was essential in helping me to research and to write this novel. Finally, thanks once again to my wife and best mate, Karn.

PART ONE

"It is odd, is it not, that a person's worth to society is measured by their wealth, when instead their wealth should be measured by their worth to society."

– A Cygni

DAN CHURACH

1

Thursday, 1 September; Columbia Heights, Washington DC

Sunlyn opened one eye and could see a ray of sunlight cutting through the bedroom window. She knew it wouldn't be long until the technoserver would awaken them. She rolled right next to her mate, put her arms around him and whispered in his ear. "Nicolás… I love cuddling up to you when we fall to sleep at night." She embraced him tightly, looked him in the eyes and kissed him deeply. "I love cuddling you when we wake up in the morning, when we…"

Her words were cut short by the technoserver. "I heard talking Nicolás, so I imagine that you two are awake. I have a Cat-5 message coming in, and I would have had to wake you anyway." The technoserver glowed red, indicating the severity of the message.

"Time, Shockey?"

"Five fifty-seven AM."

"Okay, Shockey – who's it from?"

"Your editor – Norm."

"Why is he calling me now?"

"Should I ask him?"

"No, no, Shockey." He looked at Sunlyn and whispered, "Stupid technoserver! I should have turned her off last night." He rolled his legs over the side of the bed. "Put him on, Shockey."

"Right away, Nicolás." A click or two was all that separated the technoserver's voice from that of Norman Crawford, Editor of the *DC POST*. "Sorry Ramos – are you awake?"

"That's a silly question since I'm talking to you... it's six o'clock in the freaking morning. I'm still lying here in bed."

"Fair enough. I'm sorry to call so early, but things are happening."

"Things? Happening?"

"Seems the Eights – maybe the *Los Ochos*..."

"Same difference!"

"Whatever – it seems they are blocking Constitution Avenue and have been most of the night."

"Blocking?"

"Yeah blocking... between the Washington Monument and the Ellipse."

"Is it still all kids?"

"Yeah, mostly – teenagers as far as I can tell."

Sunlyn sat up, dangled her legs next to him and gently put her hand on his naked shoulder as he continued. "Now wait, Norm. What the hell are they blocking Constitution Avenue with? I mean, do they have stalled trucks? Buses? Barriers of some sort?"

"Nope, just the kids as far as we can tell."

Nicolás shook his head. "So, I'm not following you here, boss. Why don't the DC Police or the Secret Service or the

Army or whoever... why don't they just move them out of there? It sounds pretty peaceful to me – they're not armed or anything, are they?"

"It's not that simple. There are thousands of them... maybe as many as ten thousand. And they are peaceful... almost too peaceful. They're basically just lying down there in the street, on the sidewalks, across the lawns..."

"Lying down?"

"Yeah. We have a reporter over there – Collins – and she's telling me she hasn't even been able to talk to any of them individually because they're asleep or in a trance or whatever..."

"Asleep? A trance? Damn... Must be drugs." Nicolás stood and grabbed his robe. He was still trying to wipe a combination of sleep and desire from his eyes.

"Frankly, I'm not sure it's confined to just Constitution Avenue. There seem to be smaller gatherings of Eights around town."

"So why are you calling me now... at SIX IN THE FREAKIN MORNING?"

"Have you looked outside your window this morning?"

"Have I looked outside my window? Aw, come on, Norm – I told you I'm still in bed. Just access Skynet. I'm sure they have a dozen cameras looking in the street outside everyone's house."

"Of course, of course. I'd like you to get into the office early, that's all."

"Okay, fair enough. If you need me, I can get in there."

Sunlyn let out a sigh in silent protest of the sudden transition from that quiet time just after waking to the cruel reality of a workday routine. She watched as he pulled the robe's cord tight around his waist. He looked at Sunlyn as she mouthed the words "I love you" to him.

Nicolás crossed the room and peeked between the closed slats on the window. The street wasn't blocked off, but there were dozens of people sitting, lying on the sidewalk and overflowing into the street.

"What's happening, hon?"

"I don't know, Sunlyn."

"Well, it ought to be pretty obvious, Ramos." Crawford's voice reminded both of them that he was still transmitting through Shockey."

"Obvious? I didn't realise..." Nicolás's words were cut off mid-sentence. A thunderous bash on the door in the next room threatened to knock the wall down. "Holy hell! You stay here, Sunlyn." He quickly ran out of the bedroom and into the adjacent living room. He looked up at just the moment the door was bashed in and fell to the floor.

Two people wearing ski masks and balaclavas burst in and fired a torrent of bullets as Nicolás dropped to the floor. He lay hidden behind the sofa, his ears humming from what sounded like semi-automatic weapons. Within a few seconds, the shooters shouted *"Larga vida Los Ochos!"*, quickly turned and ran out the door.

2

Thursday, 1 September; Mauna Loa Observatory, Hawaii

André pulled the jeep up to the charging station next to central staff building, stepped out of the car and turned towards the charging stand next to his rental vehicle.

"André! Aloha, old buddy!" The door closed behind one of the station operators as he walked over with his outstretched hand. "Good to see you."

"Same here, Russ. How you been?"

"Couldn't be better." Russ grabbed a heavy cord from its hanger and plugged it into the jeep's power socket. "This is a quick charge power point here, André – it'll top your charge up *wiki wiki*."

"Thanks for that, Russ."

"No problem. How was your flight?"

"The flight was good, but the last part of the ride up the mountain from Hilo was pretty bumpy. Don't you guys ever fill in the potholes here?"

"Aw, man... ever since the government decided to sell-off the land under the Mauna Loa Observatory, it's dropped to the bottom of the list as far as county, state or federal funding for infrastructure goes. At least we have the solar-charge battery system working overtime, or I fear we'd have to take a collection for the power bills." Russ Koyama tapped the power cord draped from the side of the jeep.

"Yes, I did hear about that."

"Damned government will sell the US Army if they can get away with it."

André grabbed his bag and closed the door of the rental. "It sure is a bit cooler up here than down at the Hilo Airport."

"Yeah, amazing what over 11,000 feet will do to the temperature... okay, okay – 3,400 metres to damned Frenchmen."

"...and I believe those SI Units work pretty well even for you Americans, too!" André patted Russ on the shoulder.

The two men entered the staff building. "How about a cup of Kona coffee, André?" He motioned to the staff table, and André dropped his bag next to it and pulled out a chair.

"I'd love one. Plenty of cream, yes?"

"I remember, André. You like a little coffee with your milk, right?"

"Right." He unzipped the side of his bag, pulled out a paper-thin technoserver and unfolded it. The technoserver flashed to life as it automatically connected with his SAM.

"That really folds up pretty tight, yeah? Does it handle anything your SAM can give it?"

"Sure can."

"Do you mind getting me a cup too, Russ?"

André turned to see a late-30-something woman enter the room. "Mikayla. Great to see you." He always thought she could easily have been a London super-model rather than a world-class atmospheric physicist. "How's Peter? ...and your baby?"

"Everyone is doing just fine, thanks for asking." She placed her more-traditional tablet technoserver on the table. "How was the flight?" She pulled up a chair to the small, steel meeting table and extended her hand towards another chair.

"Non-eventful, thankfully. It was a long one though." André sat across from her. "The flight from Casey Station to

Hobart is only about five hours or so. I spent a couple of days at the Australian Antarctic Division there in Tasmania, then through Melbourne and Honolulu to Hilo. The Melbourne to Honolulu flight was an SST, but the others were all old jet service and took forever! I think I could sleep straight through for a couple of nights just about now."

"Travel does that to you, supersonic or not. I trust that Amélie is fine, yes?"

"Yes, yes... she's doing just fine, thanks. She's still teaching — always did love being in the classroom."

"And the kids?"

"Growing like weeds and that's a bit of an understatement."

Russ returned with three mugs and placed one in front of his two colleagues. He pulled up a chair and seated himself. "Damn — that thing is small and flat." Russ looked at André's technoserver. "You always seem to have the latest gadgets."

Mikayla laughed. "That's for sure, André — I thought you have been resisting the temptation to get one of those fancy new Subdermal Angel Microchip implants."

"A SAM?" André knew she was teasing him as he threw his arms up in mock horror. "Well, you got me, lady. I never thought I'd agree to it either, but it's just so damned difficult not to join the SAM set, especially when you're on the road as much as I am."

Russ sipped his coffee as he looked at her quizzically. "So, you gave in... you've had a SAM implant? I've read about them, but I don't think I could go that route."

"Where have you been, my friend? It's the latest craze among the beautiful people back in Mikayla's London — Camden and Notting Hill and all those arty-farty places, yes?" He didn't wait for an answer. "And now they're even avoiding the need for an external technoserver. I hear the latest is a small chip with a receiver and transducer implanted in one of your molars. The chip constantly links with the SAM under the skin in your hand and carries tooth vibrations to your inner ear."

"NO WAY, MAN! Please tell me you are freaking kidding me..." Russ's eyes went wide.

"That's what I say, too, but I'm not kidding, and it is happening. In theory, you can hear crystal clear sound that way with nobody else even aware that you were listening to anything." André smiled.

"All right, you've got me. I agree that the molar implant idea IS crazy as crazy can be, but that's no reason to be picking on the more creative parts of my home city." Mikayla's radiant smile lit up the room. "As far as I'm concerned, I'm never getting any transducer implanted in my molar, but I couldn't survive anymore without my SAM. Besides, as long as you have the right technoserver, they are always there, you never forget them, and you never lose them, they can't be stolen, and they are always backed-up into Skynet. That's a damned sight better than the old-style cell phones, wouldn't you agree?"

"Yes, I agree." The Frenchman sipped his coffee. "What's the latest CO_2 reading up here?"

"We had 468.52 ppm this morning, but it's September. As you know, we always peak in May or June, just before the Northern Hemisphere growing season gets going in earnest. We hit 472.02 the end of May."

"Man... can 500 ppm be that far off?" André shook his head from side to side.

Her expression turned more serious as she looked toward their visitor. "So, what did you learn down in Antarctica, André?"

"It's not good, Mikayla." His frown deepened.

She slowly swirled her coffee mug, letting the froth spin on the top. "Well, to say the least, your concern was obvious in your last message, André. What kind of measurements are you seeing coming out of the Ross Station now?"

"In short, the entire West Antarctic Ice Sheet is in more trouble than we thought." André scratched his head. "The temperature numbers are increasing faster than modelling indicated, and mass and volume measurements don't look good. Besides that, the ocean currents aren't behaving as they usually do, either."

"Lots of calving?"

"It's worse than that, Russ. The sheet itself is increasingly beginning to simply disintegrate. There is increasing heat coming from below, coming from the water."

"Like the Larson sheet series?" Mikayla's facial expression revealed her alarm.

"Like Larson, but I don't have to tell you how much greater the volume and mass numbers are at Ross Station. We're talking metres of sea level increase if even a partial portion of the Ross ice melts." André tapped his flattened technoserver, and a beam of light raced across the room, projecting onto the white wall across from them. "Let me show you the numbers."

* * *

Both sat in disbelief at the data André just presented to them. "Can we have a copy of those numbers?"

"Sure thing, Russ." André swept his hand over his technoserver. "You should have them now."

"If what you say is even partially correct, our models may have been off by a factor of 2 or 3. How'd we underestimate

11

the outcome."

"Come on, Russ. You know how we model any physical system. We have to fit things within the parameters we have. Think back to your old doctoral studies, calculating standard deviations, having your software insert the error bars we are all so fond of, adding our cautions and suggested research to the end of our papers. You know as well as I do that we try our best to come up with the most accurate data sets possible, but we are always constrained by the limitations of our measurements. For that matter, I don't know about you, but I always try to err on the lower side of things so that I'm not accused of scaremongering. I know that you know this too well, but science, by definition, has a degree of uncertainty that can never be overcome."

"I blame old Werner Heisenberg for that one." Mikayla smiled.

"Somehow, I think that Heisenberg was pontificating on uncertainty at the quantum level, but you are correct that the result is the same. We just can't measure things perfectly. When you add to that the multiplication effect of thousands and thousands of measurements, it's obviously possible to be a long way off sometimes. And regrettably, that often causes us scientists a great deal of embarrassment and provides our friendly politicians with a great deal of fund-cutting ammunition. Over the past several decades, we have tended to be off by underestimating the effects of a warming Earth."

Russ nodded his head in agreement. "True enough, André, but now that you mention politicians, they are probably the one factor that is least conducive to modelling. Every time we thought the global community would respond to warnings based on the scientific data, it seems the politicians tended to do the exact opposite..."

"Yeah, threw their hands up and said let the other countries do it so that we don't wreck the home economy." André hung his head, tired of both travel and politicians.

Mikayla tried to manage a smile. "You look downright bushed, André."

"The flying gets to me more and more each year I do it." He used his hand to cover a yawn. "Look, I have to catch up on some sleep. Between the travel and the altitude here on the mountain, I just need to get a little shuteye. If it's okay with you two, we can finish this up in the morning."

"So be it, André... you know where the guest bunks are located."

3

Thursday, 1 September; Columbia Heights,
Washington DC

Grimms would have knocked, but there wasn't enough of the door standing for him to do so. He stepped across the rubble and into the front room. "Grimms... Detective Harry Grimms." He held his badge for Nicolás to see Metropolitan Police Department, District of Columbia inscribed on it. His partner occupied himself in the hall, recording images from every imaginable angle.

"Please, come in, Detective Grimms. I'm Nicolás Ramos, and this is my partner, Sunlyn... Sunlyn Singh." Nicolás stood up from the sofa the two of them were sitting on the far side of the room. He reached out to shake the detective's hand.

Grimms seemed almost old fashioned, taking notes on a small tablet he pulled from his pocket. "Are you sure you're both okay, Mr Ramos?"

"Yeah, yeah... we're okay, detective. They sure did a job on the wall here though, didn't they?"

"It looks like they were the world's worst shots!"

"Nah, they didn't want to shoot me. I have no doubt that I'd be dead had they wanted to take me out. I mean, look at the holes on the wall – all up near the ceiling. They wanted to make a lot of noise... wanted to send a message."

Sunlyn rubbed his shoulders. "They certainly did send a message! Dear lord... I was so afraid they WERE going to kill you, Nicolás."

"Did you see him... them?" Grimms ran his hand against a bullet hole in the wall.

"Yeah, I did see him... them. There were two of them, but I never saw their faces. They both were covered up pretty tight in balaclavas and ski masks – I think they were ski masks because I never got a look at their faces."

"Did they both have a weapon?"

Nicolás scratched his head. "You know, I can't answer that. I saw both of them, but by the time I came in the living room, the bullets were flying, and I hit the floor. I guess the sound of it all scared me so much that I just can't confirm if both had guns. I will guarantee you that they both wore the balaclavas and masks though."

"Did they say anything?"

"Yeah, yeah – they screamed out *'Larga vida Los Ochos!'* I have no doubt they wanted me to hear that."

The detective scratched his chin. "Humm... *'Larga vida Los Ochos!'* I don't speak much Spanish, but I do know that means 'long live the Eights.'"

"Yep. I do speak Spanish, and you're right on the money there. You know, the funny thing is, that's why I was convinced from the start they didn't want to hurt me."

"You mean by advertising the Eights?"

"Exactly right, Detective Grimms. Why would they want me to know they were with the Eights?"

Grimms bobbed his head in the affirmative as another policeman entered the room. He looked towards him. "This is Officer Bradshaw... Ryan Bradshaw. What do you make of it, Ryan?"

"It looks like it may have been a semi-automatic weapon, Harry, but that's unconfirmed at this point. Look at all the rounds that hit the wall here. But why you?" He looked at Nicolás. "Why would they go after you? Even if their purpose was to scare you? Would you have known them?"

"Nah – there's no way I'd have known these kids... That just doesn't make sense."

Grimms looked to his partner. "It sounds like they were Eights from what Ramos is telling us."

Before Bradshaw could speak, Nicolás was quick to reply. "No, no... I am NOT convinced that they were actually with the Eights no matter what they yelled out. They sure as hell wanted me to BELIEVE they were Eights though."

Bradshaw ran his fingers through his hair. "Why would you say that, Mr Ramos?"

Nicolás shook his head. "Look, both Sunlyn and I are journalists. I'm a managing editor at the *DC Post,* Sunlyn is a producer for GNN News Division, and both of us are based here in DC. I mean, depending on who they were, I guess either one of us could have been a target technically, but I have no reason to believe that is the case." Nicolás looked towards Sunlyn.

"I just did a rather unflattering piece on the Eights last week, though I can't say we had much feedback on it and certainly not from kids." Sunlyn volunteered her thoughts.

"And I know Nicolás has done a few pieces in the *Post* on them, too – haven't you, hon?"

"Yeah, a bit, but more from the academic point of view of why these kids are withdrawing."

"So, it could have been a story that particularly pissed a few of them off, no?" Grimms moved his head to within inches of the bullet holes in the wall.

"I guess so, detective." Nicolás gritted his teeth. "It's just that I've done a lot of background work on the Eights and from everything I know about them, they just haven't shown much outwardly aggressive behaviour. How about you, honey?"

"Yes, that's exactly right. It's the strangest thing with these kids... We've found the same thing in several of our GNN reports as far as a lack of aggression. For that matter, I'd bet you anything that none of them ever even read a news piece or watched any broadcasts at all. They just seem to veg out of everything for the most part."

Grimms tugged on his chin. "It's that bad, huh?"

"For sure... Honestly, I wish we could just get a few of them to talk. I think I'd do better interviewing zombies than these young folks." Sunlyn rolled her eyes to the ceiling. "But whatever, they sure scared the hell out of me – of us – this morning. Still..." She shrugged her shoulders and shook her head. "It just doesn't add up."

"Why's that, Ms Singh?"

"Honestly, Detective, it simply doesn't seem to fit the Eights' *modus operandi*. These kids don't seem interested enough to want to send any message. Frankly, I have to concur with Nicolás's belief that for whatever reason, they wanted us to believe they were with the Eights."

Bradshaw spoke up. "So, we have no suspects?"

"Except for the street out there." Grimms tilted his head

towards the window. "I mean, we have the street littered with dozens of semiconscious kids strewn about here and there."

"Have you spoken with any of them?" Sunlyn asked the obvious. "Maybe someone saw the shooters enter or exit the building."

"Agreed, Miss Singh, but we tried that already." Bradshaw fidgeted with his belt. "Frankly, in that respect, we're no different from you news folks. Don't think for a minute the cops are any more successful at getting any of those kids to say a word. I'd tell you they were all spaced out on something, but we know they aren't. The Department has had a team over on Constitution Avenue all night long, and it's the same thing there, only with thousands of kids. They haven't turned up one positive test for any pharmaceuticals or recreational drugs, and several hundred have been tested so far."

"Journalists, huh?" Grimms was thinking out loud. "I wouldn't have thought they know where you live. That's not the sort of thing that would be public knowledge, right?"

"No, of course not, Detective. I mean, other than friends at my office or at Nicolás's, no one would have access to our home address."

"Unless they dropped a GPS chip on one of you." Grimms tapped at his data band. "Where's your bag, Miss Singh?"

Sunlyn grabbed her bag from the bureau and handed it to him. "I see you don't trust having a SAM in your hand, detective."

"They will have to implant one of those things in my dead body, ma'am. I stick with my tried-and-true data band for communications and my paper notebook for my memory, thank you. Do you mind?"

Sunlyn nodded her approval. "No, please check it."

"Good. Now, let me see here." Grimms held his wrist over

her purse. Almost immediately, his data band started to beep. "Aha."

"Don't jump to conclusions, sir... I am a journalist, and I do use a data recorder. Your... your data band might be reading that."

"Can I have a look?" Harry pointed into her partially open bag.

"Go right ahead."

He rooted his hand around briefly, arched his brows as he pulled out a rice-grain-size pellet and held it up for Nicolás and Sunlyn to see. "Looks like I was right – I'm sure we'll find that this is a GPS tracker." Grimms looked around the room. "Do you have a technoserver in here?"

"I do."

"Would you mind if I used it?"

"No, no problem... Are you still online, Shockey?"

"I am, Nicolás."

"Shockey, could you please help Detective Grimms?"

"Certainly, Nicolás."

"Shockey?" Grimms tilted his head and looked questioningly at Nicolás as he repeated the technoserver's name. "Shockey."

"Yes, Detective."

"Could you contact District Two Go-Team."

"I have them, sir."

"This is Detective Grimms."

"We have your coordinates, sir."

"I need a Go Team over at this address ASAP."

"We'll be there in minutes, sir."

"Thanks, Shockey." He looked back at Ramos. "So, are you both really okay?"

"Yep."

"You might want to clear out of here while the Go Team is doing what they do – forensic evidence, you know."

"I can shower at work, that's no problem. I just need to get out of my robe and into some clothes."

"Likewise."

"Well okay then, Bradshaw and I will get out of your way. Oh, and please just leave everything as is until the Go Team does a sweep of the place. I'd say leave the door unlocked, but I don't think that will be a problem." Grimms smiled at his poor excuse for a joke.

"There's one more thing, Detective Grimms. Besides the balaclavas and ski masks, I remember one other thing... I noticed one of them had an old-style data band on their wrist."

"Humm..." Grimms stroked his chin. "A data band and not a SAM?"

"To be honest, I obviously don't know that they had no SAM, but I do remember one of them had a data band. I never saw any skin on the other fellow's wrist."

"You say the other fellow, so you're sure they were male?"

"I'd bet on it."

"And the second fellow had no data band?"

"I don't know that since I never saw his wrists."

"Yeah, okay. The wrist band detail could be important, but we need to find out more." Grimms took two steps towards the shattered doorway, stopped and looked back at Nicolás. "By the way, Mr Ramos... why did you name your technoserver

19

Shockey?"

Nicolás grinned. "Well, her full name is *Xochiquetzal*, but we call her Shockey since she's part of the family."

"*Xochiquetzal*? What the hell..." Grimms had no success at all in attempting to pronounce the name.

Now it was Sunlyn's turn to chuckle. "It's all in deference to Nicolás's Mexican heritage, Detective. *Xochiquetzal* is the Aztec goddess of everything feminine... beauty, fertility, sexiness..." She leaned over and gave Nicolás a kiss.

4

Thursday, 1 September; Transit between Alpha Colony and Gale Crater Outpost, Mars

"You may as well settle in. We're gonna be in our MRT for nearly two entire days." Joe Robinson had racked up more kilometres driving on the Martian surface than anyone else at Mars Alpha Colony.

"The MRT?"

Joe grinned. "Yeah, we fondly call it Mars Rapid Transit."

Lochie was mesmerised by the reddish landscape outside the bus-sized, six-wheeled rover and chuckled. "Rapid! We must be moving along at all of 50 kilometres an hour, mate."

"Hey, this is the fastest long-range vehicle we've ever had on Mars. Actually, it's the only long-range vehicle we've ever had on Mars, but it's faster than you think. We can hit 70 clicks an hour at top speed, and we never get caught in traffic." He smiled at his own sense of humour.

"On top of that, I assume the MRT is all-electric and self-driving?"

"Spot on. Powered by hydrogen fuel cells and self-navigated by both MPS – that's Mars Positioning Satellites – and small radio beacons we have put in place over the most heavily travelled trails such as this one. So, just sit back and relax. Regrettably, we haven't gotten to the point where we can have a few cold ones while travelling." Joe broke into a good laugh. "Well, I guess we could, but we'd be violating all the regs."

"No worries, mate. I can survive without a beer right now. Frankly, I just find it difficult to believe I'm actually here on Mars in the first place. I can't begin to tell you how much I'm looking forward to the journey down to Gale Crater. I should apologise in advance for being like a little kid in a playhouse here. I'd love to hike over to the site if I could, but I know it's a long, long way. I guess it's the curse of a geologist – let me feel the rocks, break the rocks, analyse the rocks..."

"Understood, Dr Greenbank. Obviously, you'd never be able to carry the amount of life support supplies you would need to walk that far, but you will have the chance to do some exploring near the outpost."

"Well, first of all, it's Lochie, please. And yes, I'm happy to stick with the MRT then. She's a beauty of a dune buggy."

"Thanks for that, Lochie." Joe's face was flushed with pride. "We basically built her here. Thank goodness we can get relatively 'cheap' transport for so many of our Earth-sourced supplies. I use the term 'cheap' loosely since the actual dollar cost is way high. Still, using the supply craft from Earth on the Hohmann orbit does help. You're familiar with the Hohmann orbit?"

"Well, sure... at least enough to follow what you're saying. Besides that, I just spent 259 days coasting along a Hohmann orbit, so I know only too well that it's the natural arc between a moving Earth and a moving Mars. Seems that's the only energy-efficient way of getting here."

"Or back to Earth, for that matter."

"Got you."

"It's funny, but the average, non-scientifically-minded person thinks you just get in a rocket and shoot straight towards where you want to go. The reality is that you simply need to follow a wider or tighter orbit until you catch up with where you want to go and hence the Hohmann orbit."

"Yes, we learned that in the training program, along with thousands of other things. As you know, they wouldn't even consider certifying anyone space-ready without that orientation program we all had to go through. Anyway, one of the instructors must have told us a hundred times that Albert Einstein made just that point more than a century ago, namely, that there are no straight lines in space. His logic made good sense when he said it, and it still does now – gravity makes everything move in an arc."

"True enough. Pardon me if I digress, but I was trying to make the point that we've gotten the more sophisticated bits for the MRT from back on Earth – electric motors for each wheel, the basics of the power plant, basic life support, some of the electronics and so forth. Then we put that all together in our own Martian-built vehicle that houses it all into one of these MRTs. You'll be impressed with just how much we are mining, refining, and manufacturing right here on Mars. Metals are easy. Plastics are more challenging since they still require a great deal of energy to synthesise carbon polymers since we have to take the carbon from the atmosphere. We keep getting more and more efficient and more and more self-sufficient."

"You mentioned fuel cells – how about the hydrogen?"

"No worries – we electrolyse water to get the oxygen for

breathing and also collect hydrogen for fuel cells."

"Who'd have ever thought there'd be enough water."

"Well, for a few dozen people here and there, there's more water than we could ever use. If you're talking about a mass migration to the Red Planet like in the old sci-fi novels, that just ain't gonna happen! Never! This planet is a god-forsaken wasteland to my way of thinking... no breathable air, cold as cold can be, radiation doses that can fry your brains, no standing water, no arable soil..."

"You don't sound too fond of Mother Mars, mate."

"We'd probably call him Father Mars, but no, that's not really the case. I really don't dislike the place... I actually like it up here in a way, but I am a realist. Let's be serious; there ain't never going to be billions of people here. In that respect, it is definitely a hellhole, but a kind of lovable hellhole." Joe laughed at himself.

"Fair enough. It's funny, but you just don't realise how much folks back on Earth follow what's happening up here. Well, at least folks on Earth who might have a bit of a technical curiosity, anyway. And for a geologist... this countryside reminds me so much of my home state of Western Australia. There are spots in the Kimberley that are every bit as red as what I see here and for the exact same reason... iron. The iron oxides make everything red."

"You damned geos are so easy to please! Just show you a few rocks, give you a hammer..." He laughed. "And don't forget, Misha Romanov was one of the original eight, so through her, I've gotten to know what a geologist is like very well." Joe Robinson got up from his seat and walked behind his passenger.

"Hey mate – what are you doing?" At first, Lochie forgot that the MRT was self-driving. "Bloody hell... sorry... I almost forgot that you don't have to pilot this thing. We're both sitting in the front of a bus-sized rover, and you walk away! Okay, I KNOW this baby drives itself, but it still is a bit shocking to see you get up like that."

"Yep, she drives herself!" Joe walked over to a pantry and grabbed a couple of squeeze bottles.

"For some reason, we've all just sort of fallen into thinking of our MRT as a girl. Is tea okay?"

"That'd be great, mate. You mentioned Misha. I chatted with her yesterday... well, I chatted with her over the holovision at least. For that matter, we have known each other for several years now, but it'll be good to finally meet her face to face. She sure knows her stuff. She's been cranking out paper after paper with all the work she's done up here, and we have traded more interplanetary transmissions that I can count."

"Understood." Joe sat down again next to Lochie. "I think you academic-types tend to measure all of life in numbers of papers you crank out."

"You found us out, by crikey! Just remember it isn't the papers that matter, rather the discoveries we make. The papers are just the bean counter's way to justify paying us a living wage."

"Gotcha. Well, you'll get to meet Misha face to face in another day or so. Lately, she's been spending way more time at Gale Crater Outpost than at Mars Alpha Colony."

"Quite understandable considering the ground-breaking Mars geology she's getting into over there.

"You don't know the half of it!"

"Well, I do know what an adventure you folks have been on. I don't just mean being the first people to live on another planet, but the decision you all made with the one-way ticket."

Robinson sipped his tea as he turned towards Lochie.

"Well, of course, that was a tough decision, but I think for most of us, it may have been a drawing card."

"How do you mean that, Joe?"

"Aw, I guess the shrinks could go on about that decision for decades – and they have – but we all had our personal reasons for choosing such a radical path. I mean, you have to admit, few decisions anyone could make were ever so irreversible."

Lochie nodded, "Oh yeah – one-way or no way! But hey, that's exactly what Jacob Jacobi put his billions up for – a one-way trip to Mars to establish a colony. I often wondered if he'd gone too far with that."

"Too far... well, don't be overly harsh on old Jake. I mean, are you blaming the guy for becoming the world's first trillionaire? The sound of that always astonishes me – a trillionaire... A TRILLIONAIRE!"

"Well, I'm not blaming him, but I've always wondered when too much wealth is too much wealth."

Joe shook his head. "I'll say this much, Lochie, you and I aren't going to solve that little dilemma of who's too rich and who's too poor even if we rode this little dune buggy from here to Alpha Centauri!"

"You're spot on about that. I didn't mean to be overly critical of him. Hell, I wouldn't be here if he hadn't been so determined at landing humans on Mars."

"Exactly! In the end, the whole point is that to have somehow built an old-style NASA system like the Americans used to do, you would need to have spent a factor of twenty, fifty, a hundred times more to add the return capabilities. For that matter, even cutting out a few of the triple and quadruple redundancies allowed the upfront money to get closer to twenty or thirty billion rather than hundreds of billions." Joe squeezed a bit of tea into his mouth.

"True, but it sure was no certainty you were even going to live long enough to even land here let alone live on the surface for so many years now."

"We all knew what we signed up for."

"I know, but I still admire you for doing it. Let's face it – that really took a lot of guts! The way it turned out, within four or five years the engineers managed to develop the return capability, anyway."

"Sure thing, but none of us could have known that when we volunteered. Return just wasn't a part of the decision-making equation. I mean, none of us thought for one minute we would ever have the chance to go back. As you just said, we were all doing a hell of a lot of 'assuming' just thinking we'd live long enough to make it down onto the Martian surface."

"I gotcha. At the time you made it, your decision was pretty damned final."

"To be redundant, it was totally final!"

"I know you haven't been back to earth, but do you think you will return someday?"

"Nah. Actually, of the original eight of us, only Elaina went back a couple of years ago. Damn... she had a heap of trouble trying to reacclimate."

"Yes, I know. Elaina Chandra – I met her briefly once about a year ago at a briefing. She had a hell of a time trying to readjust to Earth gravity. It seems she lost a lot of bone density and calcium."

"Hell, physical adjustment – that was the easy part! I think her biggest challenge was dealing with the psychological issues of being a freak – the 'first Martian' back to visit Earth!"

"So sad. I understand Mr Jacobi really has helped her out."

"Well, the best that he could. No doubt he feels responsible for all of us – the original eight for sure. I have a world of faith in Jake. Damn, I wouldn't have ever volunteered for a one-way trip if I didn't believe in him, but I suppose the man can't change human nature. It was always going to be a real carnival act having any of the first colonists go back there. That's why I'd never do it. Mars will be my final resting place."

"You'd never change your mind?"

"What... and have old Joe Robinson wind up being another museum piece. Not on your life, mate. And then there's the whole disintegration of our species happening back there..."

Lochie could read the concern on Joe's face. "I've travelled to China and to the States recently, and I hardly think it's fair to say the species is disintegrating. I mean, for sure there are lots of those crazy Eights and *Los Ochos* running around the place, but they seem more like silly kids to me. For that matter, it's not so organised, and from what I know, the kids are more regressive than aggressive, don't ya think?"

"Regressive, aggressive, organised, disorganised... I thought that by definition, disintegration means falling apart. It seems to me that if the young aren't socialised to carry on the species, then that's the end of the species, no? Hell, Australia is going through the same thing, isn't it?"

Lochie nodded yes.

"Whatever, I don't have the slightest desire to ever go back into all that. Maybe if I were an Aussie like you, I'd feel differently about it."

Lochie smiled. "As you are quick to point out, Aussies aren't immune – we have Eights, too. Every country has kids, and they all seem to be way too much into this Eight thing no matter what name they might give it..."

"Still, probably not as much as the Americans or the Chinese, ya reckon?"

"Fair enough, Joe, though the Europeans aren't far behind." He took in the Martian landscape from one horizon to the next, still coming to terms with the fact that he was actually here. "I guess in the end, you and the original eight will be a hot subject of academic study for the next century or two. For whatever reason, it all seems to have worked out. I mean, plopping eight people down in a confined, highly sterile environment with no chance of ever leaving was a feat in itself. The fact that you all more or less got along pretty well and never killed each other is quite amazing, don't you reckon?"

Joe smiled. "That's what you think, huh?

"What do you mean, mate?"

"Well obviously, that's what people back on Earth think cause that's what we transmitted from here. I don't want to overdo it since we did all get along mostly, but we had our tough times. They'll make a hell of a soap opera based on it someday." He laughed. "But I think that to the last one of us, we all made the decision to make it work before we boarded that first mission to come out here. I mean, we all knew that old Jake had confidence in us and we in him. Until this day, we all owe one hell of a lot to that man. Besides, not one of us wanted to be seen as the one who mucked things up for the whole Mars community."

"How about all the newbies? Do ya think they all feel the same way?"

"Well I sure as hell can't speak for everyone, but we're only talking what... five or six dozen mostly scientists counting the eight of you who just got here on Mission 10. As far as I can tell, we all seem intent on making this place work, even for those who reckon they'll go back in a few years. We all have a vested interest in making Mars Alpha Colony successful."

"I'm glad you are doing just that."

"But I still think humanity is disintegrating..." Joe

muttered under his breath.

"Come on, Joe, it's not as bad as you think."

"Look, I don't really mean it's bad – I mean not THAT bad – but I've just grown away from it all. You wouldn't realise that I just made 19 years in June, 19 years living away from Earth. I'm 53 years old, so I've practically spent half my adult life on Mars. I just think so much has changed. I like being out here with no one looking over my shoulder. I enjoy the people I work with, the sense of independence I have. Frankly, I don't want to be in the middle of all that hustle and bustle. For example, every time I read about those freaking SAM chips, I get queasy."

"Ah, come on, Joe... it isn't as nasty as you think."

"Do you have one?" Joe's eyes lifted in surprise.

"No, no... not now. I did have one, but they took it out before we left. I don't think SAMs would be so valuable up here."

"Hell, I can't quite figure why they're valuable back there."

"Come on, Joe, it's the 2040s... It's just that the SAMs are so reliable, I guess. You don't lose them... you don't forget them... they're always with you."

"But you still need a device of some sort, don't you?"

"Well yeah. You need a technoserver of some type, but it all depends on what you need."

"Techno, scmechno... it doesn't make sense. How do you know what you need?"

"If you want to read, you use a reader, and those things are so small now they're like carrying a piece of folded paper. As for audio, holovision, projection, 3D vision masks and whatnot, almost everywhere you go they have those generic technoservers there for you to use, *gratis*. It's just that your own, personal SAM has all the data storage and links you can possibly use, and the technoservers are the outlets. You needn't carry the technoservers with you."

"Well, thanks for that explanation, Lochie. It all sounds so nice and so safe and so un-hackable." Joe rolled his eyes in disbelief. "I think I'm still happy to be a Martian. You know, in light of these sort of things, I think many of my fellow adventurers out here are starting to think the only intelligent life in the solar system might be right here on Mars." It was noticeable to Lochie that Joe didn't smile.

5

Thursday, 1 September; GNN Offices, Washington DC

Sunlyn walked into the office just as a half-dozen colleagues gathered around the big holographic image in the middle of the room. One of the assembled staff members called out, "Look at this..."

She joined the group as a holovision image of a GNN reporter appeared. The young woman stood amid thousands of young people with the White House visible in the distance.

"...Holly Banks reporting from in front of the Ellipse on Constitution Avenue here in Washington DC. This mass of young people started building yesterday afternoon and by nightfall had grown to thousands. DC Metro Police are telling us there are several thousand people here and, to this reporter's eyes, I'd estimate that nearly all of them that I have seen are between the ages of maybe 13 or 14 and 17 or 18."

The off-image voice of a news anchor asked, "Holly, have the DC Police or any other law enforcement people tried to move the crowds?"

The reporter held one hand to her ear and nodded once she heard the question. "Dennis, I have spoken to several officers this morning, and I can tell you that they have tried to do just that, but they have not been successful."

"Why is that, Holly?"

"Most of these young people just don't seem interested... in listening, in talking, in moving..." The reporter bent down until she was within a foot or two of several adolescents who appeared to be sleeping. "Have you been here all night? Are you planning to stay all day?" She held her microphone towards them, but there was no verbal response. One drowsy young girl looked up with half-open eyes. She moaned, slowly waving her hand as if to say, 'go away.' The reporter again tried to ask similar questions of another girl and then a boy. They both responded in a similar fashion, namely, with little or no response.

"You can see, Dennis, that the police definitely have their hands full here. I've been told that the current plan is to treat this as a medical emergency and attempt to evacuate these young people to emergency facilities. The difficulty, of course, is that it seems the only way that can happen will be to carry these people out and into an ambulance using stretchers. One problem they face with this plan is that there are not enough gurneys, ambulances or professional staff to move the hundreds, even thousands of young people here, along with even more around other parts of the city. A second obstacle is where could they possibly take that many kids. The reports we are getting from local DC hospitals is that they are overflowing and just don't have space for this many people."

"Is there any indication of casualties, Holly? Is there any evidence of poisoning or drug use?"

"From everyone I have spoken to, Dennis, there have been no reports at all indicating drugs, poisons or any other chemical factors involved here. Usually, in large crowds like this that form to protest or demonstrate, we generally witness so much energy, so much spirit amongst the participants. As a journalist, I'm used to having people WANTING to talk to me, to voice an opinion about which they feel strongly. In all my years of reporting, I have never witnessed so many people so lethargic... so lifeless. I will continue to monitor the story and report back as soon as I have more information."

"Man, this is so bizarre." Bureau Chief Glenn McDermott turned away from the holovision, waved his hand, and the volume went down. "We've been getting reports like this for the past few months now – little groups of teens in varying degrees of stupor simply lying down and refusing to respond to anything."

One of the staff reporters let out a deep breath. "My contacts are telling me it's a global happening now."

"You're not the first to tell me that. We've had the same reports from across the country and even out of China, Europe, Australia now... The numbers involved were mostly smaller overseas, and generally, many of those incidents have been confined to a few dozen kids at most, but this isn't limited to just the States. I think in Beijing the other day there were 20-25 kids reported as comatose in a park there. But for some reason, right here in Washington seems to be ground zero for whatever this outbreak is with a literal explosion of kids joining in. What the hell is going on?" He noticed that Sunlyn had come into the office at the beginning of the broadcast. He looked right at her. "Hi, Sunlyn. Did you find any hint of what this is all about in that piece you did last week?"

Her head bobbed around almost as if to gesture both yes and no. "Well, you are correct, chief, in that the District is a particular hotbed for these kids, with way higher numbers involved here than anywhere else so far. As for the behaviour... I cannot give you anything definitive, but we certainly can confirm the lack of aggression. Damn... we actually used the term 'regression' in describing their behaviour. The kids are NOT aggressive, they ARE regressive."

"Amazing. Regression... talk about a whole different problem from what we're used to."

"Well, don't go too far down that trail. It's not ALL regression." Sunlyn looked at the small group of colleagues there in the staff room. "Around six this morning, Nicolás and I woke up to noises in our hallway. He got out of bed headed for the living room. No sooner did he get there than the front door was knocked down, and shots were fired into the room."

"My god Sunlyn!" McDermott gave her a closer look. "I thought you were a bit frazzled. Are you both all right?

"Yes, yes – we are both fine and uninjured, but I admit it was a hell of a way to wake up!"

"Any indication of who could have done it?"

"Well, the two guys – we think they were guys – who were the shooters yelled '*Larga vida Los Ocho*' loud and clear."

"Oh boy, 'long live the Eights'... so, it was the Eights."

"I don't know... don't know..." She raised her open hand as if to wave off the suggestion. "Nicolás was more doubtful that they were actually Eights as much as thinking they wanted us to believe that they were Eights. Consider Holly's report there. Think about the trend we are all seeing, the regressive behaviour. Shooting up our front door really doesn't seem to fit with other actions these kids are displaying. I'm not ready to say there is no connection, but the people who shot up our front room and the kids piled up in the streets are coming from very different mental spaces."

A young-ish intern hurried into the room and handed a note to Glenn. "For you, Mr McDermott."

Glenn glanced at the note for a few seconds and then grimaced. "Well, son-of-a-bitch... that didn't take long!" He looked up as he absent-mindedly folded the note. "From sea to shining sea. Our LA office is reporting a very similar scene unfolding out there... a few hundred kids behaving the exact same way." He folded the note and dropped it into his shirt pocket. "Okay, would you all start working your phones and pounding the pavements. We need to get to the bottom of this. Something is happening, and I want to know what the hell it is."

The little groups quickly broke up. McDermott turned abruptly. "Singh, please come into my office. I have a new assignment for you."

* * *

She preceded him into the office as Glenn closed the door behind him. "A new assignment? I thought you'd let me follow up on the Eights, boss."

"I know you did... but I have something bigger in mind — much bigger."

"Bigger? What could be bigger than a, a..."

Glenn didn't allow her to finish her question. "You've obviously heard of *Thánatos*."

"Obviously. That's the big asteroid that is heading towards Earth coming in over the North Pole."

"That's correct."

Sunlyn looked at her boss as she squinted her eyes. "Wait a minute... meteors? Look, I've heard and read about *Thánatos*, but this is me you're talking to, chief... I'm not a scientist."

"Stay with me here, Singh. That meteor – I think the astronomers are calling it an asteroid – may be more than it seems."

"More than it seems? Ah yes, the marches, protests... I saw on our feed last night that maybe 50,000 marched in Paris yesterday, and similar numbers are coming out around the globe. There were tens of thousands of 'the-end-is-near' demonstrators in New York City yesterday."

"Well yes, you're right about all that, but I am thinking beyond that. Forget the demonstrations for a minute. We have it from the experts that the asteroid may break into pieces. No doubt we'll find that out in the next few hours. I've been told it will release a huge amount of energy, and no one knows just what the hell that all means. Quakes? For sure... Tsunamis? Obviously, that depends where they impact. Every indication is that these will hit way up in Siberia and few people are around there to feel the immediate effects from it all. The problem is that we hear that quakes up there may behave in some very peculiar ways on a more global scale."

"Now wait a minute, Glenn... It sounds as though I have to say this again – you KNOW I'm not a scientist, right?"

He nodded his head yes.

She continued. "I mean, I certainly know that when a quake or tsunami occurs, the damage caused can be quite substantial. I also understand what you are saying here is that we are fortunate that the impact and the after-effects will most likely happen in a place that has way more reindeer than people."

"Well that's true, but as I said, the peculiarity isn't with the local population." Glenn was intent.

"Well, what's the 'peculiar behaviour' you are talking about here?"

McDermott took a deep breath. "It seems there could be some very unusual geological events that happen up there, and I'm not sure it's all so obvious as to exactly what they are. That said, we hear that this could be the story of the century."

"Story of the century?" Sunlyn was immediately interested. Her curiosity was aroused though as to why her Bureau Chief was talking to her about this. "Jeez, thanks boss, but asteroids, seismic events, geological oddities ...I think you probably should have Yates in here? Not only that, but we've known about *Thánatos* for months now and surely you and GNN would have people on assignment already."

"Don't get ahead of me here, Sunlyn. Of course, we assigned a couple of teams to this a while ago. And yes, Owen is a science guy, and I've already spoken to him about it. He reckons this is a big deal – a VERY big deal – and he has already accepted this assignment. I already have him coming at this from the technical side exactly as you are suggesting here. If this is as big as he's telling me though, we need to put another team on it with a different slant on things than just the science. We need to come at this from more than one perspective... more than strictly the technical side of things. Frankly, your lack of scientific background will be POSITIVE for us. You have a pretty strong background in social science, yeah?"

"Journalism."

"But your résumé shows you did a lot of psychology, yes?"

"Sure, boss. I did a double major – journalism and psych, but what in god's name does that have to do with asteroids? Astronomy? Seismology? They are so far out of my training, my..."

"Well, that is exactly what I'm saying, exactly what we need. Save for the big city demonstrations, I think everyone else is looking at this as a science-only story. I think GNN has to go beyond that... has to look at the human side of it all. You know that millions and millions of people couldn't give a rat's ass about an asteroid's chemical make-up or it's orbital mechanics or any of that. They want to know what the consequences are for their families, their jobs, how it will affect their everyday lives... the psychological, social and political effects of this thing could be huge."

"I think you're absolutely correct, Glenn, but I..."

McDermott refused to let her protest. "Look, I've got to level with you here. Nominally, the story is *Thánatos*, but that's only part of it. For that matter, I've already confirmed your suspicions that we already have teams of reporters in place to cover the actual impact and whatever the aftermath might be. I want you and Owen to take a different slant on this, to do the 'rest of the story' story, as it were. What do you know about the Global Holistic Summit?"

"Not much... only that it will take place in China in the next week or two and a lot of very bright people will be attending."

"Yes, exactly – Shanghai, China. That's where I want you and Owen to start. I want you to look at the angles no one else will be looking at. I have a feeling the Global Holistic Summit is going to be the focal point of a lot of news in the next few weeks."

Sunlyn's expression transformed from concern to curiosity. "So, do I hear you saying no asteroid?"

"Not so fast, Sunlyn. *Thánatos*, yes, in a way... but I want you and Owen to cover it from the perspective of the Global Holistic Summit, rubbing shoulders with the top brains on this planet. I think that coming at this story from the angle I'm suggesting can best be done in China, at least for a start. I've made some contacts with this Australian ecopsychologist, Professor Kylie Childs, and I've organised for her to speak with as many of the staff that we can round up here. I think you will like Kylie."

"Ecopsychologist, huh? Sounds like you know her, boss."

"We've met. I heard her speak before and I thought she was great value, which is why I invited her here today... this afternoon. I know it's a last-minute thing, but she just happened to be here now. She seems to fit right into what we're looking at here. She's also about to head off to Shanghai herself, so better you make contact here in Washington. Besides that, you'll be fascinated with her work. That's why I double-checked your résumé and noted that you did a double major with the psychology. Childs is a psychologist of some renown."

"This is sounding better and better, boss."

"Well, that's what I was hoping. I just figure that your non-physical-scientist point of view will allow you to dig into corners of this story that will go way beyond the technical. So often we do these assignments that involve a lot of scientific happenings in such a matter-of-fact style that makes the average viewer bleary-eyed. We need to bring this highly technical event to the non-technically minded, to bring this story to life, as it were. Like I said, we need to connect with the average woman, the average man. We've been missing that human side of science and technology for decades."

Sunlyn scratched her head. "I think I'm flattered, boss, but why me?"

As if it suddenly dawned on Glenn that she had just been through a shattering ordeal, he seemed to catch himself as he shook his head from side to side. "I'm an insensitive bastard, aren't I?" He didn't give her time to respond. "I can't ask you to leave Nicolás after what happened this morning."

Sunlyn had mixed emotions, but she couldn't bring herself to refuse what could be a chance of a lifetime. "Look, boss, I'm not saying no... I'm not saying yes... I'm only asking why you want to put me on a science story."

"Singh, this is WAY more than a science story. I think this might be the biggest story ever... EVER! You see, I reckon you are a true journalist. You know, the broadcast news business is filled with pretty reporters, but I always respected your work because you are a true journalist who is not afraid to roll your sleeves up and get to the bottom of things. You've gone from reporter to producer and haven't skipped a beat. You're the best I have... probably the best I've ever had. I want you to share the lead up there because I know you'll put together a story that all our viewers will understand. How's that for a challenge?"

"Damn! It sure sounds like one hell of a big challenge to me."

"Look, you know as well as I do that young grads break into this business making interesting stories seem important. But you've been around long enough to also know that the mark of a truly great journalist is taking stories that are of great importance and writing them in an interesting enough way so that the masses will understand them. You can do that, Singh... we NEED you to do that, Singh."

Sunlyn ran her fingers through her hair and paused long enough to cogitate on McDermott's words. "Thanks for that vote of confidence, boss." Sunlyn's head was slowly nodding her understanding. "You've really piqued my interest, and I'd consider it an honour to accept this opportunity... but I do need to talk with Nicolás about it first."

"Totally understood."

"I can do that ASAP though."

"Good thing... we're damned close to impact, so if it's at all possible, maybe you could do that sooner than later. It's just that you'll be on the road for a bit. If I were you, I'd be packing enough for a few weeks at least."

She slowly bobbed her head in understanding. "Thanks, chief... I think. I'll get back to you this morning."

He smiled. "Sunlyn..."

"Yes"

"Good luck."

6

Friday, 2 September; Gale Crater Outpost, Mars

While the two passengers slept through most of the Martian night, the rover ceaselessly rolled over the alien landscape. Shortly before dawn, Lochie awoke to a spectacularly glowing sky. He sat up next to the big front window and let himself be awed by the brightening sky until a noticeably smaller sun poked itself over the horizon. It was another 45 minutes until Joe stirred and noticed Lochie riveted to the window. "That's one hell of a view, isn't it?"

"You can say that again."

"How about I fix tea for both of us?"

"That would be great, mate."

"Have you tried the bubble?" Joe waved his hand at the

pop-up glass dome in the middle of the rover.

"No, but I'm onto it now." Lochie moved over to the small ladder and took three steps up into the glass observation bubble protruding out of the rover's roof.

"How's that for a panorama... I love the three-hundred-and-sixty-degree perspective you get out there."

"For sure, mate." Lochie looked down and saw Joe handing him the tea. "I mean, I know exactly what to expect in terms of how things look around here from all the photos and holographs, but the emotive feeling of actually seeing all this with my own eyes is rather awe-inspiring."

"Well, don't let me bother you. I'm going to check for updates and any news that may have come in overnight. You might as well enjoy yourself up there."

Without hesitation, the Aussie settled into his perch in the MRT's glass bubble. "Bloody hell... this is fantastic! It's still fairly dark out there, and the stars are still twinkling, though dawn is starting to chase them away."

"Of course, Mars has a pretty damned thin atmosphere compared to Earth. Look over there." Joe waved his hand towards one side of the bubble. "You see that bright, blue morning star above the mountains off in the distance?"

"Sure do."

"That's our point of origin, Lochie."

"Holy bloody... that's the freakin Earth! Again, it's all quite obvious, but actually SEEING home in the Martian sky is overwhelming."

"Yep... it sure is."

"Damn..." Lochie focused in on his home planet and let his mind wander. All he had ever known... all his species had ever known... all on that one, blue dot in the Martian sky. He was so very conscious of the contrast – the blue dot filled with water, warmth, air, life... as seen from the desolate, frigid, oxygen-starved, lifeless planet he now travelled across.

As the dawn grew brighter, he spent more time looking at the surface than the heavens, inspecting every boulder and outcrop that the MRT passed. He took the bottle of tea Joe had brought him and quietly spent a good portion of the Martian morning with his head popped up in the glass bubble, quietly captivated by the landscape over which they trekked. A few hours before reaching their destination, a ridge-like feature slowly grew across the entire vista spread before the rover. Lochie fixed his eyes beyond the ridge at the mountain peeking through on the opposite side, seemingly growing higher and higher with every kilometre they covered.

Of course, he was well aware of the fact that Gale Crater was a giant impact feature that had been formed more than three-and-a-half billion years ago. The actual basin resulted from a giant asteroid slamming into the planet and tossing rubble across the Martian surface for a hundred kilometres. He knew that he was looking at Mount Sharpe, higher than any mountain in all of his Australian home and even higher than Mont Blanc in the European Alps. Besides such prominent features as a 150-kilometre-wide crater and a 5,000-metre-high mountain in the middle of it, Gale Crater was one of the first places scientists looked for signs of life when they landed the mechanised NASA explorer *Curiosity* there some 35 or 40 years earlier. It had been apparent for many decades now that Gale Crater had once formed a giant salt-water lake and much of the terrain was shaped by running water and wind erosion. It seemed that all the ingredients for simple life had been there, though if life ever had evolved here, it most likely would have become extinct quickly once the surface water and thicker atmosphere disappeared.

Lochie eventually came down from the bubble and rejoined Joe, both of them now settled in the upholstered bucket seats with an upfront view out of the big windscreen. "Anything exciting in the overnight updates?"

"Most of Earth is abuzz with the impending impact of *Thánatos*. How the hell you can protest an asteroid is beyond me! And those crazy 'Eight' kids seem to be spreading... and doing nothing at all but lying on the streets and acting all spaced out."

"Bloody hell, I wonder what that's all about?"

"Damned if I know. If they would have been rioting, you'd reckon it was business as usual... But hell – they seem to be so quiet, so withdrawn from it all. This crazy stuff is very weird, very unsettling, don't you think?"

"I do, Joe."

The two of them sat there watching the Martian landscape roll by the MRT's windows, all the while chatting, having lunch, capturing an occasional close-up image of some feature Lochie spotted. After several hours of constant travel over varying terrain, the MRT finally neared the Gale Crater Outpost station.

"There she is, Lochie."

The new arrival had his eyes glued on the outpost for the past few minutes. "Yeah, I've been watching."

The rover's AI system doing the navigating was precise in its approach, slowly circling the station while automatically communicating with the outpost AI. The autopilot slowed to a crawl as they covered the last few hundred metres up to the station.

"Here we are, buddy."

"Oh boy – Gale Crater Outpost. Who'd have ever thought I'd be seeing what I see here, mate?"

"Well pinch yourself, Lochie, because you are in fact seeing it."

"Do you know who Gale Crater is named for?"

"Damn... I've been back and forth a dozen times, and I know all about the place, but I can't say I know where the name originated."

A flash of pride crossed Lochie's face. "Well mate, she's named after an Australian amateur astronomer, Walter Frederick Gale, from Sydney, Australia. I've read a lot about him and know that he must have spent countless nights exploring Mars with a backyard telescope he built himself in the late 19th century."

"How about that... named after an Aussie."

"Wow, we're actually here! I feel like a kid, mate." He kept his eyes glued on the expanse of the outpost. The facility consisted of two domes, one about 20 metres in diameter and the second about half that size. It was at the foot of a shallow cliff running out from the ridge, and a two-metre-high tube ran from the second dome into the side of the cliff face. "Not nearly as big as Mars Alpha Colony..."

"...but every bit as comfortable." Joe interrupted. "You also aren't seeing the whole thing since living quarters and staff emergency quarters are all below ground. That's been a mark of construction up here since it is a cheaper way to insulate and you have the added protection against any nasty radiation storms."

"That all makes perfectly good sense."

The AI brain of the rover was in total control as it lined up the vehicle with a slowly opening bay door in the side of the larger dome. "The outpost is small, but it has everything you need here and can comfortably accommodate up to fifteen people and probably more if need be. Besides that, the rover is fully automated, so it keeps a regular schedule of round trips up to Alpha Colony and back whether anyone is onboard or not. That's a real positive since they can ship whatever we might need down here within a few days." The rover entered into a small garage just big enough for the vehicle to squeeze into. Once they came to a full stop, the bay door behind rolled back into the closed position.

"Airlock?"

"You've got it, Lochie."

It was obvious the small room was pressurising from the puff of dust particles circling the side windows of the rover. The red light in front of them began to brighten to an amber colour. Greenbank nodded his head. "Pretty quick getting the pressure up."

"Sure is. That was why they designed a room with such a tight squeeze – less wasted air." By the time Joe finished his statement, the amber light had transitioned to a deep green. "Look, don't worry about your gear. The techies will unload that along with the provisions and other equipment we brought over. We never waste a trip and try to fill the storage area in the back right up to the ceiling with supplies."

"And the MRT... what'll she do now?"

"After they unload her, she'll take on more hydrogen and oxygen for the fuel cells and life support, top up her batteries and the techies will give her the once over before she heads back to Alpha to get the next load. We continuously catalogue rock and soil samples from all in and around Gale Crater and then send samples back up there. Generally, that is a much smaller load than the supplies that come down here. After a quick turnaround, the MRT heads back north again... It's one of the nice things about a totally independent rover – she just does her work and never seems to complain."

"So, in an emergency, we're on our own until she gets

back?" Lochie showed a bit of apprehension in his eyes.

"Nah, nah... we have a couple of backups, though smaller and built to just carry personnel."

"Fair enough, mate."

"Once we get past the airlock, we'll get you settled." Joe pointed out the windscreen now as the entire wall in front of the rover glowed green. A second bay door quickly rolled up revealing a much larger garage-like room with a second rover, several smaller surface vehicles and a variety of mechanical equipment neatly organised within. A techie walked toward the little rover. The door swung wide. "Hello, Professor Greenbank. Welcome to Gale Crater Outpost."

Lochie undid his seatbelt, wiggled his way out of the door and extended his hand toward the technician. "It's great being here. And the name's Lochie, mate."

* * *

Greenbank surveyed his small living quarters. He was amazed at just how large the accommodation was considering that Gale was merely an outpost and not Alpha Colony. Besides the bed, desk, a couple of comfortable chairs, a holovision port and an ensuite, there was ample space to stow what little personal gear he had. A quick glance in a drawer revealed several sets of Mars Colony coveralls. The wall cabinet across from a small basin was stocked with toothbrushes, razors, soap and toiletries.

"Lochie... We finally get to meet in person."

He turned towards the open door. "Dr Romanov... Yes, at last. I feel as though we've been video conferencing forever." He reached out and shook her hand.

"I trust your trip down to Chase was good."

"Naturally. I'm on Mars! I could have ridden shotgun on a stagecoach to get here, and it would have been a great trip!"

"I fear that's a bit of an exaggeration, but I take your point." Misha smiled at him. "We have so much to catch you up on concerning the project. We seem to be making finds every day lately. I'm happy to have you settle in. I know the trip down from Alpha Colony is a long one and fortunately, you didn't have to take a stagecoach. The MRT rover is an amazing beast, though, isn't she?"

"She is."

"And the accommodation?"

"I'm impressed. From what I have seen so far, it seems very comfortable, spacious even."

"Well, you're below the surface here in the living area, but of course that is all as much of a safety feature as it is a cheaper method of construction."

"Yes, Joe filled me in on that... all quite sensible."

Misha's expression quickly transformed from a relaxed smile to a wrinkled-eyebrow seriousness. "I wanted to speak with you alone first just to update you personally. While you were coasting out here from Earth, we made a startling find that, so far, we have not released to the public." She did not want to tease her new colleague and got straight to the point. "Almost two weeks ago now, we found life... life here on Mars."

Lochie's jaw dropped, but before he could muster up a word, Misha continued. "I apologise that you haven't been told this until now, but we decided not to broadcast via radio yet and frankly, I wanted to be the one to tell you since you are now a member of our Gale Outpost team."

Lochie's mouth was still agape, and his eyes wide open. "Did I hear you correctly? Did you say you found life?" He simply had to double-check what he thought he heard Misha say.

"Yes, you heard me correctly – we found life."

"WOW!"

"Wow is right!"

"Here at Gale Crater?"

"No, no." Misha's face was filled with excitement. "It was found while drilling for new water supplies a few kilometres from Alpha Colony. Now, I am not a biologist, and I will leave much of this for Nigella to explain, but I can tell you this – the life form is as advanced as unicellular life and way beyond mere replicase."

"Replicase?"

Misha smiled. "Yes, I know, Lochie, I am a geologist, too, and I am not familiar with all the biological jargon, either. Again, Nigella explained to us that the earliest of mother nature's attempts at life began with what the chemists – and biologists – call a 'replicase' which is basically a molecule that can make copies of itself."

"A replicase."

"For whatever reason, though, a replicase may still not be what we call alive. I can't explain any more detail to you than that, but when you meet Nigella, I am sure she can answer any questions you might have."

"Okay, I gotcha. And what you are saying is that it's NOT that, NOT a replicase whatever the hell that is – right?"

"Right! Whatever they found is absolutely alive."

"Damn! And how do they know that?"

"I'm a geologist, but I understand that a replicase is an enzyme which acts as a catalyst in replicating nucleic acids.

Yes, I know... that's all hocus-pocus to us geos... In short, I believe replicase is basically a chemical and can't do what they do without life present. Nigella tells me that, at most, they are protocells. Whatever they have found up there is actually reproducing itself and carrying out life functions in a similar way to Earthly unicellular life."

Lochie respectfully chuckled. "I forgive you for explaining biology to me as though you were a geologist. You shouldn't be surprised to hear that I understand your explanation the same way – like I was a geologist. Obviously, there's a good reason for that since we are BOTH geologists." The two of them laughed. "I guess the bottom line is that this is astounding! What is the plan for releasing this news to the public, to the Earth-side press?"

"We are keen to do that almost immediately, but there is more to the story."

"More?"

"I apologise for once again stating the obvious, but I know that, like me, you are a geologist and you came here to do geology. I promise you that will transpire in due course. You just happened to step into the middle of the biggest find anyone has ever made as far as I can tell."

"Microbial life on Mars – bloody hell, I would think that to call this the 'biggest find' may actually be an understatement."

"Well... You need to hear me out because there is more..."

"Yes, I heard you say more, but how could there be more than finding microbes? Go on..." Lochie scratched his head as a puzzled look crossed his face."

"Yesterday – after you and Joe left Alpha Colony – we stumbled across something astounding – even more astounding than the microbes at Alpha Colony."

"More astounding? Surely you couldn't top finding cellular

life."

Misha looked around the room as though she was checking for spies. "Lochie, I'm sorry for dumping all this on you at once, but we've found something way more amazing than that!"

Lochie stared intently. "Surely you aren't afraid to speak about this out loud?"

"No, no – don't be silly. It's just that... just that I almost find this hard to say so soon after..." She touched the fingertips of one hand against those of the other and took a breath. "It's totally coincidental, and as far as I can see, one find is totally unrelated to the other, but we found an artifact yesterday morning."

"An artifact?"

"We don't know what else to call it. Siti and Keegan – you will meet both shortly – were over in one of the nearby lava tubes – Tube 14B. The funny thing is that it's close to the outpost here, but we somehow overlooked it for months."

"Overlooked it?"

"Don't ask. You'll eventually see for yourself, but the mouth is well hidden by boulders and other debris. Anyway, they were just about ready to head back to the outpost when Siti saw a shiny reflection in the middle of the cave. She instinctively walked over to see what it was and found this artifact... At this point, we think it's some kind of coin-like piece or a medallion, but this is all yet to be determined. Remember, no one came down here to Gale Crater looking for life, especially intelligent life..."

"Well wait a minute, Misha..." Lochie interrupted her. "Didn't NASA land a car-sized surface rover here back at the beginning of this century – it was named *Curiosity* if memory serves me correctly."

"Exactly right..." She nodded her head. "*Curiosity* landed not far from here inside Gale Crater about 30 years ago in 2012, to be exact."

"Of course. I have read extensively about the rock and mineral samples *Curiosity* evaluated during its active time. I know that your team has followed up on that, too."

"We have."

"The whole point of landing a rover here was that Gale Crater probably had water in the past and that maybe it'd be a good spot to see if any life had developed here, right?"

"Well yes, that is true. But *Curiosity* found nothing that led anyone to believe there was life that HAD formed here. Even more, any life on Mars certainly wouldn't have evolved into intelligent life forms. Mars just never had the conditions that would have favoured that extensive pathway of evolution. Even when the atmosphere was thicker several billion years ago, it didn't last long enough for any long-term evolution to take place... at least not by any processes we know about."

"Understood."

"Now as far as reporting this find to everyone back on Earth, we find ourselves in the lead of an incredible discovery, and we'd damned well better do this right. For starters, what seems to be an artifact has obvious implications of an intelligent lifeform. We certainly have no intention of hiding this, but you can see why we can't release the find until we have a better grip on it. Can you imagine what this knowledge will do back on Earth?"

Lochie exhaled a stream of air. "Damn... no I can't. To be perfectly honest with you Misha, I don't think anyone could really imagine what it all means! So, who knows about this?"

"Of course, I already told you the cellular life is still only known to us Martians. As for the artifact, we haven't even reported this to Alpha Colony as yet, so it's just our little team here at Gale Crater."

"Is it wise to keep this quiet?"

"No, no – I swear, we won't keep it quiet. We only made the discovery within the past twenty hours or so. Frankly, I wanted to see the site with my own eyes first, and so I decided to wait for your arrival. I thought it best that we all visit together. You may be the newbie, but when we have an outpost staffed with less than ten people, we better all be on an equal footing."

"Understood and thanks for that, Misha. So, everyone at Gale Crater Outpost knows?"

"Just the science team, not the technical staff... all two of them. I won't keep it secret though and will fill them in tonight."

"Oh boy... and here I thought the biggest news of the century was the asteroid hurtling towards Earth."

"Speaking of which, when it rains, it pours... we will start the team meeting in about half an hour, and we are meant to get an update on that. I apologise in advance for putting you right to work, but there is so much happening all at once."

"No apology needed, Misha. I have travelled for 259 days of reading, sleeping and peddling the bike, all just to get to this point. Bloody hell, I can't tell you how eager I am to finally get going. To be honest, I thought there could never be anything more exhilarating than just being here... and now you tell me..." Lochie took a deep breath. "The revelation you just shared with me about first finding unicellular life... and now finding evidence of intelligence... damn."

"See you in the staff room in 30 minutes?"

"There's nothing that could keep me away."

7

Friday, 2 September; Metro Precinct Station, Washington DC

"We got the lab report back, Sarge."

Grimms looked up from his desk. "On the shoot up in Columbia Heights? You mean the Irving Street place?"

"That's the one. At least we know it's a DC branch of the Eights. The lab guys traced the GPS chip you fished out of Singh's bag back to that group we chased over K Street a couple of weeks ago. There was no definitive origin of the chip though – we only know it came from that group, but we can't trace it to a particular address... at least not yet." Officer Ryan Bradshaw tilted his head. "They are still working on it though."

"Gotcha."

"At least it does make sense that they might have wanted to scare either Singh or Ramos. Hell, you got two news people, and I guess one or both of them could have reported something that may have angered some of these kids?"

Grimms let out a sigh and grimaced. "Yeah, I guess so, but something here just doesn't add up."

"What do you mean, Harry?"

"You have to admit that we haven't seen a lot of aggressive behaviour with these kids – at least not in DC and not over the past few months."

"True enough." Bradshaw nodded agreement with his boss.

"I mean, what did we see outside their place over in Columbia Heights the other morning... and all over

Constitution Avenue?"

"Kids lying all over the place in a trance of some sort."

"The key words there, Bradshaw, are 'kids in a trance.' How many of those kids would even see a news report? How many of those kids are taking information into their heads anymore? Do they even care about Ramos and Singh's address... about the news... about anything?"

"Scary thought, Harry."

"Of course, it is. But something somewhere has got to start making some sense. I checked in with the lab folks again this morning like I do every freakin morning for the past several weeks. They ain't getting any positives for drugs... zero. I'm a bit older than you, Bradshaw, but this doesn't add up. I used to ALWAYS be dealing with kids sky high on something or other, but these kids are lower than low, and they don't seem to be taking anything at all to get them there."

Ryan slowly rocked his head back and forth. "And from what I hear – we all are hearing – this thing is growing, Harry, and it's growing fast... too fast... and it's now gone global."

"Yeah, for sure it's global, but nothing like here in the District. We're seeing thousands of these kids here while they're reporting dozens or hundreds in New York, Chicago and LA. Why here? Besides that, how the hell does a shooting fit into this? On the one hand, we can't get any of these zombie-like kids to even speak one word... not a FREAKING word! Then out of the clear blue, we get a couple of kids who – at least on the surface – appear to be related to the same group, the Eights. Next thing you know, they go shoot up an apartment. Regressive? Aggressive? I mean, it just doesn't fit!"

8

Friday, 2 September; GNN Offices, Washington DC

Glenn McDermott stood at the front of the small press room in the GNN offices. The room was used for a range of functions but was large enough to comfortably contain most of the news staff at the DC Bureau. A quick scan of the venue told him all the DC team not on assignment were there including several dozen reporters, writers, producers, a few camera people and other news staff.

"Thanks for coming in so early and on such short notice. I know that many of you have been impacted by whatever is affecting so many young people right now. That said, it doesn't matter whether you are directly working on an Eights-related story or not, I think you will find the background information being presented here today to be of value. Again, I know this was a last-minute thing, and I apologise for not giving you more of a warning, but Kylie is on the east coast here and had some time this afternoon. We are very fortunate to have her with us. Let me introduce Professor Kylie Childs. Kylie is an ecopsychologist – do I have that right, Kylie?"

She nodded her head in agreement.

"Professor Childs is on staff at the University of Sydney in New South Wales, Australia. I know she's been on a swing through the States for several academic conferences and has been good enough to meet with GNN staff in LA, Chicago and New York. She is about to head off to Shanghai – to the Global Holistic Summit – and I think she is flying out of here this evening, is that correct?"

"I've got to check my SAM, but whether it's tonight or tomorrow morning, I can guarantee it will be at some time when I know I should be sleeping, Glenn." She laughed.

"We are so happy you agreed to squeeze this into your hectic schedule. Dr Childs has done much work looking at the inner drivers and mechanisms of young people and of late, seeing how that research can enlighten us in trying to understand the Eights phenomenon. Many of you would have read some of Kylie's recent work. For that matter, you may have watched one of the numerous holovision programs that have featured her the past year or two. The whole point of her presentation today is to help us better understand why this is happening, and that will make us better able to communicate this to the public at large. Ultimately, her work is aimed at allowing governments, community groups and other non-profits to better develop a strategy to deal with this phenomenon."

Glenn looked to a paper he held in his hand. "Her expertise in anxiety disorders, particularly in adolescents and young adults, led her to establish the ACSES – that's the Australian Centre for Solastalgia and Ecopsychology Studies. I admit that is all a mouthful for me, so before I demonstrate my ignorance anymore, please let me turn this over to Professor Childs." Grimms extended his hand to the professor before he took a seat in the front row of folding chairs.

"Good afternoon – at least I'm guessing it's afternoon. You would think that in this age of SST flights that whisk us around the world in hours, we would have discovered a way to overcome jetlag. Regrettably, that has not happened, and I don't hold much hope of it ever happening. For all we like to think our modern technology can somehow shape Mother Nature to fit human desires, more often than not, we seem to be sadly disappointed.

"I guess in its simplest form, that might be at the crux of the research that I do... the problem society runs into when it tries to shape Mother Nature to fit human desires. I'd like to give you a bit of an overview of some of the studies we've conducted at ACSES. I want to reiterate Glenn's mention of the fact that I aim to provide background information to issues which our research is looking at, especially concerning our young people. Hopefully, this applies to factions such as the Eights here in North America as well as similar adolescent groupings around the globe.

"Please feel free to interrupt me at any time. I am here to answer your questions and discuss your comments, and I don't want a one-way lecture, rather a dialogue. Frankly, I do not say that lightly... I encourage you to ask questions or make comments. We can only deepen our understanding through interaction. In the end, I hope to learn as much from you as you from me.

"Let me start by making a few things perfectly clear. Firstly, I am NOT going to miraculously reveal all the answers to you this afternoon. God knows that I would like to do that, but we just don't have those answers at this point. By the way, by 'we' I simply mean the sum total of all the researchers that look into these issues globally. It's a difficult problem and, though we are making progress, we cannot honestly expect that anyone will find a magic bullet to solve it all.

"Secondly, our Australian Centre for Solastalgia and Ecopsychology Studies does not only look at young people in our research, rather at the broadest spectrum of people possible. We have tried to look at the population as a whole in Australia, Asia, North America and around the world. From these generalised studies, we have also focused in on communities in urban, regional and rural areas, various cultural and socioeconomic samples and across the spectrum of age groups.

"Thirdly, I spent my early career in counselling and working with young people before I plunged headfirst into research and academia. What we are witnessing around the world right now is not just more-of-the-same as far as adolescents and young adults go. This is different. This is far more severe and far more widespread than anything we have seen before. Even more inexplicable is the fact that we see less and less illicit drug use. Historically, over the past several generations in the western world, there has been a direct relationship between drug use and antisocial behaviour. Nowadays, we see a decrease in drug use yet more and more asocial behaviour."

Professor Childs waved her SAM at a technoserver that projected a hologram in front of the far wall. Several life-sized kangaroos – one with a small joey's head visible in her pouch – stood in front of a stand of eucalyptus trees that disappeared into the ceiling. A flock of pink and grey cockatoos flew off into the distance over a small stream meandering behind the stand of trees. A muffled chorus of oohs and aahs revealed the involvement of the news team members. The sight and sound were enough to convince many that they had been magically transported to the Australian outback.

"I come from a part of the world in which we are blessed with many tranquil landscapes very much like what you see here. This is relatively quintessential Australian bush, probably what you Americans refer to as a 'country scene' or 'rural setting.' I needn't overdo it here with the gum trees, cockatoos and kangaroos since it all pretty much takes in the most iconic bits of Aussie bushland. As a matter of fact, we have done studies that demonstrate how merely putting you into a peaceful holographic scene such as this can lower your blood pressure by ten points or more. The three-dimensional holograph certainly gives you an appreciation of the setting, but regrettably, we are missing the feel of the sun, the scent of the eucalyptus in the air... The point here is that it is essential to realise that putting you into REAL nature – physically emerging you into actual bushland – will lower your blood pressure even more significantly." A majority of the attendees were nodding their heads in agreement.

"But much like everywhere else on the planet, Australia is a land of contrasts." She snapped her fingers, and the tranquillity of the bush scene winked out and was replaced by an intense, holographic fire raging in from the far side of the office. "The terror of bush fire is as much an iconic part of Australia as was the previous peaceful vision of the endemic flora and fauna. These fires feed off eucalyptus oil, and temperatures can reach 1,100° Celsius or about 2,000° Fahrenheit. Now for those of you not used to contemplating those sorts of temperatures, that is hot enough to melt aluminium, bronze and some alloys of copper. So, in a matter of hours, it's not unusual to go from the peacefulness of an idyllic Aussie bushland setting to the horror of a raging bushfire to the burnt-out sight of a decimated countryside."

The projection changed again, panning across a blackened, desolate area with only the smallest remnants of tree stumps left to mark the original stand of gum trees. The charred remains of the few kangaroo and parrots not totally incinerated were visible on the edge of the smouldering ash, one still struggling against imminent death. Kylie could see just how rapidly the contented faces of her listeners had universally transformed into looks of distress.

"How do you feel right now?" Professor Childs looked around the group of a few dozen people in the room and noted their visible discomfort in the stark expressions they displayed. "It would be quite natural to feel a bit of shock, a bit of sadness for the loss of life, the loss of that beauty, losing that calming vision. Hold onto that feeling for a minute and realise that you have just experienced a rather stark example of solastalgia. The word has snuck into the vernacular over the past decade or two, but it really has made headlines the past year or so.

"Let me just make sure we're all on the same wavelength

here. Solastalgia is the emotional pain and anxiety one experiences when their natural environment changes for the worse with little or no hope of reversing the change or in any way making it better." The professor briefly paused to let her words sink in.

"The term was coined originally by a fellow Australian, Glenn Albrecht, an ecological philosopher and sustainability academic who finished up his academic career as a Professor in Sustainability at Murdoch University in Perth, Western Australia. This was back at the start of this century and resulted from work he had done at the University of Newcastle looking at the changes of the ecosystem in the Upper Hunter Valley in New South Wales. For those of you unfamiliar with Australia, the Hunter Valley region is a beautiful area along our east coast some 250 kilometres north of Sydney. The valley is verdant and fertile and home to one of Australia's best grape-growing regions. The locals claim the Hunter Valley is the oldest wine-producing region in Australia.

"But the Hunter also has the largest deposits of coal in New South Wales and one of the largest coal reserves in Australia. For that matter, Newcastle became the busiest coal shipping port on the Earth back at the end of the last century and at the beginning of this one. Over the years, many open-cut coal mines were developed there, which resulted in a great deal of pollution from both coal processing and coal-fired power plants. So, the coal deposits were indeed a mixed blessing with contradictory outcomes. On the one hand, the Hunter Region became one of the most affluent of all of Australia's regional communities because of the jobs and affluence provided by the coal industry. On the other hand, the effect on the local community was severe. Both the industrial damage of the local environment and a prolonged drought or two combined to inflict a hugely detrimental impact on the local community.

"Albrecht was an Associate Professor at the University of

Newcastle earlier in his career when he and his colleagues observed first-hand the changes that occurred to the psyche of residents within the local community. He coined so many modern-day terms, though I believe solastalgia must be the one we remember most. The word itself is actually a *portmanteau* that blends together 'solace' and 'nostalgia.' I would imagine we have all experienced solace, that feeling of well-being or consolation you may get in a time of great sadness or distress. And of course, nostalgia is quite an emotional feeling... a feeling that causes one to yearn for the comforts you experienced in the past but that are now lost.

"I just tried to induce positive feelings of comfort and relaxation using the synthetic holographic projection. From the looks on your faces, I believe I did succeed... at least to a certain point. Again, observing your facial expressions, I believe you also experienced sadness and unease at the view of what remained after the bush fire. Albrecht recognised that solastalgia could cause psychological distress, and he added another descriptive term – psychoterratic – to describe the mental unease caused by environmental impacts. Psychoterratic illness – that's the 'psyche' part of the term – is involved with mental health issues that are the product of our relationship with the Earth – hence, the 'terra' part."

Kylie noticed a middle-aged man with a pained look on his face that betrayed his uneasiness with something she said. "You must have a query, sir. I was serious about being open to dialogue at any time. I am only too happy to hear your question or comment."

The man was quick to respond. "Umm... yes. I guess I have a comment and a question here. I think what I hear you say is that environmental degradation and climate issues are the root cause of our kids' depression. Isn't that really way too simple? In a way, isn't that actually an intellectual copout? We all believe the environment is important, but do we really think ecological changes are the cause of such profound behavioural variations in the population? *Homo sapiens* have faced environmental changes since day one. I'm not sure that learning about solastalgia allows me to better understand why I have to step over listless kids strewn about alongside Massachusetts Avenue."

"Thank you for that..." Kylie extended her hand towards him as if to say, 'name please.'

"Oh, sorry... My name is Jorge Fernández, I'm a reporter here at GNN."

"Thanks, Jorge. I am sure if you had this question... comment... you are not alone in this room. For that matter, many GNN viewers would have precisely the same unease with what I am saying here. Trust me when I tell you that your uneasiness with the term solastalgia is shared by the population at large. Let me attempt to speak to that uneasiness with this concept using an example or two.

"If we think of running out of oxygen, drowning in floodwaters or running out of food, it is quite in-your-face understandable how that is life-threatening and would impact one's psyche drastically. On the other hand, the idea that some abstract factor like 'the environment' might have far-reaching effects on any population's mental health can seem way too nebulous, way too intangible, to have such an impact. I understand how this can easily be viewed as an academic's psychobabble copout. To many, it may seem that all of a sudden, some pointy-headed scholars are writing papers that blame such serious outcomes on ambiguous and ill-defined causes. Would it surprise you if I said this concept of solastalgia isn't a new idea? Let me explain...

"The history of both psychoterratic metal health and solastalgia go back much farther than Albrecht's work. Consider historical literature... certainly, the idea of the environment and its relationship to the human psyche has been around a long, long time. In my country, we find examples of Aboriginal rock art depicting humans and other animals and their relationship to the land. From the time I was a little girl, I learned of the Aboriginal idea that 'we do not own the land, the land owns us.' I know there are similar American Indian proverbs that say as much... 'we are part of the earth, and the earth is part of us.' I believe the indigenous peoples all over the world felt such closeness to the land, to the sea and to the sky because they lived with it... in it... from it. The more 'advanced' our technology has made us, the farther away from the land and sea and sky we have become. This is not new.

"One of your countrymen, Henry David Thoreau, wrote *"Walking"* nearly 200 years ago. You may recall that his work characterised man more as a part of nature than as a part of society. Another American, Rachel Carson, wrote *"Silent Spring"* and that certainly rocked the western world halfway through the last century. Her work pointed out just how human technology, in the form of DDT, could result in unexpected dire consequences for the greater environment. Some argue that Carson's publication marks the beginning of the modern environmental movement. We could go on with these sorts of examples. My point is not that individual well-being is somehow tied into the health of the environment, rather the point is how much more immediate these environmental impacts are today than they were 30, 50, 75 years ago. Why is that you might ask. In a word, population.

"Consider, when Carson wrote *"Silent Spring"* in 1962, there were about 3 billion humans on the Earth. Here we are in the 2040s, and we have now crowded over 9 billion people on this planet. The tripling of global population in 80 years means that human actions have rapid and drastic effects on global ecologies.

"And countless numbers of environmental 'incidents' have

tragically dotted humanity throughout historical times. Yes, the early work on solastalgia indeed had its origins in Australia. Albrecht's original reference was to the effects of coal mining, and I used examples of drought and bush fire in my opening holographic presentation to you. We can trace these kinds of situations back throughout history. At least a thousand years ago – we have no definitive dates – the *Rapa Nui* people of Easter Island developed a thriving and industrious culture. How do we know that? These Polynesian people produced enough excess resources to build some thousand stone *moai* statues and other artifacts, many of which were enormous in size. By the time European sailors arrived there in the early 1700s nearly none of the population responsible for those artifacts remained on *Rapa Nui* – what we call Easter Island now.

"Native Americans in your Midwest fundamentally survived for a thousand years by hunting the American bison in a harmonious relationship with both animals and land. Stories abound of herds that numbered into the tens-of-millions of bison ranging from the Appalachians to the Rockies. Throughout the nineteenth century, European settlers killed ninety to ninety-five per cent of the bison with the overwhelming majority of these animals just left in place to rot. Indian-American wars aside, the destruction of the bison environment had a significant impact on the indigenous population.

"We can go on with historical examples. The Great London Smog in the early 1950s resulted in four or five thousand deaths and tens of thousands of people falling ill. The Love Canal in the Niagara area of northwestern New York became a dumping ground of a toxic mix of industrial chemicals for the first half of the twentieth century and eventually destroyed an unsuspecting community. The Cuyahoga River in your American state of Ohio was so polluted that it caught on fire in the late 1960s... the RIVER CAUGHT ON FIRE!" Kylie paused and lightly hit her forehead with her open hand. "Recall one of the worst industrial accidents ever was the pesticide factory disaster in Bhopal, India in the 1980s with 5,000 dead and up to a half-million people suffering the aftereffects. The list is nearly endless... Chernobyl, the Deepwater Horizon, the Gulf of Mexico and South China Sea dead zones last decade... I will be merciful and stop there.

"In all these cases, the impact on the local environment had extraordinary effects on surrounding communities, though these early events predated coordinated scholarly work by sociologists, ecopsychologists and other academic researchers such as me to quantify outcomes. But the causes and effects of environmental damage are amplified in a world bursting at the seams with some 9 billion people.

"Because of this population pressure, we experience an increasing number of these anxiety-producing phenomena globally." The holographs kept dissolving into pictures depicting each example she gave. "The rising sea levels washing away beaches, roads and homes... the glaciers melting and receding at alarming rates... the disappearance of elephants and rhinos and tigers... the accelerated bleaching, decay and death of our Great Barrier Reef... the huge hypoxic ocean zones of death with low or no oxygen.."

One of the reporters raised his hand, not sure if he was interrupting more to ask a question or to cause a brief hiatus from the discomfort he was feeling. "Thank you, Kylie... My name is Aiden Cardona, and I fear I am in the same boat as Jorge in that I am still confused. Your point here is well made, but exactly how are you relating this specifically to the Eights or *Los Ochos*? I don't mean to underestimate the importance of your research, but what should be the takeaway for us? Referring back to Jorge's comment, we still need to 'step over listless kids scattered all over Massachusetts Avenue.' How can your work help us deal with that? Can you offer anything more definitive?"

"Good question, and thank you for asking, Aiden. If you consider that the movement of the Eights, *Los Ochos*, the *Bā*... they are, first of all..." She held one finger up, "a part of the modern-day anti-culture cult or crusade and, secondly, these movements are almost exclusively followed by the young, mostly adolescents and young adults. We have studies that indicate as high as 96% or 97% of those that identify as an Eight, or any other cultural variation of the group, are under age 20 and very nearly 100% under the age 30..."

"Again... this relates to solastalgia how?" Cardona was intent or getting something tangible, something usable in his everyday life.

"Consider for a minute that the younger a person is, the more limited their interactions are with the world. I don't want to be condescending here, but I realise many of you have most likely studied some psychology at uni... that's college here in America. Just bear with me for a minute to refresh your memories.

"Initially, an infant will function in what we call the sensorimotor stage, where everything an infant knows is limited to her or his sensory perceptions and motor skills. Somewhere around two years of age, a child begins to use language but still doesn't think the way an adult does and is just not capable of understanding another person's point of view. This preoperational stage runs up to maybe 5 or 6 years, depending on the individual. The third stage allows a youngster to begin thinking logically about concrete events, but they still have difficulty in contemplating hypothetical or abstract ideas.

"Somewhere around 11 or 12 years of age, the child reaches the formal operational stage, which allows her or him to think in the abstract and use deductive reasoning. Now for those who are driven, you can easily develop a never-ending series of PhD projects exploring the particulars of the cognitive development of a child, but fortunately, most people don't go to those extremes." The professor muffled a laugh. "I guess I'm a prime example of someone who is so possessed and has gone to such extremes!" Now her chuckle became contagious as smiles spread across the group.

"In short, solastalgia or ecoanxiety impacts the young at a higher rate and with greater force than older people. You ask why, Aiden... For starters, we all feel some effects from environmental changes. The thing is that older people have other social 'rocks' or 'life markers' upon which to lean. Older people may be more immersed in a career, a family, other life pursuits. Older people tend to have formed stronger social bonds. I am generalising here, but younger ages tend to be less settled for all the obvious reasons."

A young reporter leaned forward. "Thank you, Professor Chiles. I'm Caitlan Ferguson. It seems like a million years ago, but I am recalling the basics of what you are telling us from an adolescent psych class I took back in my undergrad days. I still don't follow exactly how ecoanxiety somehow single-handedly explains the problem we face in our society with kids dropping out... with groups like the Eights."

"Thanks for your query, Caitlan. Ecoanxiety by itself is NOT the singular cause here... it is way more complicated than that. Please let me point to the beginning of my talk here this afternoon and remind you that NO ONE has the 'answer' as it were. But it may shed light on the situation if you consider that there is a confluence of factors that I can only touch on here. Of course, the whole environmental change component is a big one, but it is not the only one. Consider also the population, socioeconomic and political influences.

"The nineteenth-century witnessed hundreds of wars across the globe with seemingly mundane arguments being fought over on the battlefield. The twentieth managed to reduce that number to dozens rather than hundreds, but amongst those conflicts were two world wars, some of the deadliest clashes that humanity has ever perpetrated. Then towards the end of the last century and into this one, we substituted the concept of cold war amongst the superpowers with shooting wars amongst smaller countries serving as proxy fights for those global contenders. Just consider how good we humans are at inventing things. We build tools that allow us to grow more food, to build larger structures, to kill more enemies, to travel to other planets... We humans actually have learned to take our planet apart piece by piece and rebuild it in ways unimaginable decades ago. But despite all this, we are pretty lousy at understanding how our technology affects the whole. We have set in motion planetwide mechanisms that will undo our handiwork."

"But we – as a global society – we know this." Caitlin seemed to plead for an answer. "We simply need to right the ship and move Mother Earth in a more positive direction. We know that our governments know that, we know that our kids know that..."

"Do we?" Kylie let out a sigh. "You know Caitlin, for as intelligent a species as is *Homo sapiens*, we just aren't always as capable of logical thought as we like to believe. Most humans don't think in facts and figures, in theories and models, in programs and equations; instead, most of us tend to think in stories. Like it or not, these stories often times have little or no foundation in what we think of as facts. I am particularly conscious of this speaking in a roomful of journos. I would think that in your chosen career, more than practically any other profession, you are painfully aware of the fact that the public no longer even agrees on what our reality is.

"Consider that over the past few decades, we have reached a point that we can't even agree on one of your nightly news broadcasts... I believe your particular version is the *GNN*

Skynet News Hour... The viewing audience has become more and more resistant to accepting anything they see for fear of video images created by 'deepfake' artificial intelligence programs. We have seen governments fall because the public no longer believes what they read and see. In the words of a century-old Marx Brothers' movie, 'who are you gonna believe, me or your lying eyes?'

"More broadly, one story tells us that we needn't worry since our governments will solve all these problems. Another story tells us that because *Homo sapiens* are at the absolute pinnacle of the evolutionary heap, we are 'free' to do whatever we like knowing that Mother Earth will always give us a pass to survival. But increasingly, there is a story that tells us we have been lied to... that these sort of 'facts' aren't real. This story voices the belief that all the marvellous technology we have created as a species just isn't about 'normal people' and especially not about young people. That story argues that adults have comfortable lives, but there isn't enough of Mother Earth left for young people to ever hope for that kind of life.

"Consider the explosion of robotics, of artificial intelligence, of self-piloted machines on the land, the sea and in the air. We've made lives 'easier' by replacing humans with our technology, but what is left for humans – especially the young – to aspire to? We face a whole new revolution that may no longer involve the wealthiest one-per cent exploiting the rest of the population. Increasingly the new revolution may now be about the most affluent elites actually declaring the other 99% of the community as irrelevant. IRRELEVANT! How do we deal with that? How do we even make sense of 99% of the population now considered irrelevant? I fear many kids today firmly believe a life story in which they are, at best, viewed as expendable and, at worst, totally invisible to the powers that be.

"So, if you are following me, Caitlin, though solastalgia is based on environmental shocks, it can never be viewed in isolation from society as a whole. We must always remember that in a crowded world of more than 9 billion people, environmental changes must be considered in the context of the socioeconomic and political milieu in which they occur. One of your famous American writers and Holocaust survivor, Elie Wiesel, once told us that 'the opposite of love is not hate, it's indifference.' Consider that indifference is the absence of passion, the inability to feel any emotion; indifference means you just don't care. I apologise for not being able to give you all 'the answer' at this point, but I believe I may better frame the question by asking 'why are our kids increasingly unable to feel? Why are they unable to care... even about themselves? Could their generation's indifference possibly be founded in their collective feeling of irrelevance?"

9

Friday, 2 September; Gale Crater Outpost, Mars

Misha Romanov placed her cup on the table and sat at one end of the staff room table. "We welcome a new team member today – Professor Lochie Greenbank from the University of Western Australia. Welcome, Lochie. I hope you at least have met Lochie at the tea kettle just now, but I intend to go around the table and formally introduce all of you to him after our chief astronomer, Dr Barlow, updates us on the latest news concerning the asteroid impact. Before she starts, please welcome Lochie Greenbank."

"Thanks, Misha." He raised one hand as a gesture of hello. "G'day. Glad to finally see all of you in person. I can't tell you how happy I am to be here on Mars – particularly at Gale

Crater Outpost – and at just how much I look forward to working with you."

"We certainly will get to know one another in ways that only a handful of scientists in a remote Martian outpost ever could!" There was a collective chuckle at her comment. Romanov looked at Lochie. "Were you able to meet Bianca back at Alpha Colony?"

"Yes, we met back at the Colony, but only briefly. And of course, Joe and I saw the limited broadcast updates during the trip down here to Gale Crater. Obviously, there wasn't a great deal to update since everyone was simply keeping an eye on a piece of rock speeding along and nicely following the laws of gravity and orbital mechanics."

A quiet beep, beep, beep could be heard from the technoserver in the corner of the staff room. "This must be Bianca. Naturally, she has been involved with the interplanetary team collecting data and helping analyse them 24-7 this past week. I believe she is ready to bring us up to date on the latest news concerning the pending impact back on the Earth. I think the data stream coming from both orbital tracking and the remote probes they've been launching from Earth may give us some better understanding of just what they are facing back at home."

A holographic image of Dr Barlow materialised next to Misha. "Hello, Misha... Lochie... Joe... I trust that you endured your ride down to the tropics."

"Endured? I loved it! The landscapes were fantastic. The observation bubble on top of MRT is quite an extravagance... great for scenery during the day and spectacular views of the heavens at night."

"It surely is, especially for an astronomer." Bianca laughed. "Did you get to see Earth? It's our morning star right now."

"Yes... yes, I did, Bianca. It was both beautiful and

71

overwhelming seeing it from here."

"And I can see the rest of Gale Crater staff are gathered there now, Misha?"

"That's affirmative." She waved her arm, and the holovision panned the meeting room showing Bianca the gathering around the table.

"Excellent. Now then, we've been monitoring *Thánatos* for the past several weeks – several months, actually – ever since Moon Base One picked it up. It's a big one too, no doubt the biggest since NASA's Object Detection and Tracking System came into existence several decades ago. Though ODTS made the original find, we are getting updates from across Earth now as well as Moon Base One and from our own observations from way out here on Mars."

"So, what have we learned?" Arya tried to be patient but was keen on hearing the latest.

"We have determined that it's a salicaceous body which is irregular in shape – nearly four times longer than it is wide or about 390 metres long and about 90 metres in diameter. Now remember, since we don't have core samples and the like, we need to do some estimating here, but we have fairly high confidence in these figures. This chunk of rock has a volume of about 2.5 million cubic meters and a density of approximately 3,100 kilos per cubic metre, so when you do the numbers, *Thánatos* has a total mass of maybe 8 megatons."

"That sounds pretty big." Lochie scratched his forehead as he spoke.

"That is big, Lochie. Eight million tonnes is way more massive than the Great Pyramid of Giza. We're going to take a hit from a pretty big rock with an impact speed of around 35 kilometres a second. Earth may be lucky in that the entry angle is going to be rather shallow, maybe around 40 degrees or so. Best of all, the earlier indication that impact might occur over Siberia close to the north pole is now confirmed. The time of impact will be around 1500 Mars Time or about four hours from now. Because of the aforementioned irregular shape and the shallow angle at which it is approaching, there are many uncertainties. We just can't be sure if it will have a strong impact, a skip off, a breakup or – most likely – a combination of all those possibilities. In the end, the final trajectory will be contingent on precise angles, frictional forces and the integrity of the stony body."

Misha took a deep breath. "So we obviously hope for a skip off the atmosphere where it'll continue along its orbit. But what are the likelihood of the other alternatives, namely a direct hit versus the breakup?"

"We just don't know yet, Misha. So much hinges on whether or not it splits into pieces. In the worst-case scenario, more pieces of rock could possibly spread the damage on impact should they all hit. In the best-case scenario, one big piece breaking into fragments could lessen damage since smaller bits tend to have higher friction per mass and thus burn up more completely. Big pieces have less friction because their mass to surface area ratio is higher, and that could increase the amount of mass that impacts the surface. At this point, that is just unknown."

Lochie raised his head and rubbed his chin. "I guess that's why they named it *Thánatos*, the Greek personification of death. Let's hope it doesn't live up to its name."

"We live in hope... I will be back to update you whenever we have anything new to report."

"Thank you, Bianca." The holovision image dissolved out.

* * *

"I've already welcomed you to our science team, Lochie, so let me go around the table from your right. First of all, you already had the chance to get to know Joe a bit – that's Joe Robinson who you shared the rover with while riding down to our outpost. No doubt you are well aware of the fact that both Joe and I were members of Mars Mission 1 and part of the team of the original 8 colonists to start up Mars Alpha Colony 19 years ago in late 2024."

"Time flies when you're having fun." Joe's contagious smile spread from ear to ear.

"Joe is an electrical engineer by training but really is a jack of all trades, a true Renaissance man. You do a bit of just about everything here at Gale Crater Outpost as well as back at Alpha Colony, right Joe?"

Robinson nodded his head.

"And I hope his modesty didn't keep him from telling you that he was the lead engineer on putting MRT rover together."

"He did mention it." Lochie chuckled.

"Next to Joe is Arya Abass, originally from Iran... Tehran, yes?"

"Pretty close, Misha. I was born in a little village just to the north of Tehran along the Caspian Sea."

"Arya has been here for..."

"Four years now – came on Mars Mission 8."

"Right, four years. Arya has a strong background in the computer sciences, and we all look at him as the Alpha Colony techie nerd." She laughed as the young Asian woman sitting beside him patted him on the back.

"Arya has spent a good portion of his career working on artificial intelligence development. Several of his breakthroughs have allowed our life support systems to become more and more aware of us colonists to the point that the systems are taking care of us rather than vice versa. I believe you dabble a bit in languages, yes, Arya? Language seems to go along with any interest in AI, yes?"

"It does, and for sure, I am interested, but I won't try to pass myself off as a linguist!"

"I guess now is as good a time as any to tell you that Lochie has been briefed both on the find of cellular life back up at Alpha Colony and of the artifact Siti and Keegan came across yesterday. This is particularly appropriate since – having never anticipated finding evidence of intelligent life – we just don't have the staff to deal with the likes of anthropology, archaeology or exopsychology. That said, we all need to dig deep to take on roles in areas of expertise one or two steps removed from our formal training. So yes, Arya, you WILL pass yourself off as OUR linguist!"

"You know I'll do the best that I can, Misha."

She then extended her hand towards the woman seated next to Arya. "Then we have Siti Jokowi whose background is in chemistry and materials science, but again, is called on to do so much more up here. Siti has been critical in analysing samples of any kind that we collect. More importantly, should you grow tired of our sometimes-bland meal menu, Siti makes some of the nicest Malaysian food imaginable."

"How long have you been here, Siti?" Lochie asked.

"I came out on Mars Mission 6, so that was eight years ago."

"I guess I might add that Siti and Keegan..." Misha tilted her head towards the man seated next to Siti, "...will no doubt go down in all of history for the find they made in 14B yesterday, the first evidence humanity has ever found of intelligent life from anywhere other than Earth. That's rather profound."

"You scare me when you say it like that, Misha." Siti squirmed in her seat.

"Speaking of Keegan, this is he – Keegan Botha..." Misha extended her hand towards the next team member. "...our geophysicist. He doubles as our mining expert as well as all things engineering. Keegan came to us from the University of Cape Town, so be very careful about ever asking him about beloved rugby Springboks – you may never get away from him. You've been on Mars for a long time, haven't you, Keegan?"

"Mars Mission 4 – that's nearly 13 years ago now." He casually tugged his coveralls neck open enough to reveal a green and gold tee shirt. "And yes, I will tell you the complete history of the South African Springboks. But please, Misha, it's not just rugby, but Rugby Union!"

Lochie had a broad grin. "So, how'd those Springboks do when they played my Wallabies the last time in Joburg?"

"I was hoping we'd be friends, Lochie..." He hung his head in mock shame.

"The last team member sitting there to your left, Lochie, is Nigella Dougan. Nigella is our Head of Life Systems. You'll quickly learn that life systems on Mars mean you need to utilise a bit of physics, chemistry, biology and engineering in very creative ways. To say that we all depend on Nigella always doing her job right is an understatement. Nigella is from the United Kingdom, more specifically..."

"From Wiltshire. I came out with Arya on Mars Mission 8 four years ago. I wanted to escape the rainy English countryside, and I surely have done that out here – it hasn't rained once here in probably more than several billion years!"

"Life Systems, huh. I'd better be extra nice to you, Nigella, since my life literally depends on it." Lochie teased her good-naturedly.

"I'm going to hold you to that, Lochie." Her smile was radiant.

"Nigella's formal title is Head of Life Systems, and her credentials are in the biological sciences. Since the discovery back at Alpha Colony about three weeks ago – 22 August to be exact – Nigella answered the call to join the biology team back up there. So far, she has spent four or five days at Alpha Colony meeting with the bio team, yes?"

"Yes, actually four days at Alpha. I just returned on the MRT supply run the last trip before Lochie and Joe came down."

"We missed her even if it was only for a week or so." Misha smiled at her. "Nigella's been here at Gale Crater Outpost pretty much since we were established. We made it perfectly clear that we need to keep Nigella with us and let the bio people up there do what they need to do. More on that in a minute. Speaking of the bio team, your colleague Professor Parisa Henning heads that bio group back up at Alpha Colony. She is from your University, yes?"

"Indeed, she is from the University of Western Australia. I knew Parisa back in Perth."

"Let me finish my around-the-table intros with Lochie Greenbank. In case the accent wasn't a dead giveaway, Lochie is a – how do you say it – a fair dinkum, true blue Aussie. Technically speaking, Lochie is a purebred geologist, and we have worked together at a distance for several years now. As coincidence would have it, he no sooner lands at Alpha Colony and heads for Gale Crater Outpost, and we discover the artifact. Though we haven't yet spent time talking about it, I am aware of the fact that he has some archaeology in his background, right Lochie?"

"Not exactly archaeology, Misha." Lochie leaned forward in his chair. "Though my PhD and most of my academic life have involved the geological sciences over the past two decades, my undergrad studies were in anthropology – physical anthropology to be specific."

"Physical anthropologist?" Siti showed her curiosity.

"Yeah, yeah... as differentiated from the classical anthropologists, the cultural anthropologists and the language guys... I've had a life-long interest in how *Homo sapiens* came to be, and that's more or less what physical or biological anthropologists focus on. I mean a great deal of this overlaps with evolutionary biology, but..." Greenbank caught himself falling into the familiar academic's trap of going on at length about things that would put the average person to sleep. "Look, at this point as far as anyone back on Earth is concerned, I'm a geologist. But even before Misha mentioned your recent find to me, I have always been interested in the evolutionary development of our species. To think that now we may possibly look at if or how another intelligent species may fit into the development of *Homo sapiens* is the chance of a lifetime!"

10

Friday, 2 September; Mauna Loa Observatory, Hawaii

"And that should just about finish it up. As usual, I've already sent you the numbers we talked about here so we can discuss anything you are uncertain of through Skynet. I already downloaded all the data you have provided. You know, no matter how inconvenient air travel may be, there is still nothing that can replace old fashioned face-to-face contact for sharing our findings."

"True enough. That said, if anyone knew discussions-at-a-distance, it would be you, André." Russ waved his technoserver off. "So where to from here, buddy?"

"Well, I am heading back to France for a very quick visit – I'll only be there for a few nights. At least I get to see Amélie and the kids for a day or two. I fear she will disown me if I don't schedule some home time."

Mikayla smiled. "...and then?"

"Shanghai. There's lots of news coming out of China lately, but more importantly, I've been invited to a big face-to-face meeting scheduled next week there, and they've given it a fancy name: The Global Holistic Summit."

"Gee... I guess just about everyone on the planet has read about that one – certainly we science-types." Mikayla leaned forward. "Congratulations to you for getting the invite. It's going to be a big deal."

"I hope. The whole idea is to bring interested parties from..."

Mikayla interrupted him. "I apologise for interrupting here, André, but you are way too modest. You and the others are not merely 'interested parties.' More accurately, you are all among the best minds on planet Earth, and the idea of the Summit is to try to reach a critical mass of Earth-conscious academics across as wide an array of disciplines as possible. I'm jealous and wish I'd be going along."

André could feel his face flush with a touch of awkwardness. "Well thanks, Mikayla, but I fear you give me too much credit. The point is that the issues we face on population and social turmoil and climate pressures transcend cultural boundaries and academic disciplines. That's why the Summit is bringing together physical sciences, biological sciences and behavioural sciences as well as a representative mix of journalists from everywhere. At least it'll be damned interesting. The holistic concept has some strong implications; we've dealt with climate science and environmental impacts for 75 years now, somehow separating social interactions, medical impacts and political influences. Too often they have been somehow looked at as separate issues rather than intricately involved problems. You know as well as I do that, by definition, the environment includes everything. Look, there are no guarantees here, but it's certainly worth a go."

"Will they consider *Los Ochos?* The Eights?" Russ looked sceptical.

"I'd sure be disappointed if the symposium didn't include that. As you know, personally I'm pretty blind to the social issues other than what I see on virtual news, but I do know we need to pay attention to it all, since the physical world has such a huge impact on how humans interact. I promise to hold up my end of the event and contribute as much as I can to the climate side of things."

Mikayla tilted her head. "I think that's the whole point. You – we – technical types have been isolating ourselves from the social impacts for way too long. I've grown convinced that we can't just separate social movements like the Eights from environmental fluctuations on a global scale."

"I'm with you, Mikayla. For that matter, I wasn't trying to 'continue my blindness', as it were... Our team contribution covers the oceanography, meteorology and climatology side of things. I'm anxious to see what some of the rumblings are up on the Tibetan Plateau." A grimace flashed across his face. "There have been several sites along the plateau there showing some disturbing methane releases associated with permafrost disintegration. Now with the impact coming in over the pole..."

"Obviously, the asteroid... *Thánatos?*" Russ interrupted.

"Yep... Who knows? Last month some big changes were

accelerating without any astronomical influences."

"Changes? How's that, André?"

"Well, I don't know the detail at this point, but conditions up there seem to have changed for the worst, temperature-wise, and at quite an alarming rate."

"Permafrost degradation? Breakdown?"

André nodded yes.

"All from the increase in temperatures?"

"Mostly temperature, yes, but pressure changes too..."

Russ shook his head. "Fever below... fever above... poor Mother Earth doesn't seem to be able to shake it all off this time."

Moureaux's attention was focused on the holovision projection. "I was ready to head down the mountain to get my connector flight, but it looks like *Thánatos* is on the home stretch to impact. Somehow I think I'd better listen to this." He glanced at the big clock on the wall. "I still have three-plus hours until boarding, and I can get to the airport in what – an hour and a half or so?"

"That's about what it'll take you. Hell, the *Thánatos* entry won't take too long. Like it or not, at 75,000 or 80,000 miles per hour, the asteroid entry isn't going to slowly glide into a gentle landing."

"I think you're right." Russ's head rocked up and down. "For that matter, depending on how the impact goes, I wouldn't be surprised if they cancel flights, especially any flying the great polar routes."

"At this point, I haven't had any communication on that, though I doubt it would interfere with the Honolulu connection."

"We always have room for one more if your flights are

affected. One way or the other, it won't be long now. We've been aware of this the past month or so, and we finally get to see how it's gonna play out. I guess we should be thankful it's happening in such a remote..."

He stopped in mid-sentence when he heard the journalist talking over the satellite feed of the asteroid now entering the Earth's atmosphere.

"...can see that the asteroid has split into several pieces that are trailing into the Earth's upper atmosphere now. Can you give us any indications of what to expect, Professor?"

"First of all, it is probably a good thing that the asteroid has broken up." The holovision showed a graphic with her name, 'Professor Kirsten Ang, Geophysicist.' "Though the cluster is very tight, it may result in less damage by having several smaller impacts over a wider area. Of course, we must wait until after the impact to read our instrumentation before saying definitively what energy release occurred. We can only hope energy is dissipated by the increased friction of smaller particles which directly equates to the greater surface-volume ratio."

"And are we sure the breaking up of *Thánatos* is what is happening?"

"Well yes," the professor waved in the general direction of the satellite projection, "...just look at the image we are getting back from orbital cameras here real-time. We still don't know exact numbers, but this much we can say: the object itself appears to be quite oblong, maybe 100 metres in diameter by up to 400 metres or so in length. The initial estimates of speed seem quite accurate, just about 35 kilometres per second as *Thánatos* enters the atmosphere. We also know that it is tumbling, which has caused our modelling software incredible problems due to the random nature of the tumbling motion once it begins to interact with the upper atmosphere. That's when the random tumbling will determine if and when the asteroid will fracture into smaller pieces and/or skip off into space. We anticipate there will be more breakage than less. That, along with the fact that the object's entry angle is very shallow – somewhere between 38 and 41 degrees relative to the ground –could both help to reduce impacts. We are still hopeful that some, or even all of it may bounce off into space like a stone skipping across the water."

"Is that possible, Dr Ang?"

"Well, of course, it is possible, but there are too many unknowns here... I mentioned the tumbling... so we just have to wait and see."

"Can you give us some idea of how much energy this could release... I mean compared to something we can equate it to?" The news anchor conducting the interview was searching for an everyday comparison knowing full well that *Thánatos* was not an everyday occurrence.

She inhaled as if trying to get up the courage to give the reporter the bad news. "Well, it is certainly bigger than any nuclear device we have ever detonated. It's also difficult to visualise an explosion since, thankfully, it is so out of our everyday experience. We equate explosive force to the equivalent explosion of dynamite or TNT. A megaton explosion would be equivalent to a MILLION tonnes of TNT.

"I won't lose you with too many numbers but will give you a few comparisons. When we consider the first nuclear bomb exploded in anger, the 'Little Boy' atomic bomb the Americans dropped on Hiroshima, that had the equivalence of about 16 kilotons or 16,000 tonnes of TNT. The most massive nuclear weapon ever exploded was the Russian *Tsar Bomba* back in the early 1960s, and that was somewhere between 50-100 megatons. Please remember, mega is million, so that's 50 to 100 MILLION tonnes of TNT equivalence. That was absolutely huge and would have made a bang equivalent to maybe five thousand Hiroshima bombs when they exploded it over an island in the Russian Arctic Sea." She lowered her head. "I'm a geophysicist, not a weapons expert. It hurts me to speak in bomb terms.

"I feel better moving to astrophysical terms here. The famous *Tunguska* event 135 years or so ago in Siberia was the most significant piece of rock or comet to hit or explode over the Earth in recent times, certainly since our scientific ability was up to making at least basic measurements of outcomes. That might have been 20-25 megatons, so only a third to a quarter as much energy as the big bomb the Russians set off.

"Maybe a geological comparison might help clarify the explosive force here. Consider a similar ballpark event to this would have been the eruptive volcanic explosion of *Krakatoa* – a series of explosions, actually. That occurred back in the 1880s and literally had worldwide effects."

The reporter's eyebrows arched. "Wow, that's big! I would assume a great deal of damage was done by all these explosive events."

"Well, the Russian blast was planned, so little or nothing that really bothered humans was felt, though the radioactive fallout drifted a long way. As for *Tunguska*, the Earth was also fortunate that it exploded where few humans lived. A great deal of damage was done there, but in Siberia, few people were killed, but an unknown number of reindeer definitely met their demise. We do have direct evidence of several thousand square kilometres of forest being flattened by the shockwaves, a remarkably positive outcome for a blast that was that big. Coincidentally, *Thánatos* will also impact very near where the *Tunguska* airburst occurred.

"That leaves *Krakatoa*. *Krakatoa* was a volcanic island in Indonesia located between Java and Sumatra. A mountain was disintegrated within minutes, and some 25 cubic kilometres of rock and soil disappeared into the atmosphere, simply vaporised. Remember, we didn't have the communications or measuring devices available then the way we do today, but probably somewhere between 35,000 and 100,000 people died from the explosion and resulting tsunamis. Reports of hearing the blast came from as far south as Perth, Australia, over 3,000 kilometres away. There were also reports of feeling the concussion from the Island of Rodrigues close to Mauritius, nearly 5,000 kilometres to the West across the Indian Ocean. Barographs measured shock waves circling the Earth several times over the next few days, and the Earth's atmosphere was so filled with dust that the sun was blocked in many places for a week or two. The entire average temperature of Earth dropped over a degree Celsius during the year after the event."

"So, could you compare that energy release from *Krakatoa* to the *Tunguska* and *Tsar Bomba*?"

The professor tossed her head in an attempt to fling a strand of hair from her eyes. "It is much bigger than both *Tunguska* and *Tsar Bomba*. *Krakatoa* probably released energy equivalent to 190 to 200 megatons, and that is only a guess."

"Two hundred megatons?" The reporter didn't wait for his rhetorical question to get an answer. "Do we think *Thánatos* will release that much energy?"

"If our size, density and velocity calculation are anywhere near correct, *Thánatos* potentially could release an equivalent amount of energy to a couple of *Krakatoa* events were it to make a full-on, direct hit into Earth." Professor Kirsten Ang's face was grim. "We are optimistic, though, and we just might get lucky. First of all, I again emphasise that first of all, the impact zone is very far up into Siberia. That area is so sparsely populated that almost no human life is at risk. Secondly, the shallow angle of entry may result in all or some of *Thánatos* skipping off into space." Professor Ang counted on her fingers. "And thirdly, the fact that it is breaking into pieces already may limit any single blast to a lesser release of energy."

"Professor, we've seen these images stream in for several minutes now. Am I correct in saying that the deeper *Thánatos* drops into the atmosphere, the more it is breaking up?" The journalist's voice sounded optimistic.

"Yes, yes... that's exactly what you see here. The deeper it *Thánatos* falls, the greater the friction. We are fortunate in that it is breaking into pieces now, and I am receiving data confirming that at least a few of the pieces have already taken trajectories that will have them skip off the atmosphere and continue on back into space. This is all good news since it will reduce the impact on far northern Siberia. I do want to caution you that though she is breaking up, we have data now that confirm some rather large pieces will certainly hit the Earth."

"My god, that is one hell of a lot of energy!" Mikayla shook her head.

André looked at his colleagues. "Let's hope Professor Ang is correct, and it is some of the bigger pieces that skip off and back out into space."

11

Friday, 2 September; Gale Crater Outpost, Mars

"So now we have gotten to learn a bit about Lochie, and he about us. I realise you have had eight-plus months on one of Mr Jacobi's Mars Transit vehicles allowing you ample time to read and learn about what we are doing out here, but I still would feel remiss if I didn't at least brief you on the basics. For the rest of you, please bear with me."

Misha looked straight at Lochie. "Gale Crater Outpost was

established a little over a year ago and was the first permanent colony located south of the Martian equator. I know you have read much about this and I needn't go into any detail here other than to say we are here about 2,800 kilometres southwest of Alpha Colony 5.4° south and 137.8° east. I'd be surprised if you weren't aware of the fact that Gale Crater was named after one of your fellow Australians a long time ago. It was formed when a very large asteroid slammed into Mars about 3.6 or 3.7 billion years ago. Keegan and I have been refining that date since we've been here.

"When the asteroid struck, it ejected debris for hundreds of kilometres. The 'Alpha-Gale Freeway' you travelled over in the MRT had you dodge a lot of that debris coming into the outpost yesterday." She laughed at her use of the term freeway. "The main interest in Gale Crater is its history of having liquid water. There are many, many signs suggesting that it was filled with water sometime in the distant past. We note erosional patterns, sediment layers... all things that we geologists dream about." Again, Misha chuckled. "That's why it always held the promise of possibly having remnants – at least fossils – of ancient life, though most argued that would have been of the microorganism variety. NASA found this site so promising that they landed the *Curiosity* rover nearby, not all that far from our position here at the outpost. I know you saw the big mountain in the middle since it is impossible NOT to see... that's Mount Sharpe, or the official name is Aeolis Mons.

"The joke has been that since we are so close to Mars's equator, our colleagues at Alpha Colony tease us for being in a tropical resort down here. Of course, that would be a tropical rain forest of the Martian-type – tropical minus the heat, minus the rain, minus the jungles and minus the animals." She grinned. "It is so tropical here on the surface at Gale Crater Outpost that we had a high-temperature yesterday of 1.8° Celsius – that's PLUS 1.8°. Now I won't bore you with any more geology of the region here since you are already well aware of so many features we have here. Also, you'll be here for a while Lochie, so I have no doubt you will be happy to explore much of Gale Crater for yourself.

"We've explored many lava tubes here over the past year and found exactly what we anticipated – pristine examples of volcanic tubes formed as hot lava drained from them. Of course, we've done the chemical analysis of the minerals, identified crystal structures and dated the rocks. Again Lochie, I know you have followed the work we posted on Skynet over the past few years along with the research you did during the months you spent in transit from Earth."

"You're spot on about all that." Lochie nodded his agreement to Misha and the other staff members.

"Aw, but the real excitement has all come in two doses and, coincidently, they pretty much just fell in our laps so very close together..." Micha snapped her fingers twice. "...bang, bang! I'm going to ask Nigella to just give you the basics right now, but you will have time to read through the early reports after we finish up. Over to you, Nigella."

Nigella leaned forward and directed her attention towards Lochie. "As Misha and I have both mentioned, I have been based here at Gale Crater since we established this outpost, save for the occasional trip back up to Alpha. Last week I learned first-hand just how the discovery happened. Our hydrology people had been reading data from ground-penetrating radar and then drilling test holes looking for water. Naturally, this has been a never-ending search for us anywhere we explore on Mars. Besides occasional finds of ice, mineral samples are taken and analysed, giving us a better three-dimensional reading of the limited spots that we have looked at so far. In mid-August, the drill team had several successful core samples they catalogued from a location about 8 kilometres from Alpha Colony. They were heartened by increasingly dense icy brine contents within the rock they were bringing up. Early on 22 August, they hit the unexpected – liquid water at a depth of some 800 metres beneath the surface."

"Liquid water? That is fairly unusual, yes?"

"Yes, it is. Generally, we find water in the form of ice. In some spots, we find water ice within a metre or two of the surface. In other places, we drill holes a kilometre deep and still find temperatures below 0° Celsius and any water discovered is in the solid-state. With the 22 August find, it all happened so quickly. They captured several liquid samples and capped the borehole. As you would know, on the Martian surface, the atmospheric pressure is so low that liquid water just won't stay liquid for long. Depending on temperatures, liquid water will either vaporise or flash freeze, and even if it does freeze, the water ice will sublimate almost immediately. Routinely all samples are taken back to the laboratories at Alpha Colony when drilling stops, but because of the unusual find of liquid water, samples were returned to home right away."

Lochie's eyes arched. "Home?"

"I forget that you're a newbie... I mean 'home' as in Alpha Colony.

"The laboratory techs there basically follow the same routine on all samples – chemical analysis, electron-microscopy studies, mass-spectrometer analysis – all of what you'd expect. Because this sample was liquid water, they ran a series of basic tests looking for microorganisms or at least for organics. They did the normal battery of tests: microscopy, biochemical tests, polymerase chain reaction. Of course, the problem was that since they were looking for totally unknown microorganisms, no one knew if the scope of analysis was adequate. To make a long story short, microscopy showed interesting targets in the sample, and chemical analysis seemed to indicate an organic nature. Within a few days, microbial cultures were showing replication of the targets. Our Martian bugs were having babies!" Nigella arched her eyebrows.

"There is so much we need to learn. Frankly, we need all the input we can get from the broader scientific community as soon as possible. Only then will we be able to analyse and categorise what we have found. At this point, I can't tell you exactly what we have here, but I can confirm that it is carbon-based, and it is living and reproducing. We think it's way more primitive than even the stromatolite colonies found on Earth and the beginnings of that date back 3.7 to 3.8 billion years ago."

"Wow!" Lochie's mouth hung open for several seconds. "So why aren't we making this public?"

Nigella continued, "Well for starters, it's not our call. Alpha Colony Director Sam Tan wanted to gather enough data before making an outrageous claim only to find it knocked down by scientists back on Earth. You are aware of false discoveries of life before."

"Of course, you refer to the false positive microbes discovered on Jupiter's moon Europa a decade ago by the European Space Agency's *Minos* lander. What a total horror show that turned out to be when they 'discovered' Earthly life that survived the sterilisation process before the probe was launched."

"Yes. How embarrassing and damaging that was to the whole scientific community. We very much want to avoid that kind of humiliation falling on us. The idea was to give it a week or ten days and then, with input from our biological group here on Mars, make the discovery public at an interplanetary press conference. But then came our little find here at Gale yesterday which suddenly complicates an already complicated situation."

Misha picked up the story. "You know, our mission here at Gale Crater is to explore, take samples, learn all that we can about the region. To that end, we have been going along now for months, opening tubes where we find them, recording what we see and taking samples to bring back to our labs for analysis. We obviously have satellite and radar data showing many of them, but we still tend to stumble across new ones while on our surface missions. In a sense, after the first several explorations, the excitement of walking in a Martian lava tube where no human has ever stepped before kind of wore off." Misha blessed herself as if violating the scientific gods that be. "God forgive me for ever saying that doing ANYTHING on Mars could somehow become boring!" There were giggles along with nodding heads around the table.

"Anyway, Keegan and Siti went into a nearby lava tube about a kilometre from here. This was yesterday, 1 September. They walked into the tube only getting back in about 200 metres from the entrance when Siti notice a flash of light reflecting the beam from her helmet lamp. Over to you, Siti..." Misha extended her hand towards her colleague.

Siti continued the story from there. "Well to say I was surprised is putting it mildly. Our mission has been to discover what forces shaped this area. Yesterday, we were looking signs of water erosion or any indicators the type and quantity of lava that flowed through that tube. Truth be told, we were actually looking for anything out of the ordinary. At first, I thought we had probably come across a crystal of olivine, but when I stooped down to see what I had found, it was quickly apparent that the object was metallic. Of course, it was difficult to make any useful judgement there wearing my surface suit, but I at once was fairly sure this was more than a naturally occurring mineral, and I called out to Keegan."

"Sure did... until I die, I will never forget it." Keegan shook his head from side to side. "I might have been fifteen metres away, and she looked towards me and said, 'Looks like someone dropped their change.' I thought she was joking at first, but as I walked over beside her, I could see the shiny reflection. Of course, we followed all protocols and immediately recorded the find with holography, photography and positioning data."

"When we were done documenting the piece in place, Keegan told me I should have the honour of picking it up since I was first to spot it.' Siti's tone revealed her excitement. "I did just that. I admit I had a chill run through me thinking of who – or what – held this object the last time. Our gloves are not that bulky, so when I actually felt this object between my fingers, it sent a chill down my spine. I raised it in front of my faceplate, and at first glance, I confirmed my earlier thought that this was not a naturally occurring object."

Lochie was on the edge of his seat now. "Why do you say that, Siti?"

"First of all, because even viewing the piece through my faceplate, it seemed almost machined... very much like something manufactured. It also seemed to have regular marks around the edges that looked for all the world like writing."

Keegan chimed in, "And when she handed it to me. I gave it a once over and immediately agreed with her assessment."

Siti continued, "Look, I did say a coin, but I only meant that figuratively. There is still no indication that this piece is associated with our concept of money, but whatever it might be, I can't conceive of any way it could be naturally occurring. Besides that, if it were a coin, it's a big one... maybe 70 or 80 millimetres in diameter."

"That's for sure bigger than any Aussie coin." Lochie turned towards Misha. "Are we able to see the object – I guess we can call it an artifact – now... I mean up close and personal... here in an oxygen-rich atmosphere?"

Misha spoke. "We've documented it in every way possible and are starting our chemical and physical analysis of it. Of course, you can see it. I think it fair to say that if it is manufactured, then it must have been manufactured by some intelligent life form. Are we all agreed on that?"

Everyone around the table slowly nodded in agreement.

12

Saturday, 3 September; GNN Offices Café, Washington DC

Sunlyn waited, lost in her thoughts. She had known Yates for several years, but they never worked on an assignment together. She did get along well with him and knew they'd have no trouble collaborating on this project. Her initial reservation with Glenn assigning her to this story quickly developed into enthusiasm for the opportunity. When she spoke to Nicolás about the proposal, she was pleased – but not surprised – by his total support of her no matter what decision she made. As soon as she finished talking with him, she let Glenn know she was excited to accept the assignment. Sharing the lead for GNN's coverage of both the asteroid impact and the Global Summit offered a dimension beyond what any technical or human-interest story alone could present. She checked the time just as Yates walked into the café.

"Hi, Sunlyn."

She stood and extended her hand towards him. "Hi, Owen."

"I don't know about you, but I was surprised that the chief

has us working on this one together." Almost as if he caught himself, he quickly added, "It certainly is a pleasant surprise, I might add."

She smiled. "After mulling this over for a day now, I'm convinced we are onto the story of the century. I think Glenn's idea of balancing your technical approach with my more humanistic point of view might just let us pitch this story in a wholly different way from what our competitors might do. Frankly, I'm thrilled about the prospects, not only career-wise, but at the whole notion of having the chance to join some of the brightest minds on the planet. I mean, it's just so exciting."

Owen looked up at the waitress as she stood next to the table. "I'll have a coffee, with cream, please." He saw Sunlyn nod her head and hold up two fingers. "Make that two, thanks."

"That's excellent." The waitress quickly scurried off.

Owen let out a sigh and his face transformed from a smile to a frown. "It could be the story of the millennium."

"Millennium? Did I miss something, Owen?"

"I just spent the past two hours in a holovision press conference. It was really aimed at the technical folks. The data are streaming in now, and we're getting some concrete numbers concerning the impact."

"Good? Bad?"

"Surprise, surprise... it's both good and bad. In the first place, the absolute best bit of luck was where the asteroid came in, up over the north pole. If this thing had hit here along the East Coast, we'd have had a million people dead in the first few minutes."

"Wow, *Thánatos* would have truly matched its namesake."

He moved his head up and down, indicating his agreement.

"The second piece of luck is that it split into a dozen or more pieces and several of the larger ones skipped off into space, and a few resulted in airbursts. Not so good is the fact that about eight or nine sizable pieces have impacted now."

"Sizable?"

"Yeah... sizable meaning 20, 30 up to maybe 50 metres in diameter."

"Wow. And you're saying most of this is good news?" Sunlyn looked a bit sceptical.

"Well sure, mostly. The airbursts caused a series of shockwaves, but again, we are lucky it all happened in the remoteness of northern Siberia. Most likely it would have flattened trees and harmed herds of reindeer more than humans, though we are still awaiting reports of the outcome. The pieces that actually hit the Earth were so large that friction was unable to vaporise all their mass before they hit. The pattern in which they impacted though is interesting... they strung out fairly close together in a more or less straight line stretching over a path a few hundred kilometres long."

Sunlyn's squinted eyes and crossed arms silently communicated her discomfort. She let out a sigh. "Look, Owen, I want to make myself perfectly clear right from the start. As I said, I didn't volunteer for this assignment, though I am thrilled to be working on it with you. I just want to remind you that Glenn was well aware of the fact that I'm not a science-type by any stretch and that I will need your help time and again. You simply need to know that I will not hesitate or feel self-conscious about telling you when I don't understand something. Are you okay with that?"

"Absolutely – I'm more than okay with that, Sunlyn." Owen immediately set her at ease with his big smile. "Glenn told me exactly that in no uncertain terms. For that matter, having known you for several years, I am well aware that you don't get put on technical assignments. You may have noticed that I don't get assigned any human-interest stories. So, we both agree to rise to the occasion and cover each other's backsides when we get stretched outside our own comfort zones. So, I don't want to hesitate when I have a question for you, okay?"

"Definitely."

"Frankly, I think the two of us will complement each other's areas of expertise very well."

"Thanks for that. I am so relieved to hear that we're both on the same wavelength with this." She let out a sigh. "I think the whole point is having a non-scientific person asking the questions that so many of our non-technical viewers might have. If we can pull that off, I agree with Glenn that it could go a long way towards communicating all this to the public at large. Well, you'd better get ready for me asking a whole bunch of silly questions on which I'll need some serious clarification."

Owen raised both open hands between Sunlyn and himself. "I've got you already, I've got you... I am fully tuned into just that. You are never going to ask me a silly question and you should NEVER feel funny when you need something explained. Concerning the assignment that we are tackling, there are no silly questions. Check?"

"Check." She let out another sigh of relief. "And that's both ways."

"Agreed. I get the feeling we're going to be learning about a hell of a lot of psychological research that I'm going to count on you to explain to me."

"Fair enough..."

"Now then... back to asteroid impacts. When *Thánatos* started entering the Earth's atmosphere, it would have been 60 or 65 kilometres high. At that altitude, the air is so thin that the rarefied gases wouldn't be detectable without specialised equipment. It would be as dark as space, and we certainly couldn't live there even if you could somehow stop from falling."

"Well, that's my first question. If there is so little air there that we may not even be able to detect it, how could that have such an effect on the meteor... um, asteroid? Actually, you say there are no silly questions, so my first 'not-silly' question is this: want's the difference between a meteor and an asteroid?"

Owen smiled. "Excellent question and we should make it a point to include just that issue in some of our reports. Asteroids are large bodies, usually of rocky and/or metallic materials, that circle our sun in orbits somewhere between Mars and Jupiter. These objects range in size up to hundreds of miles in diameter, but still way smaller than any planets. There are many more small ones than big ones and the smaller ones – only maybe 10, 20, 30 feet across – we'd call meteors. There is no clear-cut number here, but *Thánatos* is definitely big enough that astronomers are calling it an asteroid.

"There are also comets. Comets tend to be more like dirty snowballs – flying piles of water ice and gravel along with traces of other materials. Comets go in more elliptical orbits that take them far, far away from the sun and then have them make near passes very close to the sun. That's what causes such spectacular comet tails. When they get close to the sun, some of that ice boils off and stretches out hundreds of thousands of miles behind it in a tail.

"To sum up, *Thánatos* is an asteroid, but everyone knows what you mean if you call it a meteor. In our GNN journalists' style book, we'll agree to call it an asteroid."

"That all makes perfectly good sense to me, Owen. Thanks for that. Now let me re-ask my original question, how could such a thin atmosphere 60 or 65 kilometres high be able to affect *Thánatos* so much that it could cause it to break up?"

Sunlyn reached for her coffee.

"Good... good question. Remember, there is SOME air there, just very little. But even those few molecules of air rubbing against that huge piece of rock moving at speeds approaching 35 kilometres a second – that's close to 78,000 or 80,000 miles per hour – still cause frictional forces on its surface that start heating the rock and causing drag. When you were a kid, did you ever put your hand out the open window of a car and feel the wind pushing it harder and harder as the car went faster?"

"Sure – we've all done that I suppose."

"Well, that's air friction. And the speed really is the killer here. In this case, we're talking about kinetic energy or the energy of an object in motion. That energy – I promise not to 'do the math' with you too much – is quantified by the simple formula $KE = \frac{1}{2} mv^2$ or kinetic energy equals one-half the mass of an object times its velocity squared. The point here is that since the mass stays about the same, save for bits that may fall off, the velocity keeps increasing. When the velocity doubles or increases by two, the kinetic energy doesn't double because the two in the equation needs to be squared. Two times two is four, so double the velocity means four times as much energy. Triple the velocity and..."

"Increase the energy nine times."

"Far out, Sunlyn – you're spot on."

"Look, I keep saying I'm not a science-type, but I DID get through a year of calculus, a year of chemistry and a year of physics in high school! For that matter, I did pretty well in them, too. I always had the interest but studied topics other than physical science in college." She could read his curiosity. "I had a double major in journalism and psychology to be specific."

"All good, Sunlyn." He had a Cheshire cat grin on his face.

"I've known you long enough to know how competent you are. I bet you had all A-grades in high school, didn't you?"

She almost blushed. "Not exactly!"

"All right, all right... So, as I was saying, it's the friction that eventually begins to tear the rock into pieces along fracture zones within the asteroid. Remember, *Thánatos* was basically a rock the size of several aircraft carriers tumbling along at this incredible speed."

The waitress brought the two cups of coffee, set them on the table, smiled and retreated towards the kitchen.

"Did you ever skip stones off the surface of a lake or river when you were a kid."

"Yep. My dad always showed me how to spot the flattest ones we could find – they always skipped the best."

"Exactly. A few of the flatter pieces that broke off the asteroid just hit the increasingly thickening atmosphere at such an angle that they skipped just like the stones your dad tossed with you when you were a kid."

"Do they know how much skipped off back into space?"

"Well, they will have more accurate measures when the data are collected from all observation sites, including satellites, Moon Base One and Mars Alpha Colony... but probably *Thánatos* lost close to fifty per cent of the mass, some 4 megatons of rock."

"That's TONNES, not kilograms, yes?"

"It surely is."

"That sounds like a hell of a lot of rock to me."

Owen continued, "That IS a hell of a lot of rock! Actually, that's 4,000,000 tonnes to be exact! I checked it out on Skynet and found that the Golden Gate Bridge weighs a bit over 800,000 tonnes, so that would mean *Thánatos* lost maybe five Golden Gate Bridge's worth of mass! That's all the steel, all the bitumen, concrete, brickwork... gone. LOST! And probably another bridge-worth of mass would have been ablated as it hurled through the atmosphere." Owen noticed a quizzical expression on her face. "Sorry... Ablation is simply a rock that is vaporised due to friction and heat as it hurtles downward. The temperatures along the outer surface of the rock can reach over 1,600 °C – that's 2,900 °F. That doesn't just melt rock but can actually vaporise it. Now vaporise does not mean destroyed since matter can't be created or destroyed. That means that since it is already in the Earth's atmosphere and gravitational pull, the atoms and molecules of vaporised rock will eventually drift to Earth as dust."

"Asteroid... meteor... gravel... dust..." Sunlyn was thinking out loud. "Didn't the asteroid that killed off the dinosaurs create a lot of dust?"

"It sure did, though much of that was thrown up from the planet's surface after it hit. Thank god this is nothing like that one. That would have been 10 kilometres – 10,000 metres – in diameter. *Thánatos* is – or was – a measly 400 meters or so the long way. When the dinosaur-killing asteroid hit near the Yucatán Peninsula in Mexico 65 or 66 million years ago, it kicked enough dust and water into the Earth's atmosphere to cause it to be as dark as night for several years. That had such drastic consequences that it began what we call "The Fifth Extinction". The Fifth Extinction was so severe that more than three-quarters of all the species on Earth died out in just a very short period."

"The fifth? So there obviously were four extinction events before the dinosaur-killing one?"

"Exactly. Earth has had a total of five periods of great dying... anyway, the 66-million-year-ago event produced so much dust, smoke and smog that it blocked out sunlight for several years. Many plants died, and big animals that needed large quantities of vegetation for their food simply died. Probably cold-blooded animals suffered the worst because their body temperature is dependent on the sun shining, and it just didn't break through the clouds for years. A wide variety of beasts we call the dinosaurs – many big and many cold-blooded – simply died out. But guess what had been scurrying around for a few tens-of-millions of years or so..." Owen paused long enough to make his point. "...little mouse-sized mammals. The sudden disappearance of the giant lizards left a niche opening in which mammals could thrive. Little mammals led to bigger mammals which eventually led to us *Homo sapiens*."

"So, are you trying to tell me that with the 66-million-year-ago impact we were lucky?"

"I am."

"And this asteroid – *Thánatos* – would make us lucky how?"

"Now don't run ahead of the story here. I'm not saying that *Thánatos* is anything like the Yucatán event or we'd be dead and dusted already and not sitting here sipping our coffee and chatting about it all."

She let out a sigh. "I guess I'm still coming to grips with why we are – might be – lucky with *Thánatos*."

"Well, so far we are lucky. For starters, *Thánatos* was MUCH smaller than the 66-million-year-ago asteroid. We think that one hit more or less head-on, so no pieces were skipping off back into space. I repeat, but *Thánatos* is coming at a steep enough angle to avoid that kind of direct impact. Now that the meteor fragments have impacted, we just have to await word on what damage has been done."

She sipped her coffee. "With any luck, now that *Thánatos* has hit and we're all still here and mostly happy, maybe the millions of 'the-end-is-near' marchers all over the world will settle down and get back to worrying about more immediate things like rising sea levels and catastrophic storms."

"Don't hold your breath on that, Sunlyn."

"Jeez... We set off on our adventure in a few days."

"We do. No doubt Nicolás will miss you."

"And me, him." She paused. "Owen... if you don't mind me asking, do you have a mate... someone special." She paused. "I'm sorry, it's none of my..."

"No, no... if we're going to be working together, of course, it's your business." Owen's grin was genuine. "I'm – how do they say it? I guess I'm footloose and fancy-free... I did have a special mate, but that all fell apart when she was transferred to London a few years back. We tried making a go of it but being apart for long periods definitely didn't make our hearts grow fonder."

"Understood." Sunlyn finished her coffee. "To tell you the truth, Nicolás will be as busy as I am though since this whole Eights thing is getting bigger and bigger. For that matter, who knows if this whole *Thánatos* happening will have any effect on all those kids, too."

"Probably not. From reports I see, and what I read, those kids are so far out of it they don't even know what *Thánatos* is. That's all quite troublesome."

"Troublesome is putting it mildly."

13

Saturday, 3 September; Kalorama Heights, Washington DC

"I'm glad you decided to come along on this one, Harry." Maggie spoke from the backseat to her colleagues Bradshaw and Grimms belted-up in front. The car quietly hummed along Massachusetts Avenue out of Dupont Circle and past the multitude of embassies on their left. The late afternoon sun still filtered through the many trees alongside the road. "I guess I'm surprised that they traced a DNA match to a residence over here."

"Yeah, good point. You wouldn't expect to find Kalorama Heights to be a hotbed for the Eights, but the DNA match was definitive, not a partial." Grimms and Bradshaw both turned towards Maggie as their squad car rolled past embassy after embassy. "You know this area pretty well, yes?"

"Not personally, but professionally I do." She laughed. "I don't want to overstate my knowledge about Kalorama Heights, but yes, we've had several cases we worked on that brought me into the area."

"Fancy cases I bet... just look at these homes."

The police car turned off Massachusetts Avenue and drove into a squeaky-clean, obviously wealthy neighbourhood.

"Fancy? Yeah, I guess... As for what kind of crimes we find here, they'd be mostly fraud, tax evasion, white-collar crime... you know, wealthy-people dramas. We did have a case of some high-level investment banker coming home early from a business trip and shooting his wife and her lover. That's a fairly violent crime for this neighbourhood though. You don't get any riffraff living in these homes. I reckon you can't even touch one for under eight figures."

"Good one, Maggie – chasing down kids involved with the Eights, and you had to work an eight into the conversation, didn't you?"

"Yuck! That's below your level of humour, boss. Besides that, it was totally coincidental."

The car slowed along 24th Street NW as its auto-drive pilot navigated down a quiet lane until it pulled over in front of a two-story stone house. Grimms looked up at the finely manicured dwelling. "Wow... Forget the coincidence, I'll guarantee you this place is definitely worth ten-million-plus if it's worth a penny." The car set its break as the low whine of the electric motor went silent.

"Okay, how do you want to do this?"

Grimms had one hand on the door. "Look, Maggie and I will ring the bell, and you can give us some cover from outside here. It looks like that driveway goes alongside the house to a garage out in the back. The driveway is gated, but it looks like it might be partly open. As usual, we have to be ready for anything. If the young man here was involved in shooting up that apartment, Ryan, then we have to assume he could be armed."

"I got ya, boss – that's the plan. I'll cover the house from out here and be ready for anything."

The three of them got out of the car. Bradshaw walked off to the side of the house as casually as he could, putting on his best act at playing a local resident on a walk. Detectives Grimms and Patton walked up a few steps and stood before the double-doored entryway. "You set?"

"Yes, sir."

Grimms reached out and pressed the button on an intercom and looked at the camera lens.

"Can I help you?" A woman's voice crackled through the

little speaker.

"Good afternoon, ma'am. I'm Detective Sergeant Grimms, and this is Detective Patton." He held his DC Metro Police shield in front of the camera. "We're investigating a case and wondered if you could help us."

"A case?"

"Yes, ma'am. We only need a moment of your time if you don't mind."

"Um... just a minute, please."

* * *

Once Bradshaw saw his partner reach for the intercom button, he crossed the street and walked toward the corner a few hundred feet from the house. He kept his eyes glued on his partners, watched as the front door opened, and saw Grimms and Patton walk inside. When he got to the intersection, he quickly crossed over to the other side of the street and casually strolled back towards the dwelling. About a hundred feet before he approached the driveway to the right side of the target house, he saw a person moving behind the hedges and bushes around the neighbour's home. Thirty seconds later, he was nearly in front of the drive, and he saw the security gate begin to open. He unconsciously patted his chest to feel his Glock just as a young man came into view squeezing through the widening gap in the eight-foot-high fence. Their eyes met, and at once, the young man began to run towards the street.

"Wait a minute, son." He put up his hand, gesturing for him to stop, but the young man was having none of it. He bolted towards the street and abruptly stopped to dodge a pizza delivery vehicle racing down past the house. The hesitation was just enough to allow Bradshaw to run up beside the young man and grab him by the shoulders. The boy didn't offer any resistance.

"I didn't do anything, mister."

He quickly displayed his badge. "That's good. Then you won't mind if I have a word with you, right?"

"I said I didn't do anything."

"I didn't say you did." Ryan sized the young man up. From the background check they did on the person identified by the DNA sample, this boy did fit the description they had of the suspect. He was a well-built young man, seventeen years old and a senior in high school. "I want to speak with Bradley O'Keefe."

The boy jerked as if to start running again, but the detective's grip quickly stopped him in his tracks. Bradshaw still had high hopes the interview wouldn't require that he get physical with the boy. "Are you Bradley?"

The young man looked down towards the driveway. "Yes, that's me... but I told you that I didn't do anything."

"Bradley, what do you know about the group of young people associated with the Eights over there on K Street? Are you friends with anyone in that group?"

The boy kept his eyes down and didn't say a word.

"My partners are in your house right now speaking with your mother. Maybe we should go join the conversation there."

"She didn't do anything, either."

The front door opened, and as Grimms and Patton came onto the step, the woman holding the door noticed her son standing with Bradshaw. "Bradley, what are you doing out there. I thought you were in your room."

Bradshaw put his hand on the boy's shoulder, and they walked up the front steps and into the house.

14

Saturday, 3 September; The Caucus Room Restaurant,

Washington DC

The Caucus Room was one of the finest five-star restaurants in Washington. Its clientele generally would not include a couple of journalists, but Nicolás was insistent on taking Sunlyn out for a special dinner since they had no idea how long she'd be away on assignment. Normal go-to-work wear for Nicolás was an open dress shirt and a sports coat. As for Sunlyn – except when she was doing on-air broadcasting – she spent 90% of her time in blue jeans and a blouse. Tonight, he wore a suit and tie, and she wore a bright red dress along with her best jewellery. It was apparent to Nicolás that she thought the occasion special, too. Besides looking her usual beautiful self, Sunlyn wore fashionable pumps, and he knew just how much she usually hated wearing high heels. He found it a struggle to turn his attention away from her but managed to look at the wine list.

"You look absolutely beautiful tonight, Sunlyn."

"Tonight?" She lowered her head and pouted, feigning her disappointment. "And here I believed you always thought I was beautiful."

He gritted his teeth, squinted his eyes and then smiled. "I DO always think you are the most beautiful woman on Earth."

"How about the moon? Mars?"

"Sunlyn, you are the most beautiful woman in the whole

Milky Way Galaxy."

He was almost relieved to be saved by the wine steward. He looked up and order. "Could you bring us a bottle of the Dom Perignon, please."

"Excellent choice, sir."

"Oh boy... there goes our summer vacation money." She giggled.

"Only the best for you, my love." He reached along the side of the tablecloth and squeezed her hand. "Shanghai, huh? I hope you're only gone for a week or two."

"We'll see about that, hon. You know we're meant to start in Shanghai, but at this point, we have no idea where to from there. I always feel bad when we can't be together, but I admit to being excited about this assignment. Besides Glenn having the confidence in me to get me out of my journalistic comfort zone, I think we might be onto the story of the century here. This Global Holistic Summit sounds absolutely fascinating. And *Thánatos*... who knows? Besides enhancing my career path in journalism, I admit to being mesmerised by the sheer intellectual challenge of being with so much global brain-power from so many different fields."

"From what I hear at the *Post* and on the news, I think you're exactly correct. Just don't forget to come back to me." He blew an air kiss to her.

The wine steward returned and made a fuss over popping the cork from the bottle of French Champagne and handed the cork to Nicolás. He poured a bit of the bubbly and stood aside. Nicolás lifted the flute by the stem and sniffed its sparkling contents. After a small taste, he nodded his head towards the steward. "This is very good, thank you." The waiter poured into Sunlyn's flute and then topped up Nicolás's.

"Enjoy." The steward turned and was on his way to another

table.

Nicolás lifted his glass and moved it towards her. "To us – healthy, happy, successful, and soon to be together again."

"To us." Sunlyn lifted her flute and met his glass in a clink.

The couple traded chit chat as they ordered dinner, all the while sipping their Champagne. After a few minutes, Sunlyn not-so-subtly steered the conversation in a different direction. "You know, you might take a week or so of your vacation time to meet me in China... or Australia..."

Nicolás's eyes opened wide. "Aw Sunlyn – there's nothing more I'd like to do, but the *Post* is in the middle of the whole *Thánatos* impact, too. Besides that, Australia?" He cocked his head questioningly. "What do you mean Australia? How'd that come into the picture?"

"Well for starters, Kylie is from Australia."

"Kylie?"

"Yeah, yeah... I'm going to get to that. At this point, there are only some rumours floating around, but Australia might have a story in it after the Summit. Now, just maybe you need to get creative. Maybe you need to plant a seed in Norm Crawford's head that he should send YOU to China or Australia."

"Right! Now I'm planting seeds in my editor-in-chief's head."

"Well, funnier things have happened. Remember our trip to Hawaii a year or two back? I was assigned that feature story on the staff life at the Mauna Kea Telescope Precinct base camp, and you planted that seed in Norm Crawford's head. Son-of-a-gun... your boss just happens to send you on the Mauna Loa Observatory climate data piece. Somehow nobody seemed to mind that we tacked on five wonderful vacation days in Kailua-Kona, did they?"

"I love you, honey." Nicolás again reached under the table and ran his hand across her knee.

"I love you, too, Nicolás." She put her hand on top of his and pressed it tightly against her skin.

"So, I didn't say I wouldn't try to meet you somewhere." He grinned like a Cheshire cat. "China is probably out of the picture since I am pretty much booked here in DC during the time you are at the Summit. But maybe if you explain how Australia – Kylie – comes into the picture, I could figure a way to plant that seed you were talking about in Norm's head." He suppressed a chuckle as he reached for his Champagne.

"Ah, yes... Australia. We had a presentation at the office yesterday from an Australian Professor, Kylie Childs. She heads something called the Australian Centre for Solastalgia and Ecopsychology Studies."

"Oh boy – that's a mouthful."

"Well maybe, but I'll tell you this, I found her work to be absolutely fascinating and very much a part of what we've been doing concerning the kids' movement. On top of all that, she's a really neat woman. It seems Glenn knew her from a presentation he heard her give recently, and he put me on to her... or maybe her on to me... whatever. We did seem to hit it off really well. I found out over the coffee break that she will be coming to the Global Holistic Summit, too."

"Good on you, hon. She sounds interesting."

"At least I can say we got on well enough that she stopped by the office this morning on her way to the airport. Amongst other things, she told Owen and me that we were invited to a conference in Australia the week after the summit."

"Wow... that's how Australia comes into the picture. And down under conference somehow fits your assignment?"

Sunlyn's open hand turned back and forth in a maybe or

maybe-not gesture. "It's too early to tell. I don't know if we follow the asteroid story to Siberia or chase the Eights story to Australia."

"I'm all ears... tell me about her presentation. For starters, what in god's name do solastalgia and ecopsychology mean? Do those terms somehow relate to something we might be interested in?"

Sunlyn let out a sigh and took another sip of her Champagne. "Nicolás, the work she is doing has EVERYTHING to do with the Eights... maybe even the shooting at our apartment."

"How's that?"

"There is so much to tell you that I know that it's impossible to do it justice at dinner, but I'll try. To be honest, though, her presentation was very sobering."

"Sobering?"

"You do have an idea of what solastalgia is, right?"

"It'd be hard not to since the term has been all over the news for the past few years. I have to admit though that I just sort of thought it was a niche area of study and that it hadn't taken on broader implications. Ecopsychology... solastalgia... environmentally induced anxiety... has this become a bigger thing than I'm thinking?"

"I think it has, hon. I think it applies to the lower socioeconomic class as well as the middle class, to the kids, to the public at large. So much of the social issues we deal with – social discontent, domestic violence, self-harm, suicide... These disturbing stories of social decay have been getting more and more widespread of late. Many indicators point to much of this being rooted in environmentally induced distress. I guess we have all experienced the idea of – how'd she put it – 'feeling homesick when you are still at home'..."

"...because the home you live in today isn't the home you lived in yesterday."

"Exactly."

"But hasn't that gone on forever? Didn't our grandparents and great grandparents go through that?"

"Probably, but it's a matter of extremes. It is so much more pronounced today for the simple reason that, one, there are so many more people and, two, society and technology seem to move at breakneck speed. She spoke to us of the community she grew up in outside of Sydney where, as a child, she played amongst the trees in an orange grove there. By the time she got out of college, the orange grove had been cleared away, and a shopping centre was built there. So today, when she returns to visit family, there are grocery stores on that same piece of land, and they sell oranges shipped into Australia from South America or China, depending on the season. Obviously, she's an adult now, but even if she wanted to, she could never climb an orange tree there again because the orange trees have been replaced by strip malls selling imported oranges. It's like crazy stuff if you ask me, but at some level, we can all relate to that." She nodded yes to the wine waiter when he silently offered to top up her Champagne.

"Regarding your question about how this impacts on our reporting, so much of this seems to have the greatest impact on kids. It amazes me hearing about an explosion in numbers of young people displaying existential distress – almost an aloneness in facing the end of one's existence. I mean, kids! KIDS! That's the sort of thing to expect in our grandparents facing a terminal cancer diagnosis. Scientists have studied that for decades... but KIDS worrying about this!" She had obviously been affected. "You and I report on this for a living, but we just can't keep up with the speed at which it all seems to be spiralling out of control... especially for the kids!

"And she gave so many examples that emphasise this

phenomenon is not North American-centric. She talked of children in California, and New South Wales terrified to drink a glass of water because of the unrealistic fear they won't have enough to drink tomorrow... teenagers in Beijing or Delhi scared to play soccer after school because of poor air quality... Gulf Coast Floridians at Palm Beach, Sanibel and Marco Islands growing up along shoreline they are fearful of enjoying anymore because of noxious ocean sludge and carcasses of millions of fish, manatees and sea turtles... Brazilians at Copacabana and Ipanema wading through uncountable tonnes of plastic just to get wet..."

It was painfully apparent to Nicolás just how much the Australian's presentation had affected Sunlyn. He found himself wishing dinner would interrupt the sober conversation. "Look... I'm a journalist and spent my early days working the police blotter, reporting on stories of the police chasing people down who threaten society. I – we – like to think that we are lucky enough to be observers at a distance, but it still always makes me think what the world would be like if most people just decided to not follow the law. Love them or hate them, the cops have a tough job. That said, knowing WHY people behave in a deviant way often times helps law enforcement people solve the case or, better yet, maybe even prevent it from ever happening in the first place. Is that what you are saying here? Are you saying her argument is that to somehow make a positive change in the society we must come to grips with the ecopsychology of the whole situation?"

"I... I guess so." Sunlyn's frustration was palpable. "I don't want you to think that I... or she, for that matter, pretend to have all the answers. It's just that her take on WHY these things are happening seems so insightful. I mean, we all know the situation with teens has been getting worse for years. And yet there is no longer a question that casual relationships relate directly to ecopsychological and solastalgical drivers. Maybe that is the subtlety of it all.

"As journalists, we've spent our lifetimes reporting on one shocking environmental crisis after another... and listened *ad nauseum* to political gibberish explaining why it is all somehow just a one-off, that it'll all be okay tomorrow. And now – and here's the subtlety of it all – we have somehow transitioned almost unnoticed to a world in which young people are particularly sensitive to personal isolation and the global malaise that infects every area of life. It is not just an anti-corporate hatred, rather a total lack of trust in political leaders, in religious leaders, in the community at large. These kids aren't revolting against exploitation, rather they are submitting to irrelevance. The only collective reality that is connecting this cohort together seems to be their shared isolation from a world they don't perceive as having any place at all for them. They seem to share the terror of an ecosystem in decline – life support structure that keeps them alive in hopeless, terminal disruption and decay. Even more, you would think their collective perception of such a bleak future would be turning them in a more confrontational direction... but that's not what we're seeing. They are withdrawing... in masses, they are curling up in a collective ball and dropping out."

Nicolás sighed. "I think she's correct... you're correct... The weirdest thing of all though is that they are dropping out without any pharmaceuticals, any drugs..."

"Yep." Their waiter arrived with some rolls and butter. Nicolás broke a piece of bread off and began to butter it almost as a form of culinary escapism.

"But there is one detail here that just doesn't seem to add up."

"What's that, Sunlyn?"

"If the kids, including *Los Ochos* and the Eights – are withdrawing and becoming less and less aggressive, how do we explain a spray of semi-automatic weapon fire in our living room the other morning?"

Nicolás exhaled an audible breath of air and hunched his shoulders in an. 'I-don't-know' gesture.

"...and I just can't get her words out of my head when she defined solastalgia as, 'the homesickness you have when you are still at home.'" Sunlyn felt a tear in the corner of her eye.

15

Saturday, 3 September; Gale Crater Outpost, Mars

Arya, Joe, Nigella and Keegan sat with Lochie waiting for Misha and Siti to arrive. "I guess we get started when we get started."

Joe grinned. "Misha is NEVER late! She said we'd get going at 09:00 MST and believe me, we WILL get started at 09:00 MST."

"Trust me, Joe... she will be here." Nigella arched her eyebrows.

"Of course, you're right. By the way, Lochie, I know you are aware of what Mars Standard Time is, but have you ever heard the story of how it came to be?"

"I have some idea, Joe, but while we're waiting, sure, fill me in."

"Well for starters, when the original eight of us were in training – along with more than a hundred other scientists and technicians – we tried to foresee all possible challenges. The whole team believed we needed to approach every facet of life on Mars from the point of view of being cut off from Earth forever since the initial commitment was for a one-way trip.

Early on, it became apparent that we needed to standardise time somehow. I mean, there was no way it was going to work out perfectly just because of orbital mechanics, but we still needed an agreed-upon system. We needed to somehow find a common basis to apply on Mars as well as Earth. Too bad that nature's solar system clock wasn't so conducive to a common time. Consider...

"One solar day – that's high noon to high noon – at home, of course, is 24 hours exactly. Yes, yes... occasionally Earth slows down its rotation a bit, and we do add leap nanoseconds every now and then!" He held two fingers millimetres apart. "Coincidentally, a solar day on Mars is close to that on Earth: 24 hours, 39 minutes and 35 seconds. Obviously, it would have made no sense to redefine a Martian hour as a unit of time on Mars, since that would have changed minutes, seconds and so on and would have totally confused our mathematical treatment of science."

"Of course, you'd go crazy having to compare a thousand kilometres per Earth hour to a thousand kilometres per Mars hour if a Mars hour was 61.65 Earth-minutes long..." Lochie was quick to point out the problem of redefining the unit of time.

"Right. We agreed to call a Mars day a 'sol' and to divide it into 24, 60-minute Earth-hours just as at home. So far, so good... Are you with me here?"

"Yeah, but we still have more than 39 minutes unaccounted for."

"Of course. That's an extra 39 minutes and 35 seconds in a Martian sol to be exact. It was decided that this would be called a 'Martian Leap Hour' and would be inserted just after midnight MST each day. So, every night we lucky Martians get an extra almost-40 minutes of sleep! Thank god for digital clocks since it is easy for them to account for a leap hour every night. If any business occurs during the leap hour, it is simply designated as MLH, Mars Leap Hour, along with the minute number."

"Sounds complicated, but I know it works. I reckon that would be every Australian's dream at the local pub – a 'leap-hour' for drinking more beer!" The Aussie laughed at his own joke.

"Good morning Lochie." Misha walked into the staff room at a hurried pace and nodded her head towards him, "...and the rest of you. I trust you had a restful first night here." She looked at Greenbank.

"I did, thank you. Gale Crater Outpost is much more comfortable than I could have ever imagined. I also enjoyed the extra 39 minutes and 35 seconds of my first 'Martian Leap Hour' at Gale Crater to help me catch up a bit on rest."

Siti chuckled at Lochie's comment as she entered the room behind Misha. "Sounds like Joe was giving you a lesson on Mars Standard Time." She carried what seemed to be a small tool caddy, but Lochie couldn't make out what was in it. "I fear our accommodations can be too comfortable at times, especially when I want to sleep in a few extra winks beyond the Martian Leap Hour. I must admit though that I didn't have that problem today. I am very eager to catch you up on what we're finding, Lochie, and to update all of you on some analyses I've just completed."

Misha walked toward the kitchenette. "I think we should all fill up our mugs before we get started and settle in for an interesting morning." She pressed a few buttons on a beverage dispenser, and a stream of coffee was delivered to her mug. "I assume you were shown the wonders of our trusty food synthesisers back at the colony, Lochie. Yes?"

"Well, sort of. I did use one a few times, but I was only there for a short while after we arrived after our nine-month coast out from Earth. I understand the concept behind it all, but I must admit that I remain sceptical that you can basically print food using a fancy three-dimensional printer without some horrid effects to your body."

Siti looked up just as she took what appeared to be a bagel draped with cheese from the synthesiser next to the beverage dispenser. "Trust me, it works! I've been here for eight years now, and I'll be damned if I can lose any weight."

"Don't be so sceptical, Lochie... Let your taste buds tell you exactly what a food synthesizer and the right combination of raw materials can produce. Put it all together with the right programming blending the proper mix of protein, carbohydrates, fats, minerals, vitamins, flavouring, spices and colour and... bingo!" During the brief time Joe spoke, the synthesiser produced a cinnamon muffin in the middle of its stage and dropped it onto a plate.

"Well, that damned muffin sure smells good. I guess I can't be too sceptical, or I'll waste away to nothing."

* * *

"So Siti, you say it's plastic?" Lochie was totally overwhelmed at the touch of the extra-terrestrial artifact as he ran his finger over the surface and then lifted it closer to his eyes.

"Well no, it's not plastic *per se*. Plastics we make using hydrocarbons... actually using lots of carbon-bonded polymers. This stuff is metal but does display some properties of a plastic. Chemically, the medallion isn't like a metal that possesses quite orderly, crystalline structures. In this alien material, the atoms are arranged quite randomly, kind of like those in bee's wax or glass. As a matter of fact, there has been some work done in the States, China and Japan on a funny class of metal alloys called BMGs or 'bulk metal glass.'" She watched him mesmerised by the alien artifact. "I needn't patronise you, Lochie – you're a geologist and have had tonnes of chemistry. These BMGs are amorphous solids, but unlike wax or glass, BMGs have excellent electrical conductivity."

"Humm. So, tell me, Siti... what do we need to take away from your findings here?" Lochie's eyes were fixed on the medallion as he continued to nervously turn it in his hand.

"I'm telling you that this material is high-level technology. You know how we generally make medallions – or coins – back on Earth. The most economical way is to use metal 'blanks' then stamp them under a high-pressure press. Alternately, we can produce cheaper goods by blow-moulding plastic polymers. With our Martian medallion here, I am sure they were blow-moulded metals as it were, done at low pressure and relatively low temperatures. In a sense, these were manufactured cheaply and yet are made of very high-strength, durable metals."

"So, you're saying that BMGs can be thermoformed like we do with plastics?" Lochie was mesmerised at the thought of just who made the piece he held in his hand.

"Yes, I think the medallion you are looking at there was manufactured that way. At this point, I can tell you that I have analysed the material doing whatever test I can without destroying the piece, and I have learned quite a bit. Elementally, I'm finding traces of titanium, zirconium, copper and nickel, though I am unsure of exactly how the process of making it works. I can account for the material properties with the metals I have mentioned here, but we've found other constituents, too. Regrettably, I can't even speculate as to their purpose right now. I can tell you that the medallion is NOT a polymer-based plastic. Look, I need more time. We just found this and hopefully will find more. With a sample of one, I am scared to death of defacing it or – worse yet – destroying it. The best that I can answer your question right now is to say that what we all need to take away here is fairly straightforward. Whoever manufactured this piece of BMG displays a greater understanding of basic chemistry and metallurgy than our own science does today."

"Your findings here are fascinating, Siti, and you needn't apologise for just getting started." Joe was happy to let Lochie drop the medallion into his own hand. "I guess I was just assuming it was stamped out of metal blanks of some sort, but the closer you look, it definitely does seem to be different. I confess that I don't pretend to understand the finer points of the chemistry you are describing, but I can see where the BMG angle could allow for a whole different set of useful processes and materials."

Keegan pulled at his chin. "Fascinating material for sure. You know though, I still think we're missing something really fundamental here…"

PART TWO

"Our youth are not failing the system; the system is failing our youth. Ironically, the very youth who are being treated the worst are the young people who are going to lead us out of this nightmare."

— Rachel Jackson, youth advocate

16

Tuesday, 6 September; aboard Paris to Shanghai SST

André sat back in his comfortable seat on the SST, heading for China at over 2,000 kilometres per hour. He reflected on just how travel had changed over his 20-year career. With the arrival of economically affordable and environmentally friendly aircraft, these medium-sized supersonic transports easily turned 11-hour flights into two or three-hour ones. Though jetlag was still a bother, it was much easier to deal with then in the old days when he was starting out with NOAA. More importantly, though, the invitation to Global Holistic Summit was an honour for which the travel was undeniably worth the effort.

"Care for a drink, sir?"

The flight attendant almost startled him. "Ah... a white coffee, please." In an instant, she returned with his coffee and placed the cup on his tray. "Thanks so much."

"Can I get you anything else?"

"I'll have some dinner when you serve it, but right now I want to review some reports. I'm going to put my technoserver headset on, so please just tap me when we are about ready for the meal."

"Of course."

It was nice having at least a few nights home with Amélie

and the kids. After his Asia trip for this Summit, he'd promised they would take a vacation... an old fashioned two or three-week family holiday up into the mountains. André pulled his VR technoserver headset from his travel bag and fixed it over his face. He saw his field of view lighten up when his SAM completed its link with the technoserver, and the virtual reality system came to life. At once, he was lying back in his comfortable seat immersed in an auditorium filled with other scientists. A presenter came to centre stage and introduced herself.

"Good day. I'm Gillian Pickard of the Institute of Astronomy, University of Cambridge. We continue to collaborate with our colleagues in Asia, Australia, Africa, Europe, North and South America as well as Moon Base One and Mars Alpha Colony. All have been gathering tracking data on asteroid $2044DK_{156}$, now formally named *Thánatos*, since its discovery in late February." Pickard smiled. "Yes, I know the name *Thánatos* has been over-used in literature and the sciences historically, but considering the potential, this object represented upon discovery, the name still seems appropriate and is easier to say than asteroid $2044DK_{156}$.

"We will give daily updates here in Shanghai throughout the Global Holistic Summit and continuing after the Summit from our home base in the United Kingdom. This presentation will cover data collected over the first 72 hours since the initial contact of *Thánatos* with Earth's atmosphere. All the numbers I present here will be available at the end of the talk on Skynet 4 and are subject to update as more data become available. Please feel free to interrupt me should you need clarification on anything.

"Let me start by saying that the worst-case scenario has not eventuated, and the consequences from impact so far have been less we initially feared... certainly less than they could have been. When we consider all the possible outcomes from an object this size striking the Earth, we have dodged the proverbial bullet. On a scale of one to ten with ten being the worst-case scenario, the *Thánatos's* impact is probably a four or five. I must warn you, however, that we should not feel overly complacent and that we will continue to experience the effects of this impact for years to come.

"From the on-going review of the visible and infrared imagining we have amassed from ground-based equipment as well as space-based recorders, we can now better update the physical characteristics of the asteroid. It is confirmed that initially, it was irregular, oblong in shape, 405 metres in the greatest length by close to 90 metres average diameter. We observed it tumbling before it encountered Earth's thermosphere. It first displayed signs of interacting with the atmosphere at approximated 67,000 metres. Once that interaction began, frictional forces disrupted the tumbling motion and caused it to become very erratic, very unpredictable. That caused the structure of the body itself to tear apart from an altitude of about 55,000 metres. We identified 18 pieces that were large enough to track, and of these, seven skipped off into space and have continued in orbit about the sun. Three pieces exploded as air bursts with only dust and small particles hitting the Earth's surface. The eight remaining fragments that were sizable enough to track in real-time impacted the Earth over an area about 50 kilometres wide and 650 kilometres along the direction of travel, which was very close to due west to due east. These ranged in impact size from approximately 60 metres by 30 metres for the largest down to a mostly spherical 35 metre-diameter ball on the smallest of those eight pieces."

"Excuse me, Dr Pickard." The silhouette of a man standing toward the front of the auditorium could be seen as the camera panned out. "Um, Martin Taggart of the *Singapore Star News*. Could you clarify what you mean by 'eight fragments sizable enough to track in real-time', please?"

"Of course. Naturally, our systems have downloaded and stored all of these data, and we will have our AI continue to analyse them into the foreseeable future. The 'real-time' statement simply means the pieces that were big enough to actually visualise and follow by eye or camera. There were smaller pieces from truck-size down to basketball-size fragments of rock that could have fallen anywhere, and we will eventually categorise these since the data have been collected from them. I don't want to underestimate these 'smaller pieces' though since a car-sized rock falling nearby could make quite a bang."

"Thank you, Dr Pickard."

The astrophysicist nodded at the questioner and then continued. "You can see the impact zone here." Pickard turned slightly and looked towards a marked-up map behind her. "Briefly, the direction of travel stretched along a line from Dikson on the Kara Sea in the west to Tiksi on the Buor-Khaya Gulf to the east. You can see that the Buor-Khaya Gulf is this body of water projecting to the southwest from the Laptev Sea. More specifically, the western-most affected town was Dikson at 73°N and 80°E and with a population under a thousand people. In the east, the last town receiving any nearby damage from *Thánatos* is Tiksi at 71°N 128°E. Tiksi is fairly populated for this part of the world, over 200,000 people there in an industrial population centre. Fortunately, neither of these towns were in areas of direct impact with the first piece hitting some 300 kilometres east of Dikson and the last about 600 kilometres to the west of Tiksi. Towns very close to impacts are Syndassko, Yuryung-Khaya and Nordvik, and you can see them pointed out here." She again indicated a slide that showed a closer look at this area of Siberia. "Less than 1,500 people live in Syndassko and Yuryung-Khaya, and Nordvik has no known residents. At this point, there has been no communication from any of these communities, though efforts continue to establish contact.

"The eight impact fragments represent approximately forty-to-fifty per cent the original mass of the asteroid, and we were fortunate with that. Therefore, the good news I have for you is that only half or less of the total kinetic energy that could have been released actually eventuated. However, the bad news I have for you is that approximately half the mass of *Thánatos* still entered the Earth's atmosphere. Fortunately, all of that entry mass didn't remain as solid objects that ultimately reached the Earth's surface. A sizable percentage was broken off, ablated and vaporised without actually hitting the land surface. Still, a tremendous amount of energy has been released to these far northern Siberian sites. We have yet to get ground recognisance in there, but you can see the trail of primary and secondary cratering in these satellite images."

A series of high-resolution images faded in and out behind Dr Pickard. "You notice here that the two largest pieces must have been a bit over and a bit under a hundred metres in diameter and the third was around 50-60 metres across. They formed these craters of 1,400, 1,000 and 600 metres in diameter." She used a laser to point at the craters. "The other five major fragments formed these smaller craters. You can see hundreds of secondary craters scattered across the region. Some of these resulted from ground strikes of smaller fragments broken from the main body and others result from the overlap of ejecta blankets thrown from each of the impact craters after the initial collisions. When we look at this overall scatter of cratering, it is fairly symmetrical over hundreds of kilometres, though skewed west to east along the direction of flight.

"The resulting heat, concussion and debris fragments would have been fatal to most life within five to ten kilometres of the actual strikes. Greater distances than that would have absorbed lesser amounts of energy. We have been in contact with people on the ground in both Dikson and Tiksi. Dikson reported a peak seismic reading of 7.0 with severe damage to many buildings and structures. They have confirmed about a hundred injured with 12 confirmed deaths. Tiksi recorded peak seismic reading of 6.7 with many broken windows, severe damage on older buildings and ruptured water and gas mains. They have over 500 injured and 21 deaths reported at this point, though we anticipate an increase in casualties as more reports come in.

"As you may imagine, the initial impacts resulted in tremendous kinetic energy transmitted into the Earth's crust. This resulted in shifting several existing faults, setting off a series of secondary shakers still being recorded now, 72-plus hours after the initial impacts. We will update all these data from the Global Holistic Summit here in Shanghai tomorrow and every day until emergency conditions are over. Are there any questions?"

17

Wednesday, 7 September; The Bund, Shanghai, China

"So, what do you think?"

Sunlyn leaned on the railing above the glass barrier and looked out across the Huangpu River. The dense forest of hundred-plus storey skyscrapers popping up from the financial district was a familiar sight even to a first-time visitor. "It's amazing. I mean, I've seen so many holovision images of Shanghai, but my first in-person view is quite imposing. The overwhelming size of it all is enough to practically knock you over."

"They have squeezed some 40-million people in here now and – considering the decreasing land area because of seawater intrusion – the density must soon approach some limit. This is my third visit here, and Shanghai never ceases to amaze me."

"So, they call this The Bund?"

"They do." Owen was right beside her, looking across the water at the city.

"Bund... that almost sounds German."

"Actually, I think the term is Persian and is similar in meaning to an embankment or levee. You can find bunds throughout Asia and the subcontinent... China, Japan, India... I'm pretty sure though that 'THE' Bund is quite synonymous with Shanghai."

"Do they all have such broad walkways? Except for the fact that it is paved with stone, it reminds me of a boardwalk in Santa Cruz or Atlantic City."

"Certainly, they aren't all as grandiose as this." He swept his hand towards the spectacular skyline of the Lujiazui district with its iconic Oriental Pearl TV Tower still a familiar sight to people around the globe.

"You mention the decreasing land area. I assume you mean the rising water level. That's been a problem here just like in Florida, Italy, Bangladesh and anywhere else on Earth where low-elevation land meets the rising sea. Anyway, we're still on The Bund, so at least the water level couldn't have risen that much around here."

Owen shook his head. "Not exactly... Okay, let me give just a bit of background here. Look down in front of us here." He was pointing to discoloured concrete and steel remnants just poking out of the water in front of the glass guardrail they leaned against. "That heavy slanted steel railing was the top of the old barrier or seawall along the Huangpu River here. Since we're close to the South China Sea here, the river is tidal and therefore responds to tidal effects twice a day, but increasingly at high tide, the river was overflowing onto The Bund. A decade or so back, the Chinese Government spent a great deal of money just to raise the concrete base here and then finish it off with what appears to be that glass pool fence that we're looking at. My understanding is that it's some super-duper glass that is watertight and strong. When a high tide and wind occurs at the same time, it can prevent flooding. Now for how long that remedy works, who knows?" Owen hunched his shoulders and threw his hands upward. "Mitigation or not, sea levels keep on rising."

"That's not dissimilar to the Floridian projects with walls and pumps... even New York City and the lower Manhattan seawall... I just wonder how powerful we can build pumps and how high we can build walls." Sunlyn shook her head.

"D'ya want to catch a taxi or walk over to the Old Town?"

"Can we get there on time if we walk?"

"Sure – we have plenty of time. It'll only take us 15 minutes or so."

"Let's walk."

Owen turned away from the railing and then headed away from the river. "So, I'm very anxious to meet Professor Childs."

"She's a fascinating woman. As I told you, I heard her presentation and had coffee with her a couple of times before she left Washington on her way here. I quite like her, and we seemed to be very much on the same wavelength. When I found out we'd both be coming to cover the Global Holistic Summit, I was excited to think that I – we – had a head start on everyone else since we have the personal contact with her. Now son-of-a-gun... here we are."

"Well, I'm looking forward to seeing her as much as you are. Do you know who's with her, who else we'll be meeting?"

"Another professor I think – Fiona Wu from the Shanghai Jiao Tong University here in Shanghai. I never met her before, but Kylie mentioned her several times during her presentation last week. I think they do a lot of work together, and they must also be personal friends. It's such a great opportunity to get to know them both a bit better before the Summit. HURRY!" Sunlyn made a sudden dash to cross the broad street with Owen trailing behind.

* * *

They climbed two flights of old wooden stairs into a large shop that looked like a cross between a bookstore and a tearoom. There were a few people scattered about the room as Sunlyn surveyed the area looking for a familiar face. A young woman dressed in traditional, form-fitting, silk Chinese *qipao* dress walked over to them and bowed. "*Nóng hō*... Hello. Would you like some tea?"

"Thank you so much. We are supposed to meet some colleagues here."

"You are American?"

"Yes, yes, we are."

The young woman smiled broadly. "Are you supposed to meet Professor Fiona Wu?"

"Why, yes."

"Very good. Follow me." The woman turned and headed back to the stairway on the far side of the room and started to climb another flight of wooden steps. They followed her up and entered another, smaller room.

"*Nóng hō*, Sunlyn." Professor Childs sat at a small table with another woman, obviously Asian and strikingly beautiful.

The woman who had shown them up the stairs again bowed her head. "Thank you very much. Enjoy your tea." She quietly turned and walked off down the stairs.

"Hello, Professor." They walked across the room. "I'd like you to meet Owen Yates, my journalist colleague at GNN and my partner on this assignment. He's one of our best science people."

"And this is my friend and collaborator Dr Fiona Wu who is a professor here in Shanghai at the Shanghai Jiao Tong University." Kylie stood and gave Sunlyn a hug, then extended her hand to Owen. "Please, sit with us."

Dr Wu shook hands with both. "Welcome to Shanghai."

"Thank you." Sunlyn pulled her chair up to the wooden table as a tea lady came over to greet them. "I didn't realise you spoke Mandarin, Kylie."

The professor laughed. "Well, I have gotten good at saying hello in Mandarin, *Nóng hō*. Ah, but then again, I've had a good teacher." She smiled at Fiona.

"...and I have learned to say hello in Australian – 'G'day, mate." Fiona giggled at her best impersonation of an Australian accent.

"I'm so glad you could make it. I've been here at the Fenghui Tang Teahouse before with Fiona, and it's an experience like no other."

Sunlyn sat next to Kylie and reached over to pat her hand, which was resting on the table. "I'm so happy you invited us. And Dr Wu, it's so nice to meet you. Professor Childs mentioned you quite a bit a presentation which I attended in Washington last week."

"I hope when she mentioned me it was in a good light." The stunning Chinese woman's beautiful smile lit up the room. "And please call me Fiona."

Sunlyn nodded her head. "She spoke of you in glowing terms, Fiona."

Fiona Wu almost blushed as she turned towards Owen. "Have you ever been to Shanghai before, Owen?"

"I have, Fiona. This is my third trip here. I love your beautiful city and the people I've met here."

Kylie glance down at Sunlyn's hand. "You know, I noticed your data band at the GNN offices last week. That is such a beautiful one – actually a lovely piece of jewellery. Where did you ever find that one?"

"Well, of course, it's just a decorative skin – cover – over the old data band that I've had for a long time. Nicolás – he's my soulmate – gave it to me for my birthday too many years ago to admit to, and I still like wearing it. Of course, it's no longer functional since I had my SAM implant years ago. I liked the decorative cover too much to stop wearing it even though it no longer hides a functional data band."

"I guess losing the chance to have a useful piece of jewellery is just one of the many things we had to get used to once the Subdermal Angel Microchip technology exploded back whenever. You don't often see the old data bands anymore, at least not in Australia. Oh, I should be a bit more specific and say that many kids still use the thin plastic wristband, but even then, families you wouldn't think could afford SAMs still tend to give them to kids by their 15th or 16th birthday."

Sunlyn bobbed her head up and down. "That's pretty much the same in North America. How about here in China, Fiona?"

"Exactly the same. For that matter, I think you will find that about 90 per cent of all the SAMs on Earth are manufactured right here in China, so it's a no-brainer that we are huge consumers of the technology, too."

"Well anyway, I do think your non-functional data band

skin makes for a beautiful piece of jewellery, and I commend your soulmate, Nicolás. He obviously has excellent taste."

"That he does... I am hoping you will get to meet him."

"I would love that. For that matter, I hope you get to meet my mate, too. I know I told you about the conference in Sydney, but we have heard some whispers about something big, maybe in Perth, after the Summit here. Things keep changing so quickly now. Whatever, I have no doubt you'd like my Micky."

"That would be lovely. I'd love to meet your mate, Kylie."

A tea lady came to the table and introduced herself as Li Wei. She began explaining a bit about the teahouse, the types of tea they had and for what ailments each tea offered a remedy. After a brief conversation, they agreed to try a variety of blooming teas.

Sunlyn was mesmerised when the tea lady returned with a tray carrying a small glass teapot for each of them along with four glass teacups. One by one, the tea lady took a small ball of tea leaves and held it up. She assured them that each ball of leaves contained a dried flower blossom in the middle. Li Wei ceremonially placed tea balls one by one next to each teapot. Sunlyn had chosen the jasmine with amaranth and marigold and watched intently as the tea lady gently placed the flowering tea ball in her pot. The tea lady then took a kettle of boiling water from the small gas burner and proceeded to carefully pour the water into a pot. She repeated the ritual for each of them. All eyes remained glued on their own teapots as the packets unfolded in the hot water, each pod growing into beautiful blossoms over the next three or four minutes. Sunlyn was taken by the silent vigil as the group sat trance-like, watching the blooming tea brew as if a part of some mystical religious experience. Finally, Li Wei slowly nodded her head and smiled. "Enjoy."

Sunlyn filled her teacup to about two-thirds, carefully placed her pot down on the wooden mat and sipped her tea. She let the flavour rush through her nose and into her nostrils. She enjoyed the silence and let her eyes take in the serenity of the old tearoom. The walls were a muddled arrangement of shelf after shelf of teapots, teacups, tea sets interspersed with row after row of labelled jars of various teas. In amongst all of this was an array of beautiful Chinese artwork. She took another taste of her blooming tea and sighed. "Wonderful." She looked at Owen. "What did you get?"

"Lychee. It's fantastic." Owen took a deep breath. He looked quizzically across the table to the other two women.

"Guava, my favourite," said Fiona.

"Red Jasmine... yum." Kylie sipped again.

18

Wednesday, 7 September; Gale Crater Outpost, Mars

It had been a long day, and Lochie was ready for bed. He'd spent the past several hours trying to catch up on both his academic reading as well as the latest news from back on Earth. He closed his Skynet reader – maybe he'd have a bowl of ice cream before turning in. He rolled over to the side of his bed and stood; after nine months in near-weightless conditions, the 38 per cent Mars gravity actually felt good. For the umpteenth time, he surveyed his accommodation and once again was impressed with the comfortable living space the staff quarters provided. Most of the residential and working areas where the team spent their time were below ground, but they still were bright and cheery with wall light panels everywhere. It was a simple matter of telling the AI system what you wanted, and the wall could just as easily become a window looking at the ocean or a scene from a tropical rain forest. And when it was time to sleep, the same panel could project a live view of the Martian sky with all the familiar constellations. Room audio was called up in the same manner with anything from a particular genre of music to the bounding of surf to total silence. Another nice feature he liked about the smallness of Gale Crater Outpost was that nothing was far away. Within a few dozen steps, he poked his head into the kitchenette off the staff room. "Hello, ladies."

"Lochie." Nigella sat at the kitchen table with Misha, both sipping a cup of tea. "We thought we were the last two awake."

"I almost turned in for the night, but then all of a sudden thought that there was a bowl of ice cream somewhere in that damned synthesiser that was standing between me and sleep." He turned to the food synthesiser and manipulated a few buttons.

"You know, the synthesiser recognises voice commands." Misha enjoyed teasing him.

"Yes, I know, but I like to humour myself into thinking that I still have some control when I can touch a few buttons." The synthesiser pushed a bowl into place and dispensed a serving of vanilla ice cream. Lochie pulled up a chair and sat with his two colleagues.

"You've been here nearly a week... You must be settled in now Lochie."

"Well, just about. Tomorrow will be a week since I got to Gale Crater."

"So, what's your take so far?" Misha took a bite of her biscuit.

"I'm still totally overwhelmed by it all. I mean, getting onto the surface a few times this week... looking at mineral samples... chatting with my teammates here... I am still dazed by it all every time I stop and think that I'm actually on Mars."

"I doubt that wonder-of-it-all will ever go away. You know that I have been here four years now, and I still have days I am overwhelmed that way. Even more now. When I consider the past few weeks since the discovery first of simple life and now the medallion... oh boy." Misha ran the back of her hand over her forehead.

"Damn... and you're a biologist. This life thing is almost too much for a mere geologist." Misha kept a deadpan expression.

"Maybe that's what amazes me the most. Probably half the people on Mars and most of us here at Gale are academic-types one way or the other. When you think about how focused you – I – had to be to get a doctorate... there is zero room to wander even a little bit away from your goal. At least once you grab the prize and take your credentials along with you, you suddenly have more leeway to follow some broader interests at the beginning of your career. And now I find myself in a remote outpost on a remote planet nearly a year's travel from home, and suddenly it becomes blatantly apparent that I – we – have to range far and wide beyond our training. Now I don't fear that, rather I embrace that as a challenge."

"You're right, Lochie – we are all in the same boat. Like you, I'm a geo, but when I think of my days back in Russia working on my thesis, I never had a clue that I'd find myself here. And to think the biggest, BIGGEST challenge of my career might prove to be in the life sciences..." Misha's words trailed off.

"Don't get too carried away with the wandering from your area of specialisation." Nigella set her teacup down. "Though I love my biology and at times think I wander away from it more than I should, I do remind myself that the point of academia is learning the process as much as the content. Don't you think the key focus of a doctorate in any subject area at all is HOW to manage a project, HOW to design and test hypotheses, HOW to acquire new knowledge? At the end of the day, we could all use the same skills learned in our doctoral programs and apply those skills to master snow skiing or to raising a vegetable garden or whatever. I don't belittle any area of expertise that each of us may have, but it's the process of acquiring knowledge that sets us aside from the 'normal people' who don't spend six or eight years in pursuit of a PhD the way we crazy folks have." She giggled.

"Naturally, I agree with you, Nigella. I chose geology because I was interested in it, but at the heart and soul of it all, I'm just a curious bugger and love learning just about anything. Maybe that's a part of the teacher in me too, I love trying to share it all."

"Me too, Lochie." Misha put her hand to her mouth to cover a yawn. "That's probably one of the biggest things I miss up here –interactions with students... sharing so much of what we learn here on Mars. At least I do enjoy the "Talk to a Scientist" program I participate in on Skynet 2."

"Funny you mention that, Misha... the sharing part. I must admit that increasingly I feel apprehensive about keeping these earth-shattering discoveries – I should say solar system-shattering discoveries – to ourselves. Have you spoken with Colony Director Sam Tan about this lately?"

"Actually, yes I did. We spoke just before dinner this evening."

"And?"

"Well, he has been conferring with our Science Counsel, and they are confident enough now to 'tell the world' as it were, though the strategy is to do so in two parts. At this point, the plan is to send a holovision presentation conducted by the biology people back to Earth. As for you, Nigella, it hasn't been determined if you will join the presentation remotely from here or go back up to Alpha Colony. Timing-wise, Director Tan reckons that presentation will be shown shortly after the Global Holistic Summit."

"After the Summit?"

"Yes, after. They still need to work out details, but your biology boss, Professor Parisa Henning, will let us know once it is decided." Misha looked at Lochie. "I believe you confirmed that you know Professor Henning. She's one of your colleagues back in Western Australia, yes?"

"Of course, I know her. I've known Parisa for years now, though our academic paths rarely cross. We at least had dinner together in my very brief stay at Alpha Colony."

"Anyway, the actual presentation particulars are still all up in the air. Believe me, timing decisions, who gets invited, where it is held Earth-side... decisions like these have zero to do with science and one hundred per cent to do with politics. No matter the details, the announcement will be a big deal. I imagine they will follow the normal Mars press conference protocol with the incorporation of journalist questions into the presentation. Of course, the time delay with telecasts always makes for a creative approach to all that. After all the particulars are worked out, the bio team will present all they have deciphered about the Martian microorganisms to date. Finally, that will allow interaction of the world's biological community and all of its branches to access the data and request whatever new information that may be possible to get. The more brain-power, the better."

"And the medallion?" Lochie scooped a spoonful of ice cream.

"Of course, this will all be publicised and publicised soon, but we have to do that separately. Now that Sam Tan and the Counsel know of our find, they agree with us that we should take another few days searching the caves. Thank goodness we're all on the same page here. We all hope to discover more supporting evidence that'll shed light on the mystery we've stumbled upon. If we don't have any more findings to reveal by the time the Summit ends, we will make our discovery public anyway. Of course, without more items similar to what we have so far, I believe we are all fearful of misinterpreting what we found."

Lochie squinted at Misha as if that would somehow help him better understand her words. "How do you misinterpret an intelligently-design medallion?"

"The better question is how DO we interpret it?" Misha tilted her head to the side. "We just need to work double-time now. I will let the whole team know of all this in the morning. I think it best that we plan surface expeditions the next few days, even splitting into smaller teams of two or three to cover more possibilities. The answer is out there somewhere on the surface Lochie, Nigella... I can feel it."

19

Wednesday, 7 September; Fenghui Tang Teahouse, Shanghai, China

The four of them had long finished their blooming teas and now replaced them with a larger pot of a jasmine-scented green infusion tea they all shared.

"It's no different here in Shanghai... in all of China, for that matter. Amazingly enough, the anxiety we see – especially in our young people – mirrors what Kylie tells me of her experiences in Australia and what I know you two are familiar with in the States. This is not a localised problem; this is a global phenomenon. It transcends language, culture, politics... there are truly worldwide consequences which seem to be getting more drastic."

"And what do you call them in China?"

"Well, the Mandarin word for eight is *bā*, but honestly, you won't hear *bā* nearly as much as locals use the term Eights or even *Los Ochos*. When I say the problem is global, the communication is, too. Though so many kids are 'out of it' as it were, they still maintain a low level of constant chatter amongst Chinese young people and young people around the world. Whatever happens in Ohio or Sydney is heard here in Shanghai in real-time. No doubt whatever happens in Shanghai or Beijing or Guangzhou is on your GNN within minutes, and the kids in Melbourne or Buenos Aires are already interacting with it at the same time. It may not be through holovision, but whether through SAMs or data bands, the word does get around. It is not trite saying that we really do live in a global village today."

It was evident to Sunlyn that Fiona had her finger on the pulse of her home country. Increasingly it seemed that 'home country' was losing its meaning as all the peoples of planet Earth shared so much common culture. "Is it the same as the incidence of self-harm, domestic violence, suicide?"

"Looking at all recent statistics, it is. The numbers are going up and going up quickly – they are rising exponentially. I'll get to that in a moment, but consider... how did we as a species think it would be any different?"

"Any different?" Owen absent-mindedly ran his finger around the rim of his teacup. "That sounds a bit philosophical, Fiona. Exactly what do you mean by 'how did we as a species think it would be any different?' How would what be any different?"

Fiona let out a breath of air. "Have you ever heard of John Calhoun?"

"I can't say that I have."

"He was one of your countrymen, Owen. Calhoun was an ethologist and a behavioural researcher during the last century."

"An ethologist?" Sunlyn's tilted head communicated her unfamiliarity with the term.

"Yes, sorry... an ethologist is one who studies animal behaviour. What we remember Calhoun for specifically is – and I have no doubt you will recall his work even though you don't know his name – his studies with rats... well, rats and mice. I always present his story in my undergraduate lectures.

"I guess his seminal work was carried out about 75-some years ago, back in the 1960s or so. He built what he called a 'mouse utopia' at the National Institute of Mental Health in your state of Maryland. The utopia was an empty mouse city composed of hundreds of little mouse apartments connected with tunnels, burrows and open spaces. The actual structure was the size of a small room with several interconnected floors, and Calhoun made sure that it had everything a mouse could ever want. As part of the experiment, he made sure there was always excess food and water in all cubicles and that all waste and dirt was regularly cleaned and removed. The temperature was kept at a comfortable constant, and veterinaries monitored the environment to assure it was kept disease-free. He created what was essentially a mouse paradise, hence the moniker utopia. The only limitation the mice faced in this experiment was the finite space provided. Calhoun's calculations indicated that based solely on food, water and space requirements – the physical needs for life – the habitat could probably handle a maximum of about 3,000 mice. He called this super mouse utopia 'Universe 25' simply because it was his 25th go at this particular experiment. He started the experiment by introducing four pairs of healthy mice into his mouse utopia.

"Of course, with all that room and unlimited provisions, the population proliferated, doubling every 55 days at first. Within ten months, the mouse population had surpassed 600. Now remember, the theoretical maximum number of mice that could live sustainably in the mouse utopia was 3,000. So, when the population started to edge beyond the 600 animals, a very surprising thing happened: the birth rate dropped by two-thirds and food and water consumption also dropped in some cubicles. Additionally, this was not uniform across the entire community even though all the compartments were connected. Think about this now... Some apartments were overcrowded beyond hope, other apartments were sparsely populated, and a few rooms were even vacant. So, pardon my repetition, but though he had calculated that 3,000 mice could physically live there, by the time the overall population neared a thousand, this unbalanced distribution of mice became obvious."

Owen's inquisitive expression announced a question. "So, you're saying the surprise here is that we'd expect the population to happily increase more or less uniformly at least until it approached 3,000 if that's the theoretical maximum. I take it that you are saying that the reality was that the population did NOT continue to increase that way?"

"Exactly." Fiona continued. "The demeanour of many of the mice suddenly changed and some – but not all – displayed truly deviant social behaviour. A portion of male mice stopped defending their territory and even began to abandon their pregnant female companions. In a natural environment, mice that displayed these behaviours tend to emigrate to other broods, but that didn't seem to happen here. Universe 25 mice didn't move to different compartments and tended to wander about aimlessly while spending their days mindlessly eating and sporadically fighting. The most dominant males became more vicious and violent, attacking others without provocation. There were even displays of males mounting – almost raping – other mice, male as well as female. Nondominant males became so meek they were repeatedly attacked without defending themselves at all. It got to the point where cannibalism began to occur even though unlimited food was always available.

"The females didn't do any better. With males not protecting them, many females became aggressive on their own, some even attacking and killing their own offspring. Like their male counterparts, some became meek and totally submissive. Birth rates declined, and infant mortality skyrocketed towards 90%. In short, mouse utopia had become a mouse hell."

Fiona's story had certainly piqued Sunlyn's interest. "For sure, I have heard of this project. I remember reading about it in an undergraduate social psychology course I took years ago. Possibly it's just a fuzzy memory on my part, but I thought the mice society collapsed when the population literally outgrew the space provided, no?"

"You are partially correct, Sunlyn. It did collapse eventually, but it never outgrew the space provided and never even reached the 3,000-theoretical-limit that biological modelling indicated." Fiona continued, "Calhoun coined the term 'detached death' to describe the mice that exhibited a lack of will and societal involvement. Moreover, he carried the experiment on for nearly three years, but the colony never rebounded. The last baby mice were born just after 900 days, and the population continued to crash until the colony became extinct.

"During the decline of mouse civilisation, Calhoun identified several 'beautiful ones' – mice that were totally detached from the mouse society. These 'beautiful ones' completely lost touch with normal mouse behaviour and became self-centred while spending all of their time eating, drinking and grooming themselves. They outwardly had a healthy and robust appearance, though it all appeared to be a ruse. These mice lived apart from the rest in less crowded areas and remained detached from society. Calhoun called these mice 'empty on the inside.' His last experiment in this series was to place several pairs of these 'beautiful ones' into a separate, clean, adequately resourced mouse utopia to see if they would regenerate their mouse society under the new conditions. They didn't and refused to take part in any social interactions or even to mate in that new utopian environment. The experiment ended when the last of the 'beautiful ones' died of old age having never fostered offspring."

Kylie patted her Chinese friend on her hand. "I could tell you have lectured on Calhoun many times. I know that he originally used the outcome of his mouse society experiment as a metaphor for the possible fate of mankind in light of a crowded and increasingly impersonal world. Over time, Calhoun backed away from the comparison to *Homo sapiens* and argued extensively that humans are much more psychologically intricate and possess a deeper self-awareness and ability to solve problems."

Owen reflected on the implications of the experiment. "So, I hear you saying that Calhoun himself drew the line at comparing the mouse experiment to a crowded Earth. And yet I think that Fiona started by responding to Sunlyn's question on self-harm, domestic violence and suicide in young people by saying 'how did we as a species think it would be any different?' Help me here... Surely you aren't saying we behave in the same way that the mice did, are you?"

Fiona ran her fingers through her long hair and pulled it back over one shoulder. "Well no, I certainly am not arguing that there is any direct parallel between humans and any other species, most certainly not the mice. That's exactly one of the biggest dangers of comparative psychology, namely, to study the behaviour of one species – in this case mice – and then try to generalise those findings to another – in this case humans.

Over the years, some have used Calhoun's work to forecast the doom of humanity. I would argue against carrying these comparisons too far. As Kylie mentioned, humans are so much more complex, so much more self-reflective, able to foresee consequences and capable of changing behaviour to affect outcomes."

Kylie picked up the conversation. "In saying that, we still can glean some insight into the problems of crowding. Owen, I don't believe you were at my GNN presentation the other week, the one at which I met Sunlyn."

"No, I wasn't there regrettably, but I know you met Sunlyn that day. She shared a great deal of your presentation with me on our flight over to Shanghai, and I'm very sorry I didn't hear you."

"Well I don't want to be too repetitive, but I mentioned in that presentation the *Rapa Nui* people on Easter Island. Some argue that when they first arrived in 900, 1000, 1100 AD, the island was to them very much like Universe 25 was to the original four pair of mice in Calhoun's experiment. Of course, no one can be certain because there are no written records. That said, we do know from other islands in that general part of the Pacific that it should have had ample food, water and vegetation to offer a resource-rich world to sailing Polynesians. We also know that Polynesian sailing canoes could never have had more than a few dozen travellers aboard. So, at most, a few dozen humans are introduced into an island paradise and... A few hundred years later – we have no records of the exact timeline – they're all gone. Somehow we wind up with a barren, empty island strewn with hundreds of giant stone *moai*, artifacts that must have taken extreme resources to build. We are left to scratch our heads in wonder exactly why all the resources were depleted, and that entire population disappeared."

"Okay, you needn't convince me that human beings and

mice are wildly different. You did pique my interest when you mentioned Calhoun's 'beautiful ones' that seemed so outwardly healthy but seemed to totally lose touch with normal mouse behaviour. I can't help but think of that 'beautiful on the outside, but empty on the inside' idea. Was Calhoun talking about the Eights across 75 or 80 years of human history?"

"Oh boy... I see what Owen's saying, but I fear we might not want to go down that path. I see big flashing sign screaming 'people are not mice'!" Sunlyn looked to Fiona.

"Of course they're not the same. That doesn't mean we are unable to draw anything from Calhoun's work."

"Okay, Sunlyn... Fiona... I think I'd be the last man on Earth to look at Calhoun's study and attempt to apply that to our human situation on planet Earth. That said, I am curious – at least for the sake of argument – let's consider a projected maximum number for *Homo sapiens* here on planet Earth. I wonder what our ideal number might be and when we might reach that population." Owen rubbed his chin. "Of course, I don't mean to look at exact numbers, but have you ever wondered about a comparison."

Fiona smiled. "Owen, Owen, Owen... I am a hopeless academic who has prepared way too many lectures over the years."

"I can attest to that," Kylie chimed in.

"I hope I don't offend you when I say that my undergrads ask that question just about every time I give this lecture." Fiona's smile was radiant. "For the sake of argument, I did a search on global population back to 1968 approximately when Calhoun did his work with Universe 25. At that time, the global population was reported in United Nations statistics as about 3.5 or 3.6 billion people. Fast forward to today – about 75 years later – and we have a world population of between

8.9 and 9.0 billion people. That's a 250% increase or so in just 75 years even though the rate of increase has slowed."

"Those numbers are staggering!" Sunlyn shook her head. "Didn't China even have a one-child policy through many of those years?"

"Yes, that dated back to the 1970s and was modified a few times over the years. It is estimated that probably 400 million less Chinese were born because of it. And yet as a world, we still managed to nearly triple the global population."

"For sure," Owen agreed with Fiona, "...but if we are playing this game of relating us to Calhoun's work, what is the biological limit to our own Universe 25, namely Earth. How many humans can live here in a sustainable way?"

"I fear I'm the numbers women here, and I don't want you to go groggy over it all, but as I said, since my undergrads ask these same questions, I have worked out our best-guess answers." Fiona took a deep breath. "I'll start with the ridiculous... if we just say how many humans could fit on Earth, our mathematician friends tell us that the planet has about 500 trillion – TRILLION – square metres of land, though that number keeps dropping because the sea-level is rising. Still, if we allow a square metre for each human, we could potentially fit about 500 trillion souls standing shoulder-to-shoulder."

"But that's silly of course simply because there'd be no food, water, waste removal, etc." Though Kylie knew were the story was going, she played along to make the point.

"Exactly. To sustainably support any population, things like food production, water purification waste removal, etc., all need to be considered. You told us you studied chemistry, Owen, and this is a chemist's dream: energy and matter in, energy and matter out, what is the limiting reagent... There have probably been too many PhD projects dealing with how to arrive at valid numbers here, but to no one's surprise, scientists have compiled answers to your question from literally hundreds of studies. Whenever there are so many scientific studies with varying numerical results, the most effective technique employed to arrive at a number in which we can have some degree of confidence is called a meta-analysis. Basically, meta-analysis is a statistical procedure that evaluates the results of all of the studies in question. I'm over-simplifying here, but if you imagine a bell curve with the results of all these studies on it, the tails of the curve are around 4 billion on the low side to 16 billion on the high side. The peak of the curve is skewed a bit towards the low side and is somewhere around 8 or 9 billion with an absolute maximum of about 10 billion."

"WOW! Did I hear you correctly here? In a Calhoun experiment with humans, we have already reached a population at or over the theoretical maximum?"

Fiona slowly nodded her head. "Yes Owen, that's exactly what I am saying."

20

Thursday, 8 September; Gale Crater Outpost, Mars

Nigella stared wide-eyed as she grasped the medallion in her hand. "I would never kid anyone about my understanding of archaeology since I have never studied it on a formal level. I am totally overwhelmed by this, though... the thought that the medallion I am holding was made by... by whom? It's almost a spiritual experience. How long ago was this made? What did the makers believe? What did they know? Where were they from? What did they feel? Are any of their descendants alive today? Where did they go?"

It was obvious that they all felt the weightiness of the moment. Siti picked up Nigella's stream of thought. "Did they marry? Did they have families? What were their hopes? Their dreams? How did they die?"

Silence fell over the meeting room as all were lost in their own thoughts. Lochie finally interrupted the quiet. "I trust we are all feeling this on that same emotional level, Siti... Nigella... You needn't apologise for your shortage of training in anthropology. I mean, none of us have studied ancient civilisations on any advanced level, but that doesn't matter. Bloody hell – you could be a cattle herder in the middle of Timbuktu and have similar feelings. We all share the same human spirit, which means we all share the depth of feeling about this.

"I was lucky enough to be part of a team on an archaeological dig in Tanzania as an undergrad. I also have had experiences way up in the north of Western Australia, up in the Kimberley area there where we found Aboriginal rock paintings in a cave. I remember that as though it were yesterday, and quite honestly, we experienced the same feelings then. The emotion you describe must be universal, Nigella. Our job is to answer all the questions you have asked."

"Agreed, we're all experiencing the same wonder." Misha concurred. "I don't want to rain on anyone's parade, though, but we must accept the fact that we may never find those answers. We need a great deal of luck to help us uncover what we don't know here. I guess one of our biggest challenges is to decide exactly where to start."

"I've taken the liberty to get a bit of a jump on the where-to-start thing, Misha." Arya had walked over to the beverage dispenser and jabbed a finger at the controls. "I've entered all the markings from the medallion into our database. Let me start by saying there isn't what we'd call a picture on any of the patterns. Considering most human cultures, we tend to put a picture on coins or honorary medallions. Even the simplest of hieroglyphics are comprised of some level of pictographs. I honestly find it surprising that there are no pictures here."

"Good point, mate. Now that you mention it, that is strange."

Arya nodded. "Exactly, Lochie. Now, as I said, I loaded a scan of the few symbols we have into our database and have written a program to categorise, sort and compare the symbols. That's exactly the type of task our AI excels at, but the problem we face here is obvious..."

Siti tilted her head. "Obvious?"

"Yes, obvious... we have a total sample of one. AI can do lots of things, but it's an impossible task to organise anything when your sample only consists of one artifact, even considering that it has several symbols on it. AI excels when you hit it with big data sets... HUGE data sets. AI thrives on massive data sets. Regrettably, the best way to stump my AI program is to give it a sample of one."

"That makes sense, Arya. We somehow MUST find more artifacts. We have all been through the cave of discovery along with all its branches... we need a plan here." Misha was determined. "Go take care of whatever you need to take care of and let's meet back here in the staff room in twenty minutes."

* * *

"We're going to double our efforts here today. I think we all agree with Misha that we need to go all out in the little time we have in the hope of finding more artifacts." Keegan Botha was itching to get back out on the surface.

"Spot on. I think we are looking forward to the challenge." Lochie couldn't hide his eagerness to finally walk on the Martian soil.

Misha stood at the head of the table. "I appreciate your enthusiasm, but we still need to follow all the regulations."

Keegan noticed Lochie quietly searching his mind for what regulation applied here. The South African looked at the newest team member to explain Misha's reminder. "Project regulations require a minimum of two people for any surface activities. Anything in the tubes is considered surface, since we still have the same Martian atmosphere and environment inside them. Ideally, we'd have one group of three on a surface team, but we're under some pressure here and want to cover more ground. That said, we can split into two pairs and still follow all regs. Oh boy – two geologists, a chemist and an AI nerd." Keegan laughed. "How are we going to split that crew up?"

"Be nice, mate. Your life could depend on this nerd!" Arya took his dig in good humour as he turned both hands towards his chest and pointed at himself.

"I obviously mean 'nerd' in the most positive of ways, Arya."

Misha took the joking as a positive noting the team spirit was high. "So, I think it best that Keegan, Arya, Siti and Lochie will head out onto the surface and Joe, Nigella and I will stay back to man the outpost."

"You're speaking my language, Misha." Keegan was only too happy to be heading back outside. "So, what do you think as to pairings? I know we all agree that staff need to fill two, three, four roles. So, Lochie and I are both geos by trade, and Siti is a chemist. And Arya... Arya is our computer science genius." He grinned broadly as if to make up for his earlier teasing. "I know that both Lochie and Siti have anthropology backgrounds, too. And Arya has valuable specialties in artificial intelligence and linguistics. I think we can assign teams covering as many specialties as possible."

"How about you, Keegan. Where do your interests lie beside being a rock hound?" Now it was Arya's turn to have a little fun.

"I think I'd surprise you if I told you I dabbled in rock and roll." Keegan's laugh was loud. "All right, all right... I'll be serious with you, mate. I dabble a bit in physics and astronomy and even a little in hydrology."

"Fair enough... Now it sounds like we got it covered."

"But I really wasn't kidding you about the rock and roll..."

* * *

Keegan was still laughing as they had left the staff room and walked a hundred metres down a pressurised, tight, three-metre-wide fabric-covered tube. At the end of the tube was a bubble that enclosed a small area large enough to squeeze in half a dozen people. The periphery of the dome had several lockers, and there was an airlock at the far side of the room.

"Here you go." Keegan opened one of the lockers and pulled out what looked like a parachute silk duffle bag marked SURFACE GEAR on the side. "These aren't exactly one-size-fits-all, but there is a lot of stretch in them." He grabbed a second bag for himself, and the two men sat on a bench in the middle of the room.

Lochie opened the bag and followed Keegan's lead. They both stripped down to underclothes and then pulled on the pressure-rated surface coveralls. "You came on Mission 4, right? Wow, 13 years on Mars..."

"Yep, just about 13 years... where's the time go when you're having so much fun?" He grinned.

"Has it? Has it been fun, I mean?"

"Oh yeah, mostly. It's offered an intellectual challenge every day, and the community has been excellent, mostly. It's just big enough – Alpha Colony at least – that if you really don't get on with someone, you can figure a way not to come into contact all that much. Now Gale Crater Outpost is a different story. You can see it'd be pretty difficult to get away from anyone here. Fortunately, this group really has gotten along just fine, and that's a real positive."

"Did you ever think this would happen... I mean humans on Mars?" Lochie watched Keegan unpacking his gear and mimicked his preparations.

"Not a chance. I think back 25 years or so and the way global politics was going, I reckoned there was zero chance of anyone ever setting foot on Mars. I mean the moon was a natural – almost like an Antarctica base. That said, I never thought that as a species, we humans would ever see Mars up close and personal."

"Agreed. We Aussies were way too small a country to even consider going there on our own. Frankly, when the Americans even pulled out of the International Space Station, I reckoned that was the end of the Americans in space. At that point, if anyone was going, it seemed it would be led by the Chinese. Damn... I never considered corporations or billionaires – trillionaires!"

"You're exactly right. Who would have predicted a Jacobi-like character 20 or 30 years ago? I mean, who in god's name would think that a trillionaire's bragging rights would extend all the way to Mars? We agree that no single government would have come here, not because of the technology, but because the politics wouldn't have allowed for it to happen. In retrospect, the only possible way a Mars mission was ever going to work was with the backing of a multi-billionaire."

"Or in Jacobi's case, a trillionaire," Lochie added.

"Right!" Keegan's eyebrows arched high. "As you said, the Americans dropped out of the running when they decided to knock themselves off the global political pinnacle. The Russians never had the wherewithal to even try. The tighter resources have become, the less and less has been available for such folly as travel to Mars. I mean, the Chinese kind of stepped in, but they only have a small Mars base here with a handful of *taikonauts* now, and frankly, even that wouldn't have happened without Alpha Colony. Their little base is more a marketing scheme to the rest of the world announcing that 'we're China and we can go anywhere we want to go.' Jacobi's determination and his insistence on a one-way trip is the only reason we are sitting here now. In a sense," Keenan looked around to see if anyone else had come into the locker room yet, "...it's as much as saying 'no one's dick is as big as mine is', don't you think?"

Lochie broke into a big grin. "Fair dinkum, mate. I think that's probably exactly what it was all about. I seem to remember a couple of other trillionaires at least making noises about a Mars shot, but Jacobi beat them all. Talk about bragging rights!"

"That he did."

"How about day-to-day living here, Keegan? I mean, how about just normal, interactive human stuff. I mean, with such small numbers, you'd think maybe interpersonal relationships – and their breakdown – could cause some big headaches."

Keegan's head tilted to one side. "Nah... When you are here long enough, the unwritten rules become apparent. You'd be surprised how few of those kinds of problems we have had.

Relationships? Oh yeah... they happen all the time. The truth is that everyone knows how explosive that all could be, and everyone has found ways to avoid the explosions. Sam Tan has helped with that, too. Our numbers are small, but everyone seems to allow for separation of tasks whenever that is needed. Over twenty-some years now we have somehow made it all work."

"Damn... sounds like some great fodder for the social scientists." Lochie smiled.

"Oh yeah. I have no doubt there are many PhD research projects looking at these kinds of things right now." Keegan bent over and tightened a pull where his pant leg and boot overlapped. "Make extra sure you have a good seal here. Of course, we will check it before we depressurise the airlock, but better that you do a self-check now. Once the others get here and we're all suited up, we'll let the SOC check us out under pressure."

"SOC?"

"Yeah, SOC – Surface-Outpost-Communicator. Seriously, SOC isn't just our communications line, but tends to handle all things critical while we're on the surface." Keegan grinned. "We all treat SOC like she's our mother because, in many ways, she gives us life like a mother."

"Maybe you should call SOC mom..."

They could hear Siti and Arya chatting as they walked down the connecting tube to join them.

21

Thursday, 8 September; Holovision link between Washington, DC and Shanghai, China

"I'm so glad to get a hold of you. The time zone issue is a problem. I'm just going to bed, and you just woke up."

"But thank god we can at least talk with each other... see each other..." Sunlyn's SAM linked with the hotel room's technoserver as Nicolás's image visualised in the centre of her room as clearly as if she were sitting at home in her living room with him.

"How's it going so far?"

"I couldn't tell you if we spoke over the holovision all day. I've learned so much already. I REALLY want you to meet Kylie and Fiona."

"Let's just say I'm working on it." He smiled.

"Things are just getting started here. I swear though, I don't know what becomes of all the *Thánatos* impact worries, but I have gained so much insight to the Eights movement. I guess it's a movement. The more I learn, the less I even know how to label it."

"I miss you so much."

"Me too, Nicolás." She reached her hand to touch his projected likeness and was disappointed at cutting through his image as though he were a ghost.

"I only wish that worked, hon."

"Umm." She closed her eyes and exhaled deeply.

"I did talk to the police today... to Detective Grimms. He told me they did track down one of the boys who shot up our living room last week."

"And..."

"His name is Bradley O'Keefe, a seventeen-year-old high school senior, and he lives with his family in Kalorama Heights."

"Fancy schmancy... Kalorama Heights. That's a pretty elite neighbourhood tucked in amongst all the embassies, former presidents and Washington elites, yes?"

"It is. And young Bradley absolutely exudes everything that screams 'preppy.' But they seem to have had him dead-to-rights... the crime scene team found the same DNA of his on one of his dad's guns as they found on a shell casing in our living room. They also identified that weapon as the gun used at our place because they matched rifling impressions on one of the spent bullets in our wall to the gun. Surprise, surprise... they found the weapon neatly tucked away in a gun safe."

"The gun? Did they figure out if it was just one gun or did both have weapons?"

"Well, all the bullets they recovered came from the same weapon, so the police have now concluded there was only one weapon used. Grimms said they couldn't check the kid's hands for gunshot residue since it was too long since he would have fired the gun and he'd have cleaned up several times since. He did check the gun though and found fresh carbon on the bolt. I didn't realise how easy that is since fresh carbon just wipes off on a cloth. When he asked the father the last time the weapon was fired, Mr O'Keefe claimed it'd been at least a year since he had it out on the shooting range he belongs to over in Virginia. They checked that out too and confirmed it. The detective tells me that if a gun is not cleaned and sits like that for a while, the carbon cakes on and you can't just wipe it off. I think they are pretty confident that young O'Keefe is one of the perpetrators and probably the only shooter."

"Wow – DNA from a shell casing... rifling impressions on a bullet... carbon on the gun's bolt..."

"Yep. I wouldn't want to mess with Detective Grimms. He and his team sure sound competent. Anyway, they took the kid into headquarters and had a long chat with him."

"His lawyer allowed that?"

"After a bit of coaxing, yes, though the lawyer might not have mattered in this case. Grimms said they reminded him of FETA..."

"FETA?" She interrupted...

"Yeah, the Federal Emergency Terrorist Act which pretty much negates just about every constitutional right anyone suspected of terrorism ever had. If you ask me, that legislation has gone way too far, but that's the law right now. Anyway, it allowed them to pry quite a bit out of him, though we haven't discovered just who was with him as yet."

"So, what was the motive?"

"Well, your original guess may prove correct – at first glance, he seems to be with the Eights and seems to be one of the ringleaders, though they have no real support for that theory as yet. He did indicate that he heard your GNN report the other week and seemed – like many of his crowd – to be upset because you 'trivialised' the Eights."

"Well, as you'd imagine, I didn't trivialise anything. For that matter, you included a lot of 'seems' in that last sentence or two. Sounds like they are sure he fired the gun, but unsure of what the motive might have been."

"I think that's a fair assessment, hon. Grimms admits that several things still don't seem to stack up."

"Things... like what?"

"Well, for one thing, young Bradley doesn't fit the typical

Eights MO of being regressive. Obviously, shooting up our apartment is about as aggressive as you can get."

"True enough. I take it there's another thing?"

"Well yeah... I DID see one of those old data units on O'Keefe's wrist when he was shooting. I mean I was scared as hell, and it all flashed in front of me so fast, but I DID see it, and as you know, I reported that to the police. At this point, it doesn't seem to make sense since a kid living in a family house worth over ten million would surely have asked mom and dad to spend a few bucks having a SAM implanted in his hand. Grimms said the kid doesn't have a SAM and he didn't seem to get a straight answer about a data band."

"How about the other shooter? Umm... the other person?"

"I think we can say O'Keefe was the only shooter, but they do have a lead on another boy. Grimms says they are now onto him too, but I have no report to give you there."

Sunlyn frowned. "These kids live in an alternate reality. That's what really scares the hell out of me. Owen and I had such a meaningful conversation with Kylie and her Chinese academic friend Fiona today, and it is all so disturbing. These kids – the Eights, *Los Ochos*, *Bā*, whatever name they go by – are dropping out. They are more and more removed from almost anything, feeling more and more irrelevant. That's as true in Australia or here in China as it is there in the States."

"Strange. Dropping out, I mean. O'Keefe is doing anything BUT dropping out."

"You are correct on that. The fact that he IS involved... involved enough to find where we live, involved enough to get into his dad's gun safe and come to shoot our place up. All of that was premeditated. He obviously had no intention of hurting anyone this time, but who knows. Maybe it was all just a big scare. But I think he – they – are using the shoot up to enhance their bragging rights with the other kids."

"Or something else... Obviously, the police have got a lot more to find out."

Sunlyn pushed back her hair. "Is he in custody?"

"Yep. Will be for a few days at least. Even at 17, shooting up an apartment is still a pretty serious offence here in DC."

"Keep me up to date on this, hon."

"You know that I will." Nicolás nodded his head. "So, how's Shanghai?"

"It's exciting. As I said, I wish you were here with me. The city is great. The people I have met so far are really nice and very interesting. I can't tell you what I'm learning because I'd need a week – there's just so much."

"And Owen?"

"Owen's great. He's really helping me when we hit some of the more technical areas. Oh, and I spent a fascinating time in a teahouse this afternoon with Kylie and the professor I mentioned."

"Fiona?"

"Yes, Fiona."

"Sounds like I need to meet her as well as Kylie." Nicolás smiled.

"No doubt you will, eventually. So, you mentioned you're working on it... does that mean you've planted that seed... with Norman yet? Surely the *DC Post* can spare a Managing Editor for a week or two, especially if you were on assignment."

He smiled broadly. "Yes, the seed has definitely been planted."

"I love you, Nicolás." She blew an air kiss through the holovision to the other side of the Earth.

"Stay safe, hon."

"I will." She pouted. "Nicolás."

"Yes, hon."

"I miss you."

"I miss you." He reached his hand out as did she and once again, their virtual images just passed right through each other.

"Love you."

"Love you too."

22

Thursday, 8 September; Surface excursion, Gale Crater Outpost, Mars

They walked several hundred metres from the airlock door. Keegan came to a cluster of house-sized boulders stretching along the escarpment. He ducked into a narrow path between two of the largest ones and led the group towards the cliff face. "Here we are, tube 14B. This wasn't the easiest tube to find initially, which is probably why we missed it so many times."

After weaving through several more tight-fit passages between rocks, they finally came to a large, grotto-like opening. Lochie estimated the mouth would have been nine or ten metres high. "Wow... that's a pretty big entrance to have missed for several months, but I can see it really is well hidden by those giant stone blocks across the front and the overhang up on top."

Siti stood right beside him. "It would have been easy to see if we had x-ray vision." Her smile was visible through her faceplate. "I'll show you where we found it."

Siti entered the tube with the other three closely behind her. The cavern narrowed within the first 50-60 metres until the diameter was a comfortable four or five metres across. Lochie turned slowly, surveying the cave with the eyes of a geologist. He was fully aware of the physics involved in lava tube formation from the few years he spent as chief scientist at Hawai'i Volcanoes National Park on the Big Island in Hawai'i. Hot basaltic magma from Kīlauea or Mauna Loa could reach temperatures of 1,500° C, but once it was out of the depths of Earth, the molten rock began to cool. Naturally, the lava that was in contact with air started to cool the quickest. The top layer of the river of lava was the first to harden to a solid. Once this crust of solid basalt formed on the surface of the flow, it acted as an insulator to the still molten lava below. Over time, the surface crust became thicker and thicker until the only lava flowing was deep inside the original river of molten rock, well-insulated by the solid rock over the top of it. When the lava supply eventually cut off from the magma chamber feed deep inside the Earth, the remaining liquid lava within drained by gravity leaving a hollow tube behind. He felt as awestruck as he felt privileged to be one of this small handful of people to have the opportunity to walk through a Martian lava tube. The four-or-five-metre-diameter cave seemed to remain constant for as far as the beams of light from their helmets penetrated the blackness. "How far back in have you been?"

"I think we've gone in probably half a kilometre. We have the exact number on file back at the outpost, and we can call that up on the SOC if need be."

"Does the tube maintain this diameter all the way back?"

Siti responded. "Nah... it narrows down to just about nothing way in the back there."

"Look over here." In addition to their helmet headlights, each had a bright touch attached to their waist. Siti was shining hers toward a wall 12-15 metres away. "We found the medallion right in this area."

"Lying right on the surface though, yes?" Lochie walked towards her light beam.

"That's correct."

"You know, I noticed the dusting of that fine, Martian powder on the floor as we came in. I find that really interesting. Since Mars atmosphere is so thin – maybe about a hundredth that of Earth – it makes it correspondingly difficult to pick up dust and blow it. Still, there is dust a hundred metres back into the cave. Did you notice dust on the piece you picked up, Siti?"

"No. As I said though, I've recorded the find, so we can go back and look if you like. I think I'd have noticed it though."

"That either means the piece was put here since the dust blew in or..." He shook his head. "Man... I just don't know, mate." Lochie smiled as he caught himself scratching his helmet, suddenly realising that his helmet didn't have an itch!

The four of them walked another several hundred metres back into the tube. It was noticeable that the surface of the lava had a smoother texture than out towards the entrance. Eventually, they came to a fork in the tunnel. Keegan pointed to the one on the left. "We've been down that one a long way. Our MPS data tells us we went nearly 350 metres from here, but we didn't find anything more than you are looking at here."

"Did you reach an impasse?"

"Yep... narrowed down to nothing more than a crack. At this point, we need to penetrate deeper on the right fork."

Siti looked at the small screen on her faceplate. "We can go another hundred metres or so, but our oxygen reserves are low. Regulations dictate that we need to turn back in about fifteen minutes."

Lochie was nearest the entrance to the right fork and started in. As he led the group down the tube, he realised that no one had ever stepped on this path before... unless the aliens did. They walked another fifteen minutes until Siti announced they had to turn back. They regrettably would have to leave the right fork for another day.

23

Thursday, 8 September; Metro Precinct Station, Washington DC

Bradshaw and Patton jogged up the steps of the Metropolitan Police Department precinct station. "O'Reilly was his name – Sergeant Bernie O'Reilly. We are supposed to meet him right at the first-floor front desk."

The two detectives walked into the front reception area. The big room was dingy, but the lighting was bright. A few police officers mulled around quietly, talking to some young people several metres behind the desk. There were a couple of dozen more teenagers sitting on benches toward the back of the reception area. A young woman in uniform sat at an office chair with a computer screen in front of her. Ryan arched his eyebrows and looked towards his partner. "Wow... Is it quiet in here with this many people or is it me?"

Maggie nodded yes as a uniformed woman sitting behind the front desk looked at them. "Can I help you?"

"Sergeant O'Reilly, please – Bernie O'Reilly."

"Oh sure, I'll..."

"I'm here, thanks, Jenny." A rather heavyset uniformed

officer walked towards them and extended his hand towards Maggie. "Agent Maggie Patton, I presume."

She shook his hand. "You presume correctly. This is Detective Ryan Bradshaw."

"Good to meet you, Ryan." He tilted his head. "Is Ryan okay?"

"Please... Ryan is just fine, sir."

"Follow me, please." O'Reilly led them past the few dozen teens sitting quietly on the benches. O'Reilly took them into a small office twenty metres from the receptionist and closed the door. "Have a seat. We'll do away with all the formalities here – please just call me Bernie."

"That's good – all first names here." Maggie sat across the desk from him.

"So, I updated Ryan with what you told me on the phone, and we thought we'd better follow up on it."

"Yeah look, it was the strangest thing. I generally wouldn't make a run on a suicide call, but we were pretty short-staffed the other night and one of my officers – Thompson – got a call. You both know that it's Department regs that no one goes on a callout without two officers in the car anymore, so I thought it'd be good to get my butt out of my chair and go along for company. We headed over to Brentwood – Adams Street NE. The call was very vague – kids milling around, a possible suicide. You know, it's not the nicest area of town, that's for sure, but it's been better the past few years. Anyway, we had a call reporting a funny kind of demonstration."

"Funny?"

"Yeah, funny. There sure as hell were a lot of kids there – probably most were 12, 13... up to maybe 16 years old. There were hundreds of them. Actually, you just saw a bunch of kids just like them out there when you came into the station." He pointed toward the door they just came through. "They were basically strewn around the block, lying on lawns, sitting on kerbs, hanging out on peoples' front steps. It wasn't necessarily hostile or really threatening, but the kids had settled in and didn't seem interested in moving on."

"Not interested in moving on?"

"I'm telling you... it seems as though they're all stoned or in a heroin stupor or something like that. I mean in past years I'd have said they were doing downers of some sort, but we just aren't finding any chemicals in their systems. We did random saliva tests on several dozens of them and found nothing, nada, zero, zilch... not even marijuana. I mean, the saliva tests aren't a hundred per cent, but you'd think that out of that many tested, someone would have been using something."

Maggie nodded her agreement. "Besides cannabis, a saliva test would also show MDMA, right?"

"Ecstasy... yeah, but that didn't show that either. Hell, that would at least make the kids more talkative, and that's not happening. That is also the case for meth or any uppers, but with the trance-like behaviour, I can't see that any uppers would show positive. Nah, no sign of any pharmaceuticals."

"Maybe it's something new," Ryan added.

"Could be, but this aloofness isn't new. So help me god, I never thought I'd say this, but the silence drives me crazy! I have never seen so many kids being so quiet in my life! We're increasingly seeing kids this age – maybe 12 to 18 or so – in this toned-down, nearly comatose state. I'd say we've seen it grow over the past year or so."

"Well, we're finding the same thing in our neck of the woods, Bernie. Frankly, we have been getting these reports from not only around DC but from other cities now, too. I almost wonder what we're missing here."

O'Reilly rocked back in his office chair. Maggie couldn't help but think if he'd have pushed a little bit more, his ample weight would have toppled him backwards. "I also mentioned the suicide report when I spoke with Detective Patton."

"Right."

"That was yesterday, and you know, that's a funny one, too. Five people killed themselves. We still haven't ID-ed them all, but they are all kids."

"Wow, five deaths..."

"Yeah, wow for sure. I think it's pretty unusual. Look, I'm no authority on suicide, but you'd have to be oblivious not to realise the suicide rates are going up and up and up, especially amongst the young folks. We've had an FBI shrink... ah, psychologist, look into this for us." O'Reilly apologised as he glanced down to a notepad on his desk. "She – Tracey Jankowski, that is – tells us the incident of multiple suicides isn't all that common. I mean you had the obvious big ones most of us know about. There was the Peoples Temple in the 1970s in Guyana with nearly a thousand people dead. You may remember the Solar Temple cult deaths in Switzerland in the 1990s where almost a hundred people died. Then there was the mass suicide of hundreds of Rohingya people in Myanmar just a few years ago. All those seemed based on some religious cult or something like that. According to Jankowski, group suicide like that has been happening from Greek and Roman times right up to today.

"Jankowski also went on about a long history of suicide pacts when two people – often lovers – agree to top themselves together. You can also find incidents of families either suiciding or murder-suiciding, especially with seniors... the healthy one kills the sick one and then kills themselves..."

Maggie picked up where the sergeant left off. "I don't pretend to be an expert either, but I am aware of groups of people organising this sort of thing over Skynet – kind of suicide by social media."

"You're correct on that. The thing here is that there are none of these obvious things leading up to the act. As far as we know, these kids weren't part of any cult, weren't lovers or related directly in any way. Of course, we need to finalise our investigation here, but all the obvious motives are absent at this point."

Bradshaw looked up from his note scribblings. "How can we organise a session with Tracey Jankowski? It seems she has a hell of a background in this Eights stuff."

"She does. We'll stop at the front desk, and I'll have Lisa get you her details. I know she'd be more than happy to help you guys out. I sometimes think that's why the FBI exists – to show us cops that they know more than us even when they don't know shit!"

Maggie got up and extended her hand towards O'Reilly. "Thanks for the update, Captain."

"Don't mention it."

Ryan followed her lead. "One more thing, Sergeant. What was the cause of death with these kids?"

"Funny thing about that. We have five bodies sitting in the freezer, and so far, there isn't any apparent COD."

24

Thursday, 8 September; Global Holistic Summit, Shanghai, China

The last thing André needed was to head straight into a press conference after flying halfway around the world. He reminded himself that was why he came all this way – Global Holistic Summit. The point – to interact with the brightest minds on the planet and to discover ways of communicating findings to the general public. At least the hour nap and the long shower had perked him up, along with the nearly empty mug of hot coffee in front of him. He looked down the long table that stretched across the dais. He recognised several of the scientists that had been invited to participate in the Q & A session after the UN Chief Scientist's presentation. Every participant had a water glass, a notepad, a pen and a headphone set able to deliver any of the six recognised United Nations languages. He smiled to himself – the notepaper and pen seemed to be such a throwback to the old days.

A woman wearing a traditional Chinese silk dress appeared from behind a curtain on the right side of the stage and strode up to the podium. "Good morning, ladies and gentlemen. Welcome to Shanghai and welcome to the Global Holistic Summit. I would like to introduce the Chief Scientist of the United Nations, Dr René Riemann." She extended her hand as Dr Riemann traced her steps across the stage. As he neared the podium, the woman turned, shook his hand and then retreated behind the same curtain from which she had come.

Dr Riemann adjusted the microphone. "I welcome all to this Global Holistic Summit. This conference has been a long time in the making, but the reasoning behind it is quite simple. The problems we face as a species have not been created by any one people, one culture or one political system. We have all contributed to the full scope of problems we face, and it is only through cooperation that we will solve them. After literally centuries of painstaking laboratory work, academic study and scientific breakthroughs, it is clear that science alone will not save the day. The arguably greatest scientist of all time – Sir Isaac Newton – once famously said 'If I have seen further, it is by standing on the shoulders of giants.' Of course, Sir Isaac did see so very far, and he was right to recognise all the work of those before him.

"Today we also recognise the contribution of all those who have invested their hard work, their dedication and their careers into our fundamental understanding of the physical, biological and social world that some nine billion of us share. But it is not merely our science that will answer the most fundamental questions. For that matter, it's not our technology alone that'll ever solve these problems. We scientists have learned time and again that in the truest sense, science and technology are the easiest tasks we face. I fear I am repetitive when I say the technical problems are many times the most straightforward ones to solve. The scientific method assures us of that; it assures us that the best answers to the most challenging problems result from peer-reviewed research. In the final analysis, the greatest task of our time is not in doing the research, it's not in finding solutions. Rather, the greatest challenge is one of communication – of transferring that technology to the community at large for the betterment of our world.

"In summary, the science is the easy part; communicating complex solutions to policymakers and the public at large is the hard part. It is the teacher, the university lecturer, the journalist, the opinion editor and the documentary producer that is at the crux of conveying our science and technology to all nine billion *Homo sapiens* whose lives depend upon the application of this knowledge. It is to this end that I declare the Global Holistic Summit officially open."

* * *

André reached for the nearby water jug and topped up his glass. The first presenter stepped up to the podium and introduced herself as a journalist. She gave an interesting presentation that discussed the need for a global agreement on coverage of scientific research, pointing out that several countries were still blocking access to the sharing of scientific data. The second speaker was a climatologist who summarised the latest global temperature and pressure readings with correlations to greenhouse gases. The speaker noted that most of what he presented was not in great depth, but in light of the eclectic nature of the audience, the need for such a basic presentation was obvious. The third presenter was Gillian Pickard of the Institute of Astronomy, University of Cambridge. She headed a team of astrophysicists and geophysicists that was assigned to tracking *Thánatos* and then following up on the impact and effects of the asteroid. André reflected on the update she gave yesterday that he had listened to while aboard the SST. He was anxious to hear her latest summary of the impacts.

"Hello... Good morning..." She quickly glanced down at the podium clock to confirm that the time was still before noon. "My name is Gillian Pickard, and I will update you from the presentation I broadcast yesterday – now about 30 hours ago. Since that time, we have processed a great deal more data, and I can report that to you at this time.

"Data continue to flow into our computers, and the latest analysis reports that the eight largest impacts covered a zone now measured at approximately 580 kilometres long by approximately 30 kilometres wide. This zone stretches from about 72 degrees 18 minutes north and 90 degrees 3 minutes east to 72 degrees 33 minutes north and 107 degrees and 47 minutes east." A large map appeared behind the dais with the impact zone highlighted.

"I mentioned in yesterday's update that the largest craters that are now reported were 1,350, 1,050 and 600 metres in diameter. The largest crater – a bit less than a mile in the old system – is similar in size to Meteor Crater in northern Arizona to the east of Flagstaff. There are well over one hundred impact craters now mapped down to 15 metres in diameter.

"Even though this is a very sparsely populated area, we have regrettably received reports of several casualties in the small Russian villages of Syndassko and Yuryung-Khaya. To date, there have been about 100 deaths in Syndassko and another 15 or so in Yuryung-Khaya. These fatalities resulted from both concussion and earthquakes. There were also several tsunami waves reported along the Laptev Sea coastal area, but all were in very sparsely populated areas. We were also fortunate in that none of the major fragment impacts occurred in water since that could have produced much more widespread waves. The larger communities of Dikson to the west and Tiksi to the east have experienced severe seismic events, but at this time, no deaths have been recorded. The revised Richter reading at Dikson has been lowered from 6.7 to 6.5, but that of Tiksi has been revised upward from 7.0 to 7.2. We continue to monitor those communities.

"There were also several large airbursts that resulted from fragments that superheated and then exploded before any impact. Those airbursts, along with the biggest impacts, created concussion effects that were powerful enough that they were detected in Moscow, some 3,500 kilometres away. Authorities there have reported rattled buildings, shattered glass and collapses of several concrete walls and roadways.

Fortunately, other than that, there was no significant damage nor serious casualties in Moscow. Several other cases of concussion effects have been documented from around both western and eastern Europe. There were even a few reports of concussion and shaking here in metro Shanghai, and we are over 5,200 kilometres away. Again, fortunately, we have no confirmation of actual damage recorded here.

"We are now getting widespread seismic data, and it seems that earthquakes continue along a line running through the coordinates I reported here, but some 350 kilometres to the west and another 250 kilometres to the east. Historically, there is no known fault running through this area. That said, our geophysics team now report that they hypothesise that deeper, historically inactive faults may have been disturbed due to the *Thánatos* shockwave. We are now over 100 hours after the impacts, and geophysical data indicate seismic activity has actually increased along the fault. Within the past few hours, a 7.5 Richter reading was recorded with its epicentre 100 kilometres west of Tiksi. If this is confirmed, it will support the hypothesis that a previously dormant fault is now active. More troublesome is the fact that this earthquake more than 100 hours after the original impact caused a seismic event beyond the initial *Thánatos* energy input.

"I can take a few questions."

André raised his hand.

"Yes... Dr Moureaux."

André nodded his head. "Thank you, Professor Pickard. I'd like to make a comment first, please. If the 7.5 measurement is correct and the newly awakened fault line is taking on a seismic life of its own, that indeed can be troublesome. We need to continue to monitor the situation there.

"There are other related problems, however. My colleagues and I at the National Snow and Ice Data Centre have been doing a lot of work in Siberia and throughout most of the Arctic looking at the increasing breakdown in the permafrost regions. I was wondering what data you have on the subterranean composition of tundra within the footprint you have described here."

"I'm sorry Dr Moureaux, but I don't have those data now. Are you able to add to our understanding of the permafrost there?"

"Quite possibly we could help there. The National Snow and Ice Data Centre with which I am affiliated have two geophysicists here at the Symposium today." André tilted his head towards a woman a few seats to his left, "I am confident they will be able to speak to your enquiry throughout the Summit."

André's teammate acknowledged herself by raising her hand.

Pickard looked at her "Please, go ahead."

"Thank you, Dr Pickard. I'm Rosalyn Richards, a geophysicist, and, as Dr Moureaux has indicated, one of his colleagues at the NSIDC. I think it's important to mention the threat posed by the permafrost in this area. We are trying to update data, but you have already indicated how difficult that is until the earth settles from the seismic contortions she is going through. Regrettably, we are not yet able to report what effect *Thánatos* has had concerning the permafrost degradation in this area, but we have been monitoring the situation for several years and have an excellent baseline on methane release there. The fear, of course, is that the impacts and subsequent earthquakes could accelerate the release of this potent greenhouse gas."

Gillian Pickard nodded her head. "Of course, Dr. Richards. Thank you very much for that input. I can see that it may be a little early to raise this fear, but in keeping with the underlying theme of this summit, it is important to at least introduce this possibility to the public. This is exactly why we have such a broad array of expertise here at the Summit."

25

Thursday, 8 September; Waldorf Astoria on the Bund, Shanghai, China

Sunlyn and Owen walked into their hotel lobby. "Wow — what a day! I even enjoyed the dinner tonight. That was some of the best Chinese food I've ever had."

"Well, you came to the right place for that." Owen chuckled.

"It was a busy day, but it was also such an incredibly enlightening start to the Global Holistic Summit, at least for me. Want to have a drink before you retire, Owen?"

"A drink sounds great. We can deprogram a bit."

"Always nice when the drinks are on GNN."

They pulled up two stools at a high-top table looking out onto a Chinese garden behind the hotel that featured a waterfall pouring down over a fern-covered rock wall. The indirect lighting highlighted the beautiful garden without overpowering the scene. "I'll have a gin and tonic, please." She smiled at the waiter.

"I'll have a Tsingtao Beer, thanks."

The waiter looked at Sunlyn. "Bombay Sapphire gin for madame?"

"That would be great." She looked back at Owen as the waiter scurried away.

"So, what did you think?"

"I agree with you, Sunlyn, it was a fantastic day."

"What did you like... what did you find best?"

"I don't know... that's a tough one. You might not be surprised that I found the opening presentation – the correspondent – discussing the merits of a better agreement amongst journalists on how we have to stick together."

"That fair enough, but you must admit so much of that depends on a handful of countries that still don't accept the whole idea of a free press."

"That's hard to argue, but how do we ever get past that? I reckon we would need to change entire political systems to change that." The waiter returned with Owen's beer and Sunlyn's gin and tonic. He tipped his head, thanking the waiter.

"I guess the other eye-openers were the very brief comments made by Rosalyn Richards and André Moureaux from the NSIDC – that's the National Snow and Ice Data Center – concerning the methane release from permafrost. I mean, we have been watching and wondering about the impact of methane for decades, but I can see how the seismic shockwaves set off by *Thánatos* could wind up triggering a huge impact on the Earth's atmosphere over a very short period."

"From one small area of the Earth's surface?"

"Well, it's not impossible. There are such things as feedback loops where one thing leads to another... but I'm sure we'll get to feedback loops this week. How about you? What piqued your curiosity today?"

"Oh, I don't know – many things, I guess. As you already know, I'm not a technophobe or anything like that, and I most certainly did find the technical presentations interesting. Thanks to you, I can always count on getting filled in on what

I don't understand. I am curious though about just how far off these science-types can sometimes be." She sipped the drink the waiter quietly set in front of her. "Yummy... How's your Tsingtao?"

Owen clenched his teeth. "I've had worse... I guess. I enjoy China and Chinese cuisine, but I'm glad they don't supply all the brew for the Oktoberfest every year." He took another gulp and then considered his colleague's question. "Well, what do you mean about 'how far off' they can be?"

"I preface this with my disclaimer about being a humanities girl in college. Of course, we had to deal with right and wrong answers, but that had a different meaning in my field of study compared to you guys. I would assume that when you took a chemistry exam, you'd better be able to crank out the right answer along with all the supporting calculations you used to get it, yes?"

"Mostly, yeah. We did write some essay answers too though if that's what you're getting at."

"Sort of. Besides stating 'our answer,' we needed to write an explanation in support of what it was we said. Here's an example close to my heart... To me, Shakespeare may have been a great writer, but I always thought he was such a blatant misogynist that it got in the way of letting me appreciate his works. I especially remember his play, *King Lear*. Frankly, the man was a pig..." Sunlyn's eyes drifted towards the ceiling as she shook her head in disgust. "Now if I wrote that on an exam all by itself, it might get me an 'F' grade. However, by supporting my contention using Shakespeare's own writing, I could wind up turning that same answer into an 'A' mark. I remember writing about The Bard's use of derogatory lines to anything female, damning his daughter to sterility and his repeated use of vile language about women... Mentioning things like this could go a long way to raising my grade. I even remember writing about how he was bitter because he had contracted syphilis, though I was never certain exactly how he justified blaming women for that. Unless things were very different then, it still took 'two to tango', so-to-speak." She smiled.

"How'd you do? Ah, I mean how'd you do on your Shakespearian essay?"

She laughed. "I got an 'A' on that one!"

"I knew it... Sunlyn, the straight-A student!" He again made her blush.

"Nah, nah... My point though is that in humanities it's not so much right or wrong, but how you make your case. But I always thought that in the hardcore sciences, there has to be a right or wrong answer... all the time, every time, no?"

Now it was Owen's turn to smile. "I think you are overly simplistic... that's just not the way it is, Sunlyn. I mean, I only did a bachelor's in the physical sciences, but even at that level, laboratory work always called for standard deviations – a plus or minus number range for just how confident you are in your measurement. Woe is me to try to teach statistics – only ever managed a 'C' in that class – but the point is we can NEVER measure anything perfectly. That said, if our measurements have an error in them, then our calculations have errors in them. For that matter, calculations may often multiply errors many times over. The mistake some people make though is to say if we can't measure perfectly, then why measure at all. That argument is used against science all the time... against the age of old Mother Earth, against vaccination, against global warming, against... well, you get the idea."

"I do, but I guess I'm specifically referring to something like *Thánatos*. I always thought that orbital mechanics was so well known that we can drop a capsule on Mars tens of millions of miles away and put it right where we want it. I think I read somewhere once that landing a spacecraft at the distance of

Mars from Earth is similar to sinking a golf ball putt from here in Shanghai into a hole as far away as the moon or something like that."

"I'm sure that's correct. Our orbital calculations are pretty damned spot-on."

"Then how could we have been so off with *Thánatos*? First, they thought it would skip, then they thought it would totally crash into Earth, then there was a chance it would break up and then... well, you get my problem here."

"Sunlyn, that all goes back to uncertainty. I mean just consider... they discover this piece of rock flying at tens-of-thousands of miles an hour maybe a couple of weeks or months out, they don't have close up data for it, no chemical samples, no drill cores telling us its makeup, no data on the precise minerals it is made of... There is so much that goes into trying to decide how strong the actual rock is. Also, because it is tumbling, we just couldn't measure it all with enough accuracy to work the parameters of that tumble into all the atmospheric friction models. Oh, and even the rarefied gases found that high up varies from day to day, minute to minute with 'waves' of atmospheric density propagating through them in unpredictable ways. If the rock begins interacting with the atmosphere a few seconds earlier or later, it could be the difference between the rock breaking or not, skipping off or not, and every variation in between."

"I guess I see what you mean, but I do feel uncomfortable with the term 'luck' in science, kind of like so much is just left to pure chance."

"Funny you mention that... One of my favourite memories in a philosophy of science class that I had way back when concerned one of Einstein's famous quotes. He once said – in reference to quantum mechanics and the behaviour of subatomic particles – something like 'God does not play dice with the universe.' The famous British physicist Stephen

Hawking decades later argued that Einstein was wrong in saying that God does not play dice. Hawking was a confirmed atheist, and he went on to say that not only DOES God play dice, but frequently goes out of his way to confuse us by throwing the dice where we can't even see them! Now Hawking was speaking about quantum mechanics, but maybe God does hide the dice with orbital mechanics and asteroids, too."

"So, are you saying that even Stephen Hawking would give me a hard time about thinking scientists should always have the exact right answer?" She finished her drink and dabbed her lips with the napkin. "Considering that God has already played dice with my sleeping schedule, I think I'd better head off to bed, Owen."

"Me too – see you for breakfast down here in the lobby around 7:00?"

"See you then."

26

Friday, 9 September; Surface excursion, Gale Cater Outpost, Mars

The small team based at Gale Crater Outpost were all very much aware of the pressure on them. Once Misha revealed that Sam Tan and the Counsel were ready to go public with the announcement of life on Mars, there was no turning back. That announcement would be made in the next few days no matter what, though the specifics of the presentation were still up in the air. Though it hadn't yet been decided when the Gale Crater discovery of an intelligently manufactured artifact would be made, the outpost staff knew it would only be a week or, at most, ten days off. Everyone understood that it would be impossible to hold the announcement back any longer. It was incumbent upon their team to do whatever they could to find something – anything – that could in any way support the discovery of the one medallion that was so obviously produced by an intelligent life form. They all agreed that finding more artifacts would go a long way towards avoiding any embarrassment of claims of a false discovery.

Forced to abandon the exploration of the right fork of the cavern two days ago, they hoped for better luck yesterday. The working party returned to the same lava tube and penetrated inward another 650 metres, but after a two-hour walk, the cave narrowed to another dead-end. They were forced to return with fallen spirits and empty sample bags.

Misha called for an early start this Friday morning. She waited until most had finished their breakfast in the staff room. "Okay. We had pretty lousy luck the past few days, but we can't let that put a dent in our spirits. We're going to keep pushing things for the next several days. I know it's tiring doing daily surface expeditions, but I also know we are all intent on pushing the limit, on doing all we can to find something more. I'm sure we all were disappointed in the lack of results yesterday in tube 14B. What's with these aliens, anyway... drop one medallion in a cave just to tease us and then leave nothing else!" Misha rolled her eyes to the ceiling. "Pardon my lousy humour, but we just have to get over our disappointment and go on from here.

"Now I want to be perfectly clear, I do not propose that we go outside of regulations in any way, but we will try to double up our surface time the best that we can safely do so. To date, we've explored 14 tubes here at Gale Crater, and our mapping from ground-penetrating radar data shows at least another 20-some tubes. It's a little tough to get an exact number since some of the networks may actually connect together. Much of that detail is hidden from the information we currently have.

"If you look here..." There was a map projected on the wall behind her. "... you can see the layout of the network of tubes. The 14 we have now investigated are shown in green. The ones we haven't been in are highlighted in red. For the sake of time, we'll split into teams of two, but we need to be extra careful. I repeat – we follow every safety regulation on the books and take no dangerous shortcuts. With only two-person teams, it is more important than ever to have each other's back. Is that understood?" She looked around the table to nodding heads. "If you look at the map, 18A is within safe walking distance. 27A is over a kilometre, and 31B is almost two kilometres. We only have the three skellies, but regulations say we must keep one here at the outpost for safety reasons. So, I propose that we split today's work schedule this way: Lochie, you and Siti take one skellie and go into 27A, and Joe and I will take the second skellie and check out 31B. Arya and Keegan will walk over to 18A. Nigella, you will maintain the facilities here and act as the backup. It is improbable you would need to use the third skellie to come to get any of us, but if that emergency were to arise, our two outpost techies, Paul and Clarissa, are here and ready to help in any way. I have already spoken to both about being on call. Any questions?"

"Yeah, what's a skellie, mate?" Lochie meekly tried to hide his face as the others playfully chuckled at him.

Joe was the first to respond. "Well, you spent two days with me on the MRT. That is sheer luxury! Basically, they're very small, basic rovers. The term 'skellie' comes from the word skeleton... you'll see why we named them that in a few minutes." Joe grinned. "These two-person mini-rovers are open-air, framework-only vehicles that can safely range to within 10-12 kilometres of the outpost. Besides cutting down the time needed to get where you're going, they also can carry some cargo and are supplied with extra life support for longer trips and emergency situations. In the event of an injury, the skellies act as Martian ambulances and definitely are life-savers. We have three skellies here at Gale, and there are more skellies back up at Alpha Colony."

"Sounds like Siti is giving me my first ride in a skellie."

27

Friday, 9 September; FBI Headquarters, Washington DC

Harry Grimms was happy to come along for the meeting with the FBI Psychologist, Tracey Jankowski. He was a step or two in front of Bradshaw and Patton as they climbed the stairs leading up to the new Federal Bureau of Investigation building. "We probably should have tried learning more about these issues months ago."

"Better now than never, chief. Besides, it's not as though we don't have anything else to do."

"Can you tell the sarge that again, Ryan!" Maggie emphasised the word sarge.

They stopped at the front desk and spoke with the receptionist. She led them through a set of doors and down a busy corridor until she stopped in front of a solid oak door. The sign read 'Dr Tracey Jankowski, FBI Psychologist.' The young woman knocked on the door and looked at the three DC Metro officers. "I know she has been expecting you."

"Come in."

The young lady opened the door and ushered the officers into the outer area of her office suite.

"Detective Sergeant Grimms? Detectives Bradshaw and

Patten?"

"Yes, Doctor." Grimms grabbed her hand before the other two did.

"Well, hello... I've been looking forward to meeting you." The tall, dark-haired woman looked to the receptionist. "Thanks, Rachel. Would you mind getting us a coffee setup? She looked at her visitors. "Is coffee okay, or would you like some tea?"

"Coffee would be great," Maggie responded, and the two men nodded agreement with her answer.

"Now then..." Jankowski pushed her office chair back from her desk.

"Dr Jankowski, I didn't want to take advantage of your offer to help us, but thanks for my late request to bring sarge along with us. I hope that wasn't a problem." Bradshaw sounded genuinely apologetic.

"Problem? Quite the opposite – that's great. I'm thrilled to be able to help the DC Police anytime at all... anytime. We're all on the same mission here." She gestured for them to follow her through the door into her main office.

Dr Jankowski's office was sizable with a sitting area large enough to comfortably seat a half dozen people around a small table if need be. She ushered them in and sat them at the table, then turned to pick up a folder on her desk. "Again, welcome. I've been with the Bureau for about twelve years now. I confess to being overly academic at times, but I spent a great deal of my career as a behavioural psych researcher and a counsellor. I think here at the Bureau, everyone thinks my role should be about 99% profiler, but I fight that expectation as much as I can." She laughed.

Maggie settled into her chair. "When we met with Sergeant O'Reilly the other day, he spoke quite highly of you and passed along several things he learned from you. We thought it important to pick your brain a bit." Her comment was interrupted by a barely audible knock at the door.

"Is that you, Rachel?" Jankowski looked towards the entrance. "Come on in."

The receptionist pushed a small serving cart through the entrance and quietly placed a mug in front of each person and poured the coffee. She put a tray with sugar, cream and a bowl of cookies mid-table. Rachel left as quietly as she had entered.

Tracey circled her spoon in the mug, watching the swirls of cream spinning. "If it's okay by you, I'd like to give you a brief overview of what I've learned over the past several months. As I said, whether it's the DC Police Department or the FBI, we're all trying to deal with the same, growing problem." She lifted her cup and took a sip, her eyes surveying the three nodding heads. "Excellent. Let me start by saying that this phenomenon we erroneously refer to as the Eights seems to be exploding around the country... around the world... I say erroneously because the Eights are a result of the phenomenon, not the actual cause of it, whatever 'it' might be. And the American manifestation of these events is, for some reason unbeknownst to me, worse right here in the District than anywhere else in the country."

Grimms nodded his head. "This is good. I think I speak for all of us in saying that we'd appreciate your overview as the best place to start. You don't mind if I take a few notes, do you?" He pulled his notepad out and flipped the cover back.

"No, no – please feel free... and don't be afraid to interrupt if you have a query. I'm not overly formal here, and your questions won't offend me at all.

"Let me start by reiterating that the name we give to the phenomenon doesn't much matter. This event, this... this... thing, is happening all over. Frankly, you will hear the Eights and *Los Ochos* across North America, *Huit* in France, *Acht* in Germany, *Bā* across China... I can think of no advantage to having us all learn to count in a hundred different languages... the point is that none of the names really matter. Frankly, the Eights is probably the most universally used name both in and out of America and the one with which I tend to stick."

"Why 'Eights'?" Maggie stirred a spoon of sugar into her coffee.

"Eights? That's a difficult one to answer. From all the research I have done, it seems to have simultaneously appeared a few years back in both Asia and North America. Australia and Europe weren't far behind. Tradition has it that the eighth day of Chinese New Year is the annual gathering of all the gods in Heaven. The Zodiacal sign Scorpio is the eighth astrological sign. In the Tarot, eight is the card for Justice or Strength. The way we write the number 8 in the Arabic form symbolises balance, time and the reoccurring travel path of energy, similar to the mathematical graphic shape of a lemniscate figure or the symbol for infinity. I could go on, but I will mercifully leave you with a few final bits. I mentioned the Chinese obsession for the number eight; the opening ceremony of the 2008 Summer Olympics in China began on 8-8-08 at 8 minutes and 8 seconds past 8 pm. That wasn't a coincidence. Oxygen is the most fundamental requirement for life, the requirement without which death comes the most rapidly. You guessed it – 8 is the atomic number for life-giving oxygen. Eight planets... eight reindeer... In Christianity, the number 888 represents Jesus, or sometimes more specifically Christ the Redeemer, which is an opposing value to 666, the biblical number of the beast."

Grimms nodded knowingly. "Right, I never thought of that. The number 888 was the source of the angel microchip. Yes?"

"Exactly."

"Wait a minute... I don't follow here. The angel chip?"

Patton squirmed in her seat.

"Not a problem, Maggie. I guess this is a matter of history for those of us of more advanced years like Detective Sergeant Grimms or myself." Jankowski quietly laughed as she looked towards Harry. "We remember back to when these things first came into existence. For younger folks – and I say that with great envy," Tracey again smiled, "...you didn't live through it all. If you don't mind my asking, how old are you?"

"Twenty-seven."

"And you have a SAM I would assume?"

"Of course." Maggie held her right hand up and pointed to the flap of skin between her thumb and index finger.

"Well you know, SAMs – Subdermal Angel Microchips – had their early roots in the memory chips they started implanting in dogs for identification 50 or 60 years ago. They were very simple transponders that carried basic ID information about the dog: name, owner's name, address, phone... These eventually started to be implanted in humans in place of old-fashioned ID cards and security keys. Sometime back at the beginning of this century these subdermal chips rapidly grew in popularity as they started to replace bank cards, car and office keys, employee IDs and whatnot. I don't mean to patronise you, Maggie."

"No, no, you're not, Dr Jankowski. I was never too clear on this bit of history."

"A few of the more extreme religious groups started to refer to these chips as 666 chips. I don't pretend to be able to explain it all, but I know this much... The system used in America was initially called the Universal Product Code, which resulted in barcodes on all retail merchandise. Half a century ago, some fundamentalist Christians claimed that the three guard bars in the barcodes were three sixes, hence the term '666 chip.' Now, you might recall that the biblical reference to the number 666 was the 'number of the beast' in the *Book of Revelation*. The 666 chip became associated with the devil, and these human implants were viewed by many of these sects as the sign of the devil. Lo and behold, in a short time, many of the more extreme religious groups started to boycott them. As the chips became more intricate and interactive, they quickly replaced the old mobile phones and eventually the data bands some people still wear on their wrists today.

"I guess it was more of a marketing scheme than anything else, but the microchips became known as 888 chips."

"Marketing scheme?" Maggie was unclear. "Were three eights found in barcodes, too?"

"No, no... it was nothing like that. The 888 chip was so named because, in Christian thought, the number 888 represents Jesus or, more specifically, Christ the Redeemer. The actual SAM is not much larger than a grain of rice and is encased in silicate glass so as not to be rejected by the body. One of the first companies that started mass producing these devices thought it expedient to name their chip the '888" to counter the negative religious connotations. There was no more to it than using an invented name – 888 – to overcome the negative impressions of the 666. Of course, keeping with the Christian numerology theme, the 888 became known in advertising as the 'Angel Microchip', the Angel designation being one hundred per cent a marketing ploy. Put all that together, and all four of us now have a SAM implanted in our hand. Now, no one ever thinks about where the name came from at all."

"How about that. I never had the foggiest idea of why a SAM was called a SAM." Maggie looked at her colleagues as both Grimms and Bradshaw bobbed their heads in agreement.

Dr Jankowski tilted her head and smiled. "I apologise for the sidetrack, but we were trying to pinpoint a reason for the number eight being so prevalent here. I wish I had a definitive answer. Whatever it is, so many of the world's children have somehow become attached to the number eight as a symbol with which they identify. I don't tell you all this to bore you, but to simply give you a few ideas as to what sort of totally irrational things some kids want to hook onto. That doesn't in any way mean there is even a hint of reasoning involved with this. I can't explain the rationale for 'eight' any more than you can explain the logic of Santa Klaus or the Easter Bunny to me. But it certainly DOES matter to so many of our children. And just consider for a moment that adults succumb to crazy notions, too. We live in a country where close to 40% of our fellow Americans believe the Earth is less than 10,000 years old. Polling tells us that between 5% to 10% of Americans are not sure the Earth is round!"

Grimms moved his head side to side. "Hey, we're cops. If there is any segment of the society that knows about the masses of irrational people out there, it would be us. Crazy, crazy…"

"Pardon me, but I would suggest a more accurate term. As a psychologist, I couldn't agree with the 'crazy' reference, but true enough, we all perceive the world in different ways. Inevitably our age, our experiences and our personal biology all have huge impacts on how we take in and interpret information. And we surely can't overlook the culture in which we live and the social interaction we have or don't have. But we can be certain that people can vest in beliefs that are perfectly sensible to one group and yet other parts of the same society may find them illogical and even abhorrent. Consider for a minute, do any of you have any tattoos?"

Grimms and Bradshaw both grunted a no; Agent Patton remained quiet.

"Do you realise that greater than two-thirds of the American population have tattoos now and that the 'haves' and 'have-nots' both believe the other group misunderstands the whole concept of why one would or would not be tattooed." Tracey sat back and had a sip of her coffee.

Playing devil's advocate, Maggie took a hard law-and-order view of the point she thought Jankowski was making. "I follow all you are saying here and agree. The problem is that much of what any of us might do is not based on any 'facts', at least in the way a scientist might define the term. Any given behaviour will still have similar outcomes no matter what the initial motivating force. If one adolescent robs a convenience store because she is hungry, and another robs a convenience store because she is amassing money to buy guns or drugs, they both have still broken the same law and face the same charges."

"The same charges, yes... but they may be viewed in very different ways by a trial judge." Grimms added.

Maggie agreed with her boss. "Well... naturally, that's true. We're all law enforcement here and what you are saying seems quite sensible to me. I'm simply asking why a worldwide movement can be solidly based on beliefs that have NO solid foundation if that makes sense."

"Are you saying that kids investing so much in the Eights or *Los Ochos* or *Bā* believe this as much as an army might believe their generals... might believe their ruler?" Bradshaw quietly set his mug back down on the table.

"Yes Ryan, that's exactly what I'm saying. Look at our country, at our world... It seems politics and even our government has been in such disarray for decades now that kids don't find any confidence in their formal leaders. Religion has been dead to this cohort since they were old enough to interact with the world. For that matter, many, many of these adolescents haven't even experimented with drugs. So, put it all together." Jankowski started counting fingers. "One, the government is dead. Two, community organisations are dead.

Three, religion is dead... and four, even the drug culture is dead."

"Jeez... that is certainly not an optimistic way of looking at our youth." Bradshaw tilted his head.

"Optimistic? You came in here telling me you were stepping over dozens... hundreds of kids nearly comatose and strewn willy-nilly around our streets. It's difficult to look at that phenomenon through any framework of optimism, don't you think?"

All three officers mumbled their agreement.

"How about the data bands, Dr Jankowski? Depending on their parents' finances, they could have SAMs, but most of these kids have old, cheap plastic data bands. We have found some kids we've taken in for questioning using their data bands in bizarre ways. We've seen kids wave a hand at their wrist and seemingly go into trances." Maggie looked to Ryan as he again bobbed his head in the affirmative. "Is it possible that there is some programming that acts similar to the way an electronic drug would behave, as it were."

"I imagine it's possible, though I have no specific expertise in this area. The FBI has been looking into this variable, too. It is difficult to pin down because the programming involved is developed to adapt to each individual. Our lab boys tell me this fact makes it almost impossible to just run a software programme to identify data bands with such applications on board. That doesn't mean it doesn't work though. Our brains are continually functioning by using electrical signals pulsing through countless clusters of nerves. We can elect to interfere with these signals by introducing various pharmaceuticals which either supply or induce a series of chemical reactions that impact on this electrical activity. Now we can interfere in a multitude of ways – to deaden pain, to relieve stress, to induce sleep, etc. In the extreme case, certain pharmaceuticals misused can actually cause a disruption of brain activity that can result in death.

"I want to reiterate that I am a psychologist, not a computer programmer or AI specialist. That said, I assume that in the case of using the data band or a SAM, it might be possible that it could work that way. If it were somehow programmed to mimic a drug, then obviously no pharmaceutical would be needed, and the device itself would be rigged to send electrical pulses to the brain. As far as the biology goes, the brain responds whether the stimulus is initiated by a pharmaceutical in the bloodstream or by an electrical signal coming from the SAM or data band on your wrist. In either case, if the signal with the human physiology is shaped in similar ways, the resulting brain activity is the same – a state of euphoria that can lead to dependence or even addiction. Consider – we have been treating pain using electrodes for decades now."

"Wow – electronic drugs." Grimms scratched his cheek with one finger. "Is that really possible?"

"I'm afraid so, Detective. But please don't carry this too far. The bulk of these kids are following the whole Eight movement, not because of electronic drugs, rather because they really believe whatever it is that they believe. We've interviewed many of these youngsters, and they are firmly set in accepting as fact that they have perfectly free will and that they choose to follow their movement. They display a textbook example of what we academics might call conformational bias or cognitive bias. At some level, all humans tend to practise this. When one has intense feelings about any issue, group or problem, the existing desires or beliefs strongly influence just where the individual searches for supportive evidence and how that evidence is interpreted. In the end, the process she or he goes through results in the validation of their pre-existing bias. The apparent error in this round-about thinking is that the individual ceases to gather any contradictory information and winds up – in their own mind – confirming what prejudices or opinions they would like to be true. This happens in terms of ethnic backgrounds, politics, religion and even football teams. In short, we can sum this up by saying that humans tend to pal around with people we agree with and who agree with us.

"Let me tell you a one hundred per cent true case that I came upon just last week. I was asked to sit in on an interview at one of your DC precincts with three young women, two 13-years old and one 14-years old. They went on at length, telling us how angels never communicate using words, but they always connect with people using signs. Here are kids who probably hate their mathematics classes, yet it seems their entire life is tied up in some weird kind of numerology. They are convinced that the essence of each one of their own souls is involved with the number eight... their life paths follow the number eight. In the situation we are talking about here, the girls went into a fast-food restaurant and ordered burgers and fries. They were given the food and then handed a bill for $38.88. One of the 14-year-old looked at the clock and shouted out that it was eight minutes past eight in the evening."

"What's the point, Doc?" Maggie looked quizzically.

"Well, to you and me, the time... the bill... that is a total coincidence. In reality, it most likely would never have even caught our attention. To these three young girls though, that was a sign from the powers that be... from the angels... whatever that may mean. They walked out of the door with the bag of food without paying. Eights or no Eights, walking out of a restaurant without paying is against the law, and that's how I wound up meeting these young women in the police station interview room."

28

Saturday, 10 September; Gale Crater lave tube 27A, Mars

Lochie enjoyed the skellie ride like a little kid on a new dune buggy. The no-frills unit travelled over the Martian landscape at no more than 20-25 kilometres per hour but was more comfortable than he imagined it would be. He was still getting used to the lower surface gravity that was only 38% that of Earth, resulting in his 90-kilogram body only weighing in at a bit over 34 kilograms. Lochie was pleased that Martian bumps in Martian gravity were much easier on his backside compared to driving back at home on corrugated, unsealed roads across the Aussie outback.

They climbed off the skellie and checked that their tool belts were secure. Siti scrutinised the virtual map her Surface-Outpost-Communicator projected in front of their faceplate. "It ought to be a hundred metres or so behind those boulders."

"Let's do it."

They both headed off towards the escarpment. Within a few minutes, they were close enough to the ridge that the sizeable bits of rock debris scattered about hid anything behind it. "This should be it, 27A."

"I'm sure that it is, but it's not so obvious from this point of view." Lochie circled a few big boulders. "I'll check this side, and you look over there. There has to be an opening." He took a few more steps and stopped. What a dream for a geologist – a walk on the Martian surface. He fought hard to suppress the urge to examine every rock he saw. He continued stepping between giant boulders, but despite his anticipation at every turn, there was no entrance to be found.

"Lochie, over here."

He glanced at his SOC and tapped on his arm control. At

once a locator indicated Siti about a hundred metres to his left. "I'm coming, mate."

"This must be it. It's fairly well hidden, but we'll be able to get in there with no problem."

"Wait until I get there before you enter."

"Will do. Woe is me to violate regulation number one: thou shalt not enter any cave or tube without a partner." Her smile somehow almost transmitted over the SOC signal.

Lochie's head poked out around one last boulder, and he finally spotted Siti. "There you are, mate."

"It's about time you got here. You see, we tried to tell you that these tube openings aren't always so easy to find." Her 'I-told-you-so' expression was easily visible through her faceplate.

Lochie ran his glove over one of the smooth, red boulders. "Man, this baby must be 7 or 8 metres high. I wouldn't have wanted to be here when it rolled into place."

"No kidding."

"Well you found the entrance, so I reckon you should have the honours. Would you like to poke your head in first?" He could see her smile through the faceplate, making it obvious that she accepted the honour. "I'm right behind you."

"This is exciting." She stepped around some small rubble and ducked under a slight overhang. She paused in front of the opening. "The tube is large here – funny how hidden it is from out front."

"Yeah, my range finder says it's twelve metres high here at the entrance." He watched her step into the opening and followed right behind.

At first, the daylight from outside lit the way into the cavern. Both were quiet as they walked the first hundred metres into the cavern. As the natural light grew dimmer, the bright light from the lamps fixed on each of their helmets cut through the darkness. The two explorers stopped beside each other.

"Wow... this is pretty big."

"Yep, it's even higher right here than at the entrance." Lochie slowly turned his whole body, the helmet lamp cutting through the dark in a 360-degree circle. "Look over there." He pointed towards the far wall.

"Looks like another fork there. Any idea of how we decide which one first?"

"Sure do. It's' one of the earliest lessons I learned in first-year geology."

"What's that?"

"Flip a coin." He laughed. "Of course, since we don't have a coin..."

"Let's try the left side first – it looks a little closer."

"Fair dinkum, Siti."

The floor was smooth, with a light scattering of dust that had accumulated over the years. Lochie found himself reflecting on how little they could know of the history of this lava tube. A *déjà vu* moment came over him wondering if he'd felt this amazement before. Could the dust have been there for centuries? For millennia? They had absolutely no idea how long ago anything might have happened here.

As they got within a few metres of the left fork, Siti's voice came over the SOC. "Your turn."

"My turn?"

"Well you let me have the honours of coming in the lava tube first, so I reckon you should go into the side branch here."

"Fair enough. But I do recognise your devious methods here."

"Devious?"

"Yep, devious in letting me go first... After all, that's the prime rule of any science fiction story, right?"

"Prime rule? What in god's name are you talking about, Lochie?"

"Well, if there's a discovery to be made, it would NEVER be in the first fork, but always in the last possible place anyone..." Lochie was only on his second step into the fork when his helmet light reflected off a scattering of shiny objects. "Holy bloody hell! Siti! Siti!" He found his pace speed up and – though not exactly running – was wasting no time to see exactly what they had found.

"Yes, I see it!" She picked up the pace behind him until she was by his side as they covered the thirty or forty metres to the first of a dozen or so reflective objects spread across the cave floor. Right next to the shiny pieces was what appeared to be a cloth bag.

Lochie stooped down and aimed his helmet cam at the flashy pieces and reached for one. He raised it eye-level. "Bloody hell! We've got more medallions, Siti. And look here." He pointed a metre or so to the side at what appeared to be a fabric sack the size of a typical shopping bag.

"Don't touch it, Lochie." Siti reached for an instrument on her toolbelt. "We want to document the entire area first." She held the device in front of her face and scanned it horizontally through 360 degrees. She then repeated the scan vertically in a full circle overhead and underfoot. After about three or four minutes, she reattached the gadget to her belt. "Okay, I've got it. The recorder gave me a positive on completing the scan." She stooped beside him, and they both gawked at the scattered medallions and the bag.

"If I didn't know better, I'd say this was a shopping bag. Do you think we can touch it?"

"Well sure, we're going to have to. At least we have documented the area. We can't get it out of here without touching it, though we should be gentle and make sure it isn't about to tear open."

The confines of their pressurised suits made it difficult to determine what the bag was made of, but the fabric-like material had a sheen similar to leather or polyurethane. "Okay, let me document this, too." Lochie quickly scanned his camera over the bag and then turned towards the back of the tube. It seemed as though there were several more bags of similar size and shape back there. "I can't believe this."

"Wow!" Siti moved on to a second bag and ran her glove over the top of it. "I'm checking my SOC, but I don't think we have enough of a signal in here to reach the outpost or the other two teams."

"No surprise there. The caves tend to block most radio signals."

"I don't think this goes much deeper." Lochie grabbed his floodlight from his toolbelt and lit up a wider area towards the back of the cave. The walls seemed to close into a dead-end only 50 or 60 metres from where they were standing. Lochie took a few dozen steps with his helmet light and hand-held floodlight moving in every which direction. After a few minutes, he was convinced they had found all that was there. He walked back to his fellow explorer where she was still occupied with recording the area in as much detail as possible.

"I'm torn here, Siti." Lochie selected a geologist's hammer from his tool belt as he crouched down beside their find. "I know we need to go back and tell the others, but I'm just so anxious to..." He lifted the bag he hovered over and pulled a flap back over one side. "Look."

Siti bent down at his side. The two of them peered into the bag. She reached in and grabbed a medallion. "Maybe we just found backup evidence beyond our wildest dreams, Lochie."

He looked over her shoulder. "Crikey! I think we've found BAGS of backup evidence, Siti!"

* * *

In total, Siti and Lochie located six bags of medallions in the lava tube 27A. They painstakingly recorded the detail of each find in place, as well as the entirety of the chamber within the cavern that contained them. Only after the documentation was completed did they begin moving the first bag out to their skellie. They had very little to say while retracing their steps back to the cave entrance. No sooner had they poked their heads out into the Martian daylight then Siti spoke up. "SOC is functioning again. I'll let the others know what we have found. Let's get this bag back to the skellie."

Lochie was lost in his thoughts as he walked the hundred metres or so back to their little rover. He set the bag on the bench seat of the skellie and again pulled the flap open to get a better look inside. His gloved hand was a bit awkward reaching inside, but just this quick look indicated there were probably four or five dozen medallions inside. He pulled one from the bag and held it in front of his faceplate, allowing his cameras to record it in great detail. It appeared to be maybe 70-80 millimetres in diameter and about 20-25 millimetres thick. The colouring was similar to the artifact Siti and Keegan found, and the markings on the surface seemed to be the same.

"Lochie."

He was almost startled when Siti came over by his side.

"Jeez... sorry, Siti. I guess I was lost in our find here."

She smiled. "It's okay. Did you think I was an alien?"

"Right!" Lochie quickly snapped his mind back to the here and now.

"Look, our Surface-Outpost-Communicator was able to get to Arya and Keegan in 18A, and they are on their way here now. I also talked to Nigella back at the outpost. I still haven't been able to get in touch with Joe and Misha, so I assume they are out of radio range in tube 31B. Nigella has SOC monitoring them until they can hear us."

"Thanks, Siti. On closer inspection, I'll bet you these are identical to what you and Keegan found. I assume yours will be the same. How many do you have there?" He looked at the pouch on her waist where she placed the medallions scattered next to the first bag.

"Ah..." She tilted her head and mouthed the numbers as she counted quietly. "Looks like ten in total."

His grin radiated towards her. "Wait until our mates see what we've found!"

"Oh boy..."

He turned his head side to side within his helmet. "O_2 is getting low. Why don't we swap over to a fresh oxygen pack and go get another couple of bags? By then, Keegan and Joe can help us get the last of them out."

29

Sunday, 11 September; Waldorf Astoria on the Bund, Shanghai, China

Owen picked up a clump of noodles with his chopsticks and placed them in his mouth. As he began to chew, his face broke into a smile. "Yummy. This is really good. So, what am I eating?"

Fiona widened her eyes. "I'm so happy you like it. It really is tasty... I knew you'd like it."

"I do, but what is it?"

Fiona's warm smile was radiant. "What do you think it is?"

"Umm... some kind of noodles? Crispy potatoes? Yams?"

She giggled mischievously. "It's jellyfish."

Owen placed his chopsticks in the ceramic holder. "WHAT? This is jellyfish? It's crunchy and spicy, and nothing like I thought jellyfish would be like."

Fiona laughed, her long hair flowing back over her shoulders now after being tucked into a bun all day at the Summit. "Well, I hope you weren't expecting raw jellyfish."

"Okay, I'm game. Let me try some of that." Sunlyn reached over Owen's plate and secured a taste of his jellyfish between her chopsticks. She lifted them to her mouth and tasted it. "It is crunchy... yum... good. Damn... I'm surprised too. Who would have ever thought jellyfish would taste like this! How do you prepare them?"

Fiona finished her mouthful. "Easy. After you rinse and clean the jellyfish, you just mix it in a bowl with some sesame oil, soy sauce, vinegar, chilli oil, sugar and ginger. I usually let it sit and marinate for 15 or 20 minutes and then toast it in a wok with a sprinkle of sesame seeds. In a minute or two, you get it to a crispy texture, and it's ready to eat."

Kylie was amused by her new-found American friends. "Good on you! You three enjoy the jellyfish. I'm sticking with the Shanghai soy duck for right now." She tasted a swallow of her wine. "Umm... this is quite good."

"Yes, it's one of the Pigeon Hills wines. We are quite proud of the Ningxia wine region right on the edge of the Gobi Desert. You might be interested to hear that one of your best wineries – Penfolds, I believe – has given so much help to Pigeon Hills on the technical side of wine production." Fiona's Chinese pride was evident.

"Well compliments to Pigeon Hills and Penfolds." Kylie sat back as her smile was replaced by a more serious look. "You know, I received an urgent message this morning from my colleagues back in Sydney. Are you familiar with the name Lochlan Greenbank?"

"Greenbank... Greenbank..." Owen's mind was spinning. "Isn't he one of the new guys who just went out to Mars?"

"What a memory, Owen. You are spot on. Lochie is an Aussie, and I happen to know him, though he's at the University of Western Australia and I'm at the University of Sydney. We tend to be as snobby about our Group of Eight as you are with your Ivy League schools."

"The Group of Eight?" Sunlyn tilted her head in question.

"Yes, yes... The Group of Eight are some of the most prestigious and oldest universities in Australia and tend to do the bulk of the nation's research. Besides Sydney and UWA, the others are Australian National University, Melbourne University, the University of New South Wales, the University of Queensland, the University of Adelaide and Monash University." Kylie chuckled. "I promise I won't quiz you on them.”

“So, what about Professor Greenbank? He’s on Mars now, isn’t he?” Owen was familiar with some of his work from before he was chosen to go to Mars.

“Yes, of course he is. From what I heard this morning though, there is meant to be a big press conference in Perth the week after the Summit finishes, and Professor Greenbank is meant to have a central role in it.”

“Perth?”

“Yes… on our west coast.”

“That’s a long way off into the wild outback, no?”

“Wild outback? Perth’s something like three million people now. I think they have five unis there and two of their academics are Martian residents right now.”

“Two?” Sunlyn asked.

“Yes, besides Lochie, Professor Parisa Henning has been there for a while now. She’s a biologist. Actually, I don’t think any other university on the planet has two Mars residents right now.”

“Well, that’s all well and good, but if I understand the time it takes for communications from Earth to Mars and then back again, I don’t know how what we’d call a ‘normal’ press conference could ever happen.” Fiona’s interest was piqued.

“Oh, over the years they’ve dealt with that fairly well I think.” Owen seemed to be making eye contact with Fiona on a more regular basis of late. “The Mars team sends along either transcripts or videos of the presentation they want to give, a select few journalists on Earth get to read or view them in private. Once they review them, any follow-up questions they may have are then recorded by video and returned to Mars for clarification. The production teams combine both the presentation and the follow-up questions all together into a fairly traditional 'press conference' format. I've watched a few of them broadcast from Mars over the years, and they work just fine."

"It does seem to almost violate the journalist's code, since the people being queried already know what the questions are ahead of time." Sunlyn squished her face.

"Like it or not, it's the only way since Mother Nature's laws of physics dictate just that. Otherwise, after the presentation, journalists would ask one question, it'd take five, ten or twenty minutes for the question to travel to Mars for an answer, then another ten or twenty minutes to travel back to Earth. You can see that it just wouldn't work out. Regrettably, no amount of modern technology is going to make radio waves travel faster than the speed of light."

Sunlyn made another funny face. "I say damn those laws of physics!"

"Well, I'm sure it must work." Kylie continued. "I confess to not knowing all the details as yet myself, but what you say seems to make sense, Owen. My spies tell me they will report a rather startling find from what they are hinting."

"Startling?"

"Yes, startling – that's the word they used. I know that Lochie is a geologist, but rumour has it that he is now involved with the biological team you mentioned that Professor Henning heads. I wouldn't be surprised if we hear from her, too." Kylie's eyes widened as she lifted her wineglass. "Your guess is as good as mine, but if the bio people are involved, could we stretch our imaginations to Martian life?"

"Martian Life!" Sunlyn gulped her glass of Pigeon Hills. "Wow!"

30

Sunday, 11 September; Gale Crater Outpost, Mars

By the time the six explorers returned to the outpost, they were exhausted and ready for a full night's sleep. But every one of them was quickly reminded that brains don't always listen to tired bodies. The collective excitement of their astonishing find boosted their energy to high levels. Save for a few hours of napping here and there, the Gale Crater team kept laboratory lights burning bright, and computer system processors running hot all night long. By late morning, the outpost science team congregated in an impromptu gathering over tea in the staff room.

"I haven't made a great deal of headway, but I can tell you I am now convinced the markings are definitely symbols of some sort."

"Can you explain that, Arya?" Siti was on the edge of her seat.

"Well, no two medallions had the same sequence of symbols, so to start with, these are probably not any type of coin. I say that because if it were coins, you would expect to see the same symbols in the same order on groups of them."

Nigella looked at him with 'why' written all over her face.

Arya picked up his now-full mug and walked back towards the conference table. "Well, just think about having a pocket full of Earthly change... we'll use Aussie coins in our example. For the sake of argument, maybe we place 20 coins on the table. Even with no understanding of any Earthly language, the alien anthropologists would easily sort them into, let's say, six piles. It would be easy to separate them into five-cent pieces, ten-cent pieces, twenty-cent pieces, fifty-cent pieces, one-dollar coins, and two-dollar coins, each sorted into their own piles. To do this, the alien archaeologist would not need to know anything of our language, of our mathematical system and wouldn't even need to know the purpose of the coins. The fact that each pile had the exact same set of symbols would indicate some level of mass production."

"How about coins of the same type with different dates?"

"Spot on, Keegan. Naturally, it depends on what country, what process, the period of time involved and so on, but the mintmark and/or dates you refer to could show slight differences between some coins, but that would simply be a subdivision. You could still easily separate five-cent coins into one pile and realise they had some subdivision even if you didn't know what it was."

"Fair enough."

"My point is that the six bags – plus the ten loose ones – contained 316 different medallions, so along with the original find, we have a total of 317 medallions."

"Did the original seem to fit with all the new ones?"

"Yes, yes… it could have come out of one of the bags with the other 316 additions. I've recorded them all and dumped those data into my AI's brain. Our program – particularly the AI interface – has some very specialised techniques it employs." Arya almost pushed his chest out, revealing the pride he had in his AI 'baby.' "If we ever are going to crack this as a language, we need to find our Martian version of the Rosetta Stone."

"I've heard of that, but I'm merely an engineer – educate me here, Arya." Joe put his hands behind his head and leaned back.

"Sure. You've at least heard of the Rosetta Stone. It literally was a stone found by French scholars during Napoleon's invasion of Egypt way back in the late 1700s. The stone had three sets of characters carved into it reporting a governmental decree. The top inscriptions were carved in Egyptian hieroglyphic symbols which are pictographic in nature and represented by small little picture-like characters. The second version of the proclamation on the Rosetta Stone was recorded in demotic writing which is simply a cursive form of hieroglyphics or cursive hieratic script. Finally, the bottom text was written using the ancient Greek alphabet.

"Now the stone itself was not meant to be a language primer. Rather, it was a record of a decree given by the new ruler of the day, kind of like an inaugural address of a new prime minister or president. So, if you follow what I'm saying here, the stone had the same text recorded in Egyptian printing, Egyptian cursive writing and Greek writing. The fact that it was recorded in all three forms allowed linguists to decipher the unknown Egyptian language from the known Greek language."

"Fair enough, that all makes good sense to me. Of course, that begs the question as to where are we ever going to find a Martian Rosetta Stone?" Siti ran her fingers through her hair.

"I don't yet have a clue, Siti, but I know we will keep looking. It's not beyond belief that there will be something like that. Consider when the American Pioneer spacecraft was sent on a journey back in the 1970s, NASA knew it would eventually leave our solar system. The project engineers agreed to put a sort of Earthling Rosetta Stone on the plaque attached to the Pioneer probe. The team that designed it went through hell trying to consider how to communicate with a totally different life form, but the thought process they went through is instructive. If you ever get the chance, read some of the debates they had which are all posted on Skynet somewhere. Anyway, they had a diagram of a man and a woman, a hydrogen atom for scale, a map locating our sun with 14 pulsars for reference, each identified by their periods of pulsation, and cross lines pointing to us. Will anyone ever find it? Probably not. But, interestingly enough, we thought enough ahead to include the attempt to communicate on the spacecraft. We can only hope our Martians – more correctly, the aliens – have done the same."

Mischa was impressed. "I guess I didn't realise how much you knew about language, Arya."

"Well, considering that artificial intelligence is my thing, you shouldn't be surprised to hear that language is a reflector of intelligence. It is difficult to learn, to socialise, to manufacture, to build civilisations without language. In many senses, language is central to intelligence, though I don't want to push that premise too far. Since my thing has been artificial intelligence, I've had to spend time studying how language immerses itself with intelligent thought.

"To that point, over a hundred years ago, a couple of anthropological linguists proposed what is known as the Sapir-Whorf hypothesis. This hypothesis has been hotly argued for and against over the past century, but let's just say that language and thought most certainly are somehow related. I have much more to learn here concerning the language. I'll keep grinding the data and see where they get me. I keep saying that I will when I actually mean the AI will. The AI program can do overnight what a hundred linguists would take a century to do the old-fashioned way! Remember, we may have had the first medallion for over a week, but I've only had overnight to work on this expanded data set."

"Siti, do we have any idea on the age of the pieces?"

"I've not been able to date the medallions at this point, Misha."

"Maybe the objects are not easily dated, but as for where they have been found, you are talking my language." Keegan's eyes lit up as he sat leaned forward in his chair. "The surrounding basaltic lava flows are laid down in sheets. Obviously one of the key tenants of geology is that in unfolded layers, the newest layer has to be on top. We've refined the dates of the surrounding flows here at Gale Crater by doing isotopic studies and find the newest layers between about three-plus billion years old."

Lochie laughed out loud. "That's fantastic, Keegan. What you're saying is the bags could have been dropped off three billion years ago or... last week. That really doesn't narrow things down too much, mate."

"Yeah, yeah... you got me, Lochie. I didn't mean I found an exact date, only that we keep getting these data that tell us Mars has been geologically dead for a long, long time."

Nigella stated the obvious. "Let's not be too tough on Keegan. Considering the microbial life discovered back at Alpha Colony and the level of intelligence displayed by our aliens, I think it's fair to say that in astronomical terms, whoever left these objects here is a relative new-comer to our solar system."

"Why do you say that, Nigella?"

"Well, Keegan has just reaffirmed that Mars has been geologically dead for at least two-thirds the age of our 4.6 billion-year-old solar system, and we know there hasn't been liquid water or a thick atmosphere here for a long, long time – maybe a few billion years. Does anyone here actually believe the aliens who manufactured these medallions evolved here on Mars?" Nigella slowly looked around at her colleagues. "I repeat, I reckon the aliens have to be fairly recent arrivals in our solar system."

Joe had been quiet for most for the conversation but finally spoke up. "Or we are latecomers to THEIR solar system!" Heads slowly nodded their agreement around the table.

"I can be more definitive in one sense, though... whoever made these pieces had capacities beyond simply possessing intelligence." Arya held a medallion up as if displaying it was somehow making his point. "Dolphins, whales and porpoises may be intelligent, and the great apes, orangutans and some of the monkeys have learned sign language. There are many ways we can conceptualise intelligence... but the animals I mention here do not seriously display technology and are not industrial." He again raised the object above his head. "We are again left with the notion that whoever produced these pieces applied their intelligence in a technical way and demonstrated the skill to utilise that knowledge to manufacturing products."

31

Monday, 12 September; Global Holistic Summit, Shanghai, China

Professor Gillian Pickard concluded her prepared remarks from her daily update to the Summit of the data collected after the *Thánatos* impact. "That is all the latest information I can give from our team of researchers around the planet. I can take questions now."

She recognised a middle-aged man standing in the press section of the audience. One of the interns handed him a microphone and moved to the side. "Good morning, Dr Pickard. I'm Malcolm Satterley from the Australian Broadcast Network in Melbourne. First of all, thank you again for your daily update here. I... we... have listened to your daily updates now all week. I'm afraid that every morning you report facts that often contradict what we were told the day before. I'm a journo, not a scientist, but I keep hearing you say that today's data indicate more dire consequences than what we were told yesterday. My question is, what aren't you telling us? Why can't the scientific community simply level with the people? Why can't you tell us what kind of long-term consequences *Thánatos* will have on Earth and on humanity?"

Dr Pickard fidgeted with some papers on the podium before raising her head to look in the general direction of the questioner. "Thank you for your question, Mr Satterley. I... I cannot stress enough that we in the scientific community are trying to present you – the people of the world in general – with the best information we have at the time it is given. Regrettably, we simply do not have all the facts. Science can NEVER have ALL the facts. In the case of the *Thánatos* strike, there are so many variables that it is impossible to know outcomes without constantly updating measurements we collect either *in situ* or remotely. My point is that no one knows exactly what long-term consequences we can expect since no one knows exactly what the inputs from such a huge energy release might be. We can only..."

The Australian journalist interrupted Dr Pickard. "Excuse me, doctor. I understand that you can't know what you don't know, but surely you DID know that the permafrost up there contains a possibly deadly store of methane gas. I have reported science and technology for a decade now, and though I knew that permafrost contains sequestered methane, it certainly has not been common knowledge of just how much of the gas we are talking about. It seems to me that you had to know this was a possibility."

"Mr Satterley, you need to understand that some things are so remote that they border on the impossible. I confess that as an astrophysicist, I have no expertise in geology or atmospheric physics."

André leaned forward and tapped his microphone. "Yes, Professor Moureaux." Gillian seemed to let out a silent sigh in the hope that her colleague would save her from the

Inquisition.

"Thank you, Dr Pickard." He adjusted his microphone. "Mr Satterley, my name is André Moureaux, and I am a climatologist working closely with the National Oceanic and Atmospheric Administration as well as with the Climate Action Network Europe. I don't mean to interrupt my colleague here, but I believe I may be better able to answer your question concerning the methane problem we seem to have encountered here.

"We obviously knew all along that with the tremendous amount of energy that the *Thánatos* asteroid strike was most likely going to impart, it was capable of producing all kinds of problems for us. We need to be thankful that the worst did not occur, namely, a full-on ninety-degree impact with the total mass of the asteroid being released into the Earth and its atmosphere. That, Mr Satterley, is simply a coincidental bit of cosmic luck. Considering orbital dynamics, a few seconds earlier and we could have courted immediate disaster... a few seconds later and *Thánatos* could have skipped off the Earth's atmosphere and been recorded as merely an incredibly close call. Scientists can measure and deduce, but we cannot play god..."

"But the methane?"

"Please, Mr Satterley, let me continue. Of course, we knew – know – that the Earth's permafrost regions store a tremendous amount of methane gas. Of course, we know that methane gas has far more substantial greenhouse potential than carbon dioxide by a factor of nearly a hundred times greater. But once the tracking of *Thánatos*'s trajectory indicated a high chance of splitting with at least some portion of its mass skipping off into space, we reported a less-than worst-case scenario. Even more, considering that the bulk of whatever mass remained appeared headed for Siberia, we again were relieved that we just might come out of this incident with a minimum of damage. The data at hand paint a more optimistic rather than a pessimistic outcome. In support of my colleague Dr Pickard, she has reported accurately and to the best of her knowledge each day this week. However, the 'best of our knowledge' is not always what actually reflects reality. Consider...

"We knew that the area of impact contained a great deal of methane stored in the permafrost. My colleagues and I have studied these areas for the past few decades. We also knew that this area was reasonably inactive seismically. That is important since seismic activity and ground movement could – under a worst-case situation – cause us some problems. Incredibly, it seems that the path along which the meteor fragments struck closely traced a line above an inactive, deep fault zone well beneath the permafrost. Unfortunately, this ancient fault zone has become reactivated and continues the tremors set off by *Thánatos*."

"But Professor Moureaux, I still don't understand missing these ancient faults. I mean, how could you get it that wrong?"

"How can we get it that wrong, Mr Satterley?" André stretched his arms over his head as his eyes widened into circles. "I fear you give us – give me – too much credit here. I think Mother Nature has a bit to do with it."

32

Monday, 12 September; Gale Cater Outpost, Mars

"So, have you made any more headway on the chemistry of whatever makes up that plastic-metal substance?"

"You mean the bulk metal glass – BMGs. I have done some refinements on constituent component materials, but I have a way to go on that yet. When we only had one artifact up until yesterday's find, I was fearful of causing too much damage to it while running our tests. Now that we have 317 artifacts – as well as the six bags themselves – I feel confident that I can be a bit more cavalier in using a standard battery of laboratory techniques."

"In other words, chipping a bit off here and there." Misha stroked her hand with her finger as though rubbing off a sample of skin.

"Well, not exactly, but... I admit that I have been very paranoid about damaging the only artifact we had."

Misha was working her way around the table, trying to encourage the team to share any new data before the next venture into the lava tubes. "How about you, Arya?"

"I think I have progressed some since I last updated the group. I told you then that I have catalogued all 317 pieces and previously reported that I was certain they weren't coins. I hold to that hypothesis. I also have my doubts that they would be any kind of award – like Olympic medals or something like that – again, simply because they are all different."

"Wouldn't that be the case if they were awards or medals, but each had a different name or something like that?"

"Possibly, Nigella. I'm not telling you that I know beyond a doubt, but they don't seem to fit that scenario. You might make some argument for the name hypothesis, though. Considering that no two artifacts are alike, groups do keep repeating common marks or symbols. Overall, there are a set of common symbols that are repeated on several groups of medallions. My AI program sorted the pieces into five clusters, each with a common set of symbols. I say symbols, but I remind you that these could be words. Those five groupings have 142, 74, 49, 37 and 15 members in their sets. The categorisation seems to be very much like we'd label things: files, accounts, stamps... something like that. Now if we are missing something big here, this idea that they are sorted like an archive may be incorrect, but at least right now, that's the best I can tell you."

"Suppose they were like Olympic medals or awards of some type. Wouldn't they fall into groups – like swimming, running, jumping – and yet all have different writing on them because they are different individuals who won them?"

"I guess that's possible, Joe. In the end, we just could really use more samples. The larger the collection of samples we can get, the better chance we have to unravel the mystery." Arya continued, "I have made some progress on trying to categorise the writing here. I want to differentiate language from writing in that the two, though connected, are not one and the same. I also want to start by stating the limitations upfront. First of all, I want to remind you that my formalised training is not as a linguist, but as a computer scientist with a great deal of work done in the area of artificial intelligence. I only double up as a linguist because I am about as close as we get to that discipline here on Mars. Second of all, because we are dealing with an alien life form, we just can't make assumptions we would make finding new, earth-based writing samples."

Siti reassured him. "I think we all realise that a small team such as ours here at Gale Crater Outpost can't have the depth and breadth we would like, but we all double and triple up on a range of disciplines. Don't apologise for any shortcoming." There was quiet agreement around the table. "I do need you to explain your last comment though, Arya... of what assumptions do we need to be wary?" She scratched her head.

"Well I only mean that considering any earth-based writing, we could relate to at least the most basic common environmental experiences we share, namely all Earthly life breathes, drinks, eats, and – by definition – reproduces and dies... I mean, when considering an alien life form, we have no idea if it has a corporeal body for god's sake. When we see a new hieroglyph on Earth with a stick figure body and a round orb above it, we are pretty damned confident it is a human with the sun or moon overhead. I mean, suppose we were dealing with a silicon-based life form that exists on an airless asteroid travelling from one solar system to the next. I know I'm being a bit radical here, but that would give us close to zero commonality to look for in written symbols. What would a transistor chip not programmed by a human use to represent voltage fluctuations? A symbol? A binary code? A string of electrons in a beam?"

"Wow." Misha grimaced. "I've never really stopped to consider that alien life could be so... well, so alien!"

"I don't mean to put you off too much. I guess the point I'm making is that we always need to be aware of our *Homo-sapien*-bias. And we need to keep looking for a cipher of some sort – our own version of the Rosetta Stone.

"Now I did mention we also can't confuse language with writing... writing can develop way later than a language, and sometimes it never develops. Consider the indigenous Aboriginal peoples in Lochie's home of Australia. They are the oldest continuous culture on Earth, dating back at least 50,000 years and possibly as long as 60,000 years. The Aboriginal people had a long, oral history passed down from generation to generation, and they produced cave drawings dating back through much of that history. But the Aboriginal Australians had no written language. It obviously has no reflection on abilities or intelligence. No civilisation could possibly survive in such a harsh environment as the Australian continent without possessing a high level of intellect and ingenuity.

"But these medallions," Arya again held one up to emphasise his point, "...indicate our aliens definitely had a written language. What can we say about it? I won't attempt to give you a lecture on the finer points of the development of written language, but I can give you a broad generalisation here. Consider the most basic *Homo sapiens* writing began as picture writing that attempted to express ideas and concepts directly – a spear in the side of an animal. When thousands of these individual symbols are standardised across a culture, we refer to this writing as ideographic, and each symbol represents a whole idea.

"A more complex method of writing would be a segmental writing system that employs symbols to represent sounds or phonics that make up words in a language. Now we are looking at the development of an alphabet. Using an agreed-upon alphabet, various combinations of letters may represent sounds in the spoken language. They can be strung together in an unlimited number of ways to represent ideas, things, etc. For example, in English, 26 symbols strung together in an almost infinite number of ways can be used to represent hundreds of thousands of unique words. I won't go beyond this point because that's as much as I can report with any degree of certainty."

Arya looked around the table, waiting for a question, but the team seemed happy with his explanation so far. "I mention the 26 letters in an English alphabet, but there is more than that. We include ten numerals, zero through nine, and a variety of other logograms such as a pound sign, asterisk, an ampersand, etc. Because most of us have grown up using that standard alphabet, we know the difference between numerals, logograms and letters and are confident in saying we have 26 letters in the alphabet. Back on Earth, we can even allow for other alphabets: for a Russian Cyrillic alphabet with 33 letters, for a Hebrew alphabet with only 22 letters, etc.

"All of this said, I can now state with a ninety-five per cent confidence level that the alien written language we are looking at is phonetic and consists of 29 'letters' or unique symbols. I cannot say at any level of confidence whether these 29 symbols include what you and I call numbers or logograms. I fear repetition, but we need to find more... we need to find a 'book' or other lengthy pieces of writing to speak with a higher level of confidence. Frankly, I wish we could stumble across an alien library."

"Maybe you have stumbled across a library, Arya. Maybe these aren't medallions at all. Could it be that they are somehow the aliens' way of storing data? Perhaps the 'medallions' ARE the aliens' library." Lochie arched his eyebrows as his colleagues contemplated his conjecture.

Misha glanced at the clock on the staff room wall. "We are nearing Martian leap hour. I realise that in the past few days, most of us haven't slept for more than a few hours. I think we need to somehow find a way to turn off our minds enough to let us get a bit of rest tonight. We have been successful in our initial quest to find more support for our original artifact. We still need to find Arya's Rosetta Stone."

One by one, each team member filed out of the staff room. Lochie thought about Misha's request for them to turn off their minds for a few hours. Right, he thought – fat chance of that happening.

PART THREE

"The difference between technology and slavery is that slaves are fully aware that they are not free."

— Nassim Nicholas Taleb

33

Monday, 12 September; Metro Precinct Station, Washington DC

"Yeah, I know we have more important cases, but then again, maybe we don't. This thing just doesn't add up. I think we are onto something big here, but I just can't wrap my head around it at this point." Grimms leaned back in his chair and put one foot on his desk. "Did we hear from Bradshaw yet?"

"Not yet, boss." Maggie shook her head no. "He and Officer Kelly are bringing the Bidwill boy in. He must live pretty close to O'Keefe over there in Kalorama Heights."

"Of course. They are the lucky ones... born into wealthy families, attending some of the finest prep schools in America, wearing the nicest clothes..."

Maggie nodded her agreement this time.

"What's with you, Patton. Didn't you tell that shrink you were twenty-seven years old?"

"I did, boss."

"Well, what's with this nervous tick you have... you keep shaking your head one time and nodding it the next."

Maggie giggled. "It's not a tick, Harry. I'm following along with you and agree that this whole thing doesn't stack up. And Kalorama Heights... I mean, you're right. These kids have all the riches of the world available to them – they have everything... Why would they be wearing old fashioned data bands? Why don't they have the latest technology, super-duper SAMs in their hands? Why are they involved with the Eights? Why are they shooting up some journalists' apartment?"

"Right. I can't pretend to explain..." Grimms' phone interrupted the conversation. He dropped his foot to the floor and leaned up to grab the call. "Grimms... yep... gotcha..." He dropped the phone back on the desk. "Bradshaw's here. Seems young Dylan Bidwill tried giving them the slip, but they got him. He's in the interview room."

* * *

"So, Mr Bidwill, we understand you and Bradley O'Keefe are pretty good buddies, yes?"

Bidwill squirmed in his seat at the big, steel table. "I know him."

"You two go to school together, yes?"

"Yeah."

"Georgetown Academy?"

"Yeah, Georgetown Academy."

"Did you ever shoot a gun before?" Grimms asked in a firmer tone.

"I don't have to answer that, do I?"

"No Mr Bidwill, you don't. It might help your cause, though... being cooperative with the police and all."

"I... umm..."

"Bidwill?

"No, I haven't."

Grimms tilted his head. "How about computers? Do you like working with computers, Mr Bidwill?"

"Sort of."

"What do you mean, sort of?"

"I do pretty well in my computer science class at school."

"And what kind of things do you like doing with computers?"

"Messing around... you know, games and stuff. I like writing programs for new games... new applications."

"So, you do have a pretty good knowledge of computers."

"I guess."

"You must have a really top-line SAM in your hand then, yes?" Grimms knew damned well Bidwill didn't have a SAM since their scanner confirmed that the minute Bradshaw picked him up.

"Ah... no, I don't. I don't have a SAM."

"No SAM. Come on, Mr Bidwill. A boy like you who is so interested in computers. A fellow whose family has enough resources to buy you any kind of SAM that you'd like. It makes no sense that you don't have a top-notch SAM in your hand."

"No, sir... I'm ah... I'm scared of blood."

Maggie leaned in now. "Scared of blood, son? Come on, Dylan. I think you know there's no blood involved with having a SAM implanted. You don't even feel it."

Dylan wiggled in his seat, obviously getting more and more nervous with every question. "I just don't want one."

"So how do you communicate? How do you stay in touch with friends?" Grimms was a bit louder now.

"I... I use a data band."

"That's pretty old fashioned, isn't it?"

"Nah, it's all good."

Grimms looked over at Patton. "We don't seem to be getting too far here. Maybe we need to let him cool his heels in the lockup overnight. Maybe he'll be a bit more talkative in the morning. What do you think, Bidwill?" Grimms looked back towards the boy.

"Sir, do you know that I'm only 17 years old?"

"Yes, son, I did know that. I also know that shooting up someone's living room falls under the provisions in FETA. Do you know what FETA is?"

"No sir, I don't."

"Well Bidwill, FETA is the Federal Emergency Terrorist Act, and according to that law, a person's age is irrelevant when dealing with acts of terrorism. Take him to the lockup, Bradshaw."

34

Tuesday, 13 September; Gale Crater Outpost, Mars

"I am sure having a day free of any surface excursions will prove beneficial in the long run." Misha leaned back in her chair. "Not only did we all have time to do lab work today, but our bodies have had some time to recover from our explorations."

"I'll agree with that. I know I'm the newbie here and, besides that, I'm a geologist. I read somewhere that geologists might just clock up the most kilometres walking as compared to all the other professions. Still, as much as I love walking around on the Martian surface, it surely does drain you. Even though we are all in pretty good physical shape, it's hard work." Lochie's point was well taken.

"It's the suits, the packs, the life support system... All that extra gear tends to weigh on you, 38% gravity or no 38% gravity. Besides that, no matter how they try to tweak the humidity in the air tank feeds, I reckon that it just sucks the moisture out of you." Nigella inhaled in an intentionally noisy breath of air.

"We will get back to the surface tomorrow, but at least now, let's review where everyone is to this point." Misha looked to Siti. "What can you tell us, Siti?"

"Well, Arya has done the classification, a total of 317 medallions now. They are all identical in physical characteristic: circular, disk-like medallions, 82 millimetres in diameter and about 21.5 millimetres thick with almost no variation in dimensions. They all have almost the exact same mass of 193.052 grams plus or minus a few hundredths of a gram, so that calculates to a density of 6.801 grams per centimetre cubed on average. They have some translucency to them, but you certainly can't see through. It's pretty strange stuff."

"How about the bags" Nigella held one of them in her hand.

"That's another mystery I'm trying to figure out here... they sure seem like leather, but the composition doesn't appear to be any leather we are familiar with. They appear like very finely woven plant material – I say plant material, but that's because I don't know what it is. At 10,000 magnification it definitely looks like a textile of some sort, I'm 99% sure it is woven, but I can guarantee you that it was not handwoven."

"Why do you say that, Siti?"

"Consider that most textiles we use are synthetics and

increasingly, they aren't woven anymore. This material was definitely woven. The fibre they used was incredibly fine and delicate. I'm hard-pressed to figure out how they manufactured it. The end product though is incredibly strong, yet quite flexible. I'm certainly not going to try it, but I bet you could fire a bullet at one of these bags and the bullet wouldn't penetrate it. So, I assume it was machine manufactured using an exceptionally high degree of technology."

Arya tilted his head. "Can you C-14 date it?"

"Oh boy... yes and no, I guess. There are at least a couple of problems here. I ran a C-14 test on it several times and get an age consistent with 150,000 years or more, but that's on Earth... too big a supposition... Maybe this was of organic origin – and that's a big if. Maybe it lived on Mars or another alien planet – another big if. I caution that this is very shaky ground. Also, when you date samples that old, the measurements need to quantify incredibly small ratios of C-14 to C-12 because of the short half-life of carbon-14... only 5,730 years. Frankly, the more I'm thinking about it out loud here, I think you would do well to forget I even mentioned C-14 since I have zero faith in whatever number I could generate from that test."

"Well, I'm not about to forget about it that fast. I certainly know generally what C-14 dating is, but could you explain the basics again to a mere engineer." Joe raised his eyebrows when he asked.

"I'm happy to do so, Joe." Siti leaned forward and took a deep breath. "Well, we're all scientists here, so I don't mean to patronise you, but C-14 is naturally produced on Earth high up in the atmosphere by the bombardment of molecular nitrogen by sun's more energetic wavelengths. Recall that nitrogen and carbon are next to each other on the periodic table. When a nitrogen atom gets beat up enough by the energetic sunlight, it actually loses a proton and drops down

228

the table to become carbon. Most carbon is C-12 and has six electrons, six protons and six neutrons. Carbon 14 has six electrons, six protons and eight neutrons. C-14 is highly unstable and spontaneously decays to C-12 at very predictable rates, half of it in the 5,730 years I just mentioned."

"But how does that give you an age. Remember – I'm an electrical engineer by trade and I haven't had a chemistry class since high school!" Joe's self-deprecating humour caused smiles around the table.

"Fair enough... As long as any plant or animal organism is alive, it constantly eats or breathes a very small amount of C-14 – that's on Earth, at least, because of the CO_2 in the air. The minute it dies, the total amount of carbon in its physical body is set, and no more C-14 can be incorporated into its remains. Forget the specifics here, but working backwards, we can date an organic sample to some 100,000 years old and – with the newest techniques and equipment we are using these past few years – maybe as far back as 200,000 years. If you go much older than that though, the results are increasingly inaccurate because there is so little carbon-14 left in the sample. But my C-14 analytical problem is extremely complex. Mars has a very different mixture of gases with less than 2.7% nitrogen compared to Earth's 78%. For that matter, Mars atmosphere is very thin – less than one per cent as dense as Earth's. Add to that the different intensity of sunlight and the lack of magnetic field to ward off the solar wind and... well, maybe all the C-14 work on these samples just becomes moot.

"Another problem is that even discussing this is ridiculous." Siti's eyes narrowed as she crinkled her nose. "If we were confident of a 150,000-year-old number, I'd still have to laugh at all this conjecture about C-14. We know that Mars hasn't had conditions here within the past few billion years in which you could grow any organic material the likes of a textile producer."

"Unless it grew in Martian greenhouses." Joe volunteered.

"Come on, Joe." Lochie turned towards him. "I don't know about Martian greenhouses, but I don't think that's what Siti was thinking anyway. The C-14 argument assumes the plant material in those bags grew on Mars. I think what you're saying is there is no way those bags originated here."

Siti looked at Lochie and nodded her head yes.

"We spin in circles right now..." Lochie laid the medallion he held on the table.

35

Tuesday, 13 September; Global Holistic Summit, Shanghai, China

"Our next presentation will be made by Professor André Moureaux, a climatologist with National Oceanic and Atmospheric Administration as well as Climate Action Network Europe. Professor Moureaux also is affiliated with the National Snow and Ice Data Centre as well as the Australian Institute for Atmospheric and Climate Science, the Chinese Research Academy of Environmental Sciences... I could go on here, but we would not have time to hear from the Professor." The young woman smiled as she extended her hand towards him as he rose from his chair and walked towards the podium. "Please welcome Professor André Moureaux."

"Good morning. This talk has been scheduled at this time for several weeks, so it was not my intention to put my hand up during Gillian Pickard's presentation yesterday. I just thought that I was able to contribute to the question from the floor at that time. Now I hope to clarify those comments and give you a more in-depth insight into what it is we are finding both before and after the impact of *Thánatos*.

"We have already heard from several speakers concerning different factors contributing to the greenhouse effect our atmosphere provides for our planet. Now, this is a good thing, namely, that without an atmosphere, planet Earth would have temperatures ranging from a daytime high of 100 Celsius to a nighttime low of minus 173 Celsius. For our American friends listening in today, that's a range from a high of 212 Fahrenheit to a low of a bit more than minus 280 Fahrenheit. I am confident in those numbers since our natural satellite, Luna, has those temperature extremes from sunlight to darkness, and the moon is, on average, the same distance from our sun as we are. Of course, Luna has no atmosphere at all and therefore no atmospheric moderation of its temperatures. Let's be thankful here on Earth for the greenhouse effect.

"Of course, if you've ever been in a greenhouse – or even an unshaded car – in the summertime, the temperatures can quite literally run away and cause any plants still inside the glasshouse to unmercifully cook to death. In short, with no greenhouse effect, life would be impossible, and with too much greenhouse effect, life would just as certainly be impossible.

"The gas that seems to get all the credit – or blame – for the greenhouse effect is carbon dioxide, namely because it seems to be the one over which we have the greatest control. You may be surprised to hear that water vapour by far causes more heat to be retained on Earth, but the amount of water vapour remains reasonably constant over time... more on that in a minute. Carbon in the form of carbon dioxide has less effect on the Earth's greenhouse effect, but unlike that of water vapour, humans are identifiably accountable for releasing long-stored carbon into the atmosphere. I will touch on that, too, in just a minute. We have become much better at reducing this carbon contribution, but still use way more fossil fuels than we should.

"This brings us to permafrost. Permafrost is found primarily in the polar regions of Earth and includes the subsurface layer of soil that remains frozen continuously throughout the year. One-fifth of the Earth's land area is covered in permafrost, though that area has decreased for decades now because of the increase in the average global temperature. Though surface layers may thaw during the year, their structure may act as an insulator, keeping the lower, permafrost strata frozen rock-solid. About yesterday's question from the Australian journalist, this is in no way new knowledge... we have known of the massive amounts of methane stored in this way for a century or more.

"In light of so much of the Earth's surface being covered in permafrost, it has become of more pressing concern over the past several decades. Why? I fear I'm redundant, but the atmospheric temperatures keep increasing. As long as they remain a frozen state, permafrost acts as a wonderful preservative for so many organic remains. We have all read the odd story of frozen woolly mammoth bodies found in ice and permafrost that remain in nearly perfect condition for thousands of years after the animal died. The permafrost acts as an excellent preservative both because of its cold temperatures and because it cuts off chemically active oxygen from the carbon compounds.

"Regrettably, the same case can be made for microorganisms. You may be aware of increasingly widespread incidents of herds of reindeer and – in some case – dozens of people being infected by thawing microbes. More specifically, we have documented incidents of previously immobile spores of *Bacillus anthracis* – the etiologic agent of anthrax – that have thawed and enter into the water, soil and food supplies in areas of melting permafrost. We have also verified animals and humans that have been exposed to anthrax and have died because of it. If the risk of spreading of long-frozen *Bacillus anthracis* isn't worrying enough, there is no doubt hitherto unknown 'zombie microbes' preserved within the permafrost are just waiting to be released from their frozen sleep.

"But my expertise is not in microbiology, and I am not here to speak of zombie microbes. Regrettably, there are more significant global risks involved with permafrost than just these nasty germs. For all the danger that ancient microbes may pose, we believe their damage can be managed and minimised. By far the more significant threat – at least in terms of volume and mass – are the trillions of tonnes of carbon and carbon compounds produced by ancient organisms and now sequestered in our permafrost freezers. Many of these are in the form of coal, peat and oil deposits acting as giant carbon sinks within the Earth. These needn't have permafrost to preserve their stability, though many underutilised deposits do exist in colder arctic-like regions. These are forms of matter almost exclusively in the solid or liquid state and, for the most part, remain in place at ordinary temperatures and pressures. By that, I simply mean that if we do not remove these stores from the ground, they could pretty much remain preserved for countless millennia.

"The threat I am here to expound on today is the gaseous deposits of these organic compounds. One in particular – methane – is a very simple molecule which can be of great benefit or great danger to humanity." André turned and extended his hand towards the molecular model projected at the front of the theatre. "Methane is a simple molecule consisting of one carbon atom in the middle of a tetrahedral shape, the four equidistant corners all occupied by hydrogen atoms. It is a perfectly colourless, completely odourless gas at room temperature and – much to our chagrin – is only about half the mass of the average density of the constituent gases that make up the air in our planet's atmosphere. This is one of the characteristics of methane gas that results in it causing us a big headache compared to other fossil fuels. Why? Simply put, since it is less dense than air, methane gas rises when released into the atmosphere.

"I want to simplify the science here in deference to the many non-technical participants in this Global Holistic Summit, but I will post all the pertinent numbers and details for those of you interested on Skynet 4 as soon as the day's proceedings end. In short, like water vapour and carbon dioxide, methane is a greenhouse gas. As I previously mentioned, water vapour is in a balanced cycle within our atmosphere and has been for millions of years. By that, I mean that approximately the same amount of H_2O molecules evaporates into gaseous form every day as condense out and fall as rain. There is a finite amount of water on Earth, and – though some may be consumed and expelled by volcanic activity – that total hasn't changed for eons.

"Not so with CO_2. As I mentioned before, Mother Earth has seen fit to sequester so much carbon inside our planet and consequently has decreased the amount available to escape into the atmosphere. Again, there is more or less an overall balance with animals breathing oxygen, eating plant life and exhaling carbon dioxide while plant life breathes in carbon dioxide and exhales oxygen. Since the start of the industrial revolution, we humans have tipped this equilibrium by unearthing greater and greater amounts of this fossilised carbon and releasing it into the atmosphere as carbon dioxide. It takes millions upon millions of years for biological processes to return it under the Earth's surface, so the net imbalance is increasing carbon dioxide.

"The same can occur with methane. Methane naturally 'leaks' from within the Earth and – given enough time – is oxidised by sunlight or lightning bolts while forming water vapour and carbon dioxide. But we know that there is a lot of carbon contained in the Earth's permafrost. How much? I will not drive you crazy with numbers but let me at least say this much. A gigaton is a billion tonnes – that's ONE BILLION TONNES. The Earth's atmosphere today contains about 850 gigatons of carbon in the form of CO_2 and CH_4 and a few other, lesser compounds. We also estimate that the world's permafrost contains about 1,400 gigatons of carbon. Said another way, there is 60 per cent MORE carbon in permafrost than there is in the entire Earth's atmosphere. Why is this a problem?

"Carbon dioxide is an excellent greenhouse gas, but nowhere as efficient as methane. Though methane decomposes faster than carbon dioxide, it is also way more effective greenhouse gas than CO_2. Actually, at what scientists call a 100-year gas lifetime, one tonne of methane is as potent as 25 tonnes of carbon dioxide in terms of keeping the sun's heat in our atmosphere and raising the overall temperature of Earth. So, to a climatologist like myself, excessive methane release isn't a good thing.

"Permafrost captures methane. Many non-chemist-types think that permafrost freezes the methane. Well, let me state unequivocally that it does NOT freeze methane, and that isn't even close. Methane can't freeze at Earth-like temperatures. Methane doesn't freeze until you get to minus 182 degrees Celsius – again, that's nearly minus 300 Fahrenheit for our American friends here today. Now, minus 182 is pretty cold, and we don't find temperatures like that anywhere on or around the Earth. So how does permafrost contain the methane?" André paused as if awaiting an answer from the audience. "Interestingly enough, the answer is found in the peculiar characteristics of the water molecule itself.

"When water freezes at zero degrees Celsius, it has the funny habit of forming crystal structures that are filled with little holes in the centre of each crystal." He extended his hand towards the diagram that filled the big screen behind the podium. "These little holes can surround and contain other substances. In the situation we are discussing here, solid water and gaseous methane can form what we call methane hydrate or methane clathrate, both words mean the same thing. Look at the diagram projected here, and you see each methane CH_4 molecule trapped within the solid crystal structure of water like a little methane bird in a water-ice cage. The only limit to how much methane you can trap is how much water ice you have. Fortunately for permafrost, there is an almost never-ending supply of water, at least relative to the amount of methane. The methane clathrate form is so stable that we find massive amounts layering the bottom of lakes and deep in the ocean, so long as temperatures within the crystal structure don't rise above water's freezing point.

"So far, so good. The methane is locked away in these miniature ice crystal cages, and, as long as the water stays frozen, the methane is safely isolated from the environment. But should we increase the temperature enough for the ice to melt, the crystal structure of the H_2O falls apart, and the less-dense-than-air methane gas is released into the atmosphere. Regrettably, over the past several decades, the Earth's average atmospheric temperature has risen, and the ocean temperature has soared at an even greater rate. This has resulted in a dramatic release of the previously sequestered methane gas.

"And this brings us to *Thánatos*... As we learned yesterday and had reinforced today, *Thánatos* disturbed ancient faults and has set off a series of earthquakes still rocking northern Siberia. The earthquakes in and of themselves don't release the methane, instead, they expose more clathrates to the warming atmosphere or ocean. Because of where *Thánatos* happened to impact, these quakes are violently shaking an area that previous measurements have already confirmed is the source of some of the greatest releases of methane gas we have ever recorded anywhere on Earth. The fear now is that *Thánatos* just might have pulled the trigger of what has been called the clathrate gun.

"The Clathrate Gun Hypothesis was named decades ago and, frankly, was quickly dismissed by many climatologists who study these sorts of things. In brief, as atmospheric temperatures increase, the ability of clathrates to contain CH_4 decreases. Similarly, as sea temperatures rise, any clathrate deposits that are below water experience greater heat, also reducing the levels of methane those clathrates can sequester. The idea of the 'Clathrate Gun Hypothesis' is that − like pulling a trigger of a firearm − the result of releasing the bullet is irreversible. As more methane goes into the Earth's atmosphere, it enhances the greenhouse effect, which in turn raises temperatures enough to release more methane, which increases the greenhouse effect, which... I trust you see the potentially catastrophic positive feedback loop the Clathrate Gun may trigger. It just could be that once this process is started, it may begin a feedback effect that leads to runaway heating. Bang! Just like pulling a trigger on a gun, the consequences are both inevitable and irreversible."

36

Tuesday, 13 September; Fenghui Tang Teahouse, Shanghai, China

"I will miss this place." Sunlyn took a deep breath. "I admit that I have been a coffee-drinker my entire life, but I still do enjoy tea. Regrettably, until you two..." She tilted her head towards Fiona and Kylie, "...introduced me to REAL tea, I just never realised what I was missing."

Owen agreed. "Sign my name to that statement too – I never knew what real tea tasted like. And you know, it's way more than the tea... it's the entire experience. I love this teahouse, and I would assume there are many, many more in Shanghai and across all of China. The atmosphere is conducive to both relaxing and to meaningful conversation."

"Me three... The Fenghui Tang Teahouse is a special spot, and we have my mate, Fiona, to thank for introducing us to it."

"No thanks needed, Kylie. I love sharing the experience with you... all of you." Fiona turned enough to look at the three of them. "I can't even remember the first time I came here, probably back in my undergraduate days. As for the Chinese tea culture, that dates back for millennia. None of you needs to 'miss' Shanghai or China for too long... I will always be your welcoming host whenever you do return."

"Thanks, Fiona." Kylie placed her hand on top of her friend's hand. "I'm glad we are all here with you now and hope to do it again sooner rather than later."

Sunlyn and Owen dipped their heads in agreement.

"You know, I think this has been such a fantastic experience. As academics, we are expected to attend this type of conference-like event *ad nauseam*, but the Summit was truly unique. The scope of attendees was so different. I mean most confabs are so spot-on specific that we never seem to mingle with a variety of people who do research across the broader spectrum of – in my case – psychology in general. The academic world is so specialised that there is rarely time to appreciate so many other areas of research being done that could have a great impact on our own fields of expertise. I'm sure this is no different no matter what discipline in which one may do research."

Owen leaned forward. "Can you give me a 'for example',

Kylie?"

"Yes, of course. By specific, I mean that we no longer submit papers to a psychology or counselling conference, or an adolescent counselling conference or even a suicide prevention conference... The academic world is now so specialised that I attended a 'complex grief' conference in Wellington, New Zealand, in February and the sole focus was postvention help of those grieving for lost loved ones."

"Now that IS specific." Owen gently swirled his teacup.

"Please don't misunderstand what I'm saying. The conference was excellent, and I can see why that focus was useful, but talk about specific!" Kylie's eyes were wide.

"For sure, I see what you mean." Sunlyn brushed a strand of hair from her eye. "I think it's obvious to those of us in journalism just how specific research can be." She looked at Owen and noted he nodded his agreement. "Now I don't mean that academia isn't a valid career path, but don't you think it may risk eventually becoming theoretical gobbledygook if we can't bring the end result to the general public at some point?"

"Absolutely!" Kylie's head rocked back and forth. "We're all on the same page with this, Sunlyn. That's the only way that academic research can somehow contribute to a better world."

"Of course, we all believe this." Sunlyn knew she had stated the obvious. "Along this same line, I very much appreciated the Chief Scientist René Riemann's opening remarks of the Summit when he said that having scientists solve technical problems is almost the easy part of coming to grips with our challenges today. The hard part is transferring that technology and science to the community at large. Only then can we actually solve some of the problems for the betterment of our world. Researchers, teachers, journalists... we can't solve the most pressing problems without all of us working in concert."

"I couldn't have said that any better myself." Fiona looked

towards her friend. "I wonder what each of us considers the most relevant takeaways from the Summit."

Sunlyn volunteered first. "Well, I've just told you mine, though the Summit definitely reinforced my feelings here. It never ceases to amaze me that many times the actual technological breakthroughs are so much easier to develop than having society embrace them. In other words, building a new mousetrap is easier than having society use the new mousetrap."

"That's an interesting metaphor, Sunlyn." Kylie smiled. "Your point is well taken though. So many difficult questions facing humanity could be solved by better understanding the core of the question and then applying physical principles to solve or at least minimise the problem. That's true whether we speak of population control, dying oceans or runaway heat in the atmosphere. The real challenge comes from how we, first of all, communicate the resulting scientific processes to the population at large and, second of all, convince people to support the solutions. A good case in point is something like the polio outbreak absolutely wrecking Yemen and a few other Middle Eastern countries right now. Or the outbreak of measles in Samoa, Madagascar, Liberia and way too many other countries... We solved these sorts of problems nearly a hundred years ago, but still seem incapable of communicating the solution to populations in need of something as simple as a vaccine."

"Or at least communicate that – in this case, vaccines – are not just a dastardly western plot to inoculate the poor with some wicked disease." Owen scoffed.

Kylie nodded at Owen's comment. "Regrettably, so much of what we do never makes it to the general public. All the discoveries in the world are meaningless if the technology is never transferred to the community at large." An almost pleading expression crossed Kylie's face. "I think that's exactly where you journos can play such a big part in the communications aspect of the issue."

"Journos, huh! I love you damned Aussies – you abbreviate everything!" Owen laughed.

Kylie smiled. "I think one of my biggest takeaways this week was how some businesses have actually funded programs to aid in mental health outreach to both staff and customers. Regrettably, I don't think this has gone far enough, but I was encouraged just to hear what some of the companies represented here are doing to be more inclusive. I believe we need to support NGOs – the non-government organisations – that take the initiative to be more open to indigenous and socioeconomically challenged groups in their communities without the government having to hit them over the head to do so. Though I confess to being a bleeding-heart liberal politically and believe governments do have a social responsibility to support programs that help the downtrodden, it is way too large a problem to tackle without private interest and funding."

Fiona swirled her tea before turning her gaze towards her friend. "I guess because I grew up in a whole different culture, my take on it all comes from a very different perspective. Possibly the nature of the shortcomings you mention, Kylie, is dependent on cultural values." Fiona seemed a bit pained as she spoke. "I feel that I should apologise upfront because I do not mean to be critical of your home countries of Australia or America, but maybe the whole concept of a 'free world' is not so free after all. By that, I simply mean that what both of you have talked about here," She gestured towards Sunlyn and Kylie. "...may be more a reflection of how your government systems function in America and Australia. Sometimes having too much freedom results in having no freedom at all. If we KNOW as a society that we understand a problem – polio in this case – and have a solution – a vaccine – don't you think it's in the greater community's interest and wellbeing to require cooperation?"

"Require? Oh boy... now that's a tough one." Kylie expressively tapped her palm to her forehead.

Owen had been quiet until now but could keep his thoughts to himself no longer. "Well, of course, that's a tough one, I think Fiona has a good point here. We might not be in as dire a situation as we find ourselves in if we – America in my case – had been more forceful in limiting carbon waste from fossil fuels 50 or 60 years ago. Again, we KNEW the problem, we UNDERSTOOD the basics of the solution, and yet we were unable to act on that knowledge to save our society, our planet. Maybe our government could have been more proactive in implementing research outcomes into policy."

"You will get no argument from me here, Owen." Sunlyn set her teacup down. "But I also appreciate Kylie's challenge to us 'journos', and that really has me thinking. Of course, I agree with you that journalists must somehow enhance the communication so often missing in these debates. I just wonder – in light of Owen's comment here – what would have been the outcome if we'd have taken a more centrist approach. Now I say 'we' even though most of these battles were fought when the four of us were still in primary school. Yet, too often over the years, it was frequently an 'I'm-right-and-you're-wrong' shouting match in the so-called climate debate. From what I've learned from history, neither side ever listened to the other. Most of the time, it wasn't as though there was ever a serious conversation."

Owen rubbed his chin with his hand. "Well maybe, but one faction was on the side of science, and the other side wasn't. There was no debate concerning the science – that was known long, long ago from scientists like John Tyndall, Joseph Fourier and Svante Arrhenius during the eighteen hundreds. The debate you're talking about was about policy, but with only one side basing their argument on science. I'm not sure what any of our forefathers could have written or said as journalists that could have ended the shouting match. The so-called two sides were the ones shouting, not the journalists. History has proven that the science was correct all along, but much of global policy never reflected that."

"My friends, I fear we come back to what I think is the cultural problem." Fiona looked directly at Owen. "You reflect on the shouting match between science and deniers as though they were somehow on one level plane, my friend. But were they? Science is not a belief, it's not an argument, it's not a debate on some news network... science is a method. Science arrives at a finding using hypothesis, repetitive experiment and peer review of that outcome. That continues with the original conclusion becoming a revised hypothesis, another series of repetitive tests which are in turn scrutinised by peer review... and on and on...

"I realise that in Australia, America, Europe and much of the western world you may find yourself in considerable disagreement with me, but the so-called deniers you speak of, Owen, tended to be operating in an entirely different dimension... a business dimension. In that realm, the 'facts' from a commercial point of view rest upon profit. The peer review for a business is found in consumers 'voting' with their wallets or shareholders 'voting' by driving share prices up or down. The shouting match that has gone on for way more than half-a-century could never end – will never end – until we all drown below the encroaching sea." Fiona's frown telegraphed her sadness. "Please forgive me for saying this, but there are limits to so-called free enterprise. Just consider – even when we may all be in danger of either burning in bush fires or drowning in rising seas, I fear that some entrepreneurial company will try to make a killing selling fire extinguishers and smoke masks or life jackets and rowboats. I repeat my mantra about the illusion of personal freedom... If we KNOW as a society that we understand a problem, do we not have a responsibility as a society to solve it and to actually implement the solution? Can acceptance of the shouting match you refer to be categorised as freedom?"

Owen sat quietly, his chin resting on both hands with his elbows on the table. After a short pause, he sat upright. "Oh boy... I have to admit that you obviously make me... make us, I guess... look at this from a whole different perspective, Fiona. I can't argue with... I can't... well, I agree with you. I agree that the argument never was carried out with both sides using the same set of rules. It was always like having a debate on gravity... this side says things fall down and the other side says they fall up. We must make sure both have equal representation and equal time, and at the end of the debate, we should follow free-market dogma and let the customers choose the winner." He glanced at Sunlyn and Kylie and could see both struggling with the efficacy of their own cultural foundation here.

"Please... all of you... Please smile. I was not trying to challenge your birth cultures." Fiona feared she had stepped in a hornets' nest. "I'm an academic who studies human behaviour. I LOVE the diversity of cultures. I only wanted you to consider looking at this situation through the eyes of one who was socialised in an entirely different values system. I don't argue that it is better or worse in any way, it's just different. Chinese history goes back five, six, seven thousand years at least. There is evidence the Romans interacted somewhat with the Chinese, but serious contact with the west has only occurred over the past 1,500 years or so."

"And obviously, that results in different cultural practices, but we still are all *Homo sapiens*, we still all behave in similar ways." Sunlyn's comment sounded more like a question.

"Yes, of course, we behave in similar ways, but thousands of years of different experiences result in drastically different ways of thinking. Have you ever travelled through agrarian areas in Asia? Specifically, have you ever seen parts of the Asian countryside where rice is farmed?" Fiona directed her question to all three of them.

"Yes. I've seen some beautifully terraced rice paddies stepping down hillsides in Vietnam... in Cambodia... in Bali... Frankly, some of the most stunning scenery I have seen has been in the terraced hillsides of Vietnam." Sunlyn wasn't sure where her friend was going with this.

Fiona continued. "Well whether Vietnam or Cambodia, Indonesia or China... you know that rice needs a lot of water. Rice is semiaquatic, so it is cultivated from planting until harvesting in flooded fields or rice paddies. Maybe you have never thought about this but keeping paddies wet and flooded with water is easy on flatlands, but quite labour-intensive on the hills and in mountainous areas. First of all, if the growing area is not on flatlands, the farmers need to initially level the terraces. Now for one moment, just consider that. Think about living in Asia hundreds or thousands of years ago and having to move mountainsides of soil and rock when the only tools available to you were simple tools such as wooden hoes, basic carts and water buffalo. A single farmer stood very little chance at developing an intricate system of level fields, irrigation ditches, simple valves to divert water flow and the like; these are all needed to maintain a rice farm. My point here is simple: if Asian farmers did not cooperate, they starved. Of course, they are all human like we are, but the onus was squarely on cooperation or starvation. One farmer doing this is not impossible, but very much unlikely for any but the smallest of scales. The philosophy of 'my water is your water' was the key to survival.

Fiona continued, "Now, consider the North American continent in the 17th or 18th centuries... The thrust of European settlers westward demanded the new immigrants 'claimed' land and more often than not, moved the indigenous out of the way. They certainly weren't about to raise rice since the climate wasn't conducive to that nor were their European roots tied to rice as a staple food. The European immigrants were more attuned to beef and maze. I believe early American laws actually encouraged claiming vast stretches of property, many times too large to even fence. How did a rancher feed his family? I think the occupational description was to single-handedly – or with a family at most – raise herds of cattle on substantial stretches of the open range. The whole mythology of the gun-toting cowboy on a roundup along with his sons is the stuff of American legend. Here the onus was on individual know-how, and the alternative was starvation. Large groups of ranchers could never have worked well together since the distances involved were too great. The philosophy of 'my water is my water, and you keep your hands off' was the key to survival."

Kylie looked at her friend. "You know, I don't think Australia was any different."

"Well, I believe Australia was different for the simple reason that it grew as a dependent child of Mother England, not as a rebellious victor against the hated Red Coats the way the American colonists did. That said, the settling of the continent was similar. I fear I've gone too far here." Fiona sat back.

"No, you haven't, Fiona. There is much here to digest. It's funny, but where you grow up has such a huge impact on your world view, and I know that's exactly the point you were making here. Obviously, the Chinese approach to a nationwide, planetwide issue like climate science would be so much different from the Aussie approach or the American approach or the European approach..." Kylie finished her tea.

"I tend to agree with all you have said here, Fiona. It's still a bit of a tough one for me to ponder though, and I need to defer for a moment or two on what you're saying." Owen fidgeted a bit in his seat like a teenage boy thinking of asking a girl to dance. "I can tell you my biggest takeaway this week though. No question at all – I have been overwhelmed by Fiona's ideas of community development, and I think what you just told us actually better explains how you arrived at what you passed along in your presentation to the Summit."

"Aw... thanks, Owen. Thanks for appreciating my presentation." Her smile towards him almost lingered too long.

"But Fiona, though I enjoyed your address to the summit, I so much more appreciated the personal presentation you gave us last week here at the teahouse." Whether by design or by happenstance, Owen changed the mood of the conversation. "I have thought long and hard all week about so much of what you said. I also understand that there is a big difference between mice and *Homo sapiens*. I still wonder if there may be more of a connection than we might think."

"For sure, we humans CAN learn from comparative psychology." Fiona picked up on his complimentary remarks. "I just must caution you in drawing any direct parallels to findings with animals that are so much less complicated than we are. Besides that, mice can't farm rice or herd cattle the way humans can."

"And it's a damned good thing that mice can't carry rifles!" Owen's laughter grew contagious, and all had a good chuckle at both Fiona and Owen's sense of humour.

"Good one, you two." As the laughter subsided, Sunlyn kept her eye on them as Fiona and Owen interacted. It suddenly dawned on her there was more going on between the two of them than might meet the eye. "I guess it's your turn, Fiona."

"My turn?"

"Yes – your turn to tell us what you're most pleased to takeaway from the Summit this week."

"Friendships." Her face radiated optimism. "I mean, the key to solving any problem might rest more on empathy... on compassion and consideration of others. That said, learning other cultures, opening to other points-of-view, making friends with people like the three of you offers me hope in the future. I guess I have been charged with optimism this week... optimism that we actually can make a difference, that we can meet these challenges."

Kyle placed her hand on her friend's shoulder and smiled. "What an encouraging perspective."

37

Wednesday, 14 September; Metro Precinct Station, Washington DC

"Hey, boss."

"What's up, Patton?" Grimms looked up from his desk. "Any word on those search warrants?"

"Done and dusted. Judge Berger approved them, the boys picked them up and they're with forensics now. They searched through the premises and collected the kids' computer equipment at both the O'Keefe and Bidwill households."

"D'ya think they had time to clean them?"

"I don't know since we took them pretty much off guard. Still, I imagine they could have. For that matter, they seem nerdy enough around computers that they could have written a self-destruct program..."

"Connected to their SAMs."

"No, not SAMs, sarge..."

"Oh, right – I mean data bands."

Maggie continued. "Yes. Both sets of parents waved search warrants on the boys' data bands, so we didn't need to see the judge for that. We've already been through the computers, and they haven't produced a thing other than phone numbers, calendars and that kind of stuff. Even there, nothing stood out when they went through all of it."

"And the data bands?"

"Funny that... there didn't seem to be anything on the data bands. The IT boys are still working on it, but they haven't found a thing at this point."

"Weird... What did you and Bradshaw find out on the parents?"

"Again, nothing much. They both sound like pretty typical upper-class families. Both boys have siblings. O'Keefe's sister is older and out on the West Coast – a sophomore at Stanford. Bidwill's got an older brother in Philly, a senior at Penn, and a younger sister at St Philomena's here in the District... ninth grade. They are all squeaky clean. All the parents are clean, too. No one in either family has any record to speak of other than Bidwill's mom getting pinged for a marginal DUI back nearly fifteen years ago – 0.09... She paid a fine and has been clean since. The dad, Lance Bidwill, had a few speeding tickets way back when and also had a marijuana conviction in college, but that was 25 years ago when it was still illegal and never came up again. Hell, cannabis is permissible just about everywhere today, so who gives a damn? Looks like some clean folks in both households."

"Did Bradshaw learn anything at the school?"

"Not really. Their teachers didn't have much to say. I guess O'Keefe has had a few run-ins with a math teacher, but nothing serious. They both seem to excel in computer sciences."

"Oh, did Bidwill's family own any guns?"

"Nope. None are registered to either parent, and none turned up when they went through the house." Maggie put both her empty hands up. "We come up zero on any second gun. From everything we have, O'Keefe was the only shooter, and his dad's gun was the only gun."

"Humm... Maybe we need to look at those school computers, too. Let's see what the boys find with the home equipment. If nothing shows there, we'll ask Berger to issue search warrants for Georgetown Academy computers. I guess we'd have to check any of the kids' personal computers and the school server then." Grimms scrunched his face as he scratched his head. "You know, on second thought, maybe we ought to start that search warrant process now, just in case the home searches turn up nothing."

"I'll get that started, sarge."

"One more thing... Did Bradshaw mention anything about what the students were like over there at Georgetown?"

"Yeah, he did, boss. I don't think most of those uppity kids are out of it like so many of the regressives we are seeing lying around the streets. Ryan said he was surprised at how normal the kids seemed to be, chatting in hallways, kids chasing each other around, just adolescents pretty much being kids..." Maggie hunched her shoulders and turned her palms up. "Sounds pretty much just what it used to be like back in the day."

Grimms nodded his head. "Go figure... it's all really fascinating, but something is still bugging the hell out of me."

38

Wednesday, 14 September; Gale Crater lave tube 27A, Mars

Two skellies pulled to a halt in front of lave tube 27A. Siti drove one with Lochie as her passenger while Keegan drove the other with his partner, Nigella. All four unbuckled and quickly put boots onto the surface. Keegan glanced at his SOC. "This is it, yes?"

"Yep." Siti looked at her own SOC and waved her hand at the control box on her arm. "We need to negotiate this boulder-strewn pathway up to the front of the cavern. It isn't that far, only a hundred metres or so, but we can't get the skellies in there. Follow me." She set off between the outcrops, and within a few minutes, the team rounded a last, house-sized boulder and stood before the gaping mouth of 27A. The four of them grouped just outside the entrance, in awe of the 12-metre-high opening.

"Quite an entrance, isn't it?" Lochie grabbed his spotlight from his belt and fumbled with the on switch. "Siti and I had a pretty good look at the branch on the left." He used the light beam to point toward the back of the immense room. "As you saw on the video, we found the bags almost immediately inside that fork. It wasn't difficult to check much farther in since the cave came to a dead-end fairly quickly. With our oxygen packs getting low and the excitement of the find, we didn't' attempt to go into the second branch. That's the plan now, so let's do it."

The four of them walked through the opening and made their way into the cavern. The large, cathedral-like ceiling of the first chamber seemed more welcoming this time. "I told you it was big." Siti pointed her spotlight towards the back of the chamber and reiterated Lochie's words. "That fork on the left is where we chose to go in first and where we found all six bags."

"Oh, wow!" Nigella was overwhelmed at her first look into the cave where they had discovered the bags, very happy to be a part of a surface excursion this time.

"So, we head to the right side." Keegan's excitement echoed Nigella's as they covered the few dozen metres and paused beside the right fork. Siti and Lochie were right behind them.

"That's the idea, mate. You two can have the honours." Lochie and Siti fell in behind the others and let them step into the right branch. They began walking into the darkness with four spotlights cutting through the blackness in every direction. Within the first few minutes, it was quite apparent there was no repeat of numerous bags scattered about the cave floor.

"It looks like this one goes back way farther than the other side where you two went." Nigella's voice betrayed her disappointment at the lack of any more easy-to-find artifacts. All four of them continued to walk deeper and deeper into the tube, their penetrating spotlights and squinting eyes competing with each other to be the first to spot more objects of interest. The silent search seemed to pick up the pace as if somehow, a faster gait would help find what they were looking for.

After some ten minutes and several hundred metres of tramping, Lochie's voice penetrated their helmets through SOC. "Wait a minute, you guys. I think we're on to something here."

All three of the others turned and realised Lochie was 40 or 50 metres behind them standing right next to the wall with his gloved hand pressed against the surface. "What are you doing back there, Lochie?" Nigella started to walk towards him, and Keegan and Siti quickly followed.

"I think we were so intent on finding more bags of medallions that we missed what was right in front of our eyes... or to the side of our eyes."

The trio of explorers walked back towards their fellow spelunker, concentrating on him continually moving his glove up and down a flat area of the cave wall. The closer they got to him, the more apparent it was that a window-sized section of the wall appeared to have a very different texture from the rest of the surface.

Keegan moved beside him, trying to work out what his fellow geo was on to. "What did you find there, Lochie?"

"Look at this, mate. Look at how smooth this area is. Not only is it smooth, but it is almost too geometrically symmetrical to have occurred by accident."

All of them aimed their spotlights at the surface as Nigella and Siti recorded the entire scene for analysis back at the outpost. Nigella pressed her glove against the wall. "What do you make of this, Lochie?"

"It's not natural."

"How can you be sure?" Keegan asked.

"Because this is the fourth one that I've found so far, though we need to go back and look at each. These areas look as though there were windows or portals cut into the side of the cavern and then sealed over with molten lava. I say that not having had the chance to run any laboratory tests on some samples at this point, but this doesn't look like a cement fill or any substance different from the lava that is here naturally. However, I would bet my geologist's credentials that this surface was in the liquid state after the rest of the lava tube was a melt. What I'm trying to say is that these areas were sealed by artificial means. I can't think of any natural process that would produce these perfectly flat in-fills appearing in a more or less normal, rugged cave wall."

"Oh boy... artificial... What are we seeing?" Excitement had now replaced the disappointment in Nigella's voice.

"Humm... I don't know exactly, but I wonder if these 'windows' for lack of a better term might be an attempt by the aliens to store something behind the walls."

"Windows... portals... wow! What could this mean?"

"Several things I imagine, Siti. First of all, it means that once again, the aliens have displayed an amazing technology in that they sealed these openings using molten lava. Now certainly we have the ability to melt lava, but not on such a small scale and in such a targeted way. If we expended the kind of energy needed to melt, place and cool lava in a narrow, closed lava tube like this, we would probably fry ourselves. Secondly, because this new lava was in a molten state when it was used to seal the holes, that resets the clock as far as dating goes. If everything in this tube dates at two or three billion years, I will bet the outpost that these windows are way younger."

"Okay, so what sort of samples should we collect and what kind of measurements do we need to take from here?' Keegan had one hand on his toolbelt.

"Well for starters, let's do what we always do, namely, gather as much detail as we can. Keegan, you and I will take some lava chip samples from the smooth area as well as from the surrounding rough areas we assume are the original walls. We'll tag all those samples and pack them for transport back to the labs. Nigella and Siti, would you find and record every surface like this within walking distance and measure the gap between them. I don't want you to wander too far. We can come back and do it all again if needed, but remember, we are dealing with a time issue. We'll learn what we can from our sample collections and data measurements today and plan our strategy in opening these windows ASAP."

39

Wednesday, 14 September; Waldorf Astoria on the Bund, Shanghai, China

"I don't know how much of my money's worth I'll get out of the breakfast buffet this morning."

"First of all, don't worry about it because it isn't your money. Second, I don't think the GNN bean counters will check whether or not you leave any toast before approving the breakfast bill, Sunlyn." Owen chuckled as he gulped his coffee.

"Let's hope not!" She buttered a blueberry muffin. "Well, we're getting toward the end of the Global Holistic Summit. I am so happy that Glenn assigned me to this story with you, Owen. It's been so overwhelming – in a good way, I mean. I just can't believe what an opportunity this has given us and how many interesting and knowledgeable people we have met."

"I agree one-hundred per cent, Sunlyn. And I'm so glad you had personal contact with Kylie... and through that with Fiona..."

Sunlyn smiled knowingly. "Fiona, huh? I think something is happening there. I think you and Fiona might be having some feelings."

Owen rubbed his chin. "Maybe. I mean, we are adults, you know."

"Of course, I know. Last I heard, you are an eligible bachelor Owen, yes?"

He felt a bit of colour rushing into his face. "Eligible... I must admit that I never think of myself that way, but... yeah, I guess you could say I am eligible."

"Well then... I'm glad we're all going to Australia from here."

"Me, too." He lifted a forkful of scrambled egg to his mouth and slowly chewed it. "You know, who'd have thought a week or two ago we were assigned to the Global Summit and the *Thánatos* impact and that somehow turned into a trip to Western Australia? Go figure..."

"Yeah, it's all very strange, Owen." Sunlyn sipped her cup of tea. "I haven't had the chance to ask you about that climatologist's presentation... Professor Moureaux."

"Yes, that was an interesting presentation. He caught my attention the day before when that Aussie journalist called him out for not making science like... like perfect. Interesting stuff. I do fear the Aussie journalist was a bit too harsh on him though."

"Maybe... the professor did seem to handle himself okay though."

"He did."

"That said, I'm still a bit curious about a couple of things there. Do you mind if I ask you a few questions?""

"Fire away, Sunlyn."

"What can you tell me about that Clathrate Gun Hypothesis? Is that really a thing? Do you think there's anything to it?"

"Oh, I'm sure there's plenty to it. I mean, to summarise his whole point, Mother Earth had an atmosphere with 4,000 ppm – parts per million – of CO_2 during the Cambrian period about 500 million years ago, but nature saw fit to hide most of that carbon away – carbon sequestration, the scientists call it. For the past several million years during the Quaternary glaciation – ice ages to you – we've stayed way below that 4,000-level, from as low as 180 up to maybe 280 ppm. Don't worry about numbers here, but just keep in mind that a couple of hundred years ago, we had maybe 5% of the carbon dioxide in our air that we had millions of years ago. I refer to that lower level of CO_2 being at the beginning of the industrial revolution in the late 1700s or so."

"I'm following you. Isn't that what the so-called sceptics have been arguing for years – that CO_2 levels were higher in the past?"

"Well yes, but there's more to it than that. Consider that since that point a few hundred years back, CO_2 levels started creeping back up. During the last century and into this, we have 'skyrocketed' in geological terms up into the mid-400 ppm. The point is that whenever it gets too high or too low, Mother Earth – read that nature – has ways of storing carbon in sinks or releasing it back into the environment. Over the past 500 million years, much has been stored in solid and liquid form within the Earth's rocks. Minus humans, that would all stay within the Earth except for the most violent circumstances such as colliding tectonic plates, rampant volcanism or maybe a *Thánatos* impact. The one store of carbon that is easily released quite naturally is methane since it is the lightest of fossil carbon sinks we have. Because it is less dense than air, it can just drift off into the atmosphere unless it is sealed deep underground, usually with oil and gas deposits or trapped as clathrates within water ice."

"So that would be the same with other gaseous fossil fuels, yes?"

"Well not really... propane, pentane and so many others are also found underground, but they are actually more dense than air. I am definitely over-simplifying here, but for all intents and purposes, without a little help from an internal pressure source, they would tend to stay put. In the case of methane, it doesn't exist in solid form on Earth since it needs to be way colder than even Antarctica is... I think he said minus 180-something degrees Celsius. But the hydrated form of methane – the gaseous state trapped in solid water crystals as clathrates – is some fascinating chemistry. All you need do is heat the water ice just like is happening now with a warming atmosphere. But on top of that, concerning *Thánatos*, the earthquakes it has generated seem to expose more of the buried clathrates to that same atmosphere that is warm enough to melt the ice. Do that, and, of course, you release more methane into the atmosphere almost instantaneously.

"As physics would have it, methane has the interesting property of allowing wavelengths of light to enter the Earth's atmosphere but insulating the longer wavelengths of heat from escaping. This acts very much like glass on a greenhouse – it lets light in on a winter day but doesn't easily allow heat out at night."

"Just like carbon dioxide?"

"Yes, just like CO_2, but – what did the Professor Moureaux say – a hundred times more effective. Now the so-called 'greenhouse effect' can be a good thing or a bad thing. As Moureaux was saying, consider that our moon is the same distance from the sun as is Earth, but with no atmosphere. With no air to insulate, the temperature in the sunlight is about the boiling point of water, yet in a shadow a few feet away, it drops to minus 180-something... just about cold enough to freeze methane! With those extremes, we couldn't live on the moon even if we had air to breathe. Add Earth's life-giving atmosphere, and our temperatures stay within moderate levels, at least as far as water goes, never getting anywhere near its boiling point and only freezing it in the temperate regions during the winter. Fortunately for us, the coldest spots are way towards the poles, and very few people need to deal with them. That's the good of the greenhouse effect.

"On the bad side of things, keep adding these greenhouse

gases and the average temperature rises. This has been a gradual thing over the past few hundred years or so since the industrial revolution has seen humanity dump billions and billions of tonnes of CO_2 into the atmosphere. Now I've pretty much paraphrased what the professor has said here. All good so far?"

"Yep. That all made sense to me."

"All of this operates over very long periods – many decades or centuries at the quickest, but usually over millennia. What's new to us in this clathrate gun idea is the speed of change that could be involved. He is suggesting that the jump in carbon could be a much more immediate threat if a gaseous flood of methane was somehow dumped into the atmosphere all at once. That winds up short-circuiting the feedback loops. Do you know what a feedback loop is?"

"Sure... I get hungry, and that causes me to eat. I become full, and that takes away the hunger urge until my metabolism uses up the food supply, and the whole thing starts over."

"Yeah, that's a good example. Look at a more mechanistic loop such as a thermostat. The little piece of coiled metal in the thermostat expands when it heats up and contracts when it cools down. Don't worry about the particulars, since there are bits like liquid mercury switches and variations for heaters and air conditioners. The upshot is that when it gets too cool in your living room, the metal spiral contracts and causes a switch to complete an electrical circuit that turns on your heater. As the room warms up, the thermostat metal expands until it breaks the contact in the switch, and that turns off your heater. Given enough energy to supply the heater, this feedback loop could go on forever."

"But you can upset a feedback loop, yes?"

"You sure can. In your hunger case, you could eat so much that you got sick. In the thermostat example, you could short-circuit the system and heat the house until it caught on fire. Unusual factors can confound the system... catastrophic occurrences can destroy the system. Concerning the Clathrate Gun Hypothesis, the more methane released, the warmer the Earth's atmosphere would become. The warmer the Earth's atmosphere becomes, the more unstable the methane trapped in water crystals – the clathrate – becomes, causing it to be released into the atmosphere. In short, more methane causes more heat which causes more methane which causes more heat, etc. This is an example of a runaway effect or positive feedback loop and hence the term clathrate gun. Once you pull the trigger, it becomes irreversible."

"Wow. Do you believe this possible?"

Owen uncomfortably pushed his head to the side and stretched his arms over his shoulders. "Look... for a few decades now most climatologists thought that under normal circumstances, this was too big of a stretch and that it would take too long to release enough methane to cause an immediate problem. The perplexing issue is that we no longer have 'normal circumstances' in this case. We just happened to have *Thánatos* strike the Earth. *Thánatos* just happened to be large enough to cause major seismic events. *Thánatos* just happened to split and impact along a path that traces previously unknown ancient fault lines. These ancient faults just happen to be in one of the most methane-rich permafrost regions on planet Earth. The energy release just happened to cause what appears to be self-perpetuating earthquakes shaking Siberia for a week now... How many 'just happeneds' did I mention there?"

"A lot. But how could so many unexpected things happen all at once?"

"That's easy – it's luck... or the lack thereof..."

"Luck? Didn't we go through this the other day with the 'science isn't perfect' idea? You're telling me that this scientific, physical occurrence just happened the way it did because of luck... because of bad luck?"

"Sorry Sunlyn, but that's exactly what I'm telling you. It's nothing new. Do you think we – *Homo sapiens*, that is – were lucky when that huge asteroid slammed into the Yucatán Peninsula some 66 million years ago? Consider... it just happened to be a one-in-a-hundred-million-years big asteroid of around eight miles in diameter. It just happened to cause a concussion that was a million times more energetic than *Thánatos*, enough so that it wiped out much of life on Earth within days. It just happened to impact almost squarely on a huge oil deposit sitting close to Earth's surface in the Yucatán, and that just happened to cause enough soot to be blasted into the atmosphere to bring a few years of near darkness to the Earth. As if the darkness wasn't enough, it just happened to cool the Earth to such levels that so many trees and ferns and plants died back or became extinct. It just happened that these consequences killed off more than 75% of the species on Earth at the time. And probably the biggest 'just happened' occurrence as far as we're concerned is the luck of the mammals."

"Luck of the mammals?"

"Yes. You see, placental mammals existed on Earth for 80 or 100 million years previous to the great asteroid strike, but they just couldn't evolve much past small-mouse size. Why? We'll never know exactly, but it seems likely that dinosaur-like reptiles filled so many existing niches that there was no convenient spot for the mammals to thrive. Once that asteroid turned the world dark for a few years, all the non-avian dinosaurs disappeared and did so very quickly in geological terms. Within a few tens or a few hundreds of years, so many of the species that had been quite successful for millions of years just vanished. Luckily for us, the asteroid 'just happened' to cause catastrophically-induced mass

261

extinctions, and that opened the door for mammals – for our ancestors – to flourish. It eventually 'just happened' to result in a line of evolution that became *Homo sapiens*. So yes, my friend... luck – or the lack of luck – has always played an incredibly huge role in the evolution of both physical and biological systems."

Sunlyn exhaled a gush of air. "So, you're saying that if that asteroid came by 30 seconds earlier or 30 seconds later, the dinosaurs could still be roaming free as far as we know."

"That's just what I'm saying. That's pretty weird, yeah? Imagine that the dinosaurs could be... probably still would be... roaming today. Of course, there could have been some other great catastrophe that might have done them in without the asteroid."

"Wow! And it wasn't just the dinosaurs... You say that maybe three-quarters of all the species then alive disappeared?"

"Yep! That's what we now refer to as the Fifth Mass Extinction in the history of life on Earth."

"Wow! There have been five mass extinctions."

"There have... and some argue it is just a matter of time that there'll be a Sixth Mass Extinction."

"*Thánatos?*"

"I doubt it – way too small."

"Another asteroid?"

Owen pushed himself back from the table to return to the buffet. "Maybe... Increasingly, some scientists even argue that we humans may play the role of the next great asteroid... and that would lead to what might be the Sixth Great Extinction, probably better referred to as the Anthropocene Extinction."

Sunlyn's eyebrows arched high as she shook her head side-to-side. "So, *Homo sapiens* could be the next great asteroid..."

Owen nodded his head before finishing his coffee.

40

Thursday, 15 September; Gale Crater Outpost, Mars

Misha was the last to pull her chair into the staff table. "It seems everyone has a smile on their face this morning... I hope that's a good sign."

"I don't presume to speak for everyone, but I think after yesterday's find, we all seem to have a lot to be smiling about this morning." Siti's grin telegraphed her eagerness to share something of importance.

"Well let's hope you are correct, Siti. We'll have this short update over tea and will then send two teams out to begin opening the lava windows. I do think it important though that we all have a firm grip on exactly what we know and what we don't know right now. Would you like to start?"

"I would." Siti leaned forward. "In my last update to you, I explained the difficulty with trying to date the organic material in the bag sample using carbon-14 dating techniques. At least I was able to categorise several amino acids within the sample. I can report on a few interesting findings here.

"I don't want to teach you all organic chemistry, but I will give you a brief overview, so you will at least have an idea of what I'm about to tell you. For starters, we refer to amino acids as the building blocks of proteins and associate them with living systems. They are reasonably complex organic molecules and are arranged in very specific orders. We have identified hundreds of different naturally occurring amino acids, but only some 20 appear in the proteins within our body, all coded by DNA. Interesting enough, because of their complexity, amino acids show what we call stereoisomerism and when synthesised in a test tube, form molecules that are identical in type and connection of atoms, but different in geometric structure.

Siti quick scan of her colleagues' faces confirmed they were following her explanation. "The best way I can explain this variation of molecular structure is to use an analogy. Think of these microscopic amino acids as looking like two gloves. Gloves and hands, show chirality, that is, 'handedness.' Actually, I believe the word chiral comes from the Greek word for hand. Anyway, chiral objects may be identical in every way, but differing geometries do not allow one to be superimposed on the other. Consider your hands." Siti held her hands up and placed the back of her right hand against the palm of her left one.

"Now then, though my two hands are perfectly identical in size, shape and number of fingers, no matter how I try, I cannot superimpose one on the other. You can spend forever trying to match a left hand and a right hand, but they will forever be chiral images, that is, mirror images of one another. Nearly all the amino acids that we can cook up in a test tube produce two chiral varieties of the same molecule when synthesized in the laboratory, both a left-handed version and a right-handed version of the same molecules. So far, so good?" She knew she was dealing with scientists who had all studied basic chemistry. Still, Siti smiled at the thought of how organic chemistry was so often known as the downfall of many budding university students.

"Chemists have a name for these. In the lab, we produce one isomer we call the laevo form or L form and the other form of isomer we call the dextro form or D form. No matter what we do, when we synthesis any one amino acid, we get a test tube filled with both forms, 50 % laevo and 50% dextro.

"Interestingly enough, though, nature produces amino acids through life processes that you and I simply call 'being alive'. Well, surprise, surprise – all life on Earth forms only one isomer when incorporating amino acids into the proteins of life, and that is the L form or the laevo version. This is true of every living organism for all essential amino acids save for glycine since that has no chirality to its molecule. I trust you are still with me." Siti's quick survey around the table seemed to indicate everyone was still with her. "Good. In short, all life on Earth – ALL LIVING THINGS ON EARTH – naturally produce the L optical isomer or the laevo amino acids. Please don't take this too literally, but all Earth life is 'left-handed' as it were, at least stereochemically.

"Now a funny thing happens when an organism dies. Quite spontaneously, amino acids begin to naturally convert from the laevo form to the dextro form. As long as conditions remain fairly constant, this transition occurs at a constant rate. To a chemist – or a physicist, I guess – whenever we hear the words 'constant rate', that implies we can use the process as a natural clock. As long as we know what the rate is, and we know what the constant conditions are, we can determine the ratio of the original 100% L-amino acid that has turned into D-amino acids. My assumption here is that the fabric bags have rested in lava tube 27A since close to the time they were manufactured using whatever organic material is in them. My dating can only be as good as my assumptions here, but I think it a safe bet to say the temperature we measured in the cave has remained constant through time – minus 24 degrees Celsius. I think we can also be confident that the cave remained dark with no wind and no humidity to speak of. Finally, nothing would indicate that the Martian atmosphere has changed over the past several million years so we can assume the composition remained reasonably close to what it is now, namely 95.3% carbon dioxide, 2.7% nitrogen, 1.6 % argon with just a trace of oxygen. So far, so good?"

"Fantastic summary there, Siti. So, what in god's name did you find?" Keegan's half-open mouth displayed his anxiousness to hear her findings.

"Well, I can give you two fascinating findings here, the most consequential one first. No one knows why Earthly life only naturally produces L-amino acids by biological processes. One of the biggest questions we have wondered about is that should other life be found in the universe that is based on carbon chemistry, would it also be biased to the L isomeric form? Well, I remind you that we found these organics in a cave on Mars, and they certainly appear to be based on L-amino acids. So, to summarise the first finding, Martian life is just like Earth life, as far as its optical isomerism is concerned – it produces L-amino acids.

"The second thing I can tell you is that I used three different amino acids – aspartic, isoleucine and alanine – and I've run as many trials as I could overnight. Using the seven trials completed, I date the material in the bag at 165,000 years plus or minus 10,000 years. Now I have to remind you that I have not corroborated this age with anything else so far... well, the C-14, but I did warn you of my shaky confidence in those data."

Lochie spoke up. "Excellent work, Siti. From everything you explained here, I think you can be fairly sure the age at which you have arrived is in the right ballpark. If you can give us another day or two, I think Misha, Keegan and I can try offering some support for your dating looking at our rock samples."

"Anything else, Siti?"

"Not right now, Misha. I am making progress on the chemical composition of the medallions, but I need more time to confirm those findings."

"That's fine. Anything else before we head off to the tube? Yes, Arya?"

"I have some good news, actually. With the much larger base of samples loaded into our AI system, we have made some excellent progress. I am one hundred per cent sure now that we have a phonetic language. The new load of medallions has added a few more symbols, up to 32 letters now, and we have differentiated 10 numbers, so it must be a decimal system. Now I find that fascinating since the coincidence is difficult to explain."

"Coincidence?"

"Well, when you consider that the only reason humans use a base-ten in our mathematics is simply that we have ten fingers – actually eight fingers and two thumbs to be correct. I mean, it's an arbitrary thing. We could just have easily had base-eight if we only had four digits on each hand or base-twenty if we wanted to include the ten toes. I find it a very, very strange coincidence that the alien system is base-ten.

"One bag did contain a rolled-up piece of what appears to be plastic, and it looks all the world like a high-tech parchment roll from ancient Rome. At this point, Siti seems to think it is a different variation of the fabric found in the bags but will let us know if she finds any variance to that. I will say this though – the fabric or parchment-like material is incredibly strong and very durable. Naturally, I was excited, hoping we had found the Rosetta Stone as it were. We can put that hope aside. This will not be all that useful in translating the language, though we are learning from it.

"It didn't take the AI program long to determine that the scroll is a timekeeper or a calendar. The alien system appears to have 19 'months', though I use the term months not having any idea if that is actually the case. Again, we get our word month from the moon, and at this point, we don't know if the alien world had a moon, no moon, a dozen moons... Anyway, each of these month-like divisions has 20 days, which adds up to a year of 380 days. We are applying human terms to an alien culture but are confident any alien culture would share some things with us. We previously mentioned some commonalities we would expect to share. Some of these would be a periodic table, a written language of some sort, some kind number system or mathematical constructs such as Pythagorean Theorem. In this case, the shared concept is a calendar probably based on an astronomical movement of some type. Until we find something to change our minds, I suggest we assume their calendar is based on the primary star in the alien system."

"Why assume that?" Nigella asked.

"Well, simply because any time system would have evolved from pre-technology days in any culture, and it's fair to assume any intelligent people would notice the greatest time-keep of all, namely day and night.

"The 'calendar' we found has twenty frames, 19 are months, and frame 20 is a summary similar to what we'd call an astronomical almanac with pictures and simple diagrams. This leads us to believe the following: The aliens' system had one central star with eleven planetary bodies orbiting it. At this point, we have no standardised unit with which to measure distance and size. Nonetheless, they show five smaller and six larger, outer planets. I guess knowing what we do today about the thousands of solar systems we have catalogued, it is safe to assume the outer ones are gas giants and the inner planets terrestrial ones. The aliens indicate that they either live on or have visited three or four – I'm still working on that. So, considering their five inner worlds, the aliens visited all but the one closest to the primary star."

Keegan put both hands on his head and interlocked his

fingers. "Pardon me for interrupting, but maybe a couple of the planets are rogue ones like Pluto is – or was before it was demoted – and maybe..." He paused, let out a stream of air, and tilted his head to one side. "I mean, have you considered that this could be our own solar system?"

"Well yeah, I did consider that, but there several things that seem to say no here. The third planet out – at least I think it is the third planet – has a 380-day year and not 365 days. They indicate there are 5 terrestrial planets, so that eliminates our solar system. Also, the fifth terrestrial planet has a ring system around it. No doubt this is a system similar to ours, but again, from all the systems we have categorised over the past half-century, we live in a rather unremarkable solar system, and there must be billions more pretty much like it. We must all agree though that for life to have ever evolved, we'd need a planet within the Goldilocks Zone where it's not-too-hot, not-too-cold and water exists in the liquid state. We just can't imagine a carbon-based lifeform that doesn't have water as its basis of chemistry. Right now, that's about it."

"Anything else? Anything on the symbols?"

"Oh yes... one thing AI has found. It cranked away all night long, and when I checked in this morning, it has confirmed that every medallion has two symbols the same on each one. When I put this together with everything I just told you, we come to this: there are 19 groups of medallions, and there are 19 months in the calendar. As for the two common symbols, AI seems to be open to one interpretation, at least coming through a human mindset. The only interpretation that makes sense for the two symbols on each is 'birth' and 'death.' Then sorting them into 19 categories is analogous to months... I reckon these medallions are either death notices or tombstones."

From the mumbles around the table, it seemed that Arya had struck a chord. Misha recognised the big Aussie was ready to spill over. "Lochie?"

"Crikey! I catalogued all the data collected by Nigella and Siti and can add to Arya's data here. We know there are 19 sealed windows in lava tube 27A. Could they be burial crypts, mate?"

41

Thursday, 15 September; Metro Precinct Station, Washington DC

"Boss."

Grimms looked up from his desk. "Patton. Come on in."

Maggie walked in with Bradshaw and another officer behind her. "I believe you know Officer Chandra, Lenny Chandra."

"Ah... yeah, we worked together on that Anderson paedophile case last year. Good job on that, Chandra." Grimms gestured towards him.

"Here's the deal." Bradshaw held some papers in his hand. "The home computers gave us nothing, right Lenny?"

"Just calendars, phone numbers... there were a few dates for meetings of the Eights, but not a lot to go on. Actually, I'm not at all sure that the couple of Eights meetings we found listed on a calendar were meant as events to attend or events to monitor. I have that all documented on the server, so you can all look it over when you like. We did find one really unusual thing, though..."

"Go on..."

"Well, in both the O'Keefe boy's room and in Bidwill's room

we found data bands."

Grimms looked questioningly at Chandra. "Yeah... That's hardly unusual except for the fact that families in that socioeconomic class would normally have bought their kids SAMs... fancy SAMs."

"True, but that's not even the strangest part." Lenny paused.

"For Christ's sake, go on, Chandra..." Grimms' crossed arms betrayed his impatience.

"Well, as I said, they both had data bands, but both had their guts disabled. By that I mean the electronics were fried... they didn't work. Why would kids keep useless data bands in their rooms?"

"And yet Ramos, Nicolás Ramos whose apartment was shot up, swore that at least one of them was wearing a data band." Grimms pawed at his cheek. "Now why would a kid, first of all, refuse a SAM that mom and dad pay for and then wear a data band that didn't function?"

"That's all yet to be determined, boss. At least you will be happy to hear that Patton did get Judge Berger to issue a search warrant for the Georgetown Academy computers." Bradshaw continued. "We served that first thing this morning – Maggie and I went over with our IT boys. Lenny's been working all day on what we brought back, and I think he's got some preliminary findings, right Lenny?"

Chandra nodded his head.

"What did you find, Chandra?"

"First of all, we followed all the protocols, so what we have will be good to go in any court proceedings. We used the search warrant to get passwords and log histories, used faraday bags to isolate equipment and cloned school servers with our proprietary DC Police forensic software. All of this means that we assured the preservation of the integrity of every piece of data collected."

"That's all well and good, Chandra, but wouldn't we expect that you followed all those rules? For Christ's sakes man, what the hell did you find?" Grimms was again showing his displeasure at dragging things out.

"Well, I think I found a lot, Detective Grimms. I found a trail a mile long as a matter of fact. Again, I have this all posted on the server, but both Bradley O'Keefe and Dylan Bidwill carried out some fascinating research over the past several months. They were very interested in SAMs and how SAMs worked, especially the Angel chip, the 888-chip. I can't say as to exactly what level of detail they actually used, but they seemed to download the lot of it: schematics, software usage, network plans and whatnot. I can also see that they learned early on – several months back – how to disable their data bands, not that that was difficult. The point is that the disabled data bands were not that way by accident. We actually were able to snag some computer chat they used – the 'Iyamhere' program kids use to hide school chats from teachers and administrators."

"You could dig that out?"

Chandra smiled as he leaned back with his hands behind his head. "Yep... you can hide things like that from the non-techie types, but everything leaves a record for us guys who know what we're doing. My point is that they have been planning something besides their role in the Eights' hierarchy. They were planning to somehow hack into data bands as well as SAMs."

Maggie looked at her hand as if she could somehow see her implanted chip. "You mean everyone's SAM?"

"I don't think so. They were actually looking at how they could target specific groups. You know, like SAMs and bands in a specific part of the city or SAMs and bands on individuals whose registration numbers indicate a certain age range... boys and girls, certain schools. I have no idea how far they got with this, but I know both of them spent way more time on this than they did on their schoolwork."

"Anything else?"

"Well yeah... I don't pretend to have any idea what this means since we just dug it up, and I haven't had the chance to delve into it, but there have been reoccurring searches into the brain, brain activity, frontal lobes, hippocampus, moods, depression, amygdala..."

"What do you mean brains, frontal lobes and depression?" Maggie unconsciously rubbed the skin between her right thumb and index finger with her left hand, seemingly a bit wary of her own SAM. "This damned thing makes me nervous enough without hearing that stuff, Lenny. I'm starting to fear we may have uncovered something bigger than we imagined."

Chandra went on. "Look, I don't know a freaking thing about brains or mental health, but O'Keefe and Bidwill downloaded a shitload of academic articles with three common search terms: iEEGs – that's intracranial electroencephalography and studies looking at the amygdala and the hippocampus – both parts of the brain." He put his hands in the air. "I'm a techno-nerd, not a brain surgeon. I have no idea what this has to do with anything, but if I was betting, it just might fit with their interest in isolating specific SAMs and bands."

It was evident that Grimms' mental wheels were turning at high speed. "Jesus... SAMs and bands, depression, brain parts..." He looked to Patton and Bradshaw. "I think we need a follow-up visit with that FBI shrink, Jankowski."

42

Friday, 16 September; Gale Crater lave tube 27A, Mars

Misha had been tempted to break regulations and take all three skellies to the 27A tube to expedite the work needed to open the nineteen sealed lava windows, but she thought better of it. God forbid that anything went wrong, she knew she'd never forgive herself. For that matter, even if all went perfectly well, she knew that Alpha Colony Director Sam Tan would have her head on a platter if he ever did find out. Two skellies would have to do. She assigned Lochie and Siti to one of them and Keegan and Joe to the other.

The short ride to 27A was uneventful. The four of them had a bit of a challenge moving the small, wheeled trolleys around the debris and boulders and into the big cavern inside the entrance. The carts were manageable enough in the low Martian gravity, but the rock debris scattered all about made the job more difficult. Once they entered and walked back into the cavern, it was straightforward manoeuvring their equipment to the base of the wall in front of the first of the sealed chambers.

"So far. So good. I'm glad we used the hand carts. That sure made getting the gear here easier than I feared, and now we'll have plenty of time and life support reserves to get a good start on this." Lochie ran his hand over the smooth surface. "I suggest all four of us see how it goes on this first one. If things go well, we can split into pairs to see how many of these we can pop open today. I know our instrumentation tells us there are hollow areas behind the seals, but we still have no idea whether or not anything is in there. Having the wheeled carts may be wishful thinking, but let's hope we fill them up with many more artifacts."

"Well okay then, let's do it." Keegan pulled a hammer drill from the skid. "We'll follow the plan we agreed on, make an initial entry with the 20-millimetre borehole and then let the instrumentation bug go in there first, sniff the air and give us a look around the chamber. Once we have that input, we will refer to those data and decide on the best way of going in."

It only took a few minutes to drill through the smooth lava with the 20-millimetre bit. The little electronic crawler was half the diameter of the borehole, already activated and feeding data to the SOC units. Siti set it on the bottom of the borehole. "The bug is ready." She confirmed it was functioning correctly before letting it crawl into the hole. Almost instantly, an image popped up on her SOC. "Are you guys getting the feed from the bug?"

"Roger." Joe's gloved thumb pointed upwards towards the tube celling. "That's a nice, clear image. Let's see what's in there."

A sidebar of data kept changing next to the image projected onto Lochie's faceplate. "Atmosphere is the same inside as out here... the pressure is a little higher... temperature is about the same... Can we increase the bug's spotlight intensity?"

"I've got it, Lochie." Siti tweaked a setting, and the image brightened up. "Let's do a pan."

All of them watched the same video feed projected within their own helmets. The bug turned through a 360-degree arc and reported distances and angles within the chamber alongside the image projected on their faceplates. The hollow was close to five metres deep and five metres wide and, though small, was large enough for them to enter should they decide to open the wall. The image suddenly crossed a blurry object along the far wall. The bug's camera focused and zoomed in.

"Oh boy... looks like more bags... several of them."

"Can we count them, Siti?"

"I'll see – give me a moment." She maneuvered the bug down the wall and across the floor, moving closer to the pile of bags. It was easy counting sacks on the surface, but impossible to get a good number for those in the middle of the stack. Siti looked towards Lochie. "I can move the bug into the pile, but we don't know what's in there. I reckon we should go in first, document the area and the bags we can see, and then start to unstack them."

"Affirmative. We don't want to unduly disturb things without at least knowing how the untouched artifacts were set in place before we entered. Do a second scan with full instrumentation recording, and then we'll take the whole damned wall out of here or at least a wide enough doorway to enter. How thick did the bug measure it?"

"About 300 millimetres or so, varying a bit from top to bottom."

"That's an easy cut. Get the scan done, Siti."

"Will do, mate."

* * *

It only took a few minutes to rescan the small chamber before Joe and Keegan began cutting through the wall. The laser tool they used was almost of surgical quality, capable of slicing through the hardest of materials, but clean enough to vacuum any molten material and dust as it cut through. By the time the cutter outlined a door-sized piece of rock, Joe had made use of a spring-loaded gun-like device for fixing several eyebolts into the slab. "Okay, my readout tells me this slab should have a mass of about 300 kilos. Of course, under Martian gravity, it only weighs a tad over 110 kilos. I think we can pop it out using the hand jack, yeah?"

"Agreed, mate." Keegan reached for the jack clamped onto the skid. "Let me snap a couple of leads on there."

Once they set the little jack into the lava floor, it easily pulled the block away from the wall. Three of them had no trouble unhitching the lines and lying the slab down and out of the way. Lochie put on a bit of fanfare, bent over at his waist and ceremoniously thrust his hand towards the now open window. He looked at Siti. "I believe the 'ladies first' etiquette remains in place here on the Martian surface."

"PLEASE!" Siti's rolling eyes were visible through her faceplate. She didn't remain to argue though and deftly stepped over the 150-millimetre rim at the bottom of the cut. She took a second step into the small space and slowly looked around the first chamber. "Wow... how long has it been since anyone stepped in here last?"

"For that matter, did that alien being even have any legs with which to step?" Keegan may have meant his question as a joke, but nobody laughed. He followed her in.

The chamber was small, with only enough room for the four of them to surround the stack of bags in the middle of the floor. All spotlights were focused on the pile as Siti stooped. She looked up at Lochie. "Should we take a peek?"

"You're happy with the scan and documentation?"

"I am."

"Well then, let's see what we have there."

Siti wasted no time in finding the flap on the top of the bag. "It seems exactly the same as the other bags we found." She pulled the flap back. "More medallions..."

"Take a look, Siti." Joe was standing right over her now.

She reached into the bag and gently grasped one of the pieces, her hand slowly pulled it from the sack. "Man, who knows how long this has sat here untouched." She raised it to eye level and immediately started to speak. "Wait a minute... this is NOT another medallion."

"Let me see that." Lochie was immediately beside her and reached for the object, the spotlight on his helmet brightly lighting the object. "Bloody hell... it looks like a perfectly transparent disk, maybe of glass or quartz... It's approximately the same size as the medallions, but it sure doesn't look like it's made of the same material. Are they all this way?"

Siti removed a second and third piece and handed one to Joe and Keegan, while finally pulling another out for her own eyes. The four explorers sat there completely silent for a minute or two, each alone with their thoughts as to what they had just discovered.

* * *

It had been a long day. Since they took two skellies along with the wheeled carts, the four of them had enough life support refills to easily last for the eight hours-plus they had been working in the tube while still having the required reserve specified in regulations. They loaded the last of the bags from the carts to the skellies. They recorded nearly a hundred sacks that they were able to move from the chambers they opened onto the wheeled carts, rolled them out of the tube and loaded them onto the skellies. This far exceeded what they initially thought they could move. They decided to save space on the skellies and leave the two-wheeled carts at the cave overnight. The team successfully opened ten chambers and removed a haul of bags from each. The chambers held from 6 to 15 bags each for a total of 92 sacks for the day. At this point, they hadn't inventoried the numbers of transparent disks in the bags since their primary aim was to get their find back to the outpost. The cataloguing of the bag contents would be done back in the labs.

"Gale Outpost... Gale Outpost... Are you there, Nigella?"

"I hear you loud and clear, Siti. Thanks for checking in once you exited the cavern and were back in signal range. We figured you had your hands full, and we were happy to wait until you were ready to go."

"Well, we are. We have everything packed up here and are about ready to come home. I did tell Misha we were parking the two carts here overnight to save the transport."

"Misha is happy with that. She told me to assure you there was no rain forecast. Good thing – I don't think you took your brollies" They could hear Nigella giggle over the SOC.

"Okay then, we'll keep SOC open on the way back to the outpost."

"Roger that."

Siti walked back next to her skellie. "I trust you're taking the wheel, Lochie?"

"If you don't mind." He was already seated at the wheel and watched as Siti climbed into the passenger side of the little rover. He checked Joe and Keegan in the other buggy. "Are we ready to roll, mates?"

"More than ready. I've got visions of a hot shower splashing all over my brain." Keegan strapped himself into the other rover next to Joe.

"Oh yeah... I think we'll all break the three-minute rule on the showers this evening." Siti sat back in her seat as she fastened her buckle. She exhaled a sigh of accomplishment.

43

Friday, 16 September; FBI Headquarters, Washington DC

"Thank you, Rachel." Dr Jankowski's PA finished setting the last cup of coffee in front of Bradshaw. "Please close the door."

"I hope we aren't taking advantage of coming back to see you so quickly, Dr Jankowski."

"Please, that's why we're here. I want to hear what you've learned about your case so far."

"Well, I think we briefly mentioned we were stuck on why our two perpetrators – alleged perpetrators – were so much more violent than most of their peers. We ranged from drugs to data bands to SAMs to electrical impulses on that visit, and we found your input very useful. I think we've hit a few walls though and would like to run it all past you to see if you can find a different angle on any of it for us."

"I'm anxious to hear what you've learned."

"For starters, our first search warrants were for Bradley O'Keefe and Dylan Bidwill. The families live in those fancy-schmancy places over in Kalorama Heights."

The doc nodded her head. "Yes, most of those places can set you back a few dollars."

"Tell me about it." Grimms rubbed his chin as he looked at Jankowski. "Anyway, we searched the rooms but concentrated on the computers and technical equipment for the most part. Our IT fellows went through it all, and there was very little useful info found on the solid-state drives. We did find a very unusual piece of evidence, though. Both kids had data bands tucked away in their rooms, but both were disabled... Weird, huh? Both bands had all the electronics, but they just didn't work... maybe they were fried or otherwise incapacitated. The victim whose place was shot up – a copy editor with the *DC Post* – swears that one of the hooded kids involved was wearing a data band. He couldn't see the other kid's wrist. Now I don't know about you, but most journalists – especially ones who have been in the business for a while – usually are pretty damned observant. I reckon if Ramos says he saw a data band, the fellow doing the shooting was wearing a data band." Grimms' head nodded his certainty.

"Now we served the second search warrant to O'Keefe and Bidwill's school, Georgetown Academy."

"Sounds like the fancy school fits right in with the fancy house."

"You got it, Dr Jankowski. Anyway, we again isolated the kids' electronic gear there. Our forensic boys also locked and mirrored the school servers and then went through it all back downtown. Now we found no smoking gun there either, but I reckon we found a lot of breadcrumbs, and I'm hoping you can help us with this. Chandra – he's our number-one techno nerd at the Department – he found lots of interesting leads while exploring the Skynet searches they were doing over the past couple of months. I'm convinced that we can learn from these leads, but much of this stuff escapes me."

Grimms was on a roll now and spoke at a hurried pace. "Some of the more obvious searches went after things like data units and SAMs and whatnot. In particular, they were looking at a lot of material concerning how to target – IT-wise that is – certain clusters of receivers, like a specific group of data bands or a specific group of SAMs."

"Specific groups?" Jankowski leaned forward in her seat.

"Yeah, like how they could do workarounds so that they would communicate with certain segments of the population.

For example, they were looking at hacking into only data bands for kids from 10 to 15 years old or only for kids who had SAMs and lived in Kalorama Heights or only data units on kids in Hartley Public School... that kind of stuff."

"I'm surprised anyone would do that... kids, I mean. I have heard of marketing companies trying to do that by targeting certain consumer groups through SAMs, but it's illegal, at least here in the States. Sounds like these kids are more advanced in their skills than most of their high school peers." Jankowski lifted her cup.

"We've gotten that same input from our IT guys." Maggie flipped her old-fashioned notebook over. "Do you mind, sarge?"

"No, go ahead, Patton."

"Grimms, Bradshaw and I have spent the past day-and-a-half mulling this stuff over, and I'm the first to admit that what we are reading is way past our knowledge base. When Chandra did his search of the data they were looking at, he, of course, used Department AI software and basically cranked through the whole of it overnight. My understanding is the AI categorises the topics looked for and then sorts the findings into first broad areas and then narrows it down into more specific groupings. It then compares that to the parameters we put in initially and then tries giving us a summary aimed at our interest. Of course, the program gives all analysis of all data collected, but that gets ridiculous since it occupies thousands of pages on our server. We're more interested in the analysis which fits our parameters. I fear I'm talking in circles here, but the AI knows we had a shooting, it knows we have an epidemic of spaced-out teens all over the city, it knows these two kids seem to be toying with other people's SAMs and data units. The AI also recognizes that we have identified an outbreak of depressed kids and multiple suicides here in the District. I'm sorry if I'm running on..."

"No, no... I follow that, Maggie. We have done a lot of work with AI programs both here at the Bureau and in my academic work. I'm quite familiar with how they can save days or weeks of work narrowing things down for you."

"Very cool. So basically, what AI has given us besides what the sarge has already told you is a bunch of stuff that seems related to mental health issues. That's exactly why we are here. O'Keefe and Bidwill were pulling down data packs on iEEGs, whatever in god's name that might be..."

"Intracranial electroencephalography..."

Maggie's eyes arched. "We obviously have come to the right place."

Tracey smiled.

"It also had repeated hits on depression, suicide, frontal lobes, the amygdala and the hippocampus."

Jankowski leaned back in her chair. "Look, I'm not surprised, but I am surprised. Let me explain... Considering all the parameters you have mentioned here, I wouldn't be the least bit surprised at what AI has found. As you can no doubt imagine, the study of depression, mood swings and their relationship to suicide has been the topic of thousands of investigations over the past decade or two. The application of intracranial electroencephalography has been an incredibly useful technique. In the old days, we used MRI, but that indirectly measures what parts of the brain had an increase or decrease in blood flow. The MRI also requires the subjects remain motionless within a magnetic core while a superconducting magnet rotates around them. Enter the technique of intracranial electroencephalography.

"In the early days, the iEEG was itself very invasive and required that electrodes be placed directly on the brain. Over the past few decades, we have gotten to the point that RREs – that's remote reading electrodes – can do the same job without the need to actually open the cranium. At first, that breakthrough still required a rather draconian looking helmet be used during the procedure. Fortunately, in the past few years, we now have sensors that are as inconspicuous as the small, self-adhesive circular pads the cardiologists use. So, this iEEG provides a remarkable tool in that we can actually measure the electrical signals involved in the communication between parts of the brain. Besides being a more cost-effective technique, it also allows for mobile testing outside of the laboratory.

"So, this technique has allowed us to learn much over the past few years. In the first instance, just being able to measure something concrete and specific relating to the feelings of depression and sadness has proven immensely important and valuable. Historically, it has been known that the amygdala and hippocampus are both involved with a person's mood, with depression and also with anxiety." Jankowski looked at them to make sure they still followed her. "I will avoid the academic details here, and I caution you that what I'm saying is way watered down, but the hippocampus is the part of the brain that involves memory while the amygdala is the part that we associate with processing our emotions. Research now indicates that somehow the interaction between emotions and memory has impacts we are only starting to learn about. If it sounds as though I am uncertain, it's because nobody pretends to fully understand all this. It's almost as though the brain of a depressed patient somehow connects negative emotions found in the amygdala to activate the recollection of sad memories in the hippocampus. It could all happen in precisely the opposite direction, too, in other words using happy memories to alleviate depressed feelings. Now please don't take this too far because sadness and depression are NOT the same things. I can't emphasise that enough – PLEASE don't confuse sadness and depression.

"All of that said though, the bottom line here is that if we can understand and interpret the pattern of activity and communication amongst the neurons in these parts of the brain, we can better understand how depression sets into a point of feeling so sad that desperate thoughts arise. Once we understand how that works, the hope is that we can begin to manage it, to somehow devise treatments for this type of mental illness."

"One more question, doc." Maggie brushed her hair back over her shoulder. "You say the iEEG used to be invasive and used implanted electrodes, but now they simply employ self-adhesive patches. Are you aware of any process – even experimental – that might attempt to use the iEEG technology without physically implanting electrodes, using the helmet or even plastering the patches all over?"

"Please understand Detective Patton that this is not my specific field of expertise, but I am aware of several research projects looking specifically at doing just that. You can see where being able to access that type of data concerning neuroelectrical activity in the brain without cumbersome equipment would be incredibly valuable."

"And if researchers got to the point of being able to read it remotely, could they maybe discover a method to go the other way? Could they maybe find a way to affect these electronic signals to cause depression rather than alleviate it?"

Jankowski's eyes widened. "My god! I can see where you're going here. Yes, I imagine that it's possible, but I couldn't give you any specifics right here and now."

Grimms listened to every word and noted as much as he could on his pad. "Dr Jankowski, that was a better explanation than I could possibly have hoped for. You even made it clear to an old bugger like me. It does sound like very highfalutin stuff though. Now you started this by saying..." The sarge looked at his notes. "...by saying 'you weren't surprised, but you were surprised.' Well, okay, you went on to tell us the academic side of things that didn't surprise you. Tell us, Dr Jankowski, what part surprises you?"

Tracey finished her coffee. "What surprises me, Sargent Grimms is that I am very sceptical that two high school students anywhere on Earth could manage this. It's just that I can't believe that they would have near enough background to even know what to research here. Remember, AI searches only work if you tell the software what you're looking for. I don't doubt that they may be incredibly bright and fantastic techno-nerdy kids, but you just wouldn't expect this level of understanding of psychological research in a fourth-year undergrad let alone a high school kid. This is state-of-the-art neurobiological research you are talking about. I've got PhD students who get lost in all this."

44

Sunday, 18 September; Shanghai Pudong International Airport Café, Shanghai

"You know, I'm feeling so overwhelmed by the sheer volume of input during the week that I think I need to let it all settle... let my mind cogitate on the whole Global Holistic Summit for a few days."

"Good luck on the cogitating, Sunlyn. I have a feeling that what we're going to hear in Australia might make the Summit seem almost trivial." Owen scanned the drinks menu with one eye looking towards Fiona.

"Really Owen... How could the Summit take a back seat to anything else?"

"I didn't say a back seat, Sunlyn. That said that, if the rumour Kylie has heard concerning the discovery of Martian life is true, it will be one of – actually THE – biggest story in all of human discoveries."

"Even bigger than finding Ardi, the nearly four-and-a-half million-year-old *Ardipithecus ramidus* fossil discovered in Ethiopia last century? Hell, she was an ancestor to all of us." Kylie added her penny's worth.

"Ardi was monumental but come on, Kylie." Owen was having none of it. "Finding alien life would surpass anything else you can possibly dream of." He looked from Kylie to Sunlyn to Fiona... and his gaze lingered there.

Fiona hesitated. Her eyes seemed to be saying one thing to Owen, but her mouth quickly pulled her back to the general conversation. "Let's not be too hasty here. I certainly agree that an announcement of finding life out there would be remarkable, but 'the BIGGEST FIND EVER?'

Owen swallowed hard, his head reminding his heart that he was in an airport café. "Look, I don't think I am exaggerating here. Consider the hundred-some thousand years *Homo sapiens* has been around more or less and the thousands of years we have developed our technology and worldwide cultures. We have speculated so long whether life on Earth is a one-time freak of nature or if the universe is teeming with life. So far, we must believe that our evidence to date says we are a freak of the universe."

"Seriously?" Kylie was trying to dissect his statement.

"Well consider, if there is life anywhere else, you'd anticipate it would be everywhere."

"How's that follow, Owen?"

"I think the best way to answer this is by telling you a rather famous story, Kylie. I think that you and Fiona will appreciate the academic side of this. Have you ever heard of the Italian physicist Enrico Fermi?"

"Of course. He won a Nobel Prize for... well, for something in the physical sciences, yes?"

"Yes, he did. He won it in physics in the 1930s for his work with neutrons and his creation of new elements using neutron bombardment. He actually created the first nuclear reactor. After he moved to America just before World War Two, he was recruited into the Manhattan Project in the mid-1940s. You probably recall that was the team that designed and built the first nuclear bombs.

"Now I can't give you the specifics here because I'm not sure anyone knows them, but sometime at the end of the Manhattan Project or shortly after, he must have been in a lunchtime conversation at the local café, not unlike we are doing right now. He basically put two and two together and came up with a quandary we remember as 'Fermi's Paradox.' That's been around for nearly a hundred years now and can still captivate the mind. I don't want to scare you with numbers, but basically, his paradox goes like this.

"The universe, including our galaxy is somewhere around 13 or 14 billion years old... now that's BILLION along with nine zeroes after the 13 or 14. That number is larger than we mere humans can ever even hope to visualise. For now, let's just leave it at this... it is a HUGE number. Now then, our solar system formed with and is dependent on our sun and we are about 4.6 billion years old – again, that's BILLION. We're talking gigantic lengths of time here, so let's just say Earth is a third the age of the universe, give or take. Fermi started there and looked at how long life has been around, which is about 3.8 billion years. *Homo sapiens* show up around one or two hundred thousand years ago, so intelligent life is really recent... I mean REALLY RECENT! Are you still with me?"

All three of his friends nodded their heads yes, but their eyes seemed to indicate he was talking too many numbers.

"All right, last of the big numbers here... We also know that solar systems seem to be everywhere in our Milky Way Galaxy, and the Milky Way Galaxy has 250 or 350 BILLION stars in it. Maybe 10% are like our sun, and 20% of those have solar systems similar to ours... I'm starting to drive you glazy-eyed with numbers, so we'll just say that we reckon there might be five or six billion – that's BILLION with a 'B' – Sol-like solar systems in our galaxy. I promise that's the last of the numbers." Owen was almost apologetic. "Do you know what a Goldilocks planet is?"

"I know the Goldilocks story with the three bears, but not with planets." Sunlyn smiled.

"Well, you have the right idea, and that's exactly where the term comes from. A Goldilocks planet sits just the right distance away from its home star so that it is not-too-hot and not-too-cold, just like Goldilocks's porridge. That's a big deal because if we assume other life would form using complex, organic molecules like those that make up our DNA, it would need water-based chemistry which necessitates liquid water. If things were too hot, that would mean water would boil, and organic life would be impossible. If things were too cold, that would mean water would be in the solid-state precluding chemistry as we know it and organic life would be impossible. Either way, life in any way similar to Earth's is impossible without a planet in the Goldilocks comfort zone around its home star."

Owen again surveyed faces to assure himself that he was making sense to them. "If we assume the Judo-Christian philosophy that a classical God created mankind, then we are unique to planet Earth. If that is true, then we needn't look for life anywhere else."

Fiona's face took on a pained expression. "But everyone doesn't necessarily believe in a God-centred universe... or God-centred galaxy as in your example."

"Absolutely, Fiona. I'm not trying to make that argument,

but it is one way of looking at the universe... ah, galaxy." He was happy to see more affirmative nods around the table. "Okay. Now assume that we aren't so special here on planet Earth and that what happened here – the formation of organic, carbon-based life – would happen anywhere in the galaxy that had similar conditions. If we just go back to where I started this story, please recall that we have billions and billions of years to work with here. There likely would be so many accidental combinations of atoms forming molecules that the odds are fairly good that eventually, life would form no matter how different it may be from Earthly life forms."

"Let me get this straight... you're saying that if life happens by chance, there is so much time available in so many other solar systems that life should occur nearly everywhere the possibilities exist, yes?"

Owen smiled. "Exactly! You should get the prize, Kylie. You are not only right but quite succinct. It took me five minutes to say what you just expressed in one sentence."

"I'm a good listener, and I hear what you're saying, mate." Kylie leaned back, arched her eyebrows and smiled.

"Well, remember, this isn't me saying it, Kylie... in our paradox story, it's Enrico Fermi saying this."

"Gotcha."

"Okay... so put another way, life is inevitable and will form – given a few billion years here and there – wherever the conditions are right. Now I'm not trying to teach a cosmology lesson here since I am ill-equipped to do so, and you would be bored to death on top of that!" Owen half-suppressed a laugh. "We are ignoring population one stars, population two stars, metal-element-poor stars and the time it took our galaxy to get cooking, so to speak. Fermi just approximated that our Milky Way Galaxy has probably had nine or ten billion years of the right ingredients in enough places to just be cooking away all that time and letting 'god play dice', so to speak. I apologise for that reference, but the other night Sunlyn and I talked about Einstein's famous quote of god not playing dice with the universe!"

"Okay, I give up! I AM blurry-eyed with all these numbers! What is your point, Owen?" Sunlyn's frustration was apparent.

"Look, our solar system is less than five billion years old, and we know the Milky Way has had a minimum of ten billion years in which it could have formed complex carbon-based organic life forms. Fermi argued that if life developed anywhere else, it most likely would have followed a similar evolutionary path as we did until eventually, intelligence would evolve. Consider, we have gone from caveman to us in 150,000 to 200,000 years. If life isn't unusual, there should be millions, maybe BILLIONS of other systems having living creatures that would evolve intelligence similar to ours. The law of averages says that some of them would have evolved for millions and millions of years longer than us. If that is true, they would be so technologically advanced that they would have mastered space travel and spread to every part of our galaxy. Fermi argues that if life developed only once before in millions or billions of years before us, that incredible amount of time would, almost by necessity, dictate that life would be teeming everywhere.... EVERYWHERE! He is quite sound in his thinking as far as I can see.

"I know you will all be happy now when I finally say, here's the paradox... Our species has never seen, never reported visitors from anywhere else in the galaxy or the universe through time immemorial. I might add, we've never credibly reported alien life."

"How about so many UFO reports?" Sunlyn asked.

"Or Biblical passages that speak of UFOs," Kylie added.

"I said, credible! UFO stories abound, but they don't tend to be corroborated. I believe you refer to some passages in the Book of Ezekiel, but again, there is no supporting evidence for that, either. There is no tangible evidence of ANY alien life apart from what we know of on our home planet. One reasonable conclusion as to why this is the case would be that humans are simply alone in our galaxy. Life – or at least intelligent life – is very, very special and it only formed once, and that was here on Earth. If life is actually as common as many in the scientific community might think, then where the hell is everyone?"

"That all made sense to me, Owen, but didn't Fermi miss a big thing here? I may be an ecopsychologist, but I also know that the speed of light is a physical constant no one can violate. Maybe life has formed all over, but since the universe is so big, no one can travel that far or that fast."

"Good on you, Kylie, you are exactly right in your thinking here. The problem is, Fermi did think of that. I kept interchanging universe and galaxy here, but Fermi actually did use our galaxy as a point of reference, meaning our Milky Way. The reason he did is that it is more manageable in size to our limited brains. Look, the Milky Way may be 100,000 light-years across, so that's pretty damned big. It would take a ray of light that long to cross it. But a spaceship travelling one-hundredth the speed of light could cross it in 10,000,000 years. At one-thousandth the speed of light, it would take 100,000,000 years. Look, those are enormous amounts of time, but Fermi thought more about stars being 100, 200 light-years away and how an intelligent species could travel at reasonable speeds in giant space colonies and reach thousands of other planets harbouring life. No one needs to break any physical laws. It's just that knowing what a strong predisposition our species, our form of life, has for exploration, it's reasonable to think other life forms would have that same drive. Given billions and billions of years, we keep coming back to Fermi's Paradox of 'where is everybody'?"

Kylie had a good laugh now. "In Australia, there is an expression, 'where the bloody hell IS everybody'! I think maybe that's what Fermi might have been saying."

"Exactly!"

"I understand what you – what Fermi – are both saying here, but I still come back to my original question which is, 'why is finding life the BIGGEST FIND EVER?'" Fiona needed convincing.

"The Martian environment is very harsh, so if they find life there, chances are it wouldn't be as complex as here on Earth. Let's suppose they did find Martian life forms that were similar to bacteria or single-celled life. That would be astounding for the simple reason that we'd forever want to know how? Why? Where? We'd be keen on discovering if it is totally different from Earth life because then we would assume it formed on Mars. You must realise that Mars only had liquid water on its surface over the first few hundred million years of its existence, not for billions of years like Earth. If we determined that life did form there, we would need to question whether or not it somehow jumped to Earth. You do know that we find Mars meteorites lying around on the Antarctic ice sheets, yes?"

"Mars rocks in Antarctica? No, I didn't know that." Sunlyn finished her cocktail.

"Well we do, and we hypothesise that over the eons, meteor and asteroid impacts on the Martian surface have knocked bits of debris into space, and some have landed on Earth. Now then, if we find that Martian life is identical or similar to Earth-based life, we might wonder how our biological molecules jumped to Mars. As far as we know, that should be less likely than Mars life jumping to Earth because our planet's gravity is stronger, and it would be more difficult to have an Earth rock getting knocked off the surface. That's the hypothesis at least, though we haven't explored Mars enough yet to confirm that idea.

"Let me sum it all up by saying that if we do hear an announcement of life being discovered on Mars this week and we can determine that it wasn't a knock-off from the Earth, Fermi's Paradox will loom even larger... I like your Aussie way of putting it, Kylie... 'where the bloody hell is everybody?'"

45

Sunday, 18 September; Gale Crater Outpost, Mars

Misha's face looked more relaxed than it had been all week. "I'm certain we are all happy just to have a day here at the outpost with no pressure on us to suit up for another surface excursion. But I also realise that since we are all scientists, we share that same determination ingrained in us to run every damned laboratory test imaginable on our samples. The thrill of surface exploration is one thing, but once we collect the artifacts, we all possess that burning desire to see just what our knowledge, our experience and our cherished equipment can coax these newly collected samples to reveal to us. I suggest we take this time so we all can learn what each team member has learned over the past 24 to 48 hours. We'll have to make do without Nigella since she is right now on the MRT and just about ready to dock at Alpha Colony for the big press conference tomorrow. I needn't remind you that once the entire world learns of the discovery of life up here, the proverbial shit will surely hit the fan. Now that still leaves us in the clear temporarily, but I doubt we can hold off the powers that be − read that Director Sam Tan − for too long.

When I last spoke to him yesterday, he was pushing for us to announce the intelligent alien find by next week."

"That just doesn't give us time to unravel the whole story, Misha." Arya shook his head.

"I know that Arya but try explaining that to the Director. Look, he does have a point when he says we may NEVER have the whole story. Seriously, we don't have the whole story on *Homo sapiens* for goodness sakes. The reality is that if we don't make the announcement in the next several days, there is no guarantee that the news won't leak out. If that happens, we will be left trying to explain why we are responsible for keeping secret the biggest discovery ever made by humankind."

"Of course, you are right, Misha. I know that you and the director are correct. We'll just have to do the most we can before we have our own press conference." Siti gritted her teeth. "Just imagine reading 'Scientists keeping a secret from the world'... I'd hate to get in the middle of that headline! On that note, do you mind if I go first today?"

"Please do, Siti."

"I'm going to tell you what more I have found on the analysis of the pieces we have. We had an original six bags with 317 medallions in them. Arya reported on categorising them before, and I gave some preliminary results of composition. I'll update that in a minute.

"After opening all 19 chambers in tube 27A, we brought back a total of 92 bags the first day and 84 more bags yesterday. These bags had no more medallions, but a total of 8,789 transparent disks. We also have several..." Siti looked at Arya for a number.

"Five." He extended his right hand out with all fingers and his thumb held up high.

"Thanks, Arya. We have five – how shall I put it – five mystery cubes. At this point, we haven't determined what they are, but Arya and his hard-working AI program keep plugging away on that.

"Now then, the transparent disks have the same dimensions as the medallions, that is 82 millimetres in diameter and 21.5 millimetres thick. There is very little variation in those numbers, less than a hundredth of a millimetre in any dimension. The composition seems to be 98% or 99% quartz. I am still checking on any trace elements in there since I am getting a scattering from gold and silver nanoparticles. Again, I will get back to you on that. The mass of each disk is fairly uniform too at 63.8 grams, and that results in a density of 2.648 which is consistent with fused quartz, pretty much pure SiO_2." Siti nodded towards Joe, who had one finger in the air, indicating that he had a question. "Joe?"

"Can you specify the difference between SiO_2 in beach sand and that found in fused quartz?"

"Sure, that's simple. Beach sand... crystalline quartz if it's pure, is silica or silicon dioxide, chemically. In that granular form, it is structured in a very orderly arrangement, in other words, in a crystalline structure. Fused quartz has had that crystalline structure broken down, usually because of heat. In that case, it is an amorphous solid and no longer has an orderly crystalline structure the way quartz does. Fused quartz is quite transparent not only to visible light but also to UV. My tests show that these transparent disks do transmit the ultraviolet spectrum.

"Now then, the mystery cubes are solid, not hollow, and have a similar material make-up but with the quartz portion smaller, about 87%. Again, I am working on a better analysis of those."

This time it was Lochie's turn with a question. "How about

the bags, Siti?"

"Well, we surely have a lot to work with now. They all seem to be identical, so I assume that however they were manufactured, they came from the same alien machine, factory, whatever... that remains to be determined.

"At least having a sample of 182 bags means I needn't be quite as nervous if I steal a piece for analysis here and there. I have confirmed everything I told you before including the application of amino acid racemisation technique of intra-crystalline protein as an alternative supplementary technique we use for dating once-living organisms. I again looked at the ratio of the initial L-amino acid that has turned into D-amino acids and confirmed my original finding of 165,000 years plus or minus 10,000 years. I have high confidence in that number now as long as my initial assumptions are correct, and that's still problematic.

"I also got to thinking of the conversations we had around this table the other day. I go back and forth on the efficacy of using C-14 here and continue to give that method more thought. I considered Lochie's comment that knowing what we do about conditions on Mars, there is no way we can be confident that whatever organic material was used to produce the bag material was grown here."

"They could have grown whatever the organic was in a greenhouse, no?" Misha considered the possibilities.

Siti shook her head. "Look... if you ask whether or not it is technically possible to grow cotton in a greenhouse or to raise sheep and sheer their wool, well then yes, it is. I say technically, because energy-wise, I can't imagine any intelligent beings would waste greenhouse space on manufacturing textiles. Any greenhouse expenditure on materials or energy would surely be used to produce food."

"You could eat the sheep." Keegan nodded his head.

"Well, you could, but why worry about wool for textiles? Consider how much simpler it would be to capture carbon from Mars's atmosphere and synthesise nylon or rayon or whatever industrially if you want textiles. Look... I am not in any way implying that the bag textile was grown on Earth, but I think it valid to at least consider any alien life form would be native to a system similar to ours. If that is the case and if they had an oxygen-nitrogen atmosphere and orbited a star of similar brightness to Sol, just maybe we'd get some reasonable answer to a C-14 test. I don't pretend to be certain, but for the sake of science, I used several small samples of the bag material to run C-14 tests."

"And what sort of date did you get on that?"

"I thought you'd ask, Lochie... I got a consistent 172,500 years plus or minus 7,500 years."

Lochie used a finger to stroke his chin. "I'm merely a geologist, but why do I seem to remember that C-14 couldn't date much past 60,000 or 70,000 years?"

"You're saying 60 or 70 thousand years? Well, you are correct in that you heard those numbers, but I fear they reflect your old age!" The whole team had a good laugh at Siti's dig at poor Lochie's expense. "I apologise, but I just couldn't resist teasing you. I know you geos wouldn't have much use for C-14 dating, right?"

"You got me, Siti."

"In the past several decades, our techniques have improved, and the sensitivity of instrumentation increased to the point where we can measure much smaller fractions of isotope ratios. We are regularly getting pretty accurate readings back to 200,000 years now."

"Damn! Fair enough, mate. I do hope you will still allow an old codger like me to report on some work that Keegan, Misha and I did last night."

"My mother taught me to be kind to my elders... Over to you, Lochie."

Lochie shook his head, but his smile indicated he was happy to go along with the ribbing. "Now then...we took samples of the lava wall sections that had been removed and ran a simple potassium-argon dating technique. With these samples, we decided this was the best method to use and that it should work as well here on Mars as it does back on Earth. Basically, the procedure measures potassium-argon ratios. Why? Well, the idea here is that when lava is liquid, it will encapsulate some atmospheric argon in its crystal structure. As long as that argon-40 stays trapped – in other words, the lava stays solid – it will decay at a regular rate into potassium-40. Our assumption is based on Mars atmosphere having 1.6% argon compared to Earth's 0.93% argon. Remember, the starting amount matters not since it is the ratio of Ar-to-K that we're are measuring. We had many trials and had consistent results that gave us a date of 175,000 years plus or minus 8,000 years."

Misha looked at the faces around the table. "So, am I putting the pieces together here properly? Siti earlier told us that she determined an age of 165,000 years plus or minus 10,000 years using the amino acids flipflopping from one isomeric form to the other. Your C-14 dating is admittedly a result in which we have less confidence, but you still have gotten results that indicate an age of 172,500 years plus or minus 7,500 years. Lochie, Keegan and I came up with the argon-potassium ratio study, which gave us an age of 175,000 years plus or minus 8,000 years. Can we conclude that we have pretty good confidence that the bags are around 170,000 years old, give or take 5,000 or 10,000 years?"

Keegan looked around the table. "I think we all seem to be in agreement on that, though we have no number for whatever 'pretty good' might be."

"Well how about that... we do make some headway. I'm sorry we haven't more time for our studies, but I believe we are certainly on the right track here. I have declared a holiday for the outpost tomorrow morning, so we can all gather and watch the press conference... silly planetary time zones make tomorrow morning today back in Australia!" A confused look raced across her face. "That said, after the conference is finished, we will continue a single two-person surface exploration every day in hopes of uncovering any other artifacts we can find. The rest of us will put our noses to our laboratory grindstones and see how much we can learn before we go public." She surveyed her colleagues' faces. "Any questions?"

46

Monday, 19 September; Forrest Hall, University of Western Australia, Perth, Western Australia

"So, this is Forrest Hall, huh? What a great view... not bad for a university's visiting researcher accommodations." Sunlyn kicked her shoes off and stretched her legs on the sofa, looking out the picture window across a broad expanse of the Swan River. "And somehow you just had these accommodations thrown into our invite to the press conference free of charge? What a surprise, Dr Childs."

Kylie grinned. "Well, don't be surprised. I'd like to take credit for the lodging, but you'd do better to thank the wealthy philanthropist who endowed the money to the university to build this place. I believe I mentioned before, the Group of Eight are the leading research universities in Australia, and UWA is one of them along with my home university in Sydney. I have many colleagues here, and we tend to work together closely. Every time I am in Perth for academic meetings or conferences, I have been lucky enough to stay here. Besides the beautiful setting here on the Swan River, the convenience is tops – we are right on campus here at Forrest Hall. Now if either one of us were going to be surprised, maybe you'd look over there." Kylie tossed her head in the general direction of the apartment next to theirs.

"Oh boy... Who would ever have thought those two would be together this time last week? Most of us came away having made new contacts, gaining new knowledge and broadening perspectives on so many problems facing the world. I'm sure Fiona and Owen also experienced that, but they also come away from Shanghai with... each other."

"I guess you Americans would understand it when an Aussie says, 'they're definitely an item', yes?"

"An item? Of course, they're an item! But I fully admit to counting the hours until Nicolás gets here."

"When? Does he get in late tonight?"

"Not too late. I think the plane gets in around nine-ish, and he'll just catch a... what do they call it here?"

"The WAT here in Perth – that's Western Australia Transit."

"Yeah, a WAT. I'm sure he can have his SAM order it while getting off the plane, and it'll be there when he grabs his bag. And your partner? I'm so anxious to meet your mate, Kylie."

"Micky... I think Micky gets in around two in the morning. With any luck, we will all see each other at brunch. Since the press conference isn't scheduled until evening, we can at least sleep in tomorrow."

"Maybe we can catch an hour's nap now. Owen and Fiona said they were keen on having a drink before dinner."

"That sounds good. I'll head over to my apartment and see you in an hour or so."

* * *

Owen opened the door. "Sorry, it took me a minute. We both just crashed for a short snooze."

"Fair enough. I hope we're not too early."

"No, we got up a bit ago, so this is good."

"We just thought it time to check on the neighbours." Sunlyn's face beamed as she and Kylie entered the apartment, a bottle of red in her hand. "I hope this will do. We just picked this up at the bottle shop across the street."

Owen took the bottle and held it up. "For sure, this will do... Margaret River. I've heard they produce some excellent wines there."

"That they do."

"Did you two have a bit of a rest, too?"

"We did." Sunlyn suppressed a yawn.

"Hi, Kylie... Sunlyn..." Fiona came into the room, wiping the sleep from her eyes.

"Hi, Fiona... glad you had a bit of a catnap." Kylie smiled at her friend.

"Yes, the little snooze definitely was what I needed. It's not as though there is any jetlag flying south to Perth, but the trip was long enough. I wish we'd have an SST choice to Western Australia."

"Don't hold your breath, Fiona. Shanghai is just a little bit too close to schedule SSTs just yet." Owen opened the bottle and checked the kitchen cabinet for wine glasses. "Let's have a drink, and we can see if Kylie's countrymen can actually produce a wine pleasant on the taste buds."

The four of them sat in the living room, an exact copy of the one next door, only flip-flopped the other way. "You have the same beautiful view." Sunlyn took the glass Owen handed her. "Your Australia surely is beautiful. From the looks of it, we might get quite a sunset down the river there."

"My Australia... I wish!" Kylie turned both hands up almost apologetically. "I must confess that I can't take credit for it all, Sunlyn. No doubt though, Perth is a lovely spot, and the Swan River can be quite spectacular. I think the sunset will be a bit out of our view, but I can tell you that I have seen some of the most spectacularly colourful skies from these apartments."

"At least the flight down was not as bad as I feared even without a supersonic transport. What was it – under nine hours? Flying supersonic really doesn't pay for that short a flight. Now when we fly back to DC from Sydney, we'll be more than happy to be on an SST."

"You're exactly right on that one, Owen... but I'm going to hate to see you go." Fiona's face telegraphed her feelings.

"I have no doubt you two can work out ways to have your travel schedules overlap somehow." Kyle was encouraging. "Maybe Sunlyn will need to give you instructions. Now seriously, are we to believe that your Nicolás just 'happened' to get an assignment here in Perth?"

Sunlyn laughed. "Well, I confess that we were hoping to pull that off somehow. Let's just say that the folks on Mars helped. Besides that, the coincidence of picking UWA as home base for the press conference tomorrow didn't hurt."

"When does he get here?"

"Around midnight... well, his flight is earlier than that, but by the time he goes through immigration and customs and catches the WAT over here, it'll probably be midnight."

"Oh boy – even flying the SST, you can't fool Mother Nature." Fiona again wiped her eyes with a hand. It's still twelve hours' time difference between here and Washington. I will guarantee you that Nicolás will have some serious jetlag."

"I'll help get him over that." Sunlyn flashed a suggestive smile. "At least we don't have to wake up early tomorrow... that will help."

"No doubt it will." Fiona enjoyed the banter.

"Besides, like all of us, whatever gets announced tomorrow will be monumental enough to make us all forget jetlag and any other travel woes." Owen's response indicated that he was having a conversation on a whole different topic from that of the three women.

"No doubt..." Kylie's expression turned more serious. "I doubt any of you checked the news feed, and for some silly reason I did that right after I woke up."

"What are you saying? What happened?" The journalist in Owen came to the fore.

"Well, it wasn't one thing, rather a series of things... First of all, it's September which means hurricane season up in your end of the planet. The third straight category-5 hurricane in two weeks, this time running up along your east coast. The flooding is the worst they have ever seen, and hundreds of lives have been lost. The media is in overdrive linking the latest air and water temperatures to the severity of the storms.

"Then there is the human side of all of this, and it is very widespread... Washington, Chicago, Los Angeles and even London, Beijing and Sydney... there are increasing reports from around the globe of spot cases of kids in group suicide events. I know we have all been sadly following this even before the Summit, but things seem to remain on a steady, downhill trajectory while we were up in Shanghai. It's one more reminder that just because you aren't able to give a problem your undivided attention, it's not going to somehow magically disappear."

"Group suicide? How big is a group?" Owen swirled his wine.

"Fairly small – three or four kids... one with half a dozen in London. Honestly, the telling issue isn't the size of the groups, but the fact that they are happening at all. I think we've been over this before, but couples enter suicide pacts, religious groups may agree to group suicide... three, four, five kids don't just go kill themselves. THAT is highly unusual behaviour."

Sunlyn set her glass on the coffee table. "So, what do you make of it all, Kylie?"

"Well, you have heard me go on at length both in my formal presentation at the Summit and more personally over tea. As an ecopsychologist who has spent the past few decades studying this, I just can't begin to separate the environment from human behaviour."

Owen interrupted. "Surely you aren't making a direct connection between a few hurricanes and mass suicide, are you? I fear you can carry this solastalgia idea too far, Kylie."

"I fear that I'm just not communicating well at all. Please, please, please don't keep looking at environmental changes as though they occur in a vacuum. Regrettably, I think that is EXACTLY what we have done for a hundred years now. We somehow believe that the Earth's environment is magically separated from everything else. Our species has had so much difficulty making the mental leap that connects the physical environment to us *Homo sapiens*. We do not exist separate from the global ecosystem. Our politics do not exist independent of the ecosystem. Our economies are not isolated from the ecosystem... nor is our culture separated... or our technology... or global population expansion... ALL exist WITHIN the worldwide ecosystem, not somehow apart from it. Honestly, we can sum it up by simply saying that ALL of human behaviour is a part of the global ecosystem.

"Can we try to look at environmental change in the context of nine billion people, in the context of decaying political systems, in the context of a failed economic system? Believe me when I tell you that our kids do. When liberal-style western democracy 'won' the philosophical and cultural battle back in the twentieth century, the whole basis was founded in a consumer-oriented society. The conflicts between races and ethnic backgrounds, amongst rich and poor, between natives and immigrants, amongst all the different religions and cultures... these all appeared to be 'cured' by a seemingly never-ending flood of consumer products. But all that was accomplished by lifting standards of living based on global growth rates of 3%, 4%, 5% a year. We now have become painfully aware of the fact that never-ending growth on one planet is a myth. We have run into the brick wall of reality; continued unlimited growth is impossible."

"I doubt you will get any argument on that here. I know that I definitely agree with you, Kylie." Owen was grasping for some common ground.

"So, consider that we are reflecting on this terrifying phenomenon of kids committing mass suicide and wonder how we got here. There can be as many reasons for suicide as there are people, but please don't think that a primary cause is sadness. We all feel sad from time to time, and that is part of being human. I'm sure I have said it before, but sadness and depression are not the same things! Suicide results in one way or another from desperation, of hopelessness, from feeling that there is no alternative left but taking one's own life. What makes it particularly painful is that we have travelled down a tragic path that finds these kids feeling dislocated from places they have never been, from memories they know only through their parents. I refer to memories of abundance, of rewarding careers and of comfortable family homes filled with kids and pets. These kids long for feelings of pride and dignity, of self-worth and relevance. Even at 13, 14, 15 years of age, we're seeing these kids believing that they will never have that world their parents talk about... never..."

"Oh boy... aren't you a bit harsh here, Kylie?" Owen's tone dropped a notch as he felt her torment.

"I don't think so. We all agree the situation is serious. Regrettably, none of us can just snap our fingers and make it all go away. Humanity doesn't work that way. But we can't just throw our hands up in defeat, either."

Sunlyn reflected on the underlying psychology she studied as an undergraduate. "So, let me see if I am following you, Kylie. You're saying that the environment is EVERYTHING, not just the physical surroundings. Even humanity is part of the environment."

"Yes, that's exactly what I am saying."

"Aha!" Sunlyn's face reflected her eureka moment of understanding. "Now I get it when you say that we as a species somehow see ourselves outside of this environment. I just remember some of my undergrad courses that introduced the whole nature-nurture debate. Modern academics want to put numbers on everything." Sunlyn arched her eyebrows while looking at Kylie and Fiona. "Trying to quantify how much of our psyches are influenced by an infinite range of internal inputs versus external inputs is a hopeless task. If you take that one step farther and try to separate out the influence of how much each part of the whole affects us, that winds up being an impossible task."

"Yes, you are spot on there. It is impossible to separate all of that out into neat pieces." Kylie agreed. "To try weighing the influence of your dad, your diet, your teachers and your community in any sort of quantifiable way is just not possible. It's way too complex."

Fiona joined the conversation. "Maybe we have a misunderstanding based on semantics here. A simple dictionary definition of an ecosystem probably says something like the interactions of all the biological organisms within a community and their interactions with the abiotic environment. We *Homo sapiens* are a bit of a different beast compared to other species. We have such a huge impact on the environment at every level. I believe what Kylie is saying is that we extend the definition of the ecosystem beyond what exists on, for example, a coral reef. Since humans evolved such an intricate social structure, all of that is included within that structure must be part of the ecosystem."

Owen nodded his head. "All right... I guess I can accept that. We humans are a complicated bunch. But we've sure outgrown the indigenous concept of being 'of the land', haven't we?"

"Haven't we?" Kylie thought she would give it one more try. "It's interesting that you mention indigenous since I believe you are precisely onto something here. Is it possible that humans stretch that term ecosystem in the sense that Fiona just explained to a point where it includes so much of our culture? Maybe the indigenous concept of 'the land' took in a broader meaning too. 'The land' even encompassed the spirit of deceased souls or elders. 'The land' was the source of water, of food, of tools, of housing. That idea so much echoes many American Indian peoples who generationally passed down the wisdom that they do not own the land, rather the land owns them. For most indigenous peoples, the ONLY inputs were 'the land' and 'the tribe'... it was that simple and yet that complex."

"All right, all right... let's step back a minute. You are my friends, and I am listening with an open mind, but I fear I hear too much psychological gibberish." Owen dropped his hand onto Fiona's in an attempt to better wade through the conversation. "I mean, these kids are killing themselves. That is a reality! They are killing themselves by the dozens... maybe hundreds when we add up all the cities... I follow what all of you had to say here and find it all quite fascinating. Actually, I agree with most of it. But regrettably though, if 'place pathology' is the disease, we could probably spend a million years and not learn how to cure it." Owen's head tilted down, almost trying to hide his fear that Fiona and Kylie would misunderstand his doubt.

Fiona quickly replied. "Oh Owen, don't be sorry for stating what seems so obvious – this is one monstrously huge problem with no easy answers."

"I believe the term is called a BHAP – a Big Hairy Audacious Problem." Kylie also wanted to reassure him. "I don't mean to make light of your criticism, Owen, since we hear this all the time at conferences, meetings and in classes... The description of the problem is real, I am convinced of that. We know kids around the globe are showing signs of suffering from the complex breakdown of their whole world, from nearly everything that surrounds them. The issue though is how we actually find a way to solve it. I refuse to believe it is impossible since, in many ways, the survival of our species depends on finding answers."

"And before we throw our hands up in surrender, please consider that we have come a long way... we DO make progress." Fiona's voice had an air of optimism.

"Exactly, Fiona. But let's give Owen his due... He makes a great point here: we surely seem to be missing something." Sunlyn's frown telegraphed her frustration.

Kylie leaned back with a finger rubbing her chin. She was

obviously reaching deep into her thought processes. "Oh, we are missing something here... missing something big. This group suicide behaviour without a cult, without a religious influence and no apparent involvement of any pharmaceutical cause, is quite inconsistent to past occurrences of collective suicide. At the fear of being redundant, I'll say it once more – we are missing something big."

47

Monday, 19 September; Metro Precinct Station, Washington DC

"Hi, boss." Patton and Bradshaw hustled into the office like two kids wanting to show their teacher the excellent work they had done. Chandra trailed in behind them. "We've dug up some interesting stuff on O'Keefe and Bidwill, sarge."

"Interesting?"

"Yeah." Bradshaw continued. "You know, the original search warrants we had for both the Bidwill and O'Keefe residences?"

"Yeah."

"Well, Chandra here spent all his initial efforts going through the computer equipment and looking for whatever he could find there. At the same time, we did the background checks on the parents – criminal records, civil cases and whatnot. We reported all that to you."

"I gotcha."

"Well... tell him, Lenny."

Chandra reluctantly shimmed to the front of Grimms' desk

and stood there. "Ah... I found a couple of bank accounts we might want to check out."

"Bank accounts? Well, come on, Chandra. Don't make me pull teeth here. What the hell did you find?"

"Well Sarge, I was doing all the routine stuff, like Ryan said here, background stuff. I looked into both sets of parents, and it all seemed to be mostly in order. I did find the IRS audited the O'Keefe folks a few times in the past several years, but their finances were all okay in the end. I figured I was about done, but there were a couple of other accounts that kept popping up. Neither one fit the Bidwill or O'Keefe family profiles, but the AI system we use kept bringing it back up. I swear that damned AI program is smarter than us a lot of times. No one algorithm can work at this level, so we used a combination of Learning Vector Quantization along with a Linear Discriminant Analysis process. Basically, the AI looks at what we know, what we're looking for and then compares that using a..."

Grimms' patience was wearing thin. "For god's sakes Chandra, I don't need a lesson in freaking computer programming, I just want to hear about the bank accounts!"

Lenny was startled at first and took a step back from where he was. "Sorry, Detective Grimms. I just got... I eventually got to the point that I was happy that I went as far as I could with all those data we had. I sort of figured, what the hell..." Chandra swallowed like he was embarrassed to use the word 'hell.' "Then I followed up on those two spurious bank accounts AI kept spitting out at me. Well boy, am I glad I did. It seems that both the O'Keefe boy and the Bidwill boy had some money stashed away in accounts they didn't think we could trace to them. Actually, they both have two Social Security numbers, and that's why it was difficult finding them in the first place. But the AI programs didn't let that stand in the way."

"For Christ's sake, Chandra — what the hell did you find out!" Grimms' voice was louder now, and he exhaled quite audibly.

"Well sir, they both were hiding pretty large sums of money."

"How large."

"Bidwill has a total of..." Chandra looked down at his flat-screen technoserver, "...$1,250,200 in his account and O'Keefe has $1,450,350."

"WHAT? MILLIONS? Ain't these freaking kids 17?" He looked at Bradshaw and Patton.

"You've got it, boss. They're both 17, and neither one turns 18 until after the new year."

"How the hell do high school kids with no part-time jobs amass over a million dollars each?"

Maggie looked at her partner. "I think Ryan can fill you in on that."

"Look, boss, when Lenny told us this, Maggie and I figured we'd do a bit of looking before we came to you. We pointed Lenny in the right direction to see if he could track sources and Maggie and I did some investigating. We tried the cameras at the bank, but that didn't help any. We also tried cameras around the school, but nothing showed there. Surprisingly, it only took Lenny a couple of hours to produce this name." Bradshaw dropped a piece of paper on Grimms' desk that read 'William MacLucas.'

"So, who the hell is MacLucas?"

"Funny you ask, sarge." Maggie folded back her notepad. "William MacLucas — 54 years old, lives not far from the boys in Kalorama Heights, married, three kids out of high school, and he goes by Bill. He has been in advertising for his whole life. The background material we have actually calls what he does 'marketing.' Seems like he has his own business registered here and also in Virginia – Sunrise Marketing Company."

"Okay, okay... this links to the case how?"

Bradshaw picked up the report. "It seems Lenny traced payments back over the past year to both boys from MacLucas. There weren't many. Ah, three or four payments to each of them and they didn't seem to be on any identifiable schedule."

Grimms leaned back in his chair. "Help me understand this. First of all, how did he know the kids?"

"The one commonality we came across was that both boys played on a basketball team MacLucas coached a few years back when they were in ninth and tenth grade. We talked to people in MacLucas's neighbourhood, and sure enough, people have seen the kids going in and out of his house. We looked at public cameras in the city park across the street from MacLucas's place and once again, we found several clips of both boys paying visits."

"You got anything else for me?"

"One more thing, boss." Maggie still focused on her notes. "We found that MacLucas has a record. Seems he was arrested for having some of his IT guys try to hack into customer SAMs back a few years ago. Someone got wise, turned him in and he wound up pleading guilty to a throwaway charge. I think he wound up paying a thousand dollar fine or something like that, but he got off with a misdemeanour."

"Did you get a warrant?"

"We didn't need one. Everything we did was either on the original O'Keefe and Bidwill warrants or public knowledge."

"Bradshaw... Patton... you two have done excellent work here. Chandra, you and your damned AI program are geniuses! I'm impressed with your initiative and methods. Now I think it's time to pay Judge Berger one more visit. We need to freeze this guy's Company computers for sure and home ones if you need more from them. We'd better have the judge include freezing any SAMs, too. Then we can bring MacLucas in for questioning and put a bit of pressure on him. Let me know when the judge issues the warrants."

48

Monday, 19 September; Forrest Hall, University of Western Australia, Perth. Western Australia

Owen climbed into bed next to Fiona. He rolled on his side and pulled her close to his body, brushing her hair away from her face. She embraced him as the two shared a passionate kiss. Owen opened his eyes and noticed a tear making its way down her cheek. He shuddered – did he challenge her academic view of the world too vigorously? "What's wrong, Fiona?"

She smiled. "Nothing's wrong, Owen... I'm happy..."

"Are you telling me I don't see that big tear trickling down your pretty face?"

"I said I'm happy." Now she leaned over and kissed him. "Please don't tell me that you science-types think all tears only show sadness."

Owen took his finger and slowly traced the tear. A sudden thought rushed into his head... an epiphany – Chinese women are absolutely no different from American women. His little voice screamed over his thoughts, 'Shut up, Owen... don't you dare say that to her.' He took his own advice, remained silent and kissed her again.

"I so anticipated the Summit and just knew I'd come away with so many positives. I never had even a clue that I would have met you, Owen."

"It's exactly the same with me, Fiona."

"Hug me... squeeze me."

He did.

Fiona pulled back just enough for him to see her beautiful smile. "I think this is where you are supposed to kiss me." She started to giggle, but Owen quieted her as he pressed his lips on hers.

They lay silently cuddling and kissing for a minute or two, enjoying the warmth of each other's bodies pressing together. Owen spoke softly without breaking their embrace. "I didn't mean to offend you today when we were having drinks. I wasn't trying to challenge you when I questioned your comments on 'heart's ease' or 'place pathology.' After I said that stuff, I was afraid I offended you."

"Come on, Owen."

"No, no... I mean it."

"I know you do. Besides, you couldn't offend me that way. I've been involved in academic arguments for decades now, and disagreements, in that sense at least, are what drive academics. I have intellectually battled some of my close friends all day long at conferences and then spent the evening happily socialising with the exact same people. You won't offend me with any robust head-to-head over the finer points of some hypothesis. Thin-skinned academics don't usually get too far." Her beautiful smile confirmed her words.

"I'm so interested in listening to you. You are as much a scientist as the geologist and astrophysicist we just heard at the Summit, but your field of study is so new to me. I just get confused out of my own ignorance concerning psychological research. I know you and Kylie have done such profound work, but it gets frustrating as hell when kids are dying. It's not fair that I want you to have all the answers, want you to make that miraculous, life-saving breakthrough. My point was never to challenge you, but to simply express my frustrations with the whole damned situation."

Now it was Fiona's turn to run her finger along Owen's cheek. "I never for one minute took your comments as a challenge. You know, I don't think your profession and mine are all that different. As an academic, we simply do what we do – the scientific method I mean – to learn more about the universe, to explore key questions. As a journalist, you may not always apply the scientific method in the same way, but your objective is exactly the same – to do what you do to learn the truth about the story. No one can search for knowledge, search for meaning, and expect to go unchallenged. I seek intellectual questioning that drives me to search harder. I don't care who challenges me to seek answers whether that challenge comes from a stranger, a friend or my lover."

They kissed and hugged... and then more.

* * *

Sunlyn and Nicolás climbed out of the shower, taking extra time drying each other off and playing silly adolescent games. They had been apart for almost two weeks, and his jet-lagged brain refused to let him calculate the time. They both brushed their teeth while standing side-by-side, neither wearing a stitch of clothing. They rinsed their brushes and Sunlyn suddenly spun around and started to run into the bedroom. "Last one in is a rotten egg!"

They both fell across the bed and embraced. "A rotten egg?" He smothered her in kisses.

"Oh, Nicolás..."

"I've missed you so much, hon." Again, he kissed her.

"Me too, Nicolás. I am SO HAPPY you have perfected your gardening skills."

"My gardening skills? What in god's name are you talking about, Sunlyn?" He pulled his face back just far enough in the hopes of seeing if she was smiling.

"God, you keep forgetting! I asked you to plant a seed in Norm Crawford's head, and it obviously germinated, grew and blossomed into a 'Yes, Nicolás, why don't you fly to Australia' flower."

"Well, maybe I'm a good gardener, but I did get a little help from the rumours running through just about every newsroom on the planet that the Mars team discovered some level of life out there."

Sunlyn's face suddenly changed from a serious look to a smile, and she started to giggle.

"I hardly think finding alien life has a funny side to it, hon." Nicolás's confusion was apparent.

"Sorry, Nicolás, but I just had the strangest thought. Considering that we have ALL heard the rumours – academics as well as journalists – everywhere across the planet. Damn! We are ALL going to be way freaking disappointed if they show us some new Martian mineral tomorrow."

Now Nicolás laughed hysterically, putting his hand to his mouth in an attempt to not wake the neighbours. "I have full faith that they will announce more than that, honey."

"I'm glad you got yourself under control. I don't want you waking up Fiona and Owen," she tilted her head to one wall, "...or Kylie." She tilted her head in the other direction, "...before you even meet them."

"Well, first of all, I did meet Owen at a GNN Christmas party a few years ago. We may not be the best of friends, but we have met, and he seems like a hell of a nice guy. You mentioned Fiona and Kylie often enough in our holovision conversations, so I am anxious to meet them in the morning. And what, poor Kylie is alone... a single woman?"

"Well, she just had a way-longer trip than I did, first to the States before flying to China. But her mate – Micky – is coming. He's meant to be here in the morning. I'm very anxious to meet him. She is so cool, so I have no fear he will be a great guy, too."

"I'm looking forward to meeting them."

"Fair dinkum, mate." Sunlyn's smile was radiant.

"Fair dinkum, mate... you're really getting with the bloody Aussie lingo, are you?"

She licked her lips. "I was hoping you'd like hearing me speak Australian. Now if you really want to show me how much you appreciate me, how about you and I have a naughty..."

"Have a naughty? I really think you need to teach me Australian..."

49

Tuesday, 20 September; Forrest Hall, University of Western Australia, Perth, Western Australia

"Brunch, huh? I was wondering if you two would ever wake up." Fiona and Owen sat on a park bench outside the Forrest Hall Café watching the sailboats dart about the blue Swan River.

"Sorry we're a little late, but Nicolás is suffering a bit from jetlag." Sunlyn smiled, knowing full well that absolutely no one was buying her jetlag story.

"Hey man, good to see you." Owen stretched his arm towards Nicolás and shook his hand. "I don't think we've met up since that Christmas party a couple of years back."

"That would be right, buddy."

Owen made the introductions. "Nicolás, please meet Professor Fiona Wu, Shanghai Jiao Tong University in Shanghai. Fiona is on staff in the School of Humanities and Social Science there. She and Kylie have been friends for quite a while, no?"

"Jeez, maybe nine or ten years."

"So nice to meet you, Professor."

"Nicolás, please... call me Fiona. Sunlyn has mentioned you often enough that I almost feel that I know you."

"Same here, I feel as though I met you weeks ago, Fiona..." He looked out towards the water. "Wow, what a beautiful view here. I've never been to Perth before."

"Nor I." Owen gestured towards the river. "I just didn't realise the river was so wide here."

"Technically it's an estuary. I believe it actually has tides and the water is brackish. Fremantle is maybe seven or eight kilometres that way..." Fiona pointed towards the west, "...and then from there, it's just the Indian Ocean all the way to South Africa." Fiona looked at Owen. "You don't mind if I tell Sunlyn and Nicolás, do you?"

He smiled. "Somehow I think they will find out, so better we tell them now than later." He placed his arm on Fiona's shoulder.

Sunlyn looked to Nicolás knowing neither of them had any

idea what Fiona was talking about. "So, tell us already."

"Owen was picked." Fiona's excitement for her mate was palpable.

"Huh?" Nicolás tilted his head. "Too many hours on a plane I fear... what did I miss?"

Owen spoke up. "Look, Fiona's just saying that my name was pulled in the journalists' draw. It's not like I did anything. The powers that be pulled my name out of a hat, and I will be one member of the pool of a couple of dozen press representatives who are sequestered tonight before the public presentation. We get to read the text or see the video of what they plan to present to the world, formulate any questions we might have and then have our questions videoed for playing during the press conference."

"Oh wow! That really is fantastic, Owen." Sunlyn was still standing, and she leaned over to give Owen a kiss on the cheek. "Owen and GNN get a chance to be part of the biggest news conference ever!"

"That IS exciting. I wonder if the *DC Post* had any of our guys selected."

"Sorry, I don't know, Nicolás. We should hear sometime this morning."

"Morning... It IS still morning, but only for a few more minutes. Believe it or not, it's nearly noon." Fiona squinted in the mid-day sunshine.

"Exactly... It's just so nice that, for the first time in a few weeks, we can sleep late, have a bit of a leisurely brunch... maybe it's lunch... and not have to worry about meetings, summits, airports or what-have-you." Sunlyn squeezed Nicolás's hand. "And of course, not have to use the holovision just to have a conversation with my soulmate."

"I hope you two aren't going to stand all day long. Why not

have a seat until Kylie gets here?" Owen and Fiona scooted to one end of the park bench and made plenty of room for Nicolás and Sunlyn. The four of them chatted for ten or fifteen minutes, all the while enjoying the mid-day sun and the warm, 20-something degree afternoon that shouted 'spring-is-here' to all the locals.

"Nicolás, I hope we can get you up to see my home in Shanghai soon."

"That would be great, Fiona. I've never been to Shanghai but have had assignments in Beijing a few times."

"Shanghai is so much more... more Chinese."

"Oh boy, I don't want to get in the middle of this conversation. Sounds like Washington and Baltimore, New York City and Philly, Los Angeles and San Francisco..." Sunlyn held onto Nicolás's hand like a teenager on her first date. "I just know that I certainly loved Shanghai. I'd like to take Nicolás to the Tang Teahouse."

"I've heard about that on one of our holovision chats."

"Well just so you know, you are always welcome, Nicolás."

"I'm really anxious to meet Kylie's mate. I just can't believe that someone as beautiful, as lovely and as smart as she is would have any guy who isn't just fantastic."

Fiona smiled. "Guy?"

"G'day." Kylie's voice called out from the doorway as she stepped onto the lawn.

"Hi, Kylie... Micky..." Fiona stood and walked towards them.

"Sorry we are a bit late, but Micky didn't even land until mid-morning." Fiona gave both Kylie and Micky a hug and kiss, and then Kylie turned towards Sunlyn. She stood hand-in-hand with one of the most beautifully striking women

Sunlyn had ever seen. "This is my soulmate, Michele Simmons, but everyone calls her Micky. This is Sunlyn, and I assume, Nicolás."

Sunlyn stood and extended her hand, but Micky leaned over and gave her a kiss on the cheek. Kylie gave them both a hug and a kiss. "Finally, we all meet together on a beautiful spring day in Perth. In light of this evening's press conference, I trust we will remember this day for a long, long time. Why don't we make our way inside and get some lunch?"

Nicolás leaned over to Sunlyn's ear and inconspicuously whispered. "What was that you said about 'have no fear – Micky will be a great GUY'?"

50

18 September; Metro Precinct Station, Washington DC

"The warrant has been served, and our boys are going through MacLucas's residence and his business offices. Bradshaw and I just brought him in for questioning, boss. Maybe you'd like to be there in the interview room." Patton stood in the doorway with her hands resting on her hips.

"Maybe! Come on, Patton!" Grimms sprung from his chair. "Let's go do it."

Maggie stepped aside, almost dodging Grimms as he stormed out of the door. She followed his fast-paced rush down the hall to the interview room. As they got to the door, Grimms turned to her and lowered his voice even though the interview room door was soundproof. "Play along with me. I might just put a paedophile scare in MacLucas's head just to see what we can shake loose."

"Right on... Gotcha, boss."

The two joined them in the interview room. MacLucas sat at the big, steel table opposite Bradshaw. "Are we rolling?"

Maggie checked the small control panel that recorded all sound and vision. "We are, sir."

"For the record, it's 8:45 AM on September 18. Detective Grimms and Detectives Bradshaw and Patton are present along with the suspect, William MacLucas."

The suspect was the first to speak. "Now, what is this all about? I'm sure there's some mistake here, sir." MacLucas seemed very much under control.

Grimms pulled a chair out and began speaking before he sat down. "Oh, I don't think there's a mistake, MacLucas. From what we're finding, it seems you have a liking for young boys. Is that the case, Mr MacLucas?"

"What! Young boys? What are you talking about?" MacLucas's calmness was shattered in an instant. "I... I don't like what you seem to imply here, Detective."

"I'm not implying anything, Mr MacLucas... I'm just following the information our investigation has turned up. It seems you like spending a lot of time with young boys."

"You're way off base, sir... I've never... never even thought about something like that. I... I just wouldn't ever do anything like that."

"Do you know a couple of boys in your neighbourhood... names..." He looked to Bradshaw.

"Bradley O'Keefe and Dylan Bidwill? They both attend Georgetown Academy." Bradshaw set his pad back down on the table.

"Wait a minute... what are you driving at here?"

Grimms continued. "Do you know them?"

"Well, of course, I know them... I know their parents, too. I was their basketball coach for a few years."

"Basketball coach, huh. What a convenient place to meet young boys... a lot of young boys... maybe in locker rooms and showers..."

"Detective Grimms, I have no idea where you would get this idea from, but I am an upstanding citizen in this community. My wife and I have been here for years. We both contribute back to our neighbourhood, to the District as a whole. Of course, I coached – coach – kids' basketball. That's only because I have an interest in sports as well as an interest in these kids' wellbeing. I'm a father for Christ's sakes. Surely you must know all of this."

Grimms was confident his ploy had worked, and MacLucas was ready to answer a few questions. "You're right – we know quite a bit about you, MacLucas. Now what you say here may all be true but rest assured that we are looking into this right now. That is exactly why you were served with the search warrant, and our investigators are going through your home and business as we speak."

MacLucas's head drooped as he nodded his understanding.

"One thing we know is that you still see O'Keefe and Bidwill fairly regularly. We know that because the security camera at the public park across the street from your residence shows both boys visiting your house frequently. We have quite a few dates here." He flipped a page over in his notebook and looked down at it. "Let's see... August 20... August 24... August 28... September 2... Surely I needn't read all of these, Mr MacLucas. Let's just say that's a lot of visits for two kids that you don't even coach anymore."

"Of course, I've seen them, but not like you're implying..."

Grimms cut him off. "Another thing I know is that you have a wife. I know that because you just told us that. Can you tell us about your wife, MacLucas? What's her name... what she does for a living?"

"Yes, sir... Katlin... that's Professor Katlin MacLucas, and she is on the faculty at George Washington University right here in the District."

"What does she teach there?"

"Psychology."

"That must be a useful discipline to have her level of expertise in for a family whose livelihood depends on marketing. Humm, marketing... I assume there'd be a great deal of psychology you would use in that business."

"My wife isn't involved in any of this."

"Any of what, MacLucas?"

"I just mean..."

Grimms never gave him the chance to protest. "And one more thing we know is that you have a record, Mr MacLucas. Do you want to tell us about that?" Grimms kept his deadpan expression while Patton and Bradshaw kept searching the suspect's face for any clue to his state of mind.

"Oh that... it was nothing... I had a couple of my technical staff who were overly ambitious to impress me, I believe. They got involved in some programming scheme trying to hack into the SAMs of people on one of our client's customer list. It was all pretty silly. They were disciplined and dealt with accordingly."

"A couple of technical staff." Grimms rubbed his chin. "And you thought you'd be the nice guy and take the wrap?"

"Hey, I was the boss... the owner. It wasn't so much that I took the wrap, but I was the guy at the top of the ladder."

"A couple of technical staff... So, who were these two guys?"

"Ah... Lee Briers was one... he's gone now."

"Briers, huh. How about a guy named Leister? Was one of your employees a Mr Steven Leister?"

"Umm... yes, Steve was an employee."

"He WAS an employee? So, you said Briers isn't there anymore. Did you fire him?"

"Yeah, sort of... I told him I had to let him go."

"Got ya. And you say you dealt with these employees... so both of them..."

"Well, yeah..."

"So that means you disciplined Leister, too, I presume? Can you tell me what became of Mr Leister? Did you fire him too?"

MacLucas shuffled in his seat and quietly took a deep breath. "I ah... I had a talk with him... made him give me his word that he wouldn't do that sort of thing again."

Maggie leaned forward, hoping to give Grimms a break. "So again, Mr MacLucas... what became of Leister?"

MacLucas turned towards her, cleared his throat and reached for the glass of water in front of him. He took a drink and wiped his lip with his finger. "Steve is still with us." The volume of his voice was much quieter now.

"And his position with your firm?" She knew the answer but wanted to hear it from him.

"He's... he's my Head of IT now."

51

Tuesday, 20 September, Octagon Theatre, University of
Western Australia, Perth, Western Australia

This was not the first so-called press conference between
Mars and Earth, though it was a first for both Australia as a
whole and for the University of Western Australia. Because
both Geology Professor Lochie Greenbank and Biology
Professor Parisa Henning were current residents of Mars and
both were UWA faculty members, Director Sam Tan
requested that the press conference be channelled through
their home university.

Over the years, a standardised system was devised for
interplanetary press conferences. Depending on the relative
position between Mars and Earth, radio signals travelling at
the speed of light took anywhere between 4 and 24 minutes to
travel between the two planets. Of course, that meant that it
took an equal time for the signals to return. The lengthy time
delay made everyday conversations impossible. Early on, it
was decided that the best communication was in the form of
radio messages transmitted in a similar way to old-fashioned
letters or emails. This practice was the same whether the
message was as text, an audio file, a video file or a hologram.
When something like a press conference or interview was
scheduled, the protocol called for the party that was the focus
of the press conference to compose whatever presentation
they wanted to give in advance. Then that presentation was
recorded, encrypted and sent back to Earth a full two or three
hours in advance. The randomly selected press members were
isolated from any outside communication and given the
presentation to either read or view. The sequestered
journalists were responsible for formulating any questions
they saw appropriate to better understand the topic being

presented. Then the queries selected for the press conference were either video or holographically recorded, sent back to Mars, responded to by the scientists holding the press conference, then finally inserted into the final presentation for broadcast to Earth.

Though it sounded a bit awkward, the system did fill the need. By time the presentations began on Mars, including the journalists' questions seamlessly pasted in at the appropriate spots, the 'newness' of the session was maintained. The only piece missing from similar Earth-side press conferences was that follow-up questions were impossible. No one had yet worked out a way to somehow circumvent the laws of physics that dictated that this time-lapsed production was the only way to proceed. It had worked successfully for some two decades now, and it seemed that the entire world had grown used to the protocol.

"This is exciting." The doorman passed a reader over Sunlyn, Fiona and Nicolás's SAMs as they entered the big theatre. Sunlyn's head scanned the theatre counting the eight walls. "How about that – it really is an octagon." She scanned the 600 or 700 seats, quickly spotted Kylie and Micky and started walking halfway down the aisle where they slipped in beside them.

"Good evening. We were saving seats for you. It sure is filling up quickly." Kylie and Micky moved over so the other three could squeeze in.

Nicolás tried to suppress a jetlag-induced yawn but was not totally successful.

"The announcement of alien life is too boring for you, my love?" Sunlyn teased him.

Nicolás made a funny face at her. "These damned time changes..."

"Besides your jetlag, Nicolás, this is pretty late for this sort of thing." Fiona looked to the big clock on the side wall as she sat down. "A 10:00 PM start is a bit of a stretch, but I guess when you make enough political compromises to keep everyone happy, silly things can happen."

"How'd they arrive at such a late time?" Micky leaned across to include her newly arrived friends.

"Fiona is spot on... politics. I heard that initially, the Mars team wanted to present while the Summit was in session, but just didn't have the data they needed before it ended. At this point, there was no way everyone could agree to make this sort of announcement in China, America or anywhere in what's left of the EU. That leaves the smaller countries. Australia was a good pick on the surface of it all since we tend to fall somewhere amongst all the more populated countries politically. Better yet, the lead scientist of the Mars biology team is on staff here at UWA, Professor Parisa Henning. Besides her, a second UWA academic is up there now too, Professor Lochie Greenbank. I don't think any other university has two staff members on Mars right now. So Alpha Colony Director Sam Tan skilfully tiptoed through all the political roadblocks and came up with the University of Western Australia. Of course, that meant that timewise, it is late evening in Perth and Beijing, 10:00 AM on the US East Coast and afternoon in London. In short, no one may be happy except for us Aussies, but everyone is accepting of the venue."

* * *

An unseen voice filled the theatre from the public address system. "Ladies and gentlemen, the President of the University of Western Australia, Professor Liam McTavish."

A medium build man in a perfectly tailored suit quickly walked to the podium on the side of the stage. A large screen stretched across one side of the octagon that served as the front of the auditorium.

"Good evening everyone and welcome to the Commonwealth of Australia, to Western Australia, to Perth and to the University of Western Australia. I am Professor Liam McTavish, and I am delighted that our university has been chosen for such an historical moment. To get started, please allow me to introduce one of our local Aboriginal elders here this evening to welcome us to country. Mr Whadjuk Thompson...."

A dark-skinned man with a full white beard walked to the podium and stood. McTavish shook his hand and stepped back a metre or two to the side. The elder appeared to be in his sixties and was casually dressed in trousers and a brightly coloured, Aboriginal designed, open-collar dress shirt. He adjusted the microphone and leaned forward.

"Good evening. I will echo President McTavish's words and welcome you to Perth. I also would like to acknowledge that the University of Western Australia is situated on the lands of the indigenous Whadjuk Nyungar people. We pay respect to their enduring and dynamic culture and leadership of Nyungar elders both past and present. The *boodjar* – country – on which the University of Western Australia is located has, for thousands of years, been a place of learning. We at the University of Western Australia are proud to continue this long tradition.

"Thank you and welcome."

He quickly turned and walked from the stage. McTavish returned to the microphone. "I realise that most of you in this theatre – close to 700 of you – represent news organisations and academic institutions from around the world. I also welcome what I understand to be the largest global broadcast audience to ever share one common event. It has been predicted that we may expect as many as five billion – that is

FIVE BILLION – of our fellow humans to watch this press conference. We at UWA are honoured to be hosting you tonight.

"Most of you have been through these interplanetary news conferences before and realise the problem we face with the limitations of the speed-of-light nature of electromagnetic waves. For that reason, a group of two-dozen of your fellow journalists were randomly chosen to be sequestered a few hours ago. There they viewed a video of the presentation given by the Mars Biology Team, had printed copies of the talk and time to digest the content. They were then charged with the task of formulating any questions that could clarify the information presented. A handful of questions were selected from the group of journalists and these will be included in the transmission tonight. Without further words from me, let me welcome our sequestered journalists as well as the Martian Biology Team headed by our very own Professor Parisa Henning."

Twenty-four journalists quietly entered the theatre and took their seats in the first row. Simultaneously the big screen came to life with the live-digitally-transmitted presentation from Mars showing a collage of images from Alpha Colony and Gale Crater Outpost. McTavish leaned towards the podium and continued. "I believe it is fairly common knowledge to all of you here that 'live transmission' does not mean instantaneous. For the sake of our global audience, let me remind you that the transmission being projected here and around the Earth left Mars some 13 minutes previously. We refer to it as 'live' because what was transmitted was exactly what would be received. The only 'tweaking' done with the presentation was the inclusion of the sequestered journalists' questions along with team members' answers. I will now let the Martian team speak for themselves."

The montage ended, and the picture was filled with a

widescreen view of the Mars Biology Team. It consisted of four scientists sitting at a metallic table wearing the now-familiar Martian leisure jumpsuits. "Good evening to all of you gathered at my home institution of the University of Western Australia and good morning and good afternoon to the billions of our fellow humans listening in around the world and at Moon Base One. Greetings from Mars Alpha Colony. I send you best wishes from our Biology Team, from Director Sam Tan and from all the rest of our growing scientific community so very far away.

"Let me introduce you to our members. Again, I am Professor Parisa Henning on loan to the Mars community from the University of Western Australia. To my far right is Dr Tong Yigong of the Kunming Institute of Zoology in Yunnan, China. To my right is Dr Nigella Dougan from the United Kingdom National Institute for Health Research and finally to my left here is Professor Scott Salazar from the University of Southern California. I would be remiss if I didn't introduce one more colleague of mine, Geology Professor Lochie Greenbank who is newly arrived here and connected to us electronically from the Gale Crater Outpost some 2,800 kilometres southwest of here. President McTavish made me promise to mention Lochie since he too is a University of Western Australia faculty member."

There was laughter around the Octagon Theatre at Professor Henning's shameless plug for her home institution.

"Let me start by ending... ending the rumours we have heard about that are being whispered all over Earth. I can confirm tonight that we have discovered life here on Mars." There was a quiet murmur in the Octagon Theatre audience. "I want to emphasise we have discovered life, not evidence of life. We have cultured living organisms found in a drill hole about eight kilometres from Alpha Colony. We will post this on a map along with all the data communicated here on

Skynet 4 after this press conference.

"We are broadcasting to a much wider audience than merely the press so I will attempt to give a full picture of what we found and how we found it, but in terms readily understandable to a broad audience. Our mission here on Mars is twofold: survival and knowledge. Survival is self-evident since the environment here is quite harsh. Our second aim is to accumulate data from every aspect of Mars and its history as we can. To that end, our hydrology people continuously search for water. I cannot stress enough the value of water to us colonists since it supplies not only what we drink, but also what we breathe. A large fraction of our oxygen comes from the electrolysis of water.

"The hydrology team continue this unrelenting search for water in every place we explore on Mars. Typically, they begin by using ground-penetrating radar which many times gives a good indication where test drilling might be successful. Whenever they drill, sample cores are examined for the mineral content, for any tell-tale history these layers might reveal and – of course – for any indication of water. In mid-August, the drill team had several successful core samples they catalogued from a location about 8 kilometres from Alpha Colony. They were heartened by increasingly dense icy brine contents within the rock they were bringing up.

"Twenty-seven days ago, something quite remarkable happened. Early on 22 August the hydrology team was drilling reasonably close by to us here at the Colony. Unexpectedly, they hit liquid water at a depth of some 800 metres beneath the surface. I say unexpectedly since usually when we find water here on Mars, it is most likely in the form of ice or as frost mixed with local soil and bedrock. We have discovered liquid water before, but that is a rarity.

"Per protocol, the team sealed several samples and then capped the drill hole. I will remind you that the standard atmospheric pressure here on Mars is about 6 millibars or less than $1/170^{th}$ of standard Earth atmosphere. Because of this rarity of atmosphere on Mars, strange things happen to liquid water. It quite naturally either vaporises almost instantaneously or rapidly flash freezes and then sublimates once released from the pressure it experiences at depth. Because of this, we would never let water flow from a drill hole for any longer than it takes to cap it.

"As regulations require, these samples were isolated as a potential biohazard and then taken to the Alpha Colony laboratory as soon as possible after discovery. The standard battery of tests was conducted almost as soon as the samples arrived. These tests include measurements of things such as pH, dissolved solids, dissolved gases, etc. Once the basic chemistry profile was completed, additional analyses were conducted using electron-microscopy studies, mass-spectrometer analysis – all the kinds of investigations you might imagine. Because we were dealing with a sample of water, our laboratory checklist also calls for a series of biological tests to determine if the sample contained any organic compounds and whether or not any microorganisms were present. These tests included: microscopy, biochemical assays, polymerase chain reaction and a few others.

"The confounding problem in looking for life on another planet is that we must begin by assuming any potential living organisms would surely be of totally unknown origin and chemistry. This means that it is nearly impossible to know precisely what it is we need to be looking for. You will no doubt understand that we cannot assume anything of alien microorganisms. Even our most basic of all assumptions – that life would surely be built from complex carbon-based molecules – may not necessarily prove to be well-founded in reality.

"We could go on with this for a long time, and I have no

doubt that future historians will do just that, but to make a long story short, we initially used chemical analysis to confirm the presence of organic molecules in the water. In short order, microscopy confirmed that the targets of interest appeared to be microorganisms. Within 48 hours of keeping our samples in our makeshift incubators, our target bodies began to replicate. I believe it was Dr Dougan here..." Parisa placed her hand on Nigella's. "... who made a comment that our Martian bugs were having babies!"

Nigella smiled as she arched her eyebrows.

"In fact, the one-celled morphology observed behaves very much like unicellular-like organisms we see on Earth." Parisa paused long enough to sip her water. "The primary purpose of this press conference is to let the world know of our find. The secondary purpose is a cry for help. Frankly, we need help from so many of the Earth's greatest scientists in every discipline, but especially biologists, microbiologists, evolutionary biologists, molecular biologists, chemists, biochemists... we could go on with this list forever. The point: we need to engage the broadest possible scientific community in this work. There is so much to study here that we may never complete all the work to be done."

"We will take questions submitted to us by the randomly selected journalists."

The question period was skilfully inserted into the broadcast feed. Anyone on Earth not aware of the process could easily be fooled – it appeared that all the participants were together in the same room rather than on different planets.

"Kirsten Imhoff of *Australian Broadcasting Network*. I'd like to ask Dr Tong Yigong about the age of the microorganisms. Dr Yigong, is there any way to determine the age of the little creatures? Do we have any idea if they evolved three billion, four billion years ago?"

"Thank you, Ms Imhoff. I don't mean to be rude, but the age of the little creatures we have incubated is a few weeks. By that, I mean that they are currently alive. At this point, we have no fossils to date, only the actual creatures. If you are asking me to compare these to Earth fossilised microorganisms, it is just not possible at this time. We will continue to look for more evidence of these one-celled creatures' ancestors, whether in fossil form or on living specimens."

"I might pick up on Dr Yigong's reply there, too." Professor Henning continued. "You may be aware that the oldest evidence of life on Earth has been found in my home state of Western Australia. But what we found there were not living microorganisms, rather fossilised forms of microorganisms in a rock that is dated at 3.5 or 3.6 billion years. And I want to emphasise the plural – it was not one microorganism, but 11 different microbial specimens found from five separate taxa. Since they were found in rocks that were 3.5 or so billion years old, it is reasonable to assume they must have been at least that old. In the case of the Martian organisms, these are current Martian residents. They live 800 metres below ground at the bottom of the core hole our hydrology team drilled. Because they are living specimens, there is no way of telling how long they have been there or from where they originated."

"I'm Owen Yates from *Global News Network*. There is little I remember about my organic chemistry classes when I was in college, but something about optical isomerism in amino acids has stuck in my memory. Please don't explain it all to me since I never understood it the first time." The people in the Octagon Theatre watching the live transmission from Mars laughed at Owen's humour even though it was recorded. "My question, though, does concern that principle. My takeaway at the time was all living organisms on Earth produced the same isomer in life processes. I think it was the left-handed variety... the laevo amino acids." The video in a box in the upper left-hand side of the big screen revealed the real-life Owen sitting in the front row of the Octagon Theatre and blushing. "The one thing I do clearly remember from those lectures was that whatever the proper orientation of the isomer, it was a dead giveaway of Earthly life. My professor even mentioned that one of the most interesting questions to ask if we ever did find extra-terrestrial life would be whether or not the alien life followed that same convention. Well, I am thankful to be able to ask just that question today. Can any of you tell me whether or not you have looked into this isomerism and what you have found?"

The camera zoomed in on Nigella's face. She obviously had had a chuckle at Owen's expense. "First of all, Mr Yates, congratulations on surviving your undergraduate organic chemistry course. Second of all, congratulations on remembering the basics of some rather fascinating chemistry. I will not bore five billion people with the details of that matter, but the thrust of your question is excellent... one of the most fundamental questions we can ask when analysing alien life forms. We have conducted the tests that you refer to. These tests look at which enantiomers – that is which mirror image of the same molecules – the chemical process favours with this alien variety of life. Yes, you did remember correctly, Mr Yates: Earthly organisms ALL produce the laevo version of amino acids coded by their DNA. We have examined that with our Martian critters and interestingly enough, they do the same, that is, produce all laevo amino acids. What we do not know is whether or not this is strictly coincidental. After all, we could toss a coin once each on Earth, Mars and Venus and come up with three heads, but that doesn't mean the outcomes are in any way related."

"Hello. I am Jae Hwa Park of the *Korea News Agency*. You have stated that the microorganisms were discovered some 800 metres below the surface. Obviously, the temperatures at that depth would most likely allow water to remain in liquid form, yes? Also, at that depth, there would be no sunlight penetrating and probably little thermal heat from the planet's interior. This would seem to indicate that photosynthesis was impossible there. Could you please comment on my conjecture here and tell us how these organisms obtain food?"

"What an excellent question, Jae Hwa. I will tackle your question." Professor Henning's face filled the big screen in the Octagon Theatre. "As for your conjecture, the temperatures found at this depth have remained around 16 degrees Celsius. We, of course, will monitor that throughout a Martian year to see if there is variation. Our geology team, in conjunction with the biology team, agree that most likely water remains in liquid form all year. I only say that because though these creatures could hibernate part of an annual cycle, we are actually in late autumn here near Alpha Colony in Mars seasons. Your speculation on the lack of sunlight is exactly right – there is no light at this depth within the Martian crust. As for internal heat, Mars does not have an active core as does Earth, but the temperature still rises with depth.

"Now then, your question on an energy source is fascinating. Most life on Earth is supported by photosynthesis using carbon dioxide from Earth's atmosphere, which is combined with water and produces the simple sugar glucose. That process uses chlorophyll as a catalyst and is driven by the sun's energy. Photosynthesis is the basis for nearly all life on Earth, but our little Martian creatures cannot use it because of the absence of light. We are confident they utilise a chemosynthetic chemical pathway to power life processes.

"Fortunately, we have some excellent examples of this since there are a variety of Earth-side chemosynthetic bacteria and animals that transform carbon and other inorganics into organic molecules using hydrogen sulphide or methane as their energy source. Organisms employing these processes were originally discovered in deep-sea hydrothermal vents some 60 or 70 years ago on Earth. After these life forms were categorised as sulphur-loving creatures, researchers started looking in places other than deep-sea vents. Today we know of many creatures found in sulphur-rich environments in decaying matter, in salt marshes near active lava vents... In all cases, these life forms thrive using hydrogen sulphide chemosynthesis. There are other chemical pathways, and we are still exploring the particulars of these Martian creatures, but the food production mechanism is certainly other-worldly."

"Karishma Patel of the *India Times*. Do these microorganisms threaten contamination or risk to life either there on Mars or back here on Earth?"

Dr Tong Yigong tapped the microphone in front of him. "I will take that question if you don't mind, Parisa. We have carried out proper procedures through every collection, transportation and laboratory procedure conducted to date. I can happily assure you that the biology team... actually, all the science teams at Alpha Colony strictly abide by every regulation governing us. You may be well aware of the fact that our regulations mimic the highest Earth-standards for biological research. Our biological containment levels are designated PC1, PC 2, PC 3 and PC 4. PC1 is basically the level we would all work at in an office – please clean your teacup at the end of the day."

There was a wave of soft laughter in the theatre.

"Because at this point, we are in the early days of learning about our Martian microorganisms, we are following PC 4 regulations which are the highest level of containment. These regulations are quite stringent and follow all the same protocols found in Earth-based PC 4 laboratories. These requirements include practices such as ventilating all laboratories and airlocks independently, filtering supply and exhaust air using HEPA filters, providing water supplies separated from the rest of the colony, as well as employing double-ended autoclaves to sterilise all equipment. We are fortunate in that we already have our biological laboratories in a separate dome from the rest of the colony, and that has allowed us to easily maintain PC4 requirements from the start. You can read the biological hazard regulations under which we are operating in total on Skynet 4. As for any possibility of Earthly contamination, I can assure you there is zero chance of that happening. There are somewhere between 80 and 150 million kilometres of space vacuum between here and there that guarantees that."

Professor Henning nodded her head and spoke into the microphone. "We will take one more question."

"I am Blaire Dawson, *British Broadcasting Company*. At this point, can you make any statement concerning the possibility that these microorganisms have – or could – evolve into any higher life forms. I wonder if we should now be looking for maybe Martian insects or Martian foxes or anything like that up there."

Henning looked at the USC professor, Scott Salazar. "Could you tackle this question, Scott."

"Thank you for that, Ms Dawson. Regrettably, we haven't seen any insects or foxes up here, at least not yet." Again, there were laughs throughout the theatre. "Your question is a good one though, but we simply have no indication that that has happened. I don't know how well you know your Martian geology, meteorology or history, but frankly, the conditions here have not been favourable to any evolutionary path like that for billions of years. Our little friends found in the well the other week may well have evolutionary roots back three-plus billion years, but they simply don't seem to have had the chance to evolve much past where they are today. It does boggle the mind to think they have gone on for billions of years just surviving underground this way, but right now we have no indication they could have evolved into more derived life forms. I am sorry, Ms Dawson, but we have no evidence of any more complex forms of alien life having ever evolved on Mars."

DAN CHURACH

PART FOUR

"Never doubt that a small group of thoughtful, concerned citizens can change the world. Indeed, it is the only thing that ever has."

— *Margaret Mead*

52

Tuesday, 20 September; Metro Precinct Station, Washington DC

"Hey, boss. I wanted to catch you before you go home." Maggie peeked her head through his doorway.

"Before I go home – you're dreaming, Patton! I may not get home tonight!"

"I know, I know... I just thought it's a crazy day. Obviously, you heard the press conference this morning... or at least heard about it. It just seems that kind of makes anything we face rather insignificant. I mean life on Mars... alien life on another planet."

"Patton, get a hold of yourself. You're going on about finding life on Mars... hell, do we have any intelligent life in Washington? I mean you're either a cop, or you're not? NOTHING makes what we do insignificant. Besides that, this O'Keefe-Bidwill case is in no way insignificant. Hell, now that we're onto this MacLucas creep, who freaking knows where it leads. I'm starting to wonder if the three of them are somehow involved with what's going on in the Eights movement. I mean, kids killing themselves left and right. Our two teenage suspects trying to hack into SAMs and data bands... now this freaking MacLucas guy and his little marketing misdemeanour... Misdemeanour my ass!"

"That's why I'm here, sir." Maggie sounded less apologetic

now. "I am a cop, and I'm happy to work on this all night if that's what it takes. We did get some results back from the search warrant, though Chandra is still trying to decipher exactly what we have. There are several interesting things here. Bradshaw is still following up on it, but he will check in with us in a bit. He and Officer Kelly are bringing O'Keefe and Bidwill back in. We didn't mean to do that without asking, but you were out of your office, and we thought we'd better be a bit proactive here."

"As well you should be, Patton! So, if you're bringing them in, you must have found something. D'ya think we can shake something more out of them? Don't keep me in suspense here... what the hell did you find out so far?"

"Well, time is an issue here. We thought we'd better bring them in immediately because we need to talk with them before MacLucas does."

"That makes perfectly good sense, but don't tell me the court order didn't jam up their SAMs and keep them from communicating that, at least."

"Yeah, yeah – SAMs are jammed for MacLucas as well as Leister, but the kids don't have SAMs."

"They can still see him in person."

"For sure, but we know they were in school today. That said, I think we're clear up until now. If they communicated at all, it wasn't face-to-face. Listen, we're finding some very weird stuff, boss. It seems that MacLucas's wife's name keeps popping up in his computer records. We keep seeing Professor Katlin MacLucas this, Professor Katlin MacLucas that... she plays a bigger role in his company – the Sunrise Marketing Company – than you'd think someone with a fulltime professorship would have."

"How's that?"

"Well, remember that he told us Steve Leister was now his IT Director."

"Yep."

"Well, for an IT director, he spends a lot of time meeting with Mrs MacLucas."

"Maybe they're doing the dirty deed..."

"No, no... I don't think that's what's happening... at least not from what we've found so far. Chandra will be digging into this stuff for days I imagine, but just looking at calendar schedules, they are using some of that high-level psycho-mumbo-jumbo way more than you would think."

"...and that bastard MacLucas – the father – says his wife has nothing to do with the business... NOTHING!" Grimms pounded his fist on his desk. "Well, she's a psychologist, for god's sake. I mean hell, marketing... ain't that all about making people do freaking stuff that they don't really want to do?" He knew the answer was obvious.

"Yeah! Like, have your customer buy your product. Well sure, boss, but how does that involve the two boys?"

"Or the Eights for that matter?"

She looked at him and grimaced. "Why would a marketing firm selling soap and cars include two high school kids in half their IT meetings. Something just ain't right here, boss."

A light flashed on Grimms' desk. "Looks like Bradshaw and Kelly have the boys here now. Let's go have a chat with them."

Maggie stood up and turned toward the door.

"And Patton... I'm gonna really turn the heat up on these two... just play along."

* * *

"Good afternoon, fellows... or should I say good evening? It is getting later than I thought." Grimms gestured to Kelly by tilting his head towards the doorway, and the young officer pulled the door of the interview room closed behind him. Patton and Bradshaw sat with Grimms across the table from the two boys. "I didn't think we'd be seeing you again so soon."

Neither boy responded.

"What can you tell me about William MacLucas?"

The boys were silent.

"O'Keefe, either cooperate, or we just might put you in lockup for a few days to let you think about it. How do you know MacLucas?"

"Umm... he's our basketball coach."

Maggie followed up. "And you, Mr Bidwill?"

"Same... my basketball coach."

"But your parents and your school records indicate you only played basketball in ninth and tenth grade. You're both seniors now, yes?"

Bidwill's head bobbed yes as he looked at O'Keefe. The second boy nodded too.

"Well now isn't that interesting. Don't you think it's unusual to be visiting your old basketball coach two years after you stopped playing on his team?"

Both boys sat there with stark expressions on their faces. To Grimms, it was apparent they had no idea just what the police knew and where they wanted to go with the interview. He leaned back in the chair and stretched his arms behind his head. "Okay... let's try a bit of a different approach here. We know you see MacLucas regularly." He looked towards his colleague. "Maggie..."

She flipped through her notebook. "Friday, September 2 after school, Sunday, August 28 in the afternoon, Wednesday, August 24 in the evening, Saturday, August 20 in the evening, Saturday, August 20 in the morning, Tuesday, August 16 after school... Do you want me to go on, sarge?"

"Well, I don't know... do we need to go on? I think Detective Patton can go back quite a long way here."

"At least a year, sarge."

Grimms stared at the boys, his face stern. "You must be really good friends with MacLucas, right?"

"Yes, sir." Bidwill was quick to answer.

"Well, tell me this, Mr Bidwill. MacLucas is a 54-year-old businessman. You and your sidekick here are 17-year-old high school kids. You claim that you're such good friends with MacLucas that you are both getting together a couple of times a week... regularly. How's that work out in the social circles. Do all your mates at Georgetown Academy have friends three times their age? Do you reckon all MacLucas's business colleagues pal around with high school kids? Do you see the problem I'm having here? I'm just having difficulty working out how this old-man-high-school-kid friendship works."

Silence.

Maggie knew exactly what direction they needed to steer this interrogation. "Are you two boys an item? Maybe boyfriends..."

"WHAT? No way!"

"Maybe the two of you would put on little performances for MacLucas... Are you maybe a bit embarrassed about any sexual matters with MacLucas?"

"NO!" O'Keefe nearly jumped from his chair. "It ain't like that at all! Dylan and I ain't gay, man... we ain't homos! Mr MacLucas doesn't get into sex with us... sex with boys... it's

349

NOTHING like that."

"Nothing like that..." Bidwill's voice trailed off as he tried for all the world to maintain a blank expression. His attempt failed, and a tear appeared in the corner of one eye and started rolling down onto his cheek.

Grimms chimed in, "Looks like you hit a sore spot, detective. You both seem pretty defensive here. Besides, it's the 21st century now, and homosexuality is just fine... it's accepted by the community, you know."

"We ain't gay, man!" This time Bidwill raised his voice.

"Damn, this seems like a touchy subject with both of you." Grimms leaned forward. "You know, somehow you both seem to be wary of us digging too deep. Did Detectives Patton and Bradshaw maybe find something you didn't want them to find? Paedophilia is a whole different story. I can't believe that you don't know that paedophilia is against the law in DC as well as every state in the country. I assume you know full well that MacLucas will burn for this, don't you?"

O'Keefe was defiant. "You know, there's gotta be a law against this. You can't just make stuff up and throw it at us. I want a lawyer... we want lawyers."

"We can do that, no problems... Just let me ask you one last question here. Do you know Mr Steve Leister?"

"Come on, Bradley..."

"Shut up, Dylan."

"Do you have something you want to tell us, Mr Bidwill? If you like, we can take O'Keefe to another room. You don't have to both sit here together, you know."

"All right, all right... We know Steve... Mr Leister." Grimms was almost surprised that O'Keefe answered and not Bidwill. "He's kind of like... like our boss."

Bingo! The word screamed out in Grimms' head. "Your boss? Now, what's that all about? You two are high school students. You don't list any part-time jobs with the Georgetown Academy office. Your folks never mentioned that their kids had jobs."

"It's only part-time."

"Umm, part-time." Maggie turned a page in her notebook, more for show than needing to read it. "Let's see... Bradley O'Keefe account balance $1,450,350... Dylan Bidwill account balance $1,250,200... You know, I had part-time jobs in high school. I think I used to get like fifteen dollars an hour at a burger place in my hometown. I might have done even better in college – I got maybe twenty or twenty-two bucks an hour working in the library... must have been inflation. Funny thing though, I just couldn't save much money from my part-time job. Can you guys tell me how you managed to save over a million dollars? A MILLION FREAKING DOLLARS?"

53

Wednesday, 21 September; Gale Crater Outpost, Mars

"The Earth-side press is going absolutely crazy with this."

"And you are surprised why?" Misha looked at him. "I think you've been living up here too long, Joe. A story like this is not as much science as it is social. This news will rip through parliaments and legislatures like a wildfire. Wait until you start getting the religious zealots reacting to all this. You remember how crazy it all got when the first SAMs started getting implanted? That was the 'devil-on-earth' movement that brought down several governments in Europe and the States."

"Bloody hell... That was all bat-shit crazy in Australia. That's all we heard – the 666 chip, the 'number of the beast' chip... Boy, we went through several years of that stuff down under. As far as I am concerned, I could give you a hundred reasons to oppose SAMs, but the devil isn't one of them." Lochie shook his head.

"Well, I know you're both correct. It's just that the news feeds have been going off their rockers from the second the press conference ended."

"I thought the crazies were marching in 'end-of-the-world' demonstrations because of the coming of *Thánatos*." Keegan threw his arms over his head.

Joe grimaced. "SAMs, *Thánatos* protests, now the discovery of alien life somehow making humanity even crazier! I know I've been off that planet for a long, long time, and this just reaffirms my intention of never going back there."

Lochie pulled on one ear. "You know, coming at this from the other side, I am the newest bloke here. I just left Earth about nine or ten months ago. I definitely agree with what Misha is saying here. We had to expect this sort of reaction. Let's just hope some clear heads prevail."

"For how long, Lochie? Until a week or ten days from now when we follow-up with the alien artifact announcements?" Misha slapped her palm against her forehead.

"Jesus, Misha... like it or not, we are all smack in the middle of this now. Worse yet, we're kind of in a damned-if-we-do, damned-if-we-don't situation. I saw a string of reports and comments concerning Professor Scott Salazar's response last night. Did he lie?"

"You lost me there, mate. Lie?"

"Keegan... you watched the transmission. Salazar said 'we

have no evidence of any intelligent alien life on Mars' and I think that's pretty much his exact words."

Misha interrupted, "I think he specifically said no evidence of any advanced alien life HAVING EVOLVED on Mars. Certainly, we all agree that is the truth, don't we?"

"Well sure, I know WE all agree with Salazar's statement, but I'd bet you a trillion Martian dollars that the press – or most certainly the bloke in the street – won't interpret it that way. I reckon Salazar's comment is going to make our job even more difficult."

"I think I'd go along with you, Lochie, and double your bet with another trillion Martians dollars. Of course, it's a good thing there is nothing like a Martian dollar, so we haven't much to lose, do we?" Siti laughed. "Frankly, I don't think it matters one way or the other what they said last night or what we say in the next week or two. If you think our mates back on Mother Earth went crazy last night, I reckon our announcement of INTELLIGENT ALIEN LIFE will multiply the insanity a thousand-fold."

* * *

"Nigella is in transit on the MRT as we speak here, so she will be back in another thirty-six hours or so. We still need to push ourselves." Misha brushed a strand of hair away from her eyes. "We'll keep rotating through our two-man-team-per-day surface excursions and just hope we find more. No matter, we need to unravel anything that the artifacts we have might tell us. Who wants to go first on updates today?"

"I will." Arya volunteered. "I've made some headway – actually, I think I've made a lot of headway. Just like any case, the most difficult part in solving a mystery is to first lift a corner and peek inside. Once you have some idea as to what your mystery might be, you can refine whatever methods you may need to more fully reveal what is there. I'm about 99% certain I have at least opened the metaphorical lid enough to know that both the transparent disks and the five cubes are some sort of memory devices. In the good old days, you might have thought of them as fancy solid-state drives. In more recent times they'd be more like quantum storage dumps. Whatever, I think these are a variation of our older 5D storage modules."

Keegan tugged on his ear. "Of course, I've heard of the 5D storage model, but I haven't a clue how that works, Arya. Can you give us some idea of how that works?"

"Don't fret – I won't leave you hanging, Keegan. The 5D storage process is a good one. It's been around for fifty years or so, and we went through a phase with it twenty-five or thirty years ago... that was all before quantum storage techniques came into play. It's fairly simple, and the numbers on it are eye-popping. For starters, we estimate that 5D storage can hold material safely for 13 or 14 billion years. I told you we'd be eye-popping here – that's BILLION YEARS. And the quantity of data is also amazing... something the size of the transparent disks we have found here could probably hold something like 500 to 600 terabytes of data. I have difficulty trying to put all of this into everyday terms."

"Well humour us, Arya... put that into everyday terms that even an average-intelligence, non-nerdy geologist could understand."

Arya snickered. "I know you aren't referring to yourself, Keegan, since you are way more than average intelligence. Besides that, could you please stop calling me nerdy?"

They all laughed at Arya's jest.

"These aren't everyday terms, but in our circle of academic-types here, I have no doubt this will make sense. As for time... consider for a moment that you geo folks tell us the age of the universe is the over-ten-billion years at this point. we're talking some long-term storage solutions here." Arya tilted his head as he stared at Keegan. "Hell... you, Misha, Lochie... you're all geologists. If anyone deals in BILLIONS of years, that would fall smack under the category of a geologist's normal day, right?"

"All right... I'll concede that to you." Keegan nodded his head. "Your reference to 13-or-14-billion years is astounding but makes sense. But 500 or 600 terabytes... just how the hell much information is that?"

Arya continued, "The best comparison that I have heard of is the United States Library of Congress. I know that is kind of outdated now with the rest of the world passing it by, but the Library of Congress contains some 30 or 40 terabytes of data. Now, remember, the 'tera' prefix is 10^{12} or a trillion, so we're talking 30 or 40 trillion! That means one of these disks," Arya held one in front of his face, "could contain ALL the books in the Library of Congress somewhere between twelve and twenty times over!"

"Wow! That IS eye-popping. How do they do that?" Now Joe's interest was piqued.

"I'll give you the basics... They use something like fused quartz, which coincidentally we have here in this disk, and then take advantage of the fact that it is birefringent." Arya held a disk up and squinted as though he was trying to see if anyone knew the term. "Well, Siti's knowing nod tells me that she understands that word, but I can see by the looks on the rest of your faces that you are drawing a blank on the concept of birefringence."

"I'm glad to see you read faces well, Arya." Joe expression was quizzical.

"I'm not going to beat the physics to death here, but birefringence is an optical property of any transparent, glass-like material. This characteristic just means the refractive properties of the substance depend on two parameters: the angle of entry and the polarization of light. Now I know you are all aware of the basics of a lens... as light passes through it, the curvature of the surface causes the light wave to bend. If you put your eye at the focus, you get to see the image magnified. So far, so good?" He was encouraged by nodding heads.

"Certain materials – like fused quartz – will refract or bend specific wavelengths more than once. That said, I have to apply some black box, fairy-tale magic here because the physics is beyond my understanding. I do know this though – the same beam of light can contain 3, 4, 5 or even more different sets of data. If you know what you're doing – and I don't as yet – you can read the beams from different angles using different wavelengths and different polarizations and eventually decode all the data contained therein.

"Bear with me here... Remember, we're using optical coding with a simple string of ones and zeros that are coded into very short wavelengths of electromagnetic energy, basically into light. Now, this new term you are hearing, birefringent, simply means that unlike a lens that bends light once, birefringent materials can bend light two, three, four times. This all depends on either the wavelength or polarization of the light we are using. What really has me stumped here is that our aliens may have developed a way to make 6D or 7D or who-knows-how-many-D storage, all based on this multitude of layers of data in the same beam of light. I have more work to do to decipher this, but I am confident I'm on the right track. For that matter, I reckon decoding the disks might be easier because disk mechanics and geometry is what we used for this on Earth."

"Mechanics, geometry?" Lochie didn't follow.

"I only mean the way we physically wrote and then read the data back home is using a spinning disk and aiming lasers at it. If the aliens have done something similar, then I know I'm on the right track, and my AI can definitely help out. Now the cube has me stumped at this point for the simple reason that we don't 'spin' cubes. Never fear — we'll figure that out too." Arya looked at his colleagues' faces and was reassured that his explanation satisfied them enough that they believed he would figure out how to read the multiple-dimension storage systems.

"How about you, Siti? Anything new?"

"Not exactly, Misha. I can only analyse these materials so much. I'm still trying to work out the fundamental difference between the darker coloured medallions and the transparent disks. I understand what Arya is saying here, but from my chemist's point of view, I'm getting no sense of data being there — in the medallions, that is — at this point. So far, we have had zero success with bringing any data out if it is stored there. I trust Arya though, and his gut tells him he's on the right track. Just keep looking, my friend... I just can't believe the transparent disks are merely some sort of alien Christmas tree ornaments."

54

Wednesday, 21 September; Forrest Hall, University of Western Australia, Perth, Western Australia

"This is going to be a first — I get to stand back here and watch you go to work."

"Oh, Nicolás... I almost feel like I was on a free ride in

Shanghai, but I know much of what I gained will come through over the next months. Anyway, I'm here, so I'm happy to be contributing to our *GNN Skynet News Hour* this evening... well, morning here in Perth. It does get confusing, but with the twelve-hour time difference, that's just how it works out."

"I checked in with my office when we woke up. Frankly, so many of the reactions here on Earth to the news of alien life are easily predicted, but a lot are quite surprising. The fighting in Eastern Europe never skipped a beat. It's a good thing the newly discovered life is 60-some million miles away from us. If not, we Earthlings might have just exterminated it this morning."

"Nicolás! Can't you be a bit more positive?"

"Pardon my scepticism, honey."

She made a funny face at him as she heard her GNN control room speak to her through her earpiece. "One minute, Sunlyn."

She kissed him. "I'll be back in a few minutes and then maybe we can get some brunch." Sunlyn walked to the spot the team had marked with the crystal blue Swan River behind her. A makeup fellow quickly dabbed at her face with a cotton ball.

"Four... three... two... one..." He dropped his arm, and the GNN music filled their earpieces.

"This is the *GNN Skynet News Hour*. I'm your host, Dennis LaPlante. The reaction to the first discovery of alien life away from Earth has been fast and furious since its announcement this morning here in Washington. We will speak with our correspondents around the globe during our *Skynet News Hour* tonight, and I will start first with Sunlyn Singh on assignment in Perth, Western Australia. Sunlyn, I realise it is already Monday morning there in Perth since the press conference transmission occurred Sunday night, Western Australia time. Tell us, what was the mood like in the Octagon Theatre amongst the invited scientists and your journalist colleagues?"

"The electricity running through the audience was undeniable, Dennis. Amazingly enough, the rumour mill had been telling us that the announcement of the discovery of alien life was imminent. However, it still seemed to be just a rumour until Professor Parisa Henning confirmed it. Her words will surely live on in billions of memories forever. I believe I speak for many in attendance and around the world last night when I say that the impact of the announcement was not at all dampened by its anticipation."

The GNN broadcast cut away, and a video replay of Professor Henning's astonishing announcement appeared. "Let me start by ending... ending the rumours we have heard about that are being whispered all over Earth. I can confirm tonight that we have discovered life here on Mars."

The broadcast again returned live to Sunlyn. "I am certain that no one in that room, no one around the globe, will ever forget where they were when they heard that statement. Frankly, most of what came after the announcement seemed almost insignificant. I don't say that to trivialise the work ahead and the challenge to scientists here on Earth and there on Mars. For that matter, the tasks our politicians and religious leaders face in the aftermath of the announcement is monumental. I have been covering the news for nearly twenty years, and frankly, in my opinion, no story even approaches the enormity of this discovery."

"And can you tell us how the people of Perth seem to be reacting to the news, Sunlyn?"

"I can, Dennis. We took a crew into the city just an hour or two earlier to get the reaction from West Australians on their way to work this morning..." Her face dissolved into a video recorded scene from the downtown mall area in Perth's Central Business District. One-by-one faces appeared with Sunlyn's voice off-camera asking them what they thought of the previous night's announcement.

A young man smiled in the morning sunlight. "Best thing ever, mate – a real ripper. My partner and I celebrated in Northbridge into the wee hours this morning."

"What were you celebrating?" Sunlyn extended a microphone into the picture.

"Hey, we're not all alone. I mean you have to wonder lately the way things are going. Finding Martian life just means that maybe we have a chance... maybe we can survive whatever it is we're going through as a world right now."

A middle-aged woman with a much more serious look faded into camera view. Sunlyn asked, "Hello madam. How did you react to the announcement last night?"

"My husband and I went to church. Our local parish had an unscheduled midnight mass and – to our surprise – the church was absolutely packed. We haven't seen that many people in church before even on Christmas Eve at the midnight mass."

Sunlyn next asked a businessman dressed in a coat and tie what he thought of last night's announcement. "My company is a medical care provider, and we're anxious to explore ways we can use this new discovery to develop better outcomes for patients. With an entirely new life form and maybe even totally new biology, who knows what that can mean to our pharmaceutical industry? There are lots of breakthroughs to be had here... lots of money to be made. I reckon the sky is the limit."

Sunlyn's face filled the image, "That's just a few of the Perthites we have spoken to this morning. I can assure you though that not everyone was so overwhelmed by it all." The camera panned to the side and zoomed to three young people who were possibly in their early-to-mid teens. All three lay on the sidewalk, one girl propped up against a rubbish bin and the other two leaning on her. "We tried to talk with these young people, but they either didn't wish to respond or else were unable to answer our questions. Back to you, Dennis."

* * *

Nicolás put his arm around her and gave her a kiss on the cheek. "I like watching you work, hon."

"And I like getting a big Nicolás kiss before I go on air and another right after I get off air." Sunlyn pulled out her earpiece and wiped the some of the excessive on-camera makeup from her face. Now I think we are meant to catch up with the others at, "she looked at a piece of paper she had pulled from her blouse, *'Eros.'* That is Kylie's recommendation, so I have no doubt it will be a good choice. It must be a little café or coffee shop, and, from what she said, it's not far from here."

"Can we walk?"

"I think we can..."

55

Wednesday, 21 September; Metro Precinct Station
Interview Rooms, Washington DC

"Okay, we're all set now, right?"

"We are, boss." Maggie had high hopes they were finally going to get to the bottom of this today. "What's the plan?"

"Well, for starters, the three of us will stick together during the interrogations. You've got Mrs MacLucas waiting in interview room one and Leister in room two, yes?"

"That's it, Harry."

"How long have they been cooling?" Grimms looked at the wall clock.

"Leister maybe forty-five minutes and MacLucas maybe half an hour."

"Okay... We'll work Leister first and let the professor think about things a bit more. Any question on how we're playing this."

"No questions at all, boss – we'll use the sex card again... it sure has worked well so far..." Maggie answered him as Bradshaw nodded his head.

* * *

Harry was the last one in, closed the door of interview room two and stood in front of the suspect. "Mr Leister... sorry if we kept you waiting. We can get this over with fairly quickly, I'm sure. I'm Detective Grimms." He dropped his badge on the table and tapped it a few inches towards the suspect without making any effort to actually show it to him. "These are my partners Patton and Bradshaw." All three of them sat across from Leister. "Now I imagine you know exactly why we have you here, right?"

"Actually, no, I don't. I have no idea why I'm here."

"Well, it's just a little thing here about you hacking into SAMs of some of your customers, some of Sunrise Marketing's customers. Umm..." He referred to his notebook. "...about a thousand of them. Hey, that's pretty clever that you could target certain SAMs. So, what were you doing, Leister, trying to persuade them to shop at your store?"

"Look, that's all over now. I wasn't ever involved anyway. Mr MacLucas pleaded on that – a misdemeanour, I believe. It was no big deal."

"Yeah, but MacLucas tells us he was saving YOUR ass."

"Nah, it's not like that."

"Well if it wasn't you, are you telling us that MacLucas knows how to hack into specific SAMs? I know he's a bright man, but I didn't know he was an IT whiz, too."

"No, no... he couldn't do that."

"Professor MacLucas then? It must be the Mrs..."

MacLucas looked at him. "Huh?"

"You and she must have had a thing going, yes? Maybe you still do?"

"No man, no!" Leister was obviously feeling flustered.

"From what we found on the other fellow – Briers, Lee Briers – maybe he was the mastermind."

"Ah, come on... if you went through the trouble of learning all that, you'd have to know Briers was basically a coffee boy. Bill let him go right after the big stink with the police a few years ago."

Grimms raised his voice. "Well listen up, Leister. Something's just not making any god damned sense here. It wasn't you, wasn't the professor, wasn't MacLucas... Ah, okay then, must have been O'Keefe and Bidwill. We know they're both on the payroll, and we know they both are some kind of technical geniuses, so it must have been them."

"No way, man! That was two years ago, it couldn't have been them... not then, for sure..." Leister knew he lost his cool as soon as he said it. He looked down at the table and awaited whatever was coming next.

"It couldn't have been them... THEN. Tell me, Mr Leister, could it be them NOW? We know O'Keefe and Bidwill are getting paid for something – getting paid BIG BUCKS for something. Can you tell us what that might be?"

"I don't know. I just do the books for Sunrise Marketing Company. I don't know what Mr MacLucas pays them for or how much he pays them. Hell, they're only kids."

"You do the books, and you don't know how much he pays them? That's rather interesting, Leister."

"I think Mr MacLucas just tries to help them out... pays them a few bucks under the table."

"A few bucks under the table... fascinating." Maggie knew it was time to go into her act. She pulled her notebook out and paged through several sheets, making sure Leister watched every turn of the pages. "Are you pretty good at what you do, Mr Leister? Are you pretty good with the computers?"

"I hope so."

"Maybe the best computer guy at Sunrise Marketing."

"Come on, that's a silly question. Mr MacLucas is the owner, and he sure thinks I'm the best man for the job. That's why he made me Head of IT."

"Humm..." She again looked down at her notes. "You know Mr Leister, when we served the search warrant and went through those books you've done such a good job with, we couldn't help but notice you're bringing in some $325,000 a year for your Head of IT position. Is that about right? You figure you make about $325,000 a year?"

"Yes, that's seems accurate. I mean if Mr Lucas puts me on another job, we have an understanding that I could get a bit more, but that's my salary as it stands right now."

"Yeah, I thought so. Well, you must obviously know that O'Keefe and Bidwill are actually on the payroll, not just getting something under the table, as you say. Do you have any recollection of how much they make a year?" She knew exactly the amounts that Lenny Chandra found in the spreadsheets he had gone through.

"Ah... it should be there in the records, but maybe ten or twelve thousand, that's a year."

"That's thousands of dollars, yes?"

"Yes, yes – ten or twelve thousand dollars."

"Humm..." Maggie looked up from her notes, knowing she had him exactly where she wanted him. "You know Mr Leister, we severed a warrant on both of them and their folks last week. You might find it interesting that we found they both had secret bank accounts. You also might be as curious as us as to how they are making a bit more than the ten or twelve thousand you referred to..."

"Maybe they have another job, flipping burgers or something."

"Maybe Mr Leister, but it must be one hell of a burger place. It seems that they have accumulated... let's see..." She again stared at her notebook and read from it. "Bidwill has, umm... $1,250,200 in his account and O'Keefe has... $1,450,350 in his. Gee, if MacLucas is paying them that much off the books, maybe he should think about eliminating your salary and hiring the two of them as the Heads of IT, don't you think?"

Leister swallowed hard and reached for the glass of water.

* * *

The three of them entered interview room one and quickly sat across from the professor. "Hello, professor, nice to finally meet you. I'm Grimms, and this is Patton and Bradshaw. I trust we haven't kept you too long?"

Her eyes rolled to the ceiling as if to say, 'it's about time.' "Detective, I should be prepping for a lecture I have to give this afternoon. I hope this won't take too long."

"So sorry about that, Mrs MacLucas." Grimms used the back of his hand to rub his cheek. "I apologise, I should address you as Professor MacLucas. I trust we can clear this up pretty quickly, Professor. Just help us understand what's going on here, and we can get you on your way before you know it. Now then... How long have you and Mr MacLucas been married?"

"It'll be twenty-eight years this year... married in 2016." She unconsciously ran her right hand over her wedding ring.

"Now I hate to be so direct, Professor MacLucas, but I know you need to get back to campus, so I'll try to speed things up here and get straight to the point." Grimms looked her right in the eyes. "Has your husband always been interested in young boys? I mean, interested in doing things with them... to them..."

"He is NOT interested in young boys, Detective Grimms!" She nearly yelled out her response.

"Okay. Well, young men then... O'Keefe and Bidwill are young men now, not boys... though I don't believe they are eighteen yet."

It was evident that Professor MacLucas's life in the ivory tower of a university campus hadn't prepared her for such DC Police hardball. Her eyes welled up with tears, and her face turned red. "Detective, I have no idea why you're saying these things, but they just are NOT true." She sobbed. "Believe me, I know William, and the last thing he would think about that way would be boys... men... William is as heterosexual as can be, sir!"

"Well, you see, I've got a problem here. I just can't figure out why your husband sees these kids so frequently. I mean, we know he was their coach, but that's a few years back. We also know he must be seeing them at least a couple of times a week, sometimes four or five times a week." He tilted his head towards Maggie.

"I have it here... sorry..." She flipped and flipped... "Here we go... Friday, September 2 after school, Sunday, August 28 in the afternoon, Wednesday, August 24 in the evening, Saturday, August 20 in the morning... I have a lot more here, Professor MacLucas."

"You don't need to read any more of those, Detective. I can explain that."

"So, he DOES see them regularly?" Maggie set her pad down on the table.

"Of course, he sees the boys. We have been friends with them for the past several years. Many of the times you have read there, I would have been at home and saw them too. You must believe me – there is nothing of a sexual nature here. That is not at all what is happening."

Grimms came back to the fore. "I'm really relieved to hear that, Mrs MacLucas. That said, can you enlighten me, please?

Exactly what IS happening?"

"So, like I said, WE like the boys... enjoy their company... both of us. They are very nice kids, very gentlemanly."

"Do you like them more than a million dollars apiece over the past year?"

"A million dollars... what are you talking about?"

"We have found a couple of secret bank accounts for both boys. The accounts were very well hidden, secret Social Security numbers and all... but our forensics team found them anyway. Both boys have been paid well over a million dollars apiece this year, and we have confirmed that it was your husband who paid it."

"Over a million dollars each?" Professor MacLucas's eyes went wide.

56

Wednesday, 21 September; *Eros* Café, Perth, Western Australia

"Wow, the *Eros* Café... methinks this is more than a café. This is such a charming restaurant."

Kylie's face glowed. "Trust me, the food is as beautiful as the surroundings, Sunlyn."

"She's right, I know. I come here every time I have to visit Perth for work."

Nicolás looked at Micky. "What kind of work do you do?"

"I'm a doctor... a surgeon."

"Surgeon... impressive. What kind of surgery?" Owen took

a menu from the waiter.

"Cardiothoracic surgery, though I spend more time teaching now than practising. I'm right in the Camperdown area of Sydney at the Royal Prince Alfred Hospital there, and we are affiliated with the University of Sydney."

"Oh great – that's Kylie's university, yes?"

"Kylie's? I beg your pardon! That's OUR university." Micky laughed.

"And what brings you to Perth?"

"There's a big teaching hospital very near to us right here in this area of the city... Sir Charles Gardiner Hospital. I have several colleagues on staff there, and we have organised trading off certain topics, certain lectures, at one another's university."

Fiona looked down the menu. "So, what's the specialty here at the *Eros* Café, Micky?"

"They have great seafood, fresh out of the Indian Ocean."

* * *

Fiona swallowed her first piece of the mud cake she ordered for dessert. "Yummy. This is great!" She looked at Nicolás's plate. "You ordered the mud cake too. What do you think?"

"Umm... it's fantastic... It's so rich, though, that I fear I might explode!"

"I wonder if there's anything new on reactions to last night's announcement." Micky glanced in Sunlyn's direction.

"Well, people are just waking up in Germany and in the UK about now. It'll be interesting to hear how they are taking it all in Europe."

Owen picked up on his colleague's thought. "Yes, that will be interesting. At least with European time 7 or 8 hours earlier than here, they did have a chance to digest news a bit last evening since the story broke there in the afternoon."

"Have you had any update on *Thánatos*? On what's happening in Siberia, Owen?"

"Funny you should ask. With all the excitement about the Martian announcement, the threat of *Thánatos* has been knocked off the front pages. Amazingly enough, the release of permafrost methane that we heard so much about up in Shanghai last week has just about drifted off into unconsciousness." Owen took a gulp of his coffee. "At least I did get an update this morning. I viewed a holovision report by André Moureaux, the climatology professor we heard several times at the Summit. Considering it's more than two weeks now and the initial impact is long over, you'd have hoped things were settled down. Unfortunately, the seismic activity it triggered has not lessened at all and they had a 7.8 or 7.9 quake along the fault line there yesterday."

"Isn't that bigger than the original quakes that were caused by the impacts?"

His face was grim. "Yes, and that's the problem. Besides the fact that quakes that powerful has them on a tsunami watch, it seems the continuing seismic activity pretty much reinforces the notion that the old faults have now taken on a life of their own. So regrettably, the worry many geologists had that *Thánatos* might kickstart geological activity along those old fractures within the lithosphere has now been confirmed by the increasing seismic instability. Also, this seems to feed the fear that *Thánatos* and these subsequent seismic events might produce the improbable... namely, a clathrate destabilisation event."

"Holy hell... You refer to the Clathrate Gun Hypothesis?" Sunlyn recalled their conversation about just that eventuality.

"Well let's not jump that far just yet. The problem with worrying about the clathrate gun is that it sounds so immediate – pull the trigger, and we all die! The reality of the clathrate gun threat is not the speed, but the inevitability. As you and I spoke earlier, that positive feedback loop was so named because like a gun, once you pull the trigger, it is irreversible. Unlike a gun, however, it isn't instantaneous. The feedback mechanism that begins with methane release leading to more greenhouse effects resulting in greater atmospheric and ocean temperatures is real. The warming atmosphere and ocean lead to the greater release of methane which in turn leads to greater heating and so on. Probably the reason that few ever lost sleep over the hypothesis is that its ultimate outcome is an Earth that heats beyond retrieval in 50 or 75 years rather than 200 years. Our steady march towards a greenhouse hell on Earth has been baked into Mother Earth's future since the beginning of this century now. Things like this just mean it all happens to your kids rather than your grandkids."

"So, you're saying 'why worry', Owen?'" Fiona's expression seemed to shout her concern.

"No, I'm NOT saying that at all." Owen almost sounded offended. "Frankly, that was the most troublesome part of the holovision broadcast I heard. If you recall that Professor Moureaux explained how increased temperatures can disturb the methane hydrates to the point where the gas is released to the atmosphere. Surprise, surprise... it seems that the shaking caused by earthquakes dislodges deposits of clathrates exposing them to warmer conditions. This happens on land where permafrost is torn open and exposed to warmer air and underwater where clathrates can be subjected to contact with warmer seawater. The issue is just how quickly this increased exposure has been because of such violent movement. This catastrophic impact has caused a cascade of events, causing way more methane being released than anyone has even modelled over such a short time."

Fiona shook her head from side to side. "I understand what you're saying and take in your scientific explanation here, Owen, but I can't help but think of the social consequences of it all. You said that maybe the worst consequence is that instead of our grandkids facing the greenhouse hell, it may fall on our kids. As Kylie and I know only too well, I fear the last thing these kids need is another stressor applied to them, either social or environmental."

"That's a big part of my concern. Just how long can we continue to..." Owen waved his hand at all the tables in the restaurant. "...not feel concern for our kids? How long can we ignore the hellish path onto which we point our grandkids?"

Fiona reached under the table and grasped his hand. Owen squeezed her back but continued his emotion-filled news update. "This morning's broadcast also indicates that the steady drumbeat of group suicide seems to be ticking up rather than down. Several hotspots are popping up around the world and Washington, DC, is probably the worst of them all."

Kylie responded to Owen but spoke to them all. "It is not now scientifically correct to draw some causal link between *Thánatos*, the clathrate gun and teen suicide, but it's nearly impossible to think they won't be – or already are – somehow related."

Owen took the last bite of his mud cake. "What a cruel, cosmic joke has been played on us today."

"Please explain, Owen." Fiona leaned back from her dessert.

He tilted his head towards the beautifully etched sign hanging over the front desk and waiters' bench. "The sign... I mean the sign."

Fiona looked up at it and read out loud. "*Eros.*" She looked back at Owen.

"Do you know your Greek gods?"

"Yes, I know my Greek gods well enough to realise that *Eros* was the god of sensual love and desire."

"And *Thánatos* was the Greek god who personified death."

"It's even worse than that, Owen." Kylie interrupted her friend. "To people with a psychology background like Fiona and I have, *Eros* and *Thánatos* are throwbacks to the early days of psychological study. Back at the turn of the last century in the early 1900s, Sigmund Freud proposed an individual's life was a constant struggle between the life instinct and the death instinct. He expounded his thoughts to include the inner battle between the pleasure principle and the pain principle, between the quest for the fulfilment of love and desire and the avoidance of pain and death. He believed we carried out this struggle throughout life and that the 'life instincts' were *Eros* and the 'death instincts' were *Thánatos*."

Sunlyn's expression revealed her melancholy. "My god Kylie, Fiona, Owen... It truly IS a cruel joke that the cosmos has played on us all."

57

Thursday, 22 September; Gale Crater Outpost, Mars

By the time that Joe and Keegan depressurised and cleaned up after their surface excursion, it was nearly time for dinner. The two of them came into the staff room and were greeted by Lochie and Siti.

"How'd you guys do today? Any luck?" Siti knew her question was moot since they surely would have excitedly shared any find over the Surface-Outpost-Communicator.

"Not really. I'm starting to think we might not find anything else before the announcement is scheduled." Joe activated the food synthesiser, and a plate dropped onto the stage.

"The announcement IS scheduled." Misha strode into the room with an empty coffee cup in her hand. "Director Sam Tan wouldn't let us put it off any longer." She looked around the room. "We don't have Arya here yet, and Nigella isn't due back from Alpha Colony until late, so I won't wait to give you the news. The Director has decreed that we will hold our press conference this time next week – 29 September. I tried to push that back, but he was adamant... Chinese this, UN that, Americans the other thing... I assume we all have some clue as to what this announcement will be triggering. My god, just look at how the carryings-on have erupted over the one-celled life discovery back on Earth. I am downright fearful of what an intelligent life announcement will wreak."

"Jeez... even without the intelligent life part, the incidence of kids' mass suicides is reportedly rising steadily." Siti sadly shook her head. "There are massive religious protests spontaneously popping up around the globe – New York, Berlin, Mumbai, Buenos Aries, Auckland..."

"Religious protests?" A quizzical look crossed Keegan's face. "Please tell me how you protest a discovery? It's not like anyone created the newly discovered life... That is, of course, unless these religious types believe their god created it, which would mean they are protesting the exact same deity they profess to worship."

"I got you, Keegan, but I fear the hordes of followers massing in the streets haven't analysed things to that point, at least not yet."

"Breakthrough!" Arya entered excitedly, took one look at his colleagues' faces and shifted gears to a more solemn mood.

"Uh oh ... Do I want to know what I missed here... or not?"

"The boss says we make our announcement to humanity next week... the 29th of September."

"Which boss, Misha?"

"Sam Tan. He's adamant that we just can't put it off any longer. Whatever we have will have to go public then."

"Damn." Arya's face went from concern at going public back to the excitement of what he had found. "I come in here all excited because I think I have made a bit of a breakthrough, but I sure could use more time."

"We could all use more time." Joe grabbed his meal and headed for the table. "Well, don't keep us in suspense – what's the breakthrough?"

"As the story goes, I have some good news, and I have some bad news... The good news is that my hunch about the transparent disks carrying super-compressed data has proven correct. I had to mess with laser wavelengths, laser angles, polarity and whatnot, but it is finally giving me a readout now."

"If it's a physical process we know of, can't you just get it to play."

"It's not that easy, Keegan. This technology works similarly to any storage medium we have used back to magnetic tapes. It's still a binary numeral system, and the only numbers that exist are zero and one. In this case, they are still storing data using little bumps the same way that an old DVD did. In glass or quartz, we refer to these small the bumps as 'nanogratings', kind of like microscopic etchings. Now I mentioned before that this technique of storage can keep data intact for billions of years. That longevity is related to the fact that glass or quartz is that stable, even at temperatures up to 150 or 175 degrees Celsius. These nanogratings change the way light is reflected, and that is what we can read.

"So, as far as the 5D aspect goes, you need to understand that we really aren't warping space or anything like that. You see, when you consider three-dimensional space – X, Y and Z axis – we are all used to that. No doubt you're all experts on birefringence now since we spoke about that yesterday. Recall that is the refractive property of this material that depends on the polarization of light and the direction it is aimed. Because of that, the same pulse of light can refract or reflect in different directions and thus give other data from the same spots and in a sense, multiplying the amount of data stored in the same place. The challenge is to figure out what additives the aliens included in the quartz and how those constituents affect birefringence. I seem to have done that, though I always have to credit my AI partner."

"So, you can read the disks?" Lochie's eyes widened.

"Look, I've worked out the refractive nature of the material the aliens have used here. I can read the disk to the point that I am downloading data including several different images all dependent on the exact angle we view it from and what enhancement of the signal we use. So far, so good. I even can print out the results if I want to... but I still have one big problem."

"And that is?"

"Well, that's the bad news... what I'm getting is gibberish. The readouts, of course, are a never-ending string of zeros and ones, but when we translate it, we just get jibberish. I recognise some of the symbols from what we have categorised so far, but we just don't know the translation. Believe me when I tell you, we – 'we' meaning our staff and the AI program – WILL translate this, but I need a technological miracle... or that metaphorical Rosetta Stone we keep looking for.

"Maybe, just maybe, the cube will reveal our Rosetta Stone.

The problem is, I have not yet worked out a way to read it. It definitely seems to have information in there, but unlike the disks, it doesn't fit our understanding of spinning it to change the orientation of the laser-to-nanogratings orientation. Just this afternoon I might have found a clue to this. I was able to scan enough of the surface layer of the cube to pick up what I think is a diagram. AI is plodding through this as we speak, and I am hoping to make sense of it, possibly before going to sleep tonight. I just need a hint as to how to read – or build a device to read – the data stored there."

58

Thursday, 22 September; Metro Precinct Station, Washington DC

"Close the door, please." As Grimms looked up, he noted Bradshaw and Patton stepping into his office. He laid his reading screen on the desk and gestured towards the chairs across from him.

"Got it, boss." Ryan grabbed one chair as Maggie sat in the other. "You know, I think this is all coming together now."

Grimms allowed a small grin to flash across his face. "I think you're right. You know, I don't want you two to be getting fat heads or anything, but you have played this thing perfectly. I swear we make a great team. I think we did a damned good job at putting the fear of god into all of them."

"Well, it worked, sarge." Maggie settled into her seat. "Chandra milked those computers and their storage for all they were worth. You'll be amazed what he's come up with in the past thirty-six hours or so."

"Well?"

"For starters, Leister was onto some interesting technical findings when MacLucas pleaded to his misdemeanour the other year. He was ingenious enough to figure a couple of things out. First of all, Leister worked out a way to isolate just the particular SAMs he wanted to hack into. By that I mean, he worked out a system to just communicate with the exact group of people he wanted to communicate with while shielding the rest of the population from his signal. Now I say communicate, but the idea was not talking to these people or even allowing them to know he was messing around with their data. The last thing Leister wanted was for anyone to know he had breached the security on people's SAMs. That was his first bit of genius – he developed a method to locate specific targets and then to surreptitiously gain access to them. And they definitely have had some success with that."

"Success? How do you know that?"

"Well, I think one of the earliest experiments – even before the misdemeanour problems – was their initial trial involving MacLucas's own employees at Sunrise Marketing. I mean it only affected a couple of dozen people, but Leister was able to remotely hack into these peoples' SAMs and disable their ability to open locked doors and gain access to computers. It worked very well, but to avoid suspicion, he ended the experiment after only two mornings. At that point, Leister was convinced he had proved the concept."

"Did MacLucas know?"

"Absolutely." Maggie continued. He must have initiated it and asked Leister if he could do it to start with. Of course, they had no trouble covering their tracks since it was in-house, and Leister just put out a memo that there were technical difficulties and he had fixed the problem. No one was the wiser."

"So, where did the legal violations come in?"

"A few months later, MacLucas had a customer who owned an appliance retailer. It was never clear whether or not the client was part of the scam, but somehow Leister worked out a way to gather SAM data from people who came into one of the several stores the client had in DC, Maryland and Virginia. It's not clear if they collected data from the retailer's records, from GPS data or from both sources. Anyway, he then used these data to hack into the SAMs with a nifty little program that would jam the electronics of certain appliances owned by these unsuspecting people when they came home from the retailer's store. If they knew this happened to all customers, they'd have easily worked out that something was wrong, but since individual customers didn't necessarily know each other, the scheme worked for a week or two."

Bradshaw picked up Maggie's story. "In other words, all of a sudden, people looking for a new refrigerator or a new dishwasher went home and – the coincidence of all coincidences – their own refrigerator or dishwasher just stopped working. Now the scheme was brilliant since probably many of these devices were already on the blink when customers went shopping for them. Still, MacLucas and Leister's scam just helped nudge the customers into making a purchasing decision. The retailer's sales went up nearly sixty per cent for the few weeks the plan was in place."

"Yeah, it was pretty much genius!" Maggie threw both her hands up to the ceiling. "Trouble is, a half dozen or so of the customers wound up shopping with friends or relatives, and when these people went home to different households, they all had the same failures. That raised suspicions and enough complaints came in that the original retailer had to defer to a police investigation. Since there was never a direct-line implication of either the retailer or Sunrise Marketing to the home failures, MacLucas agreed that somehow his electronic collection of marketing data from his client's customers list inadvertently caused electronic interference."

"Well, that's crazy... no wonder the cops got involved." Grimms sucked air between his teeth.

"Of course, it's crazy, boss. But MacLucas was bright enough not to fight so hard that someone might actually figure out what was going on. Hell, a misdemeanour and a couple thousand-dollar fines... no big deal. He knew that if he raised too much fuss, someone might realise he had an interstate business which would open the door to the FBI coming in on the case. He settled quickly, and at least it got them off the hook."

Grimms tilted his head. "Smart on his part."

"Exactly." Maggie continued. "I think that MacLucas and Leister laid low for a while and let the dust settle. Well, at least they laid low for long enough that MacLucas fired his one techie, Lee Briers, and promoted Steve Leister to become Head of IT. It seems the 'Head of IT' title had more to do with doubling his salary than it did with any changed responsibility, but we still need to dig a bit more on that. Anyway, that led to Leister's second huge breakthrough."

"The second big breakthrough?" Grimms was intrigued with the story Patton and Bradshaw had patched together here. "Go on, Patton."

"Yes, sarge, that one was to figure out a method to somehow interfere with these targets in a way that would influence their decision process."

"Now wait a minute here... Leister is a computer whiz, not an expert on how human behaviour can be influenced."

Bradshaw continued the story. "Precisely, sir. That's where Katlin MacLucas comes in. I need to caution you that so much of this is way beyond my understanding..."

"Or mine." Maggie interrupted.

"...Nonetheless, Professor Katlin MacLucas's field of

expertise is something called Brain Science and Cognitive Psychology. I didn't just make that up... they're the 'keywords' that Chandra's AI program keeps returning from the analysis of her academic papers. From everything we can find out, that kind of expertise just happens to be precisely what Leister – or the kids, for that matter – needed to know more about to influence people's behaviour. We're still looking into how that was put to use, and I have no doubt Chandra will find what we need with this motivational behaviour stuff."

"So, where'd they go from there?"

"At first, nowhere... at least not for a year or so." Maggie leaned towards Harry's desk. "That's when MacLucas got the brainstorm to get O'Keefe and Bidwill involved."

"Why the kids."

"Two reasons to start with... First of all, they were bright. MacLucas knew that and knew they'd be able to access lots of high school kids." Bradshaw checked his notes. "The second reason was that being school students, they worked on Skynet 2 networks. Just as a refresher here, Skynet 1 has all the public users, Skynet 2 is all educational users, 3 is for government users, 4 for science and research and 5 for commercial. The fact that Sunrise Marketing systems were all commercial and assigned to Skynet 5 meant that authorities would monitor them differently than what they do for the boys on the educational Skynet 2."

"Aha." Grimms rocked back in his chair. "That just might prove to be a freakin brilliant breakthrough."

A look of satisfaction flushed Bradshaw's face. "So, they started with a simple assignment or two for the kids... hack into their classmates' SAMs and stop them from getting into their school lockers."

"You say SAMs, but wouldn't some of those kids have data bands?"

"Very, very few... you're talking Georgetown Academy here – what's that, maybe sixty or seventy grand a year tuition to send your kid to that kind of private high school? Close to a hundred per cent of those kids have SAMs. Still, the hacking would work on data bands, too."

"So, did it? Did it work?"

Now Maggie picked up the story. "Like a charm... three or four times. Trouble is, the administration got suspicious and rather than blow the whole scam, Leister called off any more of those trials.

"And here's where the whole thing went off the rails, boss." Maggie's face became sombre. "MacLucas and Leister were now convinced they were ready to start some behaviour modification experiments. That's when they involved Katlin MacLucas."

"Man, don't tell me this ivory tower academic would have been that keen on making a buck."

"No sir, I don't believe money was her motivation at all. It seems she'd been doing a great deal of research into linking neurophysiology – specifically brain parts that are involved in decision-making – to desired behavioural outcomes. She was successful in getting a couple of dozen papers accepted for publication in the last few years concerning what parts of the brain can cause or alleviate depression. She obviously explained all this to her husband and piqued his interest in a whole different way... He was also very interested in motivational behaviour, though his impetus was a hundred per cent financial. So, at some point, they both must have considered how brain anatomy and physiology could affect mood and how mood could affect behaviour. Now to the academic, this meant how they could stimulate or un-stimulate a certain part of the brain and cause a depressed person to become happy. That's a Nobel Prize-winning discovery."

"But BA BING!" Bradshaw slapped his hand on the desk. "To the businessman, this could also have implications for just how they might be able to stimulate or un-stimulate a certain part of the brain and possibly cause a customer to buy a specific item. Now THAT'S a discovery that leads to making millions upon millions of dollars!"

"Wow!" Grimms was impressed with his junior partners. "You guys got this thing figured out. You know, you've really done a great job here."

"And we have to give Chandra all the credit, too." Maggie volunteered. "But we still don't know how this involved the kids... how this wound up seeing them get millions in their bank accounts..."

59

Friday, 23 September; Gale Crater Outpost, Mars

"I can sum it all up for you in one word." Arya's smile was ear-to-ear.

"Do you want us to beg?" Keegan was on the edge of his seat along with the others.

"Okay, here it is... BINGO!"

"Bingo? All you can say is BINGO!" Misha's curiosity was evident.

Arya stood and walked to the door, briefly disappearing into the hall. He returned, pushing a small cart supporting an unidentifiable piece of equipment. "Presto!"

"Arya, you're driving us all crazy. What's this Rube Goldberg machine you're wheeling in here? Spill the beans already!" Joe spoke for everyone.

"I told you a few days ago that I was having the most difficult time trying to work out how to read the cubes. Hell, we have five of them, and I've been increasingly convinced they are going to open the door to the aliens' language. Well, the good news is that I have worked out how to read them... more correctly, my trusty AI software, and I have worked it out."

Lochie pounded his palm against his forehead. "Please don't tell us there's bad news."

"Well, I won't say bad news, but it is delayed news. AI and I worked out the details late yesterday and spent the night letting the computer feed a design into the 3D printer to come up with the parts. Fortunately, there was still a small role for me since I spent the whole morning trying to work out how to assemble the whole thing. Believe me when I tell you that just because our AI designs something doesn't mean the synthesiser chamber can build all the pieces! Anyway, this is the result of many long hours, and I am thrilled to tell you that this baby can read the cubes. The delayed gratification news is that we just haven't had time to do much reading as yet, though I'm going to give you what we have found so far."

"Congratulations, Arya. I am curious though – how'd you finally work it out?"

"As is often the case, it wound up being easier than I feared, Misha. I was so hung up on moving the object with the data in it rather than moving the reading device. More specifically, we came up with a system of spinning mirrors that could aim and pick up the laser beams and then send the information to the reader's electronic brain. I won't bore you with detail, but it works!"

"Don't keep teasing us, Arya... what have you found?" Siti was so far to the front of her chair she almost defied gravity in not falling to the floor.

"Aha, our number one chemist! It's funny you ask since the first serious information we have pulled out of the cube is the periodic table. This is critical because it allows us to calibrate our machine – by that, I simply mean we KNOW what a periodic table must have on it and as we draw out those data, we can check that we are reading correctly as well as translating them right. We are. Here, my friends, is an image of the alien periodic table, though it may look a bit strange to you since it is 3D." A holographic image appeared in front of the wall at the side of the staff room.

"Oh wow... that is from the alien cube?" Misha was spellbound.

"Wait a minute – before we get to the image, how did the cube project that?" Lochie wondered about the specifics of translating the data from the cube.

"No, no... the cube didn't project it. I'm just using an everyday technoserver that's taking the translated signal from the new reader and feeding it into the projection system we always use. The method of projection is tried and true. Anyway, this is the aliens' funny looking periodic table. It does look a bit strange, Siti, doesn't it?"

"Actually, it doesn't look too strange at all to me. We Earthlings have had 3D periodic tables forever!" Siti teasingly put on the most condescending expression she could manage. "That's a periodic table organised according to each element's electronegativity. You see where elements are projected farther out of the plane of the table which is based on electronegativity. All that means is that each element has a greater or lesser proclivity to grab electrons from elements with which they bond."

"So, it isn't any different?" Arya almost looked disappointed.

"Umm…" She squinted as she studied the image. "No, everything is there and seem to be in the correct place and in the proper orders. Of course, all the names are different… actually unrecognisable. Hey, don't be disappointed. If the aliens somehow had electronegativities different from us, then we'd have a REAL problem. That would mean that either one civilisation does not understand the laws of nature or else that the alien civilisation comes from a totally different universe with different natural laws!"

"Got you." Arya's head nodded towards her. "As for the names, well, of course, they'd be different and the fact that I am using the alien system of symbols, we don't even recognise the alphabet. But it seems all the elements are in their proper places, yes?"

"Yes, though they have more than we do."

"More? What does that mean?" It seemed as though a lightbulb flashed above Nigella's head. "Aha – synthetic elements. I think they have gone beyond the elements we have synthesised, yes?"

Siti nodded in agreement. "That's very much believable since all you need is the technology, a few nuclear reactors or particle accelerators… I will have a much more detailed look at that after we finish here. Anything else, Arya?"

"Oh yeah – glad you asked, Siti. Look, this is definitely a step in the right direction, since – even though it's not the so-called Rosetta Stone we crave – it does give us a commonality we can read in two languages now, namely, Earth languages and the alien language. I say this at least as far as the periodic table goes, but it is a start. The second thing we have found here…" Another image flashed in front of the team, "…is the basis of their mathematics. We reported before that they used a zero-to-ten decimal number system, but now we have some basics of their system, though at this point it is only simple arithmetic. Nonetheless, what we find here does allow us to confirm the way we differentiated between letters and numbers. It also confirms their mathematics seems internally consistent. By that, I mean that two times two is four and two times four is eight, etc."

Misha leaned forward. "Bit by bit, this does begin to build a picture."

I need to spend more time reading this baby," He gently tapped his new machine with one of the cubes sitting on its stage, "...and seeing if there's an actual key to deciphering the language inside there somewhere. I am convinced we will unlock this, and soon."

"I hope before 29 September."

"We'll see. By the way, Siti, any luck analysing the spot we seem to see in the middle of every disk?"

"Regrettably no. I'm stumped since I can't actually sample them without destroying the disk."

"Do you actually need to destroy a disk, or simply damage it enough to get a physical sample of the material inside?"

"Well, you are right, Misha. I wouldn't need to totally destroy a disk. If I am going to gain access to the spot in the middle, though, I definitely need to drill a hole. The disk itself would still be intact, but I probably would damage it beyond being readable."

"Humm..." Misha rubbed her chin as she considered the situation. "We have over nine-thousand of the transparent disks, correct?"

"Exactly 9,117 of them." Arya chimed in.

"And you have been reading the data on the 5D disks, yes Arya?"

"Yes, Misha."

"Can you record it from one of the disks even if you don't

understand what it is you are downloading? Then maybe we can save it to our storage and then let Siti have her way with the disk?"

"We're a step ahead of you there, Misha. AI has downloaded, recorded and catalogued about a third of those disks already. It's amazing the huge amount of space they are taking up even with our quantum storage system."

"Could you double-check one of them and after you are sure you have the information recorded successfully, give maybe two or three sacrificial ones to Siti to analyse?"

"Consider it done, Misha... Siti... I'll do that this afternoon."

Siti rubbed her two hands together in anticipation of getting a bit of that sample into her laboratory equipment for analysis. "And I promise to be as careful as I can be in getting the minimal amount of sample that I need to make the analysis."

60

Friday, 23 September; Paradise Vineyards, Margaret River, Western Australia

"Look at us! We're walking like a couple of old people... I haven't had such sore legs in twenty years." Sunlyn was wrapped in the robe she put on after getting out of the shower.

Nicolás laughed at her. "I keep telling you we should ride more. Look at me, the model of perfection." Wearing only a pair of boxer shorts, he turned sideways towards her, sucked in his tummy and grabbed his right wrist with his left hand as he mockingly pumped his bicep. "Presenting... Nicolás Ramos, Mr Olympia..." He put on his most serious expression while showing off his less-than-perfect middle-aged physique as though he were a champion bodybuilder.

"Oh PA-LEASE, Nicolás! MR OLYMPIA?" Her head tilted backwards, and she rolled her eyes. "Besides that bodybuilder physique of yours, are you honestly telling me you don't hurt at all?"

Nicolás did everything he could to hide the pain screaming out of his thighs and buttocks after spending nearly half the day riding a horse through the Margaret River bushland. "Hurt? Come on, madam... you're looking at the championship horseman here, just call me cowboy..." Again, he made a muscle, this time with his other arm.

Sunlyn pulled her robe off and swung it at him, playfully hitting him across his bare chest. "Championship rider, ha! Well mister, if you're a cowboy, that would make me a cowgirl..."

"Heehaw..." He grabbed the robe, pulled her towards him and threw his arms around her. In one swooping motion, he lifted her and took two steps backwards and gently rolled her onto the bed. "Looks like I need to tame this woman!"

* * *

Sunlyn awoke and slowly opened one eye, her naked body pressed against Nicolás's side. She could see he was awake and quietly staring at his reader. She took her finger and gently ran it against his leg. "That was beautiful, Nicolás."

Realising she was finally awake, he lay his reader down on the bed and turned to her. "We both slept for a while." He hugged her again and kissed her deeply.

"Well I don't know about the cowboy you were talking about, but I am impressed with the farming prowess."

"Farming?"

"Oh Nicolás, we needn't go through this again. You planted that seed in Norm Crawford, and here we are, holidaying in Margaret River, Western Australia."

He laughed. "Oh, THAT farmer in me. Well, now I got you – I'm two for two. It worked for Hawaii, and now it's worked for Australia."

"I love you, Nicolás."

"I love you, Sunlyn."

"It's so beautiful here... with you... so many beautiful places... so much wonderful wine... Can we just ditch the Sydney conference and stay here another week?"

"Ditch Sydney... I don't know how you'd explain that to Kylie. For that matter, stay here another week... I hate to be the bearer of bad tidings, but I'm hoping we can stay another day..."

Her face transitioned from contentment to worry. "Okay... What did you read?"

"World reaction to the life announcement is absolutely nuts. I just don't even know where to begin trying to work it all out. It's not as though a few microorganisms – microbes, protozoa, whatever the hell they determine they have found – are going to magically transform the Earth. Of course, it's a huge finding, but the reactions are not congruent with the discovery. Consider, the Pope is talking about the discovery offering proof of the one and only God. Really?" He tilted his head and widened his eyes. "The President of the People's Republic of China argues that the three or four Chinese taikonauts on Mars found the life forms first. Think we can have a war over who made the discovery?" Nicolás shook his head. "And the leaders of the Eights are saying..."

"Leaders of the Eights? Now wait a minute, honey, I don't

think there is such a thing as 'leaders' of the Eights."

"Well, Sunlyn, they are reporting that these nonexistent leaders declare the life discovery foretells the end of the world. Why does this foretell the end of the world, you ask? If you can believe it, kids were touting the fact that the drill hole was eight kilometres away from Alpha Colony and that it was 800 metres deep... 8 kilometres, 800 metres... Somehow this absolutely PROVES that angels were involved with the find!"

"Angels? Maybe all this is exactly why we should stay here another week... two weeks... maybe we can become Australian citizens." Sunlyn couldn't suppress her smile.

"Honey..." He leaned towards her, and they kissed again. "I think my farming talents only go so far."

"What exactly does that mean?"

"I think Norm is going to end this holiday sooner rather than later. For that matter, I fear your editor Glenn is going to end your holiday early, too. I don't think we can hide from our either of our bosses even being here on the other side of the planet."

She bit her lip. "Aw damn... Obviously, you read something there. What is it? I guess I'd rather know now than later."

Nicolás pulled himself up enough to sit against the headboard. Sunlyn followed his lead and wiggled her way beside him. He dropped his hand and grasped hers tightly. "I don't think either one of us has gotten a call as yet, but the rumour mill is grinding away again."

"That damned rumour mill needs a monkey wrench tossed into its works."

"Umm..."

"What are you hearing?"

"Another announcement?"

"Washington? Beijing? Brussels?"

"Nah... Mars again?"

"When"

"Don't know yet, but I think soon."

"Any ideas what?"

"Nah. Your guess is as good as mine."

"Well, I'd speculate that it has something to do with the microorganism discovery." The last of the romantic mood had drained from Sunlyn now. She felt the real world come rushing back through her body.

"Fair enough, but what? Do you think the new bugs got loose and are threatening Alpha Colony?"

"Damn, I hope not."

"At least we'd be safe, insulated by 60-whatever million miles."

"But Nicolás, these people are some of the best scientists on Earth which, strangely enough, is why they are on Mars. You'd think they'd be more vigilant than that. Surely regulations would isolate any new organisms, would keep Alpha Colony safe."

"Maybe the microorganisms were just the tip of the iceberg. Maybe they found little green Martian people threatening them with ray guns."

"Don't be silly, Nicolás. But now that you mention it, maybe they did find something more... maybe not intelligent life, but maybe something more advanced."

"Like dogs or cats?"

Sunlyn smiled. "Something more, but not intelligent like dogs or cats... maybe they found Martian politicians."

61

Friday, September 23; Metro Precinct Station
Interview Rooms, Washington DC

"I think we need to take them separately... both of them. We have Bidwill here and O'Keefe in room two. Let's get to the bottom of this now, huh?

"We can do it, boss. We'll start with Bidwill, right? I bet you that several days in a holding cell will have softened both of them up." Bradshaw seemed confident. "I figure that now they should be more than ready... we can turn up some serious heat on them, and I bet they'll spill their guts."

"Yep! Thank Congress for the Federal Emergency Terrorist Act. We'd have never gotten away with this before that came in." Grimms swung the steel door open and followed Patton and Bradshaw. He made it a point to slam the door hard enough that the steel-on-steel frame clanged with such a volume that it could easily be heard and felt in the interview room next door where O'Keefe was being held. The Bidwill boy looked up, his face red and distraught.

"Good morning, Mr Bidwill. I hope we finally get to the bottom of this today. You tell us what we need to know, and we can get you out of here... today... You'd like that, yes? You'd like to go home, wouldn't you?"

"Yes, sir."

"Well, good. We're on the same wavelength then. You just have to tell us what the hell you were doing for Leister... for MacLucas..."

He leaned back and ran his fingers through his long hair. "Aw, man... I told you before... we just did what they wanted us to do. They wanted us to try some new software. They

393

wanted us to use kids as the study sample. Mrs Mac called the kids we used the target sample. I guess they thought that was easier for us to try the software than it was for them do it."

"But that doesn't explain the million-plus dollars Mr MacLucas paid you over the past year. A MILLION DOLLARS! Come on, Bidwill... that's a lot of money even for a kid who lives in Kalorama Heights."

"I don't know why he paid us that much."

"You don't know why he paid you that much? Well, I'll tell you what you'd better know. You'd better KNOW that you ain't going home if your memory is that bad!" Grimms slammed his palm on the metal table, the metallic ring bouncing off the walls.

Time for good cop, bad cop, Maggie thought. She quite intentionally spoke in a soft, caring voice. "The sarge goes off like that sometimes, Dylan. He doesn't mean to scare you. You know, you can help us clear this up by just telling us what went wrong here. I know you didn't mean to do anything illegal. I know you weren't aiming to hurt anyone. I mean, Mr and Mrs MacLucas as well as Leister are all adults, and they ought to know better. They were just trying to use you and Bradley. So, maybe they paid you a lot of money? Did they make you two take the blame? We see this sort of thing all the time, you know... the strong preying on the weak... the older folks taking advantage of the younger ones... Don't let them stick you with ten or twenty years in the slammer, Dylan."

"Ten... twenty years?" His red eyes somehow looked redder.

"Dylan, I know my boss has mentioned FETA – the Federal Emergency Terrorist Act – to you before. You know, a lot of people say that law is too harsh, too unforgiving. Personally, I don't think it's all that fair, either. But what I think has no effect on the political system, or on the way the laws are written for that matter. Over the past several years, a lot of kids under eighteen have served some tough time based on FETA. Do you remember the Santa Fe Coffee House blast in Albuquerque five or six years ago?"

"Yeah." He mumbled so softly it was difficult to hear him.

"Those boys were only fifteen – both of them. But hell, Dylan... 87 dead... I mean, what would you expect? They're sitting in Chico Supermax in Alamogordo now and will be for a long, long time yet. Do you have any idea what a supermax prison is like, Dylan?"

He shook his head no.

"They have all individual cells." Maggie's voice got even quieter now. "At least you don't need to worry about cellmates doing... well, doing you-know-what to you." She shook her head as her face registered disgust. "You're in solitary confinement... for ten, twenty, thirty years. The cells are dark. You only get a half-hour in the yard once a week. There's no cafeteria... no library... no recreation... just a dark cell, three tin plates of food a day, a chaplain on the weekends... and that's what it is until you get out... if you do get out..."

"I didn't do ANYTHING..." Bidwill's voice was louder now, and the flood of tears became quite noticeable.

"Enough already, Patton." Grimms slammed his palm harder this time. The boy nearly jumped as Grimms – voice at near maximum – started shouting at him. "To HELL with you then, kid. O'Keefe's been singing like a bird, and frankly, I think he may be worse for you than MacLucas and Leister. O'Keefe tells us you were the brains behind what you two were doing. O'Keefe said you were the one who asked if you could get involved... that you wanted to make some cash. It sounds like O'Keefe was just a victim of MacLucas, Leister and Bidwill." Grimms' voice bellowed now, and his twisted face confirmed his anger. "I sure as hell hope you know full well that this is a Federal crime we're talking about here, a

SERIOUS Federal crime. We're just about ready to turn it over to the Superior Court of the District of Columbia. Think about it – that's federal – FEDERAL, as in FBI! I hope you know what that means... For sure, you'll be eligible for a supermax prison similar to what Patton was just telling you about. Doesn't matter what age you are, though I hear your eighteenth birthday is just around the corner. Seems to me that the Federal Prosecutor will go a hell of a lot easier on O'Keefe than you, Bidwill. Hell, your buddy might get off with a slap on the wrist if he turns evidence for the Feds. He may actually get into college in a year or two."

"I don't believe you... Bradley wouldn't say that to you. I didn't do anything."

"Okay, Patton... Bradshaw... Let's get out of here now. We've got everything we need from O'Keefe and Leister." Grimms stood. "I reckon young Bidwill here might get twenty to forty, not ten to twenty. You know how hard the Superior Court – all the courts – are coming down on these kinds of cases now." As he stood, so did Patton and Bradshaw. Grimms was first to walk towards the door and grab the handle.

"No, wait... WAIT A MINUTE!" Bidwill's face was bright red with tears dripping steadily now. "All right... all right... all right... I don't know exactly what you want me to tell you, sir."

"Well, you can start with the truth." Grimms took his hand off the door latch. "Is it worth us sitting down again or are you just going to take what the court gives you?"

"No, no... no court. Ask me what you want to know."

The three of them were back in their seats now. Grimms leaned back and started tapping on one of his teeth with a fingernail. He stared right at Bidwill for 30 or 40 seconds. Finally, he spoke at a much lower volume than previously. "How'd did you get involved with MacLucas? Leister?"

"Man... they asked us. We told you before, we knew

MacLucas from basketball. He called us over to the house about a year ago and asked if we wanted a part-time job..." Bidwill put a hand on either side of his head and started to cry out loud.

"Okay, Bidwill. We already have the story, so we can just end it for you here. Bradshaw... take him back to the lockup. I want to see O'Keefe for just a minute before he goes home. I want to finalise his statement about his friend here." Grimms played his part well. His words convinced the boy that they were now done talking to him. "Bidwill, I just want you to know that we're going to recommend the court throw the book at you."

Maggie thought she could almost read the young man's face. His fear was real – he believed that he was now taking the wrap and that his Georgetown academy friend would be heading home this afternoon. "Sorry, Dylan. I didn't think it was you, but what else can we say?"

Bradshaw leaned over. He no sooner touched the boy's shoulder then the boy started talking... talking very fast. "Look, man, wait a minute... wait a minute... Bradley was the brains here. I'm not bad at computers, but Bradley is the guy who knew how to hack. You said so yourself – Bradley got way more money than me. It's because Bradley was good at programming." His speech increased in volume and speed. "Once Mr Leister started teaching us how to do it, it was Bradley who did most of the brain work. I was just the decoy more often than not. If anyone came near the computer labs after hours, I was the guy who talked them away from seeing what he was doing. I was like the lookout."

"And what exactly was he doing, Dylan." Maggie leaned across the table and touched his hand. She lifted the pitcher of water and topped up his glass. "What did MacLucas and Leister have you doing?"

"At first it was just silly stuff like we learned how to hack into just Georgetown kids' SAMs and made the devices freeze up their lockers. Another time we sent out bogus alarm notices through the SAMs to all the Georgetown kids."

"Data bands too, Dylan?"

"Well yeah, but not many Georgetown kids have data bands... they all have SAMS."

Maggie's voice was very supportive. "You say 'at first.' What happened later?"

"We met at the MacLucas's house several times a few months back, and Mrs Mac told us about how she was working to help young people – kids our age – to shake out of being depressed. She wanted to help them. She wanted us to help them... help the other kids... That's all we were trying to do... help our classmates." Again, he started to sob.

"I know she is a professor over at George Washington, so I thought she must know what she was talking about. I mean, I sure as hell didn't follow it all... Look, I'm a pretty smart guy, and I don't even mind psychology – I did have a class in that last year. But she was way over the top with it for me. I mean frontal lobes, hippo-something, anxiety, depression, intervention, some-sort-of magnetic stimulation... I remember some of the words, but I have no freaking idea what she was talking about. I just know that she said the drugs being used to treat depression stimulated certain electrical systems within the brain. Her idea was that we could program kids' SAMs and data units to feed the same electrical signals through thousands of brains at the same time and get masses of kids to escape their depression and go on to be happy and productive. Now that part I understood. We just wanted to help... to do a good thing..." He started to sob again.

Maggie was silent. She looked at Grimms and then at Bradshaw. She gently placed her hand on his shoulder. The interview room was quiet... for what seemed to be a full minute... "And then something went wrong?"

Bidwill continued sobbing... it was a quiet cry, but his tears were real and plentiful. "We didn't mean it..." He took a deep breath and dropped his head to the table.

Grimms knew the boy couldn't see him and he looked at Maggie, nodded towards the boy and pointed straight at her mouthing the words 'you do it.'

Maggie took the cue. "Mean what, Dylan?"

"We didn't mean it to go the way it did."

"What way? Tell me what happened, Dylan." Again, Maggie touched his hand.

"Man... in the beginning... the first day or two after we loaded the program, it seemed that some of the kids – at least the ones we knew – did seem happier."

"How'd you load it?"

"Well, that was the thing. We used a program Mr Leister gave us, and we broke through the administration firewall and uploaded it into the school scheduling program. That didn't just hide the software, but it also had all the kids' SAM details. Besides that – and Mr Leister had figured this out – the Georgetown computers were somehow linked into a national system. Hell, for all I know, that nationwide system could have tied in with other countries. All I can tell you is that after the first three or four times we loaded stuff, something funny started to happen."

"Funny?"

"Yeah... we noticed kids just started acting spaced out... like they were on drugs or something."

"Did it affect you and Bradley?"

"Nope. Look, we had our SAMs taken out a month or so before we started the whole project. Mr Leister told us to do that. We had data units, but when we loaded programs that we were trialling for the first time, we wore fake data units – they didn't have any electronics in them, well, at least no electronics that functioned. Leister said that was like a doctor when testing a new drug and they always took precautions to isolate themselves from the drug."

"So, how did you do all of this?"

"We went to the house and met with Leister, MacLucas and Mrs Mac. Mrs Mac was furious at Leister, but I never did figure out why. I think he took some sort of shortcut or something, but he didn't write the software to do precisely what she told him. We went back three or four times, but each time he gave us 'the fix', it didn't work."

"What were you fixing?"

Bidwill's eyes dropped down. "The kids... the kids dying. Somehow whatever we loaded into the Georgetown computer was making some kids kill themselves. Thank god it didn't work in most kids, but it was obvious that the programs we were loading were somehow causing the walking dead stuff as much as the increased suicides."

* * *

Two hours later, Grimms stood up from the desk in front of O'Keefe. Maggie and Bradshaw joined him. Maggie leaned over and pressed her hand on his shoulder. "You did the right thing, Bradley. I'm sorry my boss was so tough on you, but at least at the end of it all, you were able to get all that off your chest. It makes no sense why you should take the wrap for MacLucas, Leister and Bidwill. You didn't squeal either. You just helped us try to make a bad situation right."

The three left and closed the door behind them. Grimms

looked to the officer in the hall. "Make sure he gets back to his cell. We'll look at a release order by tomorrow. Right now, though, make sure he and Bidwill don't see each other."

The officer nodded his head. "Right away, sir."

"Oh... look, they've had a tough time here today. As a precaution, make sure the correction officers keep them on suicide watch, too. I think they'll be okay, but better safe than sorry."

"Yes sir."

Grimms, Patton and Bradshaw marched down the hall back to the sergeant's office, entered and took seats. Maggie exhaled loudly. "Man, I couldn't do that every day."

"Tell me about it! None of us could do that. How long did that take us?" Grimms looked at the clock. "...three-and-a-half hours. Damn! None of us could do that too often, Patton. Look, being a cop is hard work. You just have to tell yourself you do what you have to do to make the world a little safer. You think I don't feel it? You think I don't have emotions too? That was damned hard, but we had to do it."

"I know, boss... I'm not bitching about it. I just feel jumbled inside."

"Hey, all three of us do."

"You're right there." Bradshaw nodded as he echoed his boss.

"You both were fantastic. Look, at the end of the day, we got both of them to talk, and they confirmed each other's story. I think we have about the whole thing now, save for a few of the academic details."

"You know Sarge, I really got the feeling they seriously thought they were doing the right thing."

"Well, the two boys and the professor did, that's for sure. I

401

don't place a bit of faith in MacLucas and Leister though... true freakin capitalists! I think those two would sell their mothers if they could make a buck from it."

"I fear you're right, boss." Bradshaw stood and pulled a cup from the dispenser next to the cooler. "There is one mystery, though... why did MacLucas pay them so much money." Bradshaw filled his cup and took a mouthful.

"Come on, Bradshaw, that isn't such a mystery. You heard O'Keefe say that they both started getting scared as hell since kids their age were beginning to die. When they made noises about going to the cops to try to stop it, MacLucas thought he'd just 'raise their salary' a bit. Truth be told, that was simply a low-stress, just-among-friends form of payoff or bribery."

"Paying them off?" Maggie had a quizzical look.

"Well, it was either that or go find a hitman."

"Damn!" Maggie ran fingers from both hands through her hair. "You may be right there. Hell, I guess it was getting to that point. So where to from here?"

"In about a minute, you two will get Berger to sign one more court order that allows us to get Chandra to shut down whatever that program is in the Georgetown Academy scheduling software. If he needs any help, we have Leister sitting on ice here just waiting to offer his assistance, I can guarantee that. I don't trust that son-of-a-bitch, but we have him covered, and I'm sure he'll play ball." Grimms rocked back in his chair and let out a deep breath.

"We're right on the Judge Berger court order." Ryan crumbled his paper water cup and tossed it into the waste bin.

"When you finish that, one more thing you two."

"What's that, Sarge?"

"Let me buy you both a beer over at Clancy's Pub."

62

Sunday, 25 September; Gale Crater Outpost, Mars

"We wound up sampling three of them. Regrettably, I did damage this one more than the other two, but I didn't destroy any of them." Siti held up one of the transparent disks, and to the casual viewer, it seemed to be intact. It was clearly visible that a hole had been drilled into its centre. "Fortunately, we have 9,114 more of these that are all still perfectly preserved."

"...and I have recorded a copy of all three disks, and those data are stored to memory, too." Arya interrupted.

"So, what did you find, Siti?" Misha knew her curiosity was shared by everyone in the staff room.

Siti's eyes were wide, her expression somewhere between excitement and disbelief. "Look, I went over this again and again. I mean, the basic analysis is quite simple. It was apparent from the initial microscopic inspection that we had a sample of large organic molecules which looked a hell of a lot like pieces of DNA. I ran about every test I could from there and sure enough, the dot in the middle of the transparent disk – all three that I analysed – are exactly that – pieces of DNA."

"DNA? Pieces?" Nigella's excitement level skyrocketed since DNA was clearly the Holy Grail to a biologist.

"Yes, DNA. I'm not..."

"Oh my god!" Nigella's face went pale. "You didn't destroy the DNA samples, did you?"

"No, no, no, no... I wouldn't have done that, Nigella. I still have the samples all in one piece. Besides that, I had the AI program map them for you now that base sequencing can be done using AI technology. There are pairs of chromosomes, pairs of autosomes... I don't have all the results yet. I'm a chemist and wouldn't for one minute try to interpret these results, but for all the world it seems what we have is simply impossible."

"Impossible?"

Siti looked back at Nigella. "My friend... I will give you everything I have as soon as we finish here, but from what we can see at this point, all three samples appear to be comprised of human-like DNA... I only speak as a chemist now and not a geneticist, but the initial analysis seems to indicate these are – for lack of a better word – samples of diploid cells."

"Diploid cells?" Joe scratched his head.

"Sorry, Joe. I should defer to Nigella to explain that."

"I can explain what diploid cells are quite easily. Diploid cells have paired chromosomes, basically one from each parent. Taken all together, you can read a genome or genetic map from diploid cells. Now, as to what Siti has found here, I have absolutely zero explanation." Nigella's mouth hung open.

The hush around the table was deafening. After nearly a whole minute with no words spoke, Siti broke the silence. "I fear to say this since I am not the one to speak of the intricacies of human DNA. I only know that the analytical program I use in my lab compares the alien sample to its database and indicates a match to human samples." She slowly rocked her head side to side. "I don't have any idea how to explain this. I guess we face the same quandary with almost everything else we are unravelling, that is that we need to include the entire Earth-side scientific community to help decipher whatever it is we are finding. I am so very curious to hear your thoughts on this, Nigella."

"I haven't seen the samples, so I can't speak to that, but I am familiar with the software your analytical program uses and have great confidence in what it tells you, Siti. I... I just don't know..."

Again, silence blanketed the staff room.

"I hate to do this to you, but I have more astounding findings to report to you." Arya sat up in his seat, his tone almost apologetic. "We've finally been able to not only pull information out of the cubes – two cubes at this point – but we have begun to actually decipher some of this and as I said, what I'm finding is incredible.

"Let me start by saying we have downloaded and compiled the equivalence of thousands of pages of alien writing now. Of course, the problem is, we don't have any direct way of translating it to any language we can understand at this point."

"You're saying we didn't find a Rosetta Stone so far." Keegan tapped a finger against his front tooth.

"I'm afraid not. I also should make a point of clarification here, too. I know I've referred to the Rosetta Stone several times now and regrettably, I confess to being quite unfair with you. Forgive me if I said all this before, but the original Rosetta Stone had a decree written in three different languages, two were the Egyptian formal hieroglyphic script and the more everyday Demotic script. Additionally, the Rosetta Stone had the same decree written in ancient Greek. Fully two thousand years after the stone was engraved, French soldiers discovered it buried in Egypt. Since archaeologists of the day could understand Greek, they could use the stone to learn how to interpret the earlier two languages."

"Therein lies our problem with the alien language in question. Since we do not share ANY common language with them, we won't ever have it that easy. We need to match language to common knowledge... to things we share. That is particularly difficult since, by definition, we have zero ideas as to just what we might share with the alien culture. That's why finding the calendar and finding the periodic table have been so important. That at least opens the door to translation.

"What I can tell you today is that we have added to the initial common ground of a calendar and a periodic table, more shared experiences here." Arya waved his hand, and an image appeared in front of the staff room. "If this looks suspiciously familiar, it surely is, though I can guarantee you it is absolutely coincidental."

"Are you telling us this diagram came out of the aliens' cube?" Joe's head was tilted with a surprised look on his face.

"I am absolutely telling you just that."

"For Christ's sakes, if you put that beside the old Pioneer spacecraft plaque you mentioned a few weeks ago, they'd be identical."

"Good point, Joe, but we did that. Believe me when I tell you they aren't the same. They are sure as hell similar, though. You see the two bodies looking very much like humans. There is even an obvious gender difference which is remarkably similar to us, though the convention of long-hair-girl, short-hair-boy doesn't seem to parallel us."

Misha stared intently at the diagram. "Frankly, my memory isn't photographic by any means, but I don't see a difference."

Arya changed the projection to show the alien diagram paired with the old NASA Pioneer spacecraft plaque. "This will refresh your memories. You can see that the two 'people' standing side by side are similar, but unlike the Pioneer version, neither of the alien specimens has any hair. You also notice the Pioneer plaque has the human 'I come in peace' sign with the open hand up, and the alien diagram has both specimens with arms down by their sides. They also match the Pioneer plaque with a representation of a hydrogen atom. My AI software, as well as my personal analysis, says that image

MUST be hydrogen. But there is no spacecraft there for comparison which we humans included to communicate our species' size. There also is no representation of a solar system. Finally, there is no alien diagram showing the 'spokes' coming out which on Pioneer represented our sun's position as related to many Milky Way pulsars, those rapidly rotating objects across our galaxy that continuously emit regular pulsating radio waves. So, I do agree, this alien diagram is way close to our Pioneer plaque, but it certainly is not the same thing."

Lochie had a stressed look as he shook his head from side to side. "Bloody hell... I know the alien diagram isn't exact, but it's damn close! I mean seriously, are we to think the aliens just happen to look like humans?"

"Well let's not get too far into thinking this is coincidental beyond belief." Nigella was considering the biological aspects of this finding. "I mean there are evolutionary pressures that may cause parallel tracks leading to similar outcomes. For example, intelligent life probably couldn't be in a body the size of a flea for the simple reason that we are pretty sure this calls for greater size... at least enough room to have a brain filled with synapses that could handle what we consider to be intelligent thought. Fundamental physical principles put a limit here since atoms are atoms everywhere in the universe and to build complex molecules, you'd need a minimum amount of space anywhere. On the other extreme, an intelligent being the level of which we are talking probably wouldn't be the size of a humpback whale or an elephant because of simple heat constraints. When an organism gets that big, it has way more trouble keeping cool as well as feeding such a large body. Again, it's difficult to conceive of giant forms of intelligent life.

"I caution you though, I am just thinking out loud here. I will need to defer to my colleagues whose careers focus on these kinds of things. I'm making way too many assumptions.

If a lifeform is homeothermic, that is, it generates its own heat metabolically, then it needs to somehow dump that heat. Possibly an alien could live on a planet that is consistently warm and therefore developed a poikilothermic metabolism resulting in little heat production. And gravity would need to play a significant role, too. On Earth, whales can grow into giants because they are ocean creatures and the neutral buoyancy of the sea allows for that. Their large size also allows them to retain warmth in cold arctic waters."

Lochie looked first at Nigella and then around the room. "That's all well and good, but Arya is projecting a diagram that shows us a picture that looks very much like humanoids. I don't know that we need to make so many assumptions. Just a glance indicates the physical appearance of the aliens shows gender bifurcation, a bipedal means of locomotion, two eyes..."

"Well Lochie, I'm NOT saying the aliens have this appearance for any other reason than that we are looking at the diagram Arya has found. I'm simply trying to think of how and why it could have happened in seemingly such a similar way as happened on Earth." Nigella's tone made her frustration apparent. "I don't pretend to know what we're looking at here or why it is the way it is."

"I'm not picking on you, Nigella. Hell, I'm a geologist, and I can still understand your biological confusion even though all this talk of evolving organisms and metabolic functions and parallel adaptations are foreign languages to me. But I just can't believe that of the millions and millions of adaptations that could have happened, our aliens just so happen to pretty much look just like us. Then on top of all that, Siti just told us that the three transparent disks seem to contain diploid cells containing DNA bits that her analytical program tells her are human-like." Lochie was having none of this coincidence argument. "Seriously... did we risk our lives to come all the way to Mars just to find another King Tutt's Tomb?"

63

Monday, 26 September; The Black Wattle Café, Glebe, Sydney, New South Wales

"So, this is Sydney, huh? You sure work in a beautiful part of the city, Kylie."

She smiled. "Yes and no. Sydney is blessed with a magnificent natural harbour which is why the colony was established here in the first place. That said, you can be in most parts of the city and still be somewhere near the water.

"If you're speaking specifically of the university atmosphere, that's another issue altogether. I guess being an academic of some sort my entire career, I've grown used to this kind of atmosphere, but I'm never so used to it that I can't step back long enough to appreciate it all. I just love the young minds, the intellectual challenge, the interaction of ideas from around the world. It frustrates me when I hear the critics point to 'ivory tower' theorists. I can think of few professions where ideas are tested, and arguments listened to every day. The peer-review process never lets any personality rise above the give-and-take of the debate. Frankly, Owen, I think journalism may be one of the few other professions where what you report is always challenged, your story is constantly probed for accuracy and any facts you include call for independent corroboration and verification. At the end of the day, journos are also peer-reviewed very much like academic researchers. I guess the most significant difference is that your critics don't only consist of competing journalists but also the public at large."

Owen nodded. "Well, of course, I agree, Kylie. I admire what you and Fiona do, and humanity could never advance without academics, without research. I don't care what field piques your interest, dedicating a career to investigating, probing and learning is quite admirable as far as I'm concerned."

"As is journalism, Owen – I agree one-hundred per cent with Kylie." Fiona sat beside him, her hand clasping his. "Without the investigating, probing and learning you speak of, the masses would never know what our community leaders and government representatives do on a daily basis."

"In China, too?"

"Well, we have our own thing going there, but yes, there is a journalist core that carries out this mission in their own way."

Owen paused for a few seconds considering Fiona's claim but thought better than to challenge it just now. "Thanks, hon. I'm glad somebody understands the importance of the whole world of newsgathering." Owen finished his coffee. "Too bad Micky couldn't be here today, Kylie."

"Well, one of us has to be earning the mortgage payment. Her hospital is right over that way about two blocks, Royal Prince Alfred Hospital." Kylie pointed out the window.

Owen looked up just in time to see his colleague and her mate coming in the door. "Well look who's coming. I'm hungry enough to eat a buffalo, so I'm glad the two lovebirds have finally found the Black Wattle Café."

Kylie noticed Sunlyn and Nicolás walking over to the table at a quicker-than-normal pace. "G'day mates. I'm glad to finally see you two in my home city."

Sunlyn made no pretence of any formalities, the first words

out of her mouth delivered at full speed. "I can't believe it! Kylie... Fiona... you need to help me understand this." She almost dropped her reader onto the table.

"Calm down, honey. We'll get to the bottom of all of this, and I have no doubt that your friends here will make sure of that. Why don't we both sit down, and we can explain what happened this morning." He pulled the chair out for her, and she sat. "Sunlyn is frustrated trying to make some sort of sense of all that gobbledygook." Nicolás pushed the reader towards Kylie, and she looked down and started to read.

"At least tell us what happened." Fiona was concerned for her friends.

"Well, the morning started off on a positive note – a bit of a sleep in after the flight over here from Perth... coffee in bed." Sunlyn smiled at Nicolás, but her words were spoken so fast they were running together. "Then Nicolás had a holovision chat with his editor Norm and found out that the DC Police are close to solving the case of two boys who shot up our living room a month ago. We originally thought the whole thing had to do with the Eights gangs in DC, and that seems to be true, but it all of a sudden seems much deeper... much more sinister."

Nicolás patted her hand, trying to calm her. "Slow down, hon... slow down. We're on top of this now. As I said, we are so lucky to have Kylie and Fiona here. I am certain we will, at the very least, make some sense out of that." He gestured towards the paper Kylie was looking at on his reader.

"What is it, Kylie?"

She shook her head and looked back at Fiona. "Imagine this... 'Treatment of Anxiety and Depression Behaviours by Stimulating Electrochemical Channels in the Hippocampus and Amygdala.'" Kylie read the title out loud.

Fiona rolled her eyes. "...sounds like where behavioural

psychology meets neurophysiology and computer science."

"How did you get this paper?" Kylie scrolled through the paper on Sunlyn's reader.

"Well, that came after we talked with Norm. He put us back in touch with the original policeman we met, a Washington DC Police Detective Grimms... Harry Grimms. By this time, I was on the holovision, too. We chatted with him for... for how long, Nicolás? It must have been maybe twenty minutes or so." Sunlyn's thoughts were obviously jumbled and still held his hand tightly. "The detective told us this whole bizarre story that his team has uncovered about a marketing company and the guy who owns it. It seems that the company's head of IT as well as the two high school kids who shot up our apartment were involved. Even crazier, the wife of the marketing company's owner just happens to be a psychology professor at George Washington University."

"Professor Katlin MacLucas..." Kylie read her name out loud.

"Yes, yes... that's it." Sunlyn's head nodded her confirmation. "That's who wrote that paper and evidently several others along a similar theme. Fortunately, the DC Police have been working with a local psychologist who is an FBI agent right there in Washington – Dr Tracey Jankowski."

"Jankowski? And you say she's with the FBI there in Washington?"

"Yes. Yes."

"I've met her... Actually, we've met her. We've attended conferences with her." Kylie looked at Fiona's head, nodding in agreement.

"I wasn't able to have a chat with her, but Grimms told me she hasn't had the latest updates. He was just sending her a copy of the paper as we spoke." It was obvious that Sunlyn was upset, and she had difficulty not running on with her words.

"Please, try to calm down, Sunlyn." Fiona's soothing touch reassured her friend. "It sounds as though the police have them now, so it's under control and at least no one else will be hurt..."

"Well no, not exactly. That's the problem. The police, the IT Head, the professor... no one seems to be able to stop a program hidden in the school's administration computers. They are fearful some malware has somehow made it impervious to deactivation."

"Can you send me the paper or the link?"

"I've already done that, Kylie... and Fiona..."

"Good. Look... why don't you guys eat? I'm walking back to my office and reading through this paper. I'll try to get some understanding of what's going on here. I have Dr Jankowski's contact. Is this the George Washington professor's contact? MacLucas... Katlin MacLucas?"

Kylie looked at her reader open to the front of the MacLucas's paper. "As far as I know it is. I've never spoken with MacLucas, only the FBI psychologist, Tracey Jankowski. For that matter, I haven't spoken to her – Tracey that is – about this issue of using electrical signals to remotely stimulate brains and all."

"I understand. And the number here is Detective Grimms' contact?"

"Yes."

"So, Fiona and I will both have this through Skynet already." Kylie grabbed her bag and stood.

Fiona got up at the same time and kissed Owen on the cheek. "I'm going with you, Kylie."

"You needn't..."

"I AM going with you, Kylie." Fiona was adamant.

* * *

Kylie and Fiona spent the next few hours going through the paper, checking references, following footnotes... After they both digested the precepts and conclusions, they walked to the staff room and sat down with a cup of tea. "We need to talk to Professor MacLucas."

"Agreed... but it's three in the morning over there."

"I think this is important enough to wake her."

"Where will we go with it?"

"Well look, the science here is well-grounded as far as I can tell. I don't think the problem is in the paper's conclusion. From everything that I read, she should be able to just shut it all down."

"That's how I read it, too."

"So, then the problem isn't the theory, rather it's a behavioural issue. It seems that we have three choices... One, the professor is standing in the way, two, the kids are standing in the way, or three, the IT head is the one causing the problem."

"Then maybe it isn't the professor we should be talking with, maybe it's Detective Grimms."

"Let's go back to my office and see if we can connect with him via the holovision."

64

Monday, 26 September; Gale Crater Outpost, Mars

"I've got some incredibly exciting news to report to you today. I've gone through this several times and have shared it with my biology team back at Alpha Colony. I wanted to be particularly careful with this, so I waited for Professor Parisa Henning and the rest of the team to look at all the data with me. We are at the point that we are all in agreement here.

"Before I present you with the results, I need to give you a bit of background. Please feel free to interrupt me with questions at any time. I do not mean to be lecturing you on genetics and evolution, only giving you enough of a foundation for our results for it to make sense to you." Nigella brushed her hair back out of her face.

"Now then, when Siti was able to analyse the little dark specks encased in the three fused quartz disks, she correctly identified them as DNA molecules. They were part of a sample of diploid cells, and she correctly recognised them as appearing to be very human in nature. Well to be honest, when we speak of reading a DNA molecule, we speak of decoding or reading the genome, which is basically all the genes or genetic material that is present in a cell or organism. I will not even attempt to get into exactly how we do this – or have our AI do it nowadays – but I will simply tell you that biologists namely geneticists and molecular biologists – do this all the time. We are specifically speaking of genomics here."

Nigella looked at the team assembled around the table and was quickly reminded that not one of them was a biologist. "Look, I don't mean to patronise any of you, but on the most elementary level, DNA is the gigantic double helix molecule that contains all the genetic code – the blueprint if you will – of any life we so far know of. I promise to not get in the weeds with all the particulars here but let me summarise by saying that this DNA molecule is huge, over 200 BILLION atoms organised in a sequence of some three BILLION segments we refer to as base pairs. So, considering some of the chemical compounds that make up the minerals you geo-types deal with, DNA molecules are unbelievably gigantic!" Nigella smiled at Misha, Lochie and Keegan.

"Considering the immense complexity here, it won't surprise you that no two DNA samples from different organisms – even those of the exact same genus – are identical. Far from it. And it's not just one DNA molecule we are concerned with, but – depending on the organism – many pieces of DNA that function to map the design and function of the organism. In the case of humans, the diploid cell that contains the human genome or blueprint is made up of 46 of these huge molecules that are paired as 23 chromosomes. All of this together makes what is called the human genome.

"Even if we map all the exact sequences in your genome and compare it to my genome, we would typically expect to have some three million differences! Still, three MILLION differences out of three BILLION base pairs means that you and I are maybe 99.95% or even 99.99% the same as each other, DNA-wise. This allows us to say with certainty that our DNA confirms we are of the same species, as expressed by our reproductive isolation from other species. In the case of the three alien DNA samples that Siti has retrieved from the disks, they are so close to identical we can equally be confident that they are all from the same species.

"Now, that's not the case as we start looking at our relatives." Nigella scratched her head. "Look, I'm being honest with you when I say that I'm not at all a genetic expert, but I do at least attempt to stay familiar with the subject. That said, it's been forty-some years since the first of the great apes had their genomes sequenced, but we have known since then that *Homo sapiens* share maybe 99% of our DNA with two types of apes, namely the chimpanzees and the bonobos. Think about that – we share somewhere near 99% of the DNA we inherit, but that last one per cent makes so much difference."

Joe spoke up. "Look, I confess my lack of background here, but I thought you biologists confirmed years ago that humans are not descended from apes?"

"Good point, Joe. You are exactly correct. Humans – genus *Homo* – and the great apes – genus *pan* – were certainly on the same evolutionary pathway but diverged from our CHLCA a long time ago." Nigella smiled, knowing full well that her physical science colleagues probably wouldn't know the biological lingo. "CHLCA, that's short for 'chimpanzee-human last common ancestor.' You may not all be biologists, but you are all keen scientists and realise how often we may fit many pieces of the puzzle that we are researching together, but we may never find all the missing pieces. This is an excellent example of that dilemma. We know that somewhere between four or five million and twelve or thirteen million years ago, the line of evolution of the great apes and of humans went in two different paths. Why? We don't know. What was the last common ancestor? We don't know. There have been some fascinating fossil discoveries on the African continent in the 2030s, but they are still the focus of considerable debate. For all we know, the divergence happened over millions of years. We just don't know. But that does NOT mean our understanding is incorrect or that in fact, this is the way evolution happened."

"If you were telling this to the public at large, they'd probably challenge you and argue that you were unscientific." Lochie set his coffee mug down. "But we are ALL scientists, and we ALL deal with incomplete answers. That's probably why I, and maybe you, love being a scientist. The challenge is in knowing that we may never totally satisfy our curiosity with that final answer, but the process of searching is its own reward. I know from a geologist's point of view things like plate tectonics and the five historical mass extinctions have evidence beyond challenge supporting their occurrence... but we still cannot explain the detail of either one of those ideas to the point of the so-called 'final answer.' Sorry for the side-track – I am speaking to the converted here."

"You are exactly right, Lochie. And yes, we biologists are challenged on so many things, but probably nothing could be more controversial among the general population than the evolutionary theory about which I speak here."

"Despite what physicists would have us believe, the whole idea of a final answer may just not be possible." Misha ran her fingers through her hair. "Our physicist friends have proposed a Grand Unified Theory for generations arguing that at least three of the four natural forces are all the same thing. Good on them for continuing the search, but we are still left without their 'final answer' even as we speak."

Nigella nodded. "Another good example, Misha. In the biological issue here concerning the case of our divergence from that last common ancestor, we humanoids went through several – ten or twelve – variations. In the same vein as Lochie's geological examples, we have one hundred per cent proof that *Homo sapiens* are here... that we exist..." Nigella gestured towards her colleagues around the table, "...but do not know – probably can never know – exactly how it all happened. We can find support for our conjecture of interbreeding and migration using research utilising mitochondrial DNA. These studies seem to confirm that *Homo sapiens* did interbreed with other hominins, including *Neanderthals, Denisovans*, and *Homo heidelbergensis*."

Joe's face told her he had no idea of the names she was

using but nodded along with his colleagues.

"These are all our close relatives, Joe. We all shared Mother Earth together during the past million years or so. In the standard American vernacular, you'd call them cavemen, but they were also our relatives."

"Interbreed... you're saying they all could bonk together?" Everyone chuckled at Lochie's query.

"Well, I'd probably use a different term, but yes. The end result is that we all have many, many common DNA features we share with these relatives."

"You're saying we have *Neanderthal* DNA in us?" Joe seemed doubtful.

"Among other things, yes, of course, we do... you do. And we are fortunate that we do have that contribution to our gene pool since we know that it contributes positives to our makeup. Science is still not at the point where we can say precisely to what extent our genetic input from *Neanderthals* and *Denisovans* has affected us. That said, we are certain those genes helped us as our ancestors migrated out of Africa."

"Shouldn't that be an easy comparison we could do in an afternoon's work in your DNA lab, Nigella?" Joe's face showed some scepticism. "I followed the whole argument here, but now I'm curious... Why we haven't yet discovered the precise differences in DNA? Isn't it as easy as analysing human DNA, analysing some of our earlier relatives' DNA and letting the AI software make the comparisons the way Siti's software did here with the aliens' DNA?"

"If only..." Nigella head shook side to side. "Your question is excellent Joe, and the answer is quite easy. If only we had those kinds of DNA samples from the *Neanderthals*, *Denisovans*, and *Homo heidelbergensis*, we would be thrilled to do the analysis you describe. Regrettably, DNA is such a complex molecule that we just don't find fully preserved specimens that are hundreds of thousands or millions of years old. A good deal of what we do know comes from partially preserved specimens. To that, we add data from more recent relatives along with conjecture based on what we learn from archaeological and anthropological records.

"We are fairly certain of some things, though. It is likely that the bits of *Neanderthal* DNA we retain somehow resulted in skin and hair adaptations making *Homo sapiens* more suitable for life in Europe and Asia. For that matter, that inclusion of *Neanderthal* DNA probably allowed *Homo sapiens* to develop greater resistance to the local, Eurasian pathogens. We also have evidence that the interbreeding wasn't all good and that just possibly male offspring from the mix may have been born weaker and even sterile. In the end, though, this passed down genetic material has stayed with us over these few hundred thousand years and may still have impacts we may never fully understand."

"And the alien DNA fits into this picture how?" Keegan was happy for the background knowledge but was as impatient as the rest of them to learn what Nigella and the biology team had learned.

Nigella took a deep breath. "Well, to me, there are a couple of things that are very strange here. The first peculiarity is the quality of the preserved DNA from the aliens. No matter how those samples were collected and saved over what must have been maybe millions of years is absolutely remarkable. I just told you the problem we have obtaining even a few preserved fragments of our ancestors' DNA... It seems the alien DNA is probably much older than that and yet it's pristine. Our whole Mars biology team is quite perplexed by it all.

"The second peculiarity is what our analysis shows us. Remember that we only have three samples of the alien DNA molecules to compare at this point and we have a limited number of comparative genomic tools available even at Alpha

Colony until we announce our find to everyone. Keep this in mind concerning what I am about to tell you since sample size and limited tools both cause incredibly severe limitations to what we've found.

"That said..." Nigella paused and slowly panned the faces of her colleagues. "...we have sequenced the DNA on each sample of diploid cells and repeated the sequencing more than once. The superb preservation of the DNA samples has allowed us to read the genome as well as modern equipment allows. We have allowed our AI programs to draw comparisons and to assess parallel and divergent factors. What we have learned is astounding! Our human DNA seems to share as much with the alien DNA as it does with many of our Earthly-based ancestors."

"Crikey..." Lochie's Australian was showing, but everyone else was as much overwhelmed as he was. "If I followed everything you just told us, that means we humans may be as close a match to the aliens than we are to *Neanderthal*? Bloody hell... how could that even be possible?"

65

Monday, 26 September; Metro Precinct Station, Washington DC

Grimms put his hand to his mouth to cover his yawn. "Damned holovision links in the middle of the night."

"It's all part of the job, right boss?" Patton followed him and Bradshaw up the steps.

"Yes, it is, and I'm not complaining. It's just not every night that I get awakened by a couple of shrinks calling me from Australia." Again, Grimms used his hand to muffle a yawn.

"But hopefully they were helpful, yes?"

"For sure. There's got to be some reason we are working at this god-awful hour! We still need to wade through some way-too-complicated mumbo-jumbo here though, and that's exactly why we're coming to see Jankowski. I at least spoke to her an hour ago, and I know she had a chat with the Aussie shrinks, too."

Maggie smiled. "Maybe keep the 'shrink' moniker out of the conversation this morning, boss."

"Gotcha, Patton."

* * *

"Yes, Detective Grimms, we have agreement on much of this. Look, if I were chasing after this idea of electrochemical treatments of depression, I'd spend the next year or two running independent trials, testing Katlin MacLucas's findings and trying to see what the alternatives are. The problem, of course, is that with this sort of research, there are all sorts of restrictions on what we can and cannot do with human subjects. Some of these restrictions are in the realm of ethics, some are more of a legal nature, and most are of both ethical and legal consideration. Frankly, Professor MacLucas bypassed nearly all of those regulations. I reckon she is in some very deep-water because of this, career-wise that is. She does sound very remorseful though, and I have no doubt she will cooperate with the police – with you – in any way she can. Still, as a scientist, I am overwhelmed by the ethics – or lack thereof – involved here..." Jankowski shook her head from side to side.

"Well let's hope she will cooperate, doc." Grimms felt his chest pocket for his pen.

"Let me try to summarise here, though much of what I'll tell you will have no detail. I've spent my whole life studying things similar to what is here," she touched the academic paper on her reader sitting in the middle of her desk, "...but I still won't pretend to understand some of her work fully. I can reassure you though that I believe I understand it enough to help us try to solve our problem, namely, can her work help us understand why all these kids are killing themselves in ever-increasing numbers."

"That's our number one goal, Dr Jankowski." Maggie leaned forward.

"This all comes down to the theoretical interactions of the hippocampus and amygdala. Now when we last met ten or twelve days ago – mid-September I believe – I know we at least touched on this. Researchers have thought for a long time now that two specific areas of the brain interact in such a way as to affect anxiety and depression. Those two areas are the hippocampus which is associated primarily with short-term, long-term and special memory and the amygdala area that processes emotions and survival instincts. Please understand that I have just summarised years of study and research into two or three sentences, so please be aware that this is WAY oversimplified.

"Now, I say these areas may interact to affect anxiety and depression, but the alternative could also be true. By that, I mean that these same parts of the brain could have an impact in exactly the opposite direction, namely on feelings of happiness and contentment. Once again, here's where the years-of-study-squeezed-into-a paragraph comes in..." Jankowski paused long enough to quickly inventory their faces enough to believe they were following her explanation.

"The brain is such a complex system. Our latest research indicates that the human brain has in the order of 100 billion neurons – that's 100 BILLION – and those neurons can be connected in the order of 100 trillion different ways – that's 100 TRILLION connections! Now for me to sit here and tell you that I or any other human can explain exactly how all of this works is ludicrous. We don't! We have learned so much in the hundred-and-fifty years since Freud, but we haven't even scratched the surface of the actual way the brain works. Does that mean we throw our hands up in defeat? Well, of course not. We keep taking steps, some big and some small. We have learned to better control pain, to better deal with autism and dementia, obsessive-compulsive disorder and many others. And yes, we have made significant progress in the treatment of clinical depression and anxiety disorders.

"In the case of anxiety and depression, we have historically used a battery of pharmaceuticals as well as the original electroshock therapies. Nowadays, we call that electroconvulsive therapy or ECT, and the method has come a long way from its darker beginnings. Modern electroconvulsive therapy is used quite successfully. The only reason I tell you all of this is that nobody can explain to you exactly how any of these tools work, but they do indeed work, and we use them successfully every day.

"The leap made in this case and with Katlin MacLucas's work is fascinating. She basically devised a method to substitute the pharmaceutical effect of certain drugs on the hippocampus-amygdala interactions by using remotely controlled electromagnetic signals coming through a SAM or data band."

Grimms leaned forward. "She was using electrical signals instead of drugs?"

"Yes, that's basically what they were doing. The problem is this is a very hazardous experiment to try on unsuspecting subjects. Has the proper programming been written to allow this concept to work? Does it work?" Dr Jankowski leaned back and used her open hands to ask the question in an 'I-don't-know' gesture.

"I believe we see confirmation that it may work by looking at the effects of Leister's program loaded by the boys into the Georgetown Academy administrative computers. As to whether or not it was manageable... well, that's a whole different question. Indeed, to a point it was controllable, at least in the beginning. They seemed able to target the audience they were after, so the ability to reach selective targets seems confirmed. The early trials all supported that. Did it accomplish what was desired? Now that's where this whole thing went off the rails...

"I believe I mentioned that I had a very useful conversation this morning with my Australian colleague Professor Kylie Childs and her Chinese collaborator, Professor Fiona Wu. Both of them have done much more detailed work on this than I have. They basically tell me that as far as they can see, the experiment most likely went wrong because of either confusion on the researcher's part or malice on the programmer's side of it all. From the evidence currently available to us, all the data that your colleague Lenny Chandra has provided to us and the short time we have had to review it all, the three of us have agreed the problem might be with reversing the signals?"

"Reversing?" Grimms leaned forward.

"Yes, reversing. It's almost as if I throw a switch one way and the lights go on, then I can easily throw the switch the other way, and the lights will go off. In this case, it seems that at the very front end of this elaborate trial is a simple application of a one or a zero... that's as in binary coding in a computer program. Basically, one means on, and zero means off. I say that not knowing a thing about programming, but it seems that the signals sent out to the kids actually deepened their depression and raised levels of anxiety. I repeat, the signal sent out DEEPENED rather than lessened anxiety. The

425

cause of this had to be in what was loaded into the Georgetown computer."

It was almost as if a lightbulb went off over Maggie's head. "So doc, in police-speak, there are only four possible suspects. One would be Professor MacLucas who could have given the wrong data – the wrong on or off, I mean... The second and third suspects could have been either or both of the boys who could have somehow changed the program before uploading it. The last suspect could have been Mr Leister. He could have purposefully changed the one to zero or zero to one when he authored the program based on the professor's instruction. Does that sound about right?"

"It does for sure."

Bradshaw looked at his partner. "Why four, Maggie? Why not five suspects?"

Maggie swept her gaze across Bradshaw, Grimms and Jankowski. "Well, I thought we could eliminate Mr MacLucas from the get-go, at least as far as putting the program in place. Sure enough, he has the blame for initiating the whole scheme through his company, but I don't think he was directly involved with the Georgetown computers at all. I am NOT saying that would absolve him of any culpability, but he surely is incapable of programming and delivering high-tech electronics to switch on and off.

"If Dr Jankowski's hunch is right, Professor MacLucas – Mrs MacLucas – was honestly trying to solve a community problem as far as depressed kids go, so we can eliminate her. Obviously, she still has much to answer for since she broke so many rules and laws concerning the conduct of ethical research, but I don't believe she wanted to harm a soul."

Maggie was holding two fingers in front of her face. As she spoke, she extended a third and fourth up. "The two boys? Look, the three of us have interviewed them several times. I think they wanted to impress their old basketball coach and even make a few bucks – maybe even a few million bucks – on a part-time job, but there is nothing I've seen that tells me they wanted to hurt anyone. Actually, when the noted more kids partaking in self-harm, they seemed remorseful."

"You don't think that stealing dad's weapon and shooting up two journalists' apartment might have hurt someone?" Bradshaw made his point.

"But Ryan, they so obviously didn't want to shoot or hurt any person and just wanted to scare the hell out of a couple of the journalists. Their motive was to frighten Ramos and Singh away from one of their target groups, the Washington local Eight kids. They may have also been paranoid they'd be discovered as having a role in the SAM hacking caper. Don't misunderstand me – again, what they did was wrong, and they need to pay the price for that, but I can't believe they were the ones trying to up the suicide rate of their peers."

Ryan looked at his colleagues and leaned forward in his seat. "Good analysis, Maggie. I think you've put this together exactly right, so I guess that leaves the only likely perpetrator left... Steve Leister. But hell, he's just the Head of IT, not usually the position from which you find mass murderers working. I mean give me a break... IT guys are normally the quiet, nerdy types..." The cop in Bradshaw made him still want to test Maggie's now-obvious conclusion.

Dr Jankowski responded. "Don't be too free with your generalisations, Detective Bradshaw. There most certainly are cases of computer nerds doing more than chasing money and acting mischievously. Remember that hacker in London about ten years ago who jammed up the computer control systems in several skyscrapers in Riyadh and Mecca in Saudi Arabia, and wound up crashing hundreds of people to their deaths... wasn't that all in the name of teaching Muslims a lesson?"

"Actually, now that you mention it, that case might have

been quite similar in that at the end of the day, he simply told the electrons that 'stop' meant 'go' and the elevators just crashed into the ground." Grimms tilted his head. "You know, I think you've hit the nail right on the head, Patton. We are dealing with five people here that will eventually have to face the courts, but I'm about 99% certain that Leister's our number one perp. I just can't figure out why he'd do it... Maybe it's time we go pay Leister a visit."

66

Tuesday, 27 September; Gale Crater Outpost, Mars

"Today is the last time we meet and share our findings as a team before the press conference. In reality, even if you are shaky on today's findings, let's at least consider them here and then see what we do and don't include in the broadcast. Tomorrow we must focus on serious preparation of what we'll include in our presentation to nine billion people on Thursday."

"Do you really think nine billion people will be listening?" Siti hid her face in her hands.

"Well, if there were over five billion at the microorganism announcement, it's hard to believe anyone other than infants would miss this one, so realistically, maybe six or seven billion would be a reasonable guestimate."

"I think you are correct, Misha. Oh boy... I guess I should probably go first today since I've been hidden away with my AI for pretty close to two days now." Arya held his hand in the air.

"That's fine by me, Arya. I see you have your Rube Goldberg machine wheeled in here with you, so I assume we'll be seeing something from that."

"Your assumption is correct, Misha. Actually, I have two astounding findings to report to you today, and only the second comes from the cube reader. Honestly, I'm not even sure if the term 'astounding' conveys enough weight to either discovery, but here we go... The first thing I need to tell you comes directly from the disks."

Arya took one of the transparent disks from a shelf on the cart that held his machine and raised it in front of him. "Our AI software has now confirmed that the transparent disks are, amazingly enough, a part of the alien culture that ritualistically honours and preserves deceased friends and relatives." Arya's eyes arched high. "It seems that the incredibly dense storage capacity of the 5D system they used is capable of recording and safeguarding the 100-150-trillion-plus connections in a human-like brain. That capacity in storage results in the ability to preserve what you and I would call 'the individual.' I am assuming..."

Lochie was as startled as the rest of the team and interrupted him in mid-sentence. "Do you meant to tell us that a dead alien's brain has been stored in that disk?"

Arya nodded yes. "That's exactly what I'm telling you. Now, of course, I am assuming much here: that the aliens were similar to humans, that they could somehow do this before or shortly after death, that they conceived there would be a reason and method to restore the individual... I don't pretend to understand all of this, but I can absolutely confirm that the transparent disk contains what we would consider being the neurological contents of a living brain including the deceased's memories, knowledge, personality..."

"My god... but it isn't a functioning brain, right?" Nigella was as staggered as the rest of the staff.

"No, no... of course not. The disk simply stored all the

connections within a brain. We have no idea at this point how – or even if – it could have been reactivated or brought back to life, as it were. I wouldn't be surprised if that information is contained somewhere in the incredible store of alien knowledge in these five cubes, but we just don't have the time or manpower to extract that just yet. I will say, though, that it seems strange they would do this over and over again if they couldn't somehow replay them."

Arya still held a disk in front of himself as he talked. "Look, I am aware of this brain storage concept amongst the techno nerds back on Earth. I think the buzz word was 'whole brain emulation' or 'mind uploading.' I know there are on-going experiments with WBE, but I'm not aware that so far, any have successfully replayed what has been uploaded as yet."

"Crikey! It boggles the mind to think there may be a way to 'revive' an alien's brain. Consider... should we learn how to do that, we can circumvent so many intellectual impasses, dead ends and blind allies. We could maybe sit with an alien and have a conversation about their species, where they came from, where they have gone..." Lochie's mind revelled at the thought. "It could be a store of knowledge that would be unlike anything we have ever even conceived of before."

"Aw man, we don't know that at this point, Lochie... But there is more. You're going to have to all hold your socks on because I'm about to shake your foundations to an even greater level."

Arya waved his hand at his cube-reading machine. "These, my friends, are the first pictures we have from aliens. I am assuming they are from their homeworld." Arya turned as the first photo projected in front of the staff room. It was a colour two-dimensional photo of escarpments, depositional and erosional features, mountain ranges... He didn't speak for a minute or two as some two dozen photos were projected, each for a few seconds. There was no time to concentrate on any one picture, but the most notable thing about the alien images was that they seemed so non-alien.

"You reckon these are from the alien planet?" Siti had a quizzical expression. "Why do you believe that, Arya?"

"Come on, Siti..." He pointed with pride at the AI-designed machine now reading one of the cubes. "...the images are being downloaded directly from the cube being read right here before your very eyes."

"Could they have been sort of surveillance photos they took on Earth? I mean seriously the strangest thing about these pictures is that they are not strange."

"I follow what you're saying, Siti, but in a moment or two, you'll see they probably aren't from Earth."

The images continued until finally, the first animals were shown. A dog-like creature with a rodent-like face... a bird with two sets of wings similar to a dragonfly... There was the first slide that showed the shoreline with beautiful but quite strange-looking emerald-green waves crashing against the sands.

Lochie tugged on his chin with his hand. "Are you positive we aren't looking at Earth? At first glance here, I'd swear you were tricking us by using slides of Earth that you slipped in here. I'd need to look closer to ascertain differences, things that seem out-of-place."

"Well for starters, these are all available to you right now on the Gale Crater Outpost system. Obviously, I'm keeping these here in the outpost system only until after tomorrow's presentation. In response to Lochie's question, if the pictures really were from Earth, it wouldn't explain the funny animals. I'm not a palaeontologist or an evolutionary biologist, but I never remember seeing even fossils of some of these beasts.

"We are also reading the language reasonably well now. I

have to be honest with you – I must give all the credit for deciphering language to our AI programs. In the old days – read that fifty years ago – we'd have had teams of translators spending months trying to interpret all of this. But using our AI, we've had great results in only a few days. Realistically, part of this is because we have a wealth of samples that the 5D reader is working on now. The other factor is that these translations tend to cascade – the more we can decipher, the easier the next bit becomes because it all relates backward to our last readable text. AI is like a human kid learning from scratch in that, in the beginning, it is slow going, but the more it absorbs, the easier it becomes to expand its understanding.

"The reason I'm telling you this is that the aliens have given us some particulars on the planet... a 12,104-kilometre diameter and a mass about 81.5% that of the Earth, both just a tad smaller than our home."

"Well, obviously you have somehow gotten alien units of measure." Keegan's comment was more a question.

"That we did. Once we started understanding the language, the rest was pretty easy. We did relate both length and mass through the periodic table. Again, the similarity to Earth isn't unusual. If the planet were too small, it probably wouldn't have enough atmosphere to support life, or at least support life long enough for it to evolve intelligent forms."

Nigella nodded. "Similar to the problem that Mars seems to have had."

"Exactly. If the mass were too great, you'd have a whole set of challenges the other way. Any planet that was too large would maintain an atmosphere that could still hold onto hydrogen gas and other components that wouldn't necessarily lead to a stable place for life."

"But early Earth had a carbon dioxide, methane and ammonia-rich atmosphere." Keegan again interjected.

"Sure, that seemed to actually encourage early anaerobic life at first but was long gone after the evolution of photosynthesis by microbes and the subsequent 'oxygen revolution' that finally produced the first creatures to crawl out onto land and start their climb up the evolutionary tree."

Arya continued the slide show. Many more photos appeared showing fishes, birds and other animals. At a few points, he slowed, pointing out some noticeable contradictions to Earthly fauna. At one point, an obvious beetle could be seen on a branch, but unlike the Earthly six-legged *insecta* variety, this one had ten legs. Another showed what looked like a spider resting in the middle of a web, but divergent from an Earth-based *arachnid*, this one had twelve legs."

Arya stopped showing the pictures. "I believe these are examples of convergent evolution where two creatures that do not have common ancestors wind up evolving similar characteristics that fit in similar niches. I'm going to defer to Nigella here."

"You certainly have the right idea, Arya. The problem we will have here is all of our classifications and differentiations apply to animals and plants that have evolved on one planet, Earth. We're looking at a whole new field of study if we think of parallel evolutionary development. Wow, I'm starting to think I may have been born too early."

Misha chuckled. "Just what you need, Nigella – another PhD in comparative alien evolutionary biology!"

A look of seriousness crossed Arya's face and chased his laughter away. "If you will please indulge me, I will now get to the nitty-gritty of this presentation. I begin this part by reminding you that we now have so much information from the aliens that will take decades or more to thoroughly unpack. I am only scratching the surface here, but I believe the aliens actually wanted to put a bit of a summary upfront just in case another intelligent creature was to eventually discover it. It's the aliens' summary that I will show you here.

"The aliens called their planet Gothos – at least that's the nearest English interpretation which our AI could give us." The next images showed orbital views of Gothos featuring fluffy white clouds with orangish-yellow tops and mostly bright green oceans. After a half-dozen pictures from various angles, it became apparent that there was one large continent with many islands spotted around it. "The text tells us that two 'families' shared that one, big supercontinent." Another couple of dozen photos were shown that could have easily been taken from an Earth resource satellite of the old Landsat vintage. These photos could have been used by the aliens to track weather, aid with forestry and agriculture, find resources, aid mapping and carry out a variety of remote sensing investigations. The slides that Arya was showing now offered a wide array of alien resources, cities, ports and so forth, but showed no fine detail of structures.

Finally, a slide appeared that showed a space station. Initially, the size and scale were difficult to determine, but the structure seemed incredibly sophisticated as that kind of habitat no doubt needed to be. Easily visible were an array of docking sites and spherical modules attached to a central hub, along with many free-floating craft and platforms nearby. "The descriptions we have indicate that this habitat was home to thousands of the aliens." Arya wiped his forehead with his palm. "Interesting enough, because Gothos had no natural moon, it sounds as though the aliens needed to build such a sizable orbiting base if they were ever going to master the art of spaceflight."

"Fascinating... Space habitats like that Princeton physicist Gerard O'Neill's proposed 75-years ago for huge space colonies. I'd imagine those habitats would be complete with artificial gravity and farmland and rain." Joe was delighted. "I grew up on some of those ideas, though most people thought them financially ridiculous by the time I read about them."

"Are those some kind of giant wings?" Nigella's eyes were wide.

"They aren't wings, Nigella. If you look close enough, you'll see that they're solar panels... HUGE ones!" Arya continued. "The absence of a moon would have presented enormous challenges to space flight and reaching this level of accomplishment speaks well of the aliens. As best that we can figure, it seems that these extraterrestrial beings must have evolved at least tens of thousands earlier than we did and obviously are or were an intelligent species."

"Why do you say that, Arya?" Nigella looked at him with a curious expression.

"Just look at these images." As soon as Arya responded, a series of photos appeared showing what must have been the inside one of the space habitats. The sheer volume of the ark was impressive. Hillsides were rolling up the sides of the cylinder with a river valley running through the middle of it. "As far as we can tell, this is the interior of one of those orbiting structures we just looked at. Joe, I'm unfamiliar with this O'Neill professor you mentioned, but these habitats include just what you mentioned as far as hills, valleys, agricultural fields..."

"My god, that structure must be kilometres long and at least a kilometre or more in diameter." Keegan marvelled at the massive size of the structure. "We have never built anything nearly as big as that."

"Bloody hell, we never HAD to build anything that big... we had the moon." Lochie echoed Arya's point.

Several more pictures humbled the group. At this point, there was no doubt that Earthlings were nowhere near as advanced technologically as a quick look at these alien photos demonstrated.

Misha shared their wonder. "What an amazing spaceship."

"Don't jump the gun here, Misha. I believe we're looking at a giant space station, not a spaceship. I don't think it was ever going anywhere but in orbit around Gothos. There is no obvious propulsion system here, just the myriad of little thrusters all over which they would use to maintain their orbit." Lochie looked to their resident engineer for confirmation. "I fear I am repetitive, but with no natural moon, the aliens would have had to build something like this as a stepping stone to space travel, no?"

"For sure, that would be correct as far as I can tell." Joe nodded his agreement.

"Well, let's not be too quick to negate the aliens' ability to build spacecraft, though." Arya waved his hand, and another image appeared. This was a smaller structure with the space station off in the distance. "You can see here that this design is much different from the space station. For starters, it is much smaller – you can see two astronauts floating around and working outside there. Naturally, the ship would accommodate far fewer people than the space colony. You can also see it has some solar panels too, but less of them."

"That's just as impressive though, as you say, on a smaller scale. It's easy to see the engineering differences between the mammoth space station and the much smaller spaceship. The designs are aimed at very different purposes."

"Yes, of course, Lochie." Joe admired the engineering miracle he was seeing along with his colleagues. "I know I am too often an example of a blinded, true-blue Jacob Jacobi admirer, but looking at these structures, the aliens needed way more than the resources of a trillionaire to design and build all of this. I have no doubt this had to be a species-wide effort."

"Well, maybe not species-wide, Joe." Arya continued. "Possibly, it was a family-wide effort. Recall that we have learned that Gothos was home to two 'families.' Now maybe on Earth, we'd call them countries, but the word somehow translates as family through the AI system. Anyway, they both shared the one continent but – sadly enough – might not have shared it as well as they could have."

"Please explain."

"Well, did you notice anything in those first photos... something that just might not have fit with the comfortable 'just-like-earth' feelings you might have had?"

"Yeah, I did..." Lochie wet his lip with his tongue. "The cloud tops didn't seem right... kind of yellowish. And the oceans... they were too green."

"You win the door prize, Lochie. You are spot on there. I have great trepidation in showing you the next group of slides, but I fully agree with Misha's plea for revealing all that we can today, so we have the chance to plan how we present this on Thursday."

The next photos shown were again taken from orbit and showed brownish blots of varying sizes scattered throughout the green ocean. There was no indication of time, but the subsequent six or eight photos showed more ocean areas being covered. Another photo appeared with a few small plumes of dark smoke billowing skyward. In the next several images, it became apparent that these fires were popping up everywhere and were all large enough to be clearly visible from a thousand kilometres high.

"I'm sorry that we have to watch this but based on the planetary statistics I mentioned at the beginning of my presentation, we know these plumes of smoke are reaching a hundred or more kilometres high. The text is explicit, and I have no doubt it will be studied for centuries to come. Despite their high-level intelligence and advanced technology, the two families simply couldn't agree to a peaceful existence on their one supercontinent.

"The first slides we saw just now with the green ocean browning are quite telling. You needn't be an oceanographer to realise the algae blooms had become so widespread that these inescapable ocean 'death zones' began to appear and merge. There are no better ways of saying this other than that the aliens had killed their planet. There is a narrative describing how each family blamed the other for the catastrophe. We haven't worked out the timespan here, but eventually, the forests began to burn, the cities began to burn... Gothos became unliveable. The ecological calamity was as easily predictable as it was preventable, but the aliens failed to do so.

"Worse yet, as their ecosystem deteriorated, the more it impacted on health, on the economy, on political and social systems... Hells bells, this reads like a damned novel, but – instead of making peace to deal with a planetwide catastrophe, the families blamed each other for the failure. I apologise for the lack of time available to learn more of the story, but as you can see here," Arya almost appeared to wipe a tear from his eye. "...the continental fires are quickly hidden by the billowing, planetwide black clouds of doom."

The next two slides showed close-in enough images of the unmistakable mushroom clouds obviously caused by a series of hundreds of thermonuclear explosions. "Your eyes are not deceiving you – they are in fact thermonuclear detonations we see here, first on one side of the supercontinent and then on both sides. The text reported automated responses and whatever touched off the initial aggression triggered both sides to unleash their entire arsenals against the other. The alien text reports that some eight-billion of their species died within days."

"EIGHT BILLION! But I thought this was an environmental crisis, Arya." Siti had a tear running down her cheek.

"It was... but as we all know too well, environmental stress doesn't occur in a vacuum. Environmental stress – extreme environmental anxiety as it were – applied to a society causes people to behave in irrational ways. We so frequently confuse 'intelligent' species with the notion of a 'logical' species. Though until now, we only have a sample of one – our own – we time and again recognise that intelligence so obviously does not equate to logical behaviour."

The remainder of the slides showed Gothos with black clouds increasingly covering most of the continent. It showed the entire planet surrounded in black smoke. All were overcome with emotion. Noting the angst written on his colleagues' faces, Arya mercifully closed the picture of planetwide destruction. He replaced it with the hopefulness of the earlier image showing the alien spaceship with the giant space station floating off in the distance. He let the last picture remain on the screen.

"As I said, we need more time... maybe years... maybe decades... Much work needs to be done to sort through all the aliens have left us here about the history of their species. As a point of optimism, I'll end with this image of a ship that I believe might have been the alien's escape vessel. I imagine it could hold at least hundreds of people... ah, aliens. I am assuming a lot to say possibly they returned to wherever they came from after the planet-ending disaster. I hope I am not kidding myself, but I like to think that it may be the aliens' 'Noah's Ark' for their survival as a species."

"Wherever they came from?" Joe scratched his head. "Weren't they from Gothos?"

Lochie arched his eyes. "I don't know that we can assume that. We know the aliens were here on Mars and we know they were on Gothos, so they obviously had mastered space flight at a way higher level than we humans have. We need to learn more."

There was a minute or two of complete silence as each of them remained lost in their own thoughts. Finally, Siti leaned forward. "Wow... that was sobering, to say the least." She squirmed in her seat, full well aware of the fact that she was yet to present her latest findings.

Misha noted Siti's anxious behaviour and looked to her. "Did you have something to report, Siti?"

She let out a long stream of air. "I fear telling you about my latest finding. In light of what we have just seen, I hesitate to start with a question, but I must..."

"A question?" Misha's head tilted to one side.

"Yes, a question. I wonder why they left their burial vault behind."

Her surprise question caused everyone to sit up in their seats. "Burial vaults, Siti?" Misha uttered what seemingly all were thinking. "You obviously refer to the downloaded minds of aliens to the transparent disks, yes?"

"Well, it's more than that. I apologise for starting with the 'burial vault' question, but Arya took me off guard with this series of slides showing the demise of their planet... of Gothos...

"I must report to you on the latest analysis of the medallions I now have. Nigella shared our finding on the DNA molecule at the centre of each of the transparent disks. As she told you, we confirmed that DNA by sacrificing three of the over 9,000 disks we now have. That resulted in confirmation of the human-like diploid cells – I believe that's what Nigella called them – containing genetic material in all three of them. The biology group back at Alpha Colony along with Director

Tan all concluded it was prudent to run tests on three random samples pieces taken from the 317 medallions we have. This is quite different from the transparent disks because, as far as we can determine, the medallions are not meant to be 'played' or downloaded in the same sense that the disks are. I was both cautious and frugal with the samples I collected. Again, Arya recorded each sample in the highest definition three-dimensional imaging that we can manage.

"I've reported time and again that I was pretty confident we were looking at the BMGs – that's the 'bulk metal glass' material we talked about. I confirmed that with an analysis of mostly zirconium and beryllium with some titanium, nickel and copper. So far, so good, and that is precisely what we would expect. It is the other elements that have been blended into each medallion – at least of the three that I sampled – that had me scratching my head. I was able to identify by mass about 39% oxygen, 6% hydrogen, 41% carbon, 8% nitrogen, 4% calcium and traces of phosphorus, potassium, sulphur, sodium, chlorine, magnesium…"

Nigella rocked to the front of her seat, her head nodding as though she knew where this was going.

"I won't continue to bore you with the chemical details, but basically, I am convinced that the aliens have somehow blended the partial remains of cremated bodies into each medallion."

"But wait a minute. If the aliens are that similar to humans and humans are about two-thirds water, I think you said 30-some per cent for oxygen and maybe six or so for hydrogen. I think those masses per cent masses would total way too low for a human-like body?" Keegan was quick to pick her up on the numbers.

"You are correct in the two-thirds water argument, Keegan, but remember, these remains would have been what was left after some sort of cremation. Heat would have vaporised much of the water, so we'd expect it to be gone from the ashes. Interestingly enough, the ratio of these elements seems to mimic a human body's makeup. I think we accidentally came across an alien burial site in those lava tubes. Forget the mismatch in numbers of disks versus medallions, since we know there must be many, many artifacts that we haven't found as yet. I hypothesise that the aliens' ritual to 'bury their dead' so-to-speak included downloading their minds into 5D storage, including enough of a diploid sample to preserve that individual's unique genetics in the middle of it and then blending some of their ashes into bulk metal glass material. They finished each medallion with the individual's name, birth date and death date on the piece."

Arya nodded his head in agreement. "That would definitely work because I am certain now that each medallion does indeed include a name, a birth date and a death date."

Misha held a medallion in her hand and looked around the table. "You know Lochie, a couple of days ago you mentioned the idea that maybe we had found another, King Tutt's Tomb... you may have been way more correct than you ever imagined. I think Siti's conjecture is correct: we have found an alien burial ground."

Again, silence befell the group. The team shared the same unspoken mourning for a species they had never met, for a culture they barely knew, for individuals with whom they never shared a conversation, a laugh, a cry... There was no understanding of when the aliens last walked here on Mars or from where they came and where they went...

Suddenly Joe broke the silence. "You know, as an engineer with a lifelong interest in everything to do with space travel, I can't get my eye off the image of the alien's spaceship up there." He gestured towards the projection at the head of the table. "I'll grant you that the ship is large and beautifully designed from what we can see, but something just doesn't add up here. I've been looking at that image for ten or fifteen minutes now, and I'm telling you, there is no way the design of that ship was ever aimed at interstellar space travel. I see no evidence of an ion drive or anything like that. The large tanks on the sides and those big thrusters over there..." Joe pointed towards what was most likely the back of the ship. "...indicate chemical rockets. I reckon the large tanks are chemical fuel tanks. Solar collectors do you no good on interstellar flights... Now we don't know if they had another ship or ships somewhere, but the best they could have ever done from that design would have been travel within the confines of the inner solar system... That image definitely is not an interstellar spacecraft."

67

Tuesday, 27 September; Metro Precinct Station, Washington DC

Much to Bradshaw's surprise, neither Grimms nor Patton was in their office. He walked in the sarge's open door and sat in front of the desk and waited. It only took a few minutes until he heard his two colleagues coming down the hall. They stepped into his office together. "Good morning, Bradshaw. Nice of you to show up today. Thank god someone around here looks like they had a good night's sleep." Grimms squirmed around the side of his own desk and plopped himself in the office chair behind it.

"Hi, Ryan." Maggie sat next to him. She was a bit more sympathetic to Bradshaw not knowing that she and Grimms had been at the Precinct since early this morning. "I couldn't sleep, so I came in early. Surprisingly, I found the sarge already here, too."

"Well, don't blame me FOR sleeping. You know I'd have been here at any time at all if anyone asked me to come it early." Bradshaw couldn't figure out why he was apologising.

"Alright, enough of that. We have to wrap this damned thing up today... this morning. I have high hopes that between them, Jankowski and Chandra can somehow shut down this damned program that the professor and Leister created. That will all depend on how we finish off Leister. We know he's as guilty as guilty can be. I've been convinced of that for a while, and I know Patton has been too."

"Make that me three, sarge." Bradshaw could see the writing on the wall too.

"Well, motive, motive, motive... we need his motive... Patton and I both did a bit more digging this morning, and we found some news pieces from way back... it seems Leister had a few experiences in his background that might have caused him to dislike kids. Sadly, certain experiences can stay with you for a lifetime and maybe that's exactly what has happened with him. Somehow, we need to let him spill the beans to us. I want to tie this up in a ribbon for the DA."

"I think we got him, boss. We just need to beat him over the head with the truth and hope he'll start crying like a baby."

Grimms actually laughed at her. "You know Maggie, I'm starting to think you're watching too many cops and robbers' shows! That last statement from you sounds like a line straight from a detective movie!" They heard an uncharacteristic chuckle from the sarge. Without notice, all three started to laugh just enough to take a bit of the edge off. "Okay, we've got Steve Leister in the interview room. We'll give ourselves one coffee, and we're off to have a little chat with him."

* * *

"What do you got against kids, Leister?"

"Kids? Me? Nothing."

"Come on, Leister. We know it was all your idea to tweak the programs you had the boys upload and hoped you'd be able to kill some of the little bastards. Am I right?" Grimms leaned forward.

Leister became flustered. "What in the hell are you talking about? I didn't do any of that. I couldn't do anything like that... I told you that I admit to passing along the program."

"Passing it along. I thought you wrote the program." Bradshaw's voice was raised.

"Well I did write it, but it wasn't my idea. Mrs Mac worked all that out."

"Mrs Mac likes kids. You freaking hate kids, Leister." Grimms parted his lips and tapped his teeth together ever so slightly. "I mean, how the hell did that all happen? How the hell did you come to hate kids?"

"I told you, I don't dislike children."

Maggie remained calm. "I know about what happened to you a long time ago when you lived in Maryland."

"Nothing happened to me in Maryland."

"Aw, come on, Steve. I know about the kids there at Potomac High School in Columbia... when you were a kid going to school there. I know how the other kids treated you there."

"You don't know shit, lady."

"I know a bunch of your classmates were pretty mean to you... always called you a freak... a nerd."

"That's because I was brighter than them."

"Oh, I'll bet you were. But boys can be nasty... boys can be mean..."

"I didn't hang around with them."

"But they hung around with you that night in Blandare Park. Do you remember that night, Steve?"

He was quiet. He turned his face down towards the table and didn't respond.

Maggie leaned front but kept a calm voice. "I bet it hurt... I bet it hurt your feelings as much as... well, as much as back there." She tapped her hand towards her backside, never actually reaching it.

Leister shook his head side to side. "It wasn't like that."

"I'm sorry... sorry for what happened to you with the boys." Maggie's voice was soft... calm... "What was it? A baseball bat? A tree branch? There are a lot of trees in Blandare Park. I've been to Columbia... to Blandare Park... It's a pretty town... pretty park..."

"Shut up!"

"Did they push that branch into you? Up your..."

"SHUT THE FUCK UP!" Leister tried to jump up, but one hand was cuffed to the secure point beneath the table. "JUST SHUT THE FUCK UP, LADY!"

"Man up, Leister. For Christ's sakes, at least admit to your past." Grimms was a bit off the boil now but still showed no compassion. So, you didn't like your classmates... that's no reason to be killing kids today, is it?"

"I didn't... I didn't kill anyone."

"Do you have a brother, Leister?"

"Yeah." His voice was so quiet now he was barely audible.

"He's a few years older than you, yes?"

446

"Two."

"Are your folks alive, Leister?"

He hesitated for a few seconds... "No."

"Sorry to hear that, Leister." Grimms poured two glasses of water, stood up just enough to push one in front of Leister and then took one for himself. He gulped half the glass down in one go. "How'd your mom die, Leister?"

There was no response.

He raised the volume a level. "How'd your mom die, Leister?"

Again, there was no response.

"Your brother, ah..." Grimms thumbed through his notepad. "Umm... Garrett. Your brother's name is Garrett, right."

"Why's it matter?"

"Oh, just wondering." The sarge took his time now because he knew he found the sweet spot. "He has a son named Todd, right?"

Leister stayed quiet.

"Where's your nephew Todd now, Leister?"

Again, there was no response.

This time Grimms let the better part of a minute go by in silence. He kept staring at the suspect in perfect silence while finishing his glass of water. Finally, he got to his feet and walked right beside Leister. At first, he spoke in a very measured way. "Why can't you tell me where your nephew... where Todd is? Why don't you want to talk about this, Leister? Don't you like Todd?"

Leister remained quiet, though his face was red, and his eyes were moist.

"The fact is that Todd is in a supermax, isn't he? He's in the North Branch Correctional Institution, right? He's been there for a decade or more now, yes?"

"Let me go, man."

"Why's Todd in there, Leister? Who'd he murder, Leister?" Grimms leaned over with his face inches from Steve Leister now and yelling at the top of his lungs. "Tell me about it... TELL ME, LEISTER! TELL ME!" He brought his fist down right next to him. The loud bang from the steel tabletop frightened Maggie as much as the suspect. Leister nearly jumped out of his seat until the handcuff yanked on his arm again.

Leister mumbled, "He... he killed my mom."

"What's that, Leister? I CAN'T HEAR YOU, LEISTER." Grimms bellowed right in his face.

"Todd killed my mom. THE FUCKING BASTARD KILLED MY MOM... HE FUCKING TORTURED MY MOM!" He exploded in tears.

Grimms had returned to his seat now, his voice back to normal tones. "Funny that. Here you are the Head of IT for Sunrise Marketing Company, and you go and kill lots of kids... At least we know why you don't like kids, right. What did your nephew do, Leister? Your nephew pulled off a computer scam on your mom, didn't he? He robbed your nursing home-bound mom of her savings and her Social Security, didn't he?"

"SHUT UP!"

"He tortured her, huh? Strangled her in her bed... under a pillow. Not a nice thing to do to granny after he stole all her money."

"FUCK OFF!"

"Poor Leister... Damn... I wonder if it's in the genes. What do you think, Leister?"

"I think you're a fucking bastard, that's what I think."

"You hate Todd, don't you? You hated your school mates, didn't you? You should have killed them all... You'd just as soon all the kids died. You were never married... never had kids... Who needs kids, right Leister? KILL THEM ALL!" Again, Grimms pounded the table.

"I... I... I didn't start out to do it... I didn't think it would really work..." Leister's head dropped into his hands on the tabletop, and he started to cry uncontrollably.

Grimms grabbed his pad and walked into the hall. "Officer. Make sure that man is secure and take him back to his cell. We're booking him for first-degree murder." He took one step and stopped. "You'd better put him on suicide watch, too."

68

Tuesday, 27 September; Western Sydney International Airport, Badgerys Creek, New South Wales

"I don't even know where I am... Badgerys Creek? Didn't we fly into another airport?"

"Yes. The downtown airport is pretty much for domestic flights now. I think just about all the international flights go out of Sydney West here... have for years..." Kylie set her purse at the end of the table.

"I feel so badly about the conference, Kylie."

"Well Sunlyn, there's nothing any of us can do about that. You must admit, it's an unbelievably monumental reason to skip out of a conference that I've – I guess I can say we've – been looking forward to. Somehow, I think the conference-goers will get on without me. I couldn't skip the Shanghai announcement for all the tea in China."

Owen mocking slapped his forehead with his hand. "That was awful, Kylie. I mean, all the tea in China?"

Kylie squished her face up. "Honestly, I didn't mean it that way..." She actually blushed.

Sunlyn tried to rescue her Australian friend. "I know you didn't. And you are missing the conference too, Fiona."

"At least I get home sooner than I expected, all Chinese tea or no Chinese tea." She couldn't resist humouring her friend's misstatement.

"Well, I admit that Nicolás and I were sure that our next flight would be back to Washington." Sunlyn pouted as she looked toward Nicolás.

"And miss the biggest story ever!" Owen smiled at his colleague.

"Don't do this to me, Owen. I mean three weeks ago I'm sitting there in the Bureau Chief's office and listen to him go on... 'This *Thánatos* story will be the biggest ever'... I was happy to go on assignment with you, Owen. Then it became the Global Holistic Summit that was going to be such an 'unparalleled happening.' I mean, as far as I was concerned, Glenn was indeed sending us on a career-defining mission... Of course, then came the trip to Perth. The Mars team was making the announcement to top all announcements, and it was. I mean, it isn't every day we discover alien life on another planet. So, for the third time in as many weeks, we were on the one and only assignment never to be outdone. Now here we are, seven or eight days later and awaiting another flight, back off to Shanghai for that 'once-in-a-lifetime' assignment... AGAIN! Seriously! Four once-in-a-life-time assignments in September! Tell me, am I missing something here? Do you think there is any chance that maybe October can be a little bit slower month for journalists?"

Nicolás put his hand on her shoulder. "Well, my dear, we ARE boarding this flight, and we WILL be at the next Martian news conference. I guess that means that I am sure about what you're NOT missing, and that is the BIGGEST STORY EVER, AGAIN!" They all chuckled.

"Well, we may still be amid the biggest story ever. I mean, it's not like we know how all this comes out." Owen looked a bit more serious now.

"Comes out... Seems to me that we know that, no? Subplot one: the cops caught our shooters. Subplot two: *Thánatos* didn't end all life on Earth as we know it. Subplot three: there's alien microbial life on Mars. Done and dusted, we know how this story comes out." Sunlyn wiped her hands together in the universal gesture of indicating 'that's all finished.' "Bring down the curtain... roll the credits!"

"I know you aren't serious, Sunlyn, so I'll ignore the 'done and dusted' remark. Now that you mention it, what did come from the police case and your conversations with the psychologist back in DC?"

"Look, the cops are almost done... just trying to wrap up the last of the details. There is still the issue of whether or not the crazy professor actually was messing with kids' minds or if it was all just a very poorly run experiment gone bad. I'm sure we'll hear about that soon."

"You know Sunlyn, I've been in academics my entire adult life, and I can't say that I ever remember such an unabashed trampling of standard research practices and procedures." Kylie's face telegraphed her disgust. "It offends me that a person of such high academic standing would even think of trialling any experiment that affects behaviour in such a way, let alone targeting unknowing kids. I have no doubt you Americans have very similar codes of conduct and ethical responsibility for researchers as we do in Australia. She obviously just ignored them all." Kylie's abhorrence of Katlin

MacLucas's unethical conduct was apparent to all.

"Do you think the shooting had anything to do with MacLucas?" Fiona's tone also expressed her total loathing of MacLucas's shocking lack of academic ethics.

"I don't think so, Fiona, though we probably won't get the full details of it all until we get back home." Nicolás opened the menu. "It sounds to me as though the whole Eights involvement for those two boys was more of a distraction from their main game of hacking into their school's computer system."

"At least they caught them all... I confess that I've been trying to follow up with the *Thánatos* impact. Do you realise that since that impact – what was it, September 2, so that's over three weeks now – they are still having seismic tremors up there, Sadly, the Richter Scale intensity doesn't seem to be lessening, and they had a 6.9 shaker yesterday. I listened to a holovision broadcast this morning of Dr Gillian Pickard... the woman you all heard present at the Global Summit the other week. She still gives daily updates on the impact along with the climatologist, Professor André Moureaux, who is keeping us posted on the methane problems. You would have heard him at the Summit, too. It is pretty much accepted as fact now that *Thánatos* has indeed awakened these ancient faults and that area may remain seismically active into the foreseeable future. We're basically in uncharted territory as far as the geophysics of it all is concerned, but the methane release has increased nearly a hundredfold since the initial impact."

Kylie arched her eyebrows. "Oh boy... I know we've been through all the scientific explanations before, so obviously, we know that the methane is a real problem. Do I hear you saying we still don't know how much of a problem?"

"That's what I'm saying. Professor Moureaux keeps asking us all to stay tuned."

* * *

Their flight to Shanghai wasn't scheduled until evening, so they ordered lunch and had a leisurely conversation at one of the airport restaurants. The waiter brought desserts and set one in front of each of them. Nicolás planned his attack on his three-scoop ice cream sundae as he looked over his glasses at Kylie. "So you know, all the talk of alien life raises many issues. I mean, matters such as how far along the evolutionary line it is and Owen's press conference query as to whether the optical isomers rotate this way or that... I sort of think we might be missing a more fundamental question. I shouldn't be jumping the gun here, but I can't help but wonder what this all might mean to the human psyche? It just seems to be a huge deal. I look to you Fiona, and to you Kylie, because you have both spent your lifetimes exploring human behaviour. What kind of impact do you think this will have on us as a species? On our kids? Our behaviours?"

"Jeez... you're asking the impossible here since there is no precedent of extraterrestrial aliens... not really. I do think you can look at some analogous Earthly examples, though. We do see parallels in historical cases where a more technologically advanced culture just shows up uninvited smack in the middle of a less advanced culture." Kylie teased a morsel of her pie towards the side of her plate. "Consider the Australian Aboriginals in my country and North American Indians in your country... there's probably no exact equivalence in China. The confrontation of a more technically advanced civilisation on a less technically advanced one seems to always end in disaster for the lower technology culture. Historians can argue forever about the good and the bad of Columbus, Ponce de León, Balboa, Magellan, Tasman, Cook... No doubt they brought western science, medicine and agriculture. But they also brought unheard-of diseases, gun powder and alcohol."

Owen nodded his agreement towards Kylie. "Don't forget unbridled consumerism."

Kylie nodded her head yes. "Now I'm not addressing your question since you refer to the Martian microbial find and that has nothing to do with seeing us come to grips with an alien intelligent civilisation. We have many examples of organisms farther down the evolutionary ladder being introduced to civilisation again, mostly not without more drama. We're hard-pressed to investigate invasive species before humans were around to do the transporting. There are still some examples of organisms breaching biogeographic barriers unaided by humans. North and South America exchanged biotas that were separated previously. We see a similar event on ice bridges between Asia and North America across the Aleutians at a time of low sea levels and glaciation. These happened so slowly as to not have crisis impacts. We heard at the Holistic Summit the frightening possibility of ancient diseases returning to us through the thawing permafrost. Finally, you speak of psyches, of human responses to all this. Frankly, we have no idea what this Martian discovery is let alone what it will do the human psyche."

"I agree wholeheartedly, Kylie." Fiona continued with her thoughts. "Maybe we should look at it in another way. Up until now, you pointed out how the chance meeting of two intelligent cultures pretty much meant either absorption or total destruction of the less technical culture. But in these Earthly examples of Europeans 'discovering' the Americas and Pacific islands, we are looking at two intelligent cultures having the same DNA, so the whole competitive issue must be considered. In the Martian life case, a microorganism of differing evolutionary line of DNA shows up and does not seem to present any competitive threat, assuming, of course, that there is no biological threat to *Homo sapiens*. If humanity does not perceive any direct challenge from the Martian bugs, this 'world's greatest discovery ever' could prove a big flop much faster than we imagine."

Owen finished his cheesecake and leaned back in his chair. "Wow. So, Fiona, you're suggesting Martian life could simply become boring?"

"I don't want to overdo it, but that is a possibility." Fiona ran her fingers through her hair.

"Woe is me to comment on your expertise concerning human behaviour, but might there be a whole different way at looking at this? Might it be that for the first time in the history of our species, we are now forced to conceive of the fact that we are not alone... that Earthly life is not the only variation of reproducing organisms in the universe. Do you remember our chat at the Shanghai Airport the other week before we flew down to Perth when we talked about Fermi's Paradox? At that point, we were talking about humanity being alone in the whole universe... or at least alone in our Milky Way Galaxy in Fermi's version of things. I suggest that finding a new life – a separate chain of life that has developed and evolved apart from us – shines a whole new light on our species. What does it do to our psyche? ... to our confidence? I mean seriously, what impact does this have on Earthly religions? If God created Earth for humans, what did he create for Martian microorganisms? For Martian bacteria? I fear that merely answering 'Mars' may not be all that satisfying."

"You pose some excellent questions here, Owen." Fiona arched her eyes at him. "Regrettably, I don't know that we are any closer to finding the answers. I will say this, though, so much depends on your lot in life. When I think of our friends who do research in biological and biochemical areas, I am certain that we could never even imagine the euphoria they are experiencing about this discovery. For that matter, I could think of no way they would EVER grow bored with studying alien DNA." She maintained her eye contact with Owen as she sipped her tea.

"And rightfully so. I confess my ignorance as to what areas of biological research are currently at the forefront. Still, I know enough to say that if we had just one other biological line of evolution to compare to Earth's lines, that would offer tremendous insights to all of our own life sciences. It sounds funny, but to go from one known line of the evolution of life to two lines does more than double the input. Instead, it opens the impact of 'other life' to an infinite number of undiscovered possibilities. Frankly, I imagine that could change the entire field of biological study."

Sunlyn raised a final spoonful of ice cream and unconsciously waved it towards her mates. "I find this all downright fascinating, though I should remind you that we need to board the flight to Shanghai. To think we may be going through this Martian life presentation all over again seems unbelievable... *déjà vu* here we come. All the speculation in this world or on Mars will basically not mean a thing once the updates come down to us. In this instance, every one of our guesses is as good as anyone else's." Sunlyn finalised her words by taking the last spoonful of ice cream from her strawberry sundae.

PART FIVE

"Two possibilities exist: Either we are alone in the Universe, or we are not. Both are equally terrifying."

– Arthur C. Clarke

69

Thursday, 29 September; Metro Precinct Station, Washington DC

"I guess that about wraps it up. Thank god that you were able to at least get what you needed out of O'Keefe and Bidwill along with that Georgetown Academy IT guy..." Grimms' face looked more relaxed than it had in weeks.

"Widmeyer, sarge... Nate Widmeyer. He was their IT guy." Chandra was obviously more comfortable in front of his keyboard than talking with his colleagues.

"Was he good value?"

"Not really... Aw, well... I guess he did get me into his system. Frankly, I got more just working backward from the two boys. They were pretty good with a computer. I think one of the Georgetown IT guys mentioned there was some malware involved, but upon inspection, that didn't seem to be the case. That said, we did find a couple of Heisenbugs planted in there. I admit they had me a bit stumped until boys helped out."

"Heisenbugs?" Bradshaw scratched his head.

"Yeah, Heisenbugs." Chandra looked at their faces and realised that none of them had any clue. "Sorry. The Heisenbug gets its name from the 'Heisenberg' principle in quantum mechanics. You know..." He quickly realised from their faces that they didn't have the foggiest. "Look, the Heisenberg Uncertainty Principle simply says that in many physical systems, we can never measure things with an unlimited degree of accuracy. So, when you're writing code, the term Heisenbug relates to that. It's designed to prevent anyone from discovering a hacker messing with a program. In this case, the Heisenbug planted in a computer program is meant to either disappear or change its characteristics whenever somebody starts nosing around trying to figure out what it is. The boys put a couple of Heisenbugs in the school computer that kept that Widmeyer fellow a million miles off the trail."

"Gotcha." Maggie understood the outcome but was still shaky on the detail. "So exactly what did you accomplish after all that, Lenny?"

"Well, we took over the program and read through it a few times until I finally figured out what that Leister guy wrote. Then I used what I understood from Professor MacLucas. You did know that I had a long chat with her, yes? I took that information and made the switches back the other way. I don't profess to know a damned thing about the neurophysiological theory behind the hippocampus and the... whatever the other one is, but I know my programming. The doc seemed to think we needed to go through a cycle... let the program run with the reversal in it. By cycle, she meant an overnight run going out through the kids' SAMs and data bands. Anyway, we went overnight with it that way, and then I removed the damned program in the morning."

"What was the point? Why did Mrs MacLucas want you to go through a cycle, Lenny?" Maggie was trying to follow the rationale.

"The best I could figure, she thought that if the signals going through the SAMs and data units had turned something on or off in the kids' heads – I never got which one – that it might take a while to reverse things. I think MacLucas thought that possibly several hours after I flipped it to do the opposite, we would see some changes in the kids. Hell, I have no idea on the psychology or neurology behind it all, but I trust she was telling me the right thing."

"Well I don't know if she told you the right thing either, but just having my eyes open while driving over here this morning, there was a noticeable lack of young kids draped all over the sidewalks. I mean there were some, but I'd say the sheer volume of bodies has greatly decreased. I guess we need more quantifiable numbers before we really know, but I think you've at least defused that immediate suicide bomb to some extent, Lenny."

"And Leister, boss?" Bradshaw asked.

"The slammer... What a son-of-a-bitch! The District Attorney tells me we already have enough to put him away for a long, long time, though they still need to determine the proper charge. I'm not a lawyer, but I reckon murder one. The DA thinks the problem will be proving premeditation and that it might be impossible to do so."

"Impossible? For Christ's sakes, the kids were obviously zonked out, depressed and committing suicide." Bradshaw was indignant.

"Tell me about it... but in this country, you have to prove that beyond a reasonable doubt. The DA says it is difficult-to-impossible directly linking the program Leister wrote with anyone's death." Grimms shook his head in the negative. "I don't like it, but that's the way the system works. Look, Leister is going away for a long while no matter what... you can bet the house on that."

"MacLucas? I'm talking Mr MacLucas now.

"Damn! MacLucas was given a misdemeanour a few years back, and that didn't just go away. It had a suspended sentence with it, so that comes into play. Even more, we know that MacLucas was up to his ears in this thing. As I told you before, he had no knowledge or desire to hurt any of those kids, but his business sense was vintage 'win-at-any-cost.' Look, the son-of-a-bitch was greedy... crooked... I reckon he'll join his IT Head in the slammer for a bit."

Maggie ran her hand through her hair. "And the boys? You know, I just never got the feeling they actually knew what the hell they were doing beyond uploading the code."

"Neither does the DA, Patton. I doubt they will get off scot-free, but I also don't believe he's thinking about throwing the book at them. For starters, they'll lose their saving account from their seven-digit part-time jobs. I have no doubt the courts will take that and put it to good use. I also think they have something to answer for concerning the gun violations. You can't just use a weapon to shoot up someone's living room, scare the bejesus out of them, and then not pay some price for it. They might get off lightly if the DA decides not to prosecute under the Federal Emergency Terrorist Act. As you no doubt know, under the FETA, they treat 17-year-olds as adults, and that means a whole different set of rules. If they're lucky, they might get a slap on the hands... a serious slap, but not the full body blow they could have gotten under the terrorism laws."

"And I guess that leaves Mrs Mac, the professor. You know, I spent a lot of time talking to that woman and she strikes me as bright as can be, a very caring woman and without a violent bone in her body. But I still can't figure out why she saw fit to avoid all the ethical considerations involved with research using human subjects."

"Well, I think you are exactly right, Maggie." Grimms nodded his agreement. "What she did wasn't right. She's lucky it got stopped – at least we hope it's stopped – when it did. I have no idea what will happen to her, but I know the DA is looking into it now. Look, she didn't abide by the rules – ethical or legal – concerning academic research. The very least that's going to happen is she'll lose her tenure at George Washington University. Just think about that... I've had friends tell me a million times that the only way a college professor can lose tenure is to murder someone..."

"Damn! I think that's exactly what she might have done... whether or not she actually intended to do that." Bradshaw put his hands behind his head and leaned back.

"Well... that's for the DA to determine. Whatever though, I think she is history at George Washington University."

"I suppose you're right." Maggie looked up at the clock. "I guess we better go watch the big announcement from Mars. What do you think it's about, boss?"

"All this and you're asking me about Mars." He slapped his forehead with his open hand. "I don't know, but after the Martian bug story the other week, let's hope it's something that actually has some impact down here."

"I think they found little green men up there, boss" Bradshaw laughed.

70

Thursday, 29 September; Fenghui Tang Teahouse, Shanghai, China

"I never expected to be in Shanghai again so soon... and with Nicolás this time. I am so happy that you finally get to have blooming tea here... I'm going to miss this place." Sunlyn squeezed his hand as she was captivated at the sight of a flower bloom uncurling in a teapot of boiling water.

"It sure is every bit as mysterious and inviting as you said, honey."

"Well, you know, you needn't be strangers." Fiona was glad they were back in her home city, but sad knowing her new friends would soon be departing. "The last I heard, Washington or New York to Shanghai is only about 12,000 kilometres. How long does that take in a supersonic... maybe five hours."

Nicolás looked up from his blooming teapot. "Yes, about five hours... But Fiona, there's still this nasty little thing called work. Somehow we need to get the vacation time to come to visit."

"Vacation? Why not work time? I mean, didn't Sunlyn say you used some agricultural technique to get an assignment in Australia?"

Sunlyn laughed at Fiona's question. "You mean farmer Nicolás... how he planted the seed in his editor-in-chief's head. Well, it worked for Hawaii, and now it also worked for Australia...' She looked at Nicolás. "You know Fiona's right, honey. I could think of a million reasons you could give Norm to justify a trip back to China. As for organising trips here to Shanghai, maybe we should be more concerned about you and Owen getting together, Fiona. I think you two for sure will miss each other."

Owen smiled as he set his tea down. "Maybe, maybe not, Sunlyn. I've already spoken to our boss, Glenn, about possibilities in the GNN offices here in Shanghai. Interestingly enough, it seems there may be an opening for – now get this – a science and technology correspondent."

"Maybe the angels are watching over us, Owen." Fiona leaned over and gave him a kiss.

"Angels, huh? Farmer Nicolás and science and technology correspondent Owen..." Sunlyn's laugh touched off the group.

Kylie had a brief laugh with the rest of them and then lost her smile. "All the small talk is well and good, but I can't help but think about why we're here. In my whole life, I've never attended such a seemingly huge announcement on such short notice. This new Martian presentation seems... well, it seems we are about to learn something earth-shaking."

"Of course, you're right, Kylie. I've been a journalist my whole life and agree with you whole heatedly concerning the air of mystery and importance surrounding this press conference." Nicolás raised his teacup to his mouth.

"Let's hope it's not another biggest-story-ever announcement." Sunlyn squeezed his free hand. There were no more smiles now as the small group's mood turned more serious. "I just can't imagine what the big announcement might be. And yet to call so many here at the drop of a hat... It's difficult to believe they can ever outdo the Perth announcement... alien life found on Mars."

Owen stretched his arms out, his hands clasped together. "Who knows? What do you think, Kylie?"

"I don't know, Owen. Maybe they found more microbes. I guess that wouldn't be unexpected, but if that's what it is, I doubt there'd be another big production like this, do you think?"

Owen continued, "Nah... I doubt that, too. Do you believe that maybe your university might have had some tipoff? Isn't it strange they send you here for some unknown announcement at the expense of you not being at a conference on your own campus?"

Kylie squinted as if she were looking for a far-away answer. "I have no insight as to what inside word the University of Sydney may have. I'll say this though: it's not every day the university absorbs wasted conference fees for their academics just to send us off to more news stories. Hell, I'm an academic, not a journo... why did they want academics here, too?"

Fiona was quick to respond. "Well, it sure wasn't a blanket thing for academics. I have many colleagues at my home university just a few kilometres away who were not invited to ride the Metro line across the city to attend the news conference. Kylie's university – though thousands of kilometres away – is the same, yes?"

"Yes, that's correct, Fiona. My dean asked that I change plans specifically because of my psychology and counselling background, and since I was at the first announcement in Perth. There are two things we can be sure of... Firstly, this announcement also has to do with life on Mars. Secondly, the powers that be are anticipating a great psychological impact on the population."

"Wow." Owen had both elbows propped on the table as he rested his chin in his cupped hands. "Wow again! If your dean is aware of the expectation of 'great psychological impact', I can't begin to fathom what that could be."

"Let's not get too crazy here." Sunlyn tried to be a bit more upbeat. "Considering they found some living microorganisms there, it's quite believable that maybe more drill holes would find more life. Maybe the announcement concerns the widespread number of microbes, not of a more advanced life form."

"I don't know..." Nicolás tugged at his chin. "I mean, that certainly wouldn't require another momentous interplanetary press conference with rumours of huge psychological impacts, do you think? Wouldn't it be incredible – sad in a way – if they called the press conference to tell us it was all one big mistake and that they somehow contaminated the samples with Earth bugs?"

"Damn, Nicolás, I never thought of that! Taking back an announcement of discovery could for sure have psychological impacts on science, on journalism, on research as a whole! Damn! I hate to even think that could be the case!" Sunlyn almost looked worried. "I certainly hope that isn't the breaking news."

"Slow down... Don't take me too seriously. I'm only suggesting that it COULD be a big thing." Owen was almost apologetic. "Considering our recent conversation about just what an impact extra-terrestrial life has on the human psyche, maybe that would be of huge import. Imagine if we were forced to go back to our all-alone-in-the-universe selves again!" He whistled. "Man, would that put a huge dent in scientific research in general and in the Mars scientists specifically. That would have some psychological impacts on the population, right?"

"Well, yes and no. I mean, yes, that would have a big impact... but no, it just can't be that. I mean, they just absolutely, positively couldn't have gotten it THAT wrong." Fiona shook her head. "There's just no way..."

"Don't be too sure of that, Fiona. Consider what careless research Professor MacLucas was practising back there in Washington with her amygdala-hippocampus mumbo-jumbo. For all we know, dozens of kids could have been nudged to suicide by her thoughtless abandonment of proper scientific rules of conduct." Nicolás shook his head in disgust.

"You are correct about the off-the-rails work of MacLucas, but I don't see that with the Mars team." Owen was quick to separate a rogue Professor MacLucas from the Mars scientists. "MacLucas had a greedy husband pushing her along. The Mars team are real pros as far as I can see. They are all well-schooled in the scientific method. Talk about dedicating your life to your career – many of those people volunteered to leave their Earthly life, go to Mars and – at least with the early travellers – agreed to the prospect of never returning to Earth. Imagine... literally giving your ENTIRE

LIFE to the study of science."

"Agreed, but you can't compare them to MacLucas. MacLucas wasn't a scientist?" Nicolás eyebrows were arched high.

"Well, sure she was... is... though maybe minus the ethics of a true scientist," Owen protested. "I reckon the Mars team are fully aware of what impact their discovery will have – has had – on all of humanity. It defies belief that they would have announced this so casually. I think maybe they have found some fossils that might allow them to date some of the Martian life... even if the fossil find is not of these particular microorganisms."

"Now that's an interesting thought, Owen. Maybe they did find fossils... maybe of higher forms of life..." Fiona warmed to his speculation.

"But on Mars?" Nicolás was quick to interject. "I happily confess to not being an astronomer, geologist or planetary scientist, but all that we have heard over decades now is that Mars just wasn't liveable enough for long enough that any life much beyond microorganisms could have developed."

"Listen to us, going on with speculation. We'll find out soon enough, and then I imagine we'll laugh at these ideas." Sunlyn refused to venture another guess. "Still, I can't get MacLucas out of my head. I am outraged about Professor MacLucas's ignoring the wellbeing of those kids, though. I mean forget that we were involved with this, at least as far as the two boys shooting up our apartment. I've been following the whole Eights story for months now. I have no doubt there's been an uptick in their 'regressive' behaviour and the incidence of suicide, even group suicide."

"For sure you are correct, Sunlyn, but don't think for one minute that MacLucas's crazy scheme is the only input these kids have had. I must remind you – remind all of you – that these behaviours have been brewing for several decades now."

Sunlyn knew where Kylie was going. "Solastalgia?"

"Well sure, solastalgia... and all that goes with it, too. The explosion of population. The global sense of irrelevance our children increasingly feel. The collapse of norms, values, institutions... We'd be fools to think these impacts are somehow less than that of hacking SAMs and data units. Even with this whole crazy notion of initiating electrical signals into the brain, we aren't talking about drastically changing behaviour since the kids are already prone to anxiety, to depression. I don't deny that, at least not in theory. MacLucas's programming electrical signals into the brain is possible, but the reality is that we have had so much greater input to these kids' brains through our action as a society."

"Or inaction as a society." Owen held onto Fiona's hand as he glanced towards her. "I can never get Fiona's story of John Calhoun and his mouse utopia out of my head. I remind myself time and again that we can't make direct comparisons between humans and mice, but for Christ's sakes, so much does parallel his experiment. More and more hopeless... more and more out of control..."

"Please, Owen, don't fall into that trap. Mice are mice, and humans are humans... we are so much more mentally complicated."

"Obviously, we are more complicated, but there is still some reason that you present those experiments in your psychology lectures. I haven't been able to get that image you painted of Calhoun's 'beautiful ones' out of my mind. I just think of what you told us about how he observed those 'beautiful ones' totally detached from the rest of their mouse society.

"Consider our youth. Haven't so many of our kids completely lost touch with what we think of as normal adolescent behaviour? I mean holy hell; we're even reading studies about so many kids losing any interest in sex!" Owen had definitely taken his friend's words to heart. "At home, we keep seeing hundreds... thousands of kids lying around the streets and slumped over park benches? Are they the human version of the beautiful ones?"

Fiona shook her head. "Please, Owen... Of course, we can learn from Calhoun and can draw some knowledge from that, but where mice kind of just do what mice do, humans actually think about things." Fiona had heard these questions many times before. "Mice react, people contemplate and then act. In this example, kids take it all in and respond accordingly. I agree with Kylie – the entire milieu of social, political, economic environmental and technical developments all come together to influence behaviour."

"I admit that I see both sides to the Calhoun discussion here, Owen and Fiona. As long as we seem to be reviewing the happenings of the past few weeks, I would still like my GNN partner here to clarify the idea of uncertainty in science. You remember you went through this with me concerning the Clathrate Gun Hypothesis, Owen."

"Of course I do, Sunlyn. I think we talked about that a couple of weeks ago over drinks right here at the Shanghai Waldorf Astoria."

"Yep, that's the conversation."

Fiona, trying to switch gears from the Calhoun experiments, asked, "the Clathrate Gun Hypothesis? Please remind me again."

Sunlyn continued, "Sorry. I know you at least heard about the idea of the clathrate gun releasing vast amounts of methane gas from the presentation at the Global Summit. I asked Owen about how scientists could get it all so wrong, and he told me we need to give it time to see whether or not they had it right... By right – I mean correct here – were the scientists right as far as the methane release after the meteor impact?

"Maybe I'm overly simplistic, but I still wonder whatever happened to that old approach to science – you know, where we discovered something and then collected data showing us what happened. If no data support what we think we found, we must abandon the hypothesis and move on to a new one. I fear that we too often just carry on an academic exercise rather than following the science where it may lead. Am I on the right track here?" Sunlyn was still shaky on the lack of understanding about what *Thánatos* might have triggered. "I guess what I'm saying is that I want proof!"

"Don't we all." Owen let out a sigh. "I remember I had a chemistry teacher once who always reminded us that if you want THE TRUTH, you need to go to a minister or a politician. Religion deals in 'truth' and politicians deal in 'truth'... at least their version of the truth, whatever that may mean. Scientists, on the other hand, deal with evidence... evidence that supports a hypothesis or weakens a hypothesis. If and when a hypothesis is weakened enough, science will abandon it and replace it with another hypothesis that they can test. In that respect, there is no absolute TRUTH, no absolute PROOF, at least in science. Rather, science always deals with a process... with the scientific method. That method always attempts to increase our confidence in just exactly what we know and what we think.

"When Marconi applied Maxwell's theory of electromagnetism as it related to radio waves, he applied it to a wireless telegraph system in the 1890s, but that didn't magically produce the holovision units that we use today. When Sir Alexander Fleming discovered the first antibiotic in a mould containing penicillin in the 1920s, he didn't all of a sudden give the world 'the answer' to infectious disease. When Watson and Crick announced their discovery of the structure of DNA in the 1950s that didn't miraculously cure genetic diseases through gene editing and CRISPR technology. Science doesn't happen that way... Science is sometimes slow... sometimes boring... but it is ALWAYS methodical.

"I fear beating the proverbial dead horse, but I must echo the words of Chief Scientist of the United Nations, Dr René Riemann, in his opening talk to the World Holistic Summit the other week. Sir Isaac Newton may be the greatest scientific mind the world has ever known, yet it was he who once said that 'If I have seen further it is only by standing on the shoulders of giants.' Marconi, Maxwell, Fleming, Crick and Watson were giants, but they – we as a species – need other giants to learn from them and to carry on. Solastalgia, the clathrate release of methane, whatever great achievement is stimulated by the discovery of alien life on Mars... the researchers and thinkers behind those momentous discoveries and constructs are the giants upon whose shoulders tomorrow's scientists must stand."

"I am fascinated by this conversation and almost apologise for saying the obvious, but I believe we are just about ready to hear from some of those giants." Fiona began to stand as she noted the time. "We'd better get over to the university before the news conference begins."

71

Thursday, 29 September; Fudan University Xianghui Auditorium, Shanghai, China

People were still filing into the big auditorium located several kilometres away from Fiona's own university. She still felt as though she were on her home ground and acted the part of a host. "Fudan University is the most prestigious university in Shanghai, and I say that with all deference to my own esteemed Shanghai Jiao Tong University across the city. My friends have updated me on the procedures, and basically, everything will run as it did in Perth – same time, same rules, same random draw for journalists asked to be sequestered and then ask questions. I am surprised though that no one seems to know exactly what the announcement will be about. Speculation is all over the place." Fiona noticed the lights had dimmed somewhat. "I believe the university president will be out any minute now..."

* * *

Misha Romanov's face filled the big screen in the Shanghai theatre as well as so many other screens viewed by billions of people across planet Earth. "Greeting to everyone gathered there in Shanghai at Fudan University and to those of you watching this all-around Earth and to our fellow extraplanetary colleagues at Moon Base One. I thank President Zhang Li Shen of Fudan University for her kind words. Likewise, thank you to our Director and friend, Dr Sam Tan. I appreciate his eloquent words of thanks to our staff here at Gale Crater Outpost and to our biological team at Alpha

Colony, but I must also credit all of our Martian colleagues as well as the Earthside support staff. The work we do here on Mars could not be done without all of your contributions. Being so many millions of kilometres from home necessitates that every one of us must contribute to the whole. That said, all our accomplishments, our discoveries and even our survival must be shared jointly.

"We will be broadcasting this presentation to you from here at the Gale Crater Outpost located south of the Martian equator some 2,800 kilometres away from our colleagues up at Alpha Colony. Being an outpost, we have limited creature comforts here and have done what we could to spruce up our humble staff room." Misha attempted to keep a modicum of cheerfulness in her introduction.

"I would like to take a minute to introduce our small Gale Crater team of seven research scientists to you. I am Misha Romanov, nominally the coordinator of Gale Crater Outpost and a geologist. I am also one of the original 8 astronauts who arrived on Mars on Mission 1 back in 2025. Joe Robinson is an American engineer and also one of the original astronauts sent on Mr Jacob Jacobi's first mission to Mars." The camera panned to Joe, and he briefly put his right hand up to acknowledge her words. "This is Keegan Botha, a South African geophysicist who has been here on Mars for 13 years now, arriving on Mission 4. Our chemist is Siti Jokowi. Siti is our colleague from Malaysia who has been on Mars for 8 years, arriving on Mission 6. Our biologist, Nigella Dougan, lived and studied in England and is our Head of Life Systems. Over here is our head of IT, AI and all things computer-oriented, Arya Abass originally from Iran. Both Nigella and Arya arrived on Mission 8, which landed 4 years ago. Finally, our rookie Martian is geologist Lochie Greenbank from Perth, Western Australia. Lochie has only been with us for about a month now. I would be remiss if I didn't thank both of our support personal here at the outpost. Though they are not directly involved with the science here at Gale, we could never do what we do without them. Thank you to Paul Westfield and Clarissa Kowalczyk."

"I'd like to ask Nigella to take it from here. Nigella is our credentialled biologist at Gale Crater. No doubt, she will be familiar to you because you heard from her the other week at the Alpha Colony announcement concerning the microorganisms found near there. Nigella…"

Nigella's face filled the screen. "Good morning, good afternoon, good evening. I realise you may think it impossible to bring you news of any greater importance than the discovery of alien microorganisms from the surface of another planet." She paused briefly. "Actually, I am here to tell you exactly that: we have made an astonishing discovery right here at Gale Crater. On Thursday, 1 September 2044, Siti Jokowi and Keegan Botha were on a routine surface excursion exploring a series of lava tubes that riddle the exterior walls of Gale Crater. While inside tube 14B, Dr Jokowi noticed a reflection off a shiny object on the floor of the cavern and, upon inspection, determined that it appeared to be a medallion of some sort. She collected the sample and returned it to the outpost…"

* * *

The presentation continued for nearly 45 minutes with each team member contributing their part in the joint discovery. Joe went on at length, explaining how they systematically explored the lava tubes indicated by ground-penetrating radar and other remote sensing devices. Keegan described the details of finding the 182 bags, 317 medallions, 9,117 transparent disks and 5 cubes and how they used the skellies to transport the artifacts back to the outpost. Siti recounted her laboratory work on the artifacts determining composition as well as speculating on purpose and age. She went into detail concerning the discovery of DNA in the 5D disks, and the elements they had determined were human-like remains within the medallions. Siti also discussed the team's conjecture that the medallions and transparent disks must have been an integral part of a burial ceremony practised by the aliens to honour their deceased.

Arya described how he deduced that the transparent disks were data stores utilising the 5D process allowing for such high-density storage. He went on to explain that they appeared to contain the downloaded contents of each individual alien brain, their personalities and memories, all encoded and preserved. He also described how he and his AI program were able to decipher a workable method to read the exhaustive wealth of information describing the aliens, their language, culture and history stored in the five cubes. He then showed a representative sample of the alien photographs the team had reviewed here in the outpost staff room over the previous few days.

With that, Arya advanced the presentation to the next slide showing the alien spaceship in orbit around the death-cloud-cloaked planet. "Our AI software translates what the alien's called 'families' into what we would call countries or nations. From what we have unravelled in the short time we've had to work on this, I believe it is safe to say that alien members from both 'nations' opted to flee from planet Gothos since that presented their only means of survival. We have no detail at this point, but it seems as though the stronger group went to Baylock since it was far more habitable and therefore desirable than Zar. The second faction did flee to Zar, though that planet was much colder, much harsher and much less hospitable to life.

"We have now seen dozens of projections of the group of

aliens who escaped to Zar. This photo is representative of all of them." A slide appeared. Almost immediately the 700 or 800 people in attendance at the Fudan University venue spontaneously took one deep breath very nearly in unison. The image showed the faces of a group of individuals that appeared to be a family unit with two adults and three children. There were undoubtedly billions of more people reacting similarly to these photographic and holographic images around all of Earth. The most surprising thing about this image was just how 'normal' the aliens all looked. These extraterrestrials were not only of very familiar humanoid-like form, but they appeared to be identical to any light-skinned, African descendant humans.

"We surmise it is one of the many family units that went to Zar. This next image illustrates another of the competing nation of aliens who were typically representative of those who travelled to Baylock." Another projection could be seen of smiling adults and children identical in outward appearance to African Earthlings with much darker skin than the Zar aliens. The low volume buzz of the Shanghai auditorium audience conveyed the astonishment of those intently watching.

"Please bear with me as I present to you a narrative that our Gale Crater team believes can be deduced from all that we have seen so far. This information has been extracted from what we think is meant to be a summary of the historical records stored in the five cubes the aliens left behind. I cannot emphasise enough that this only scratches the surface and much more study needs to be done."

Arya gulped down a breath of air. "The brown and black skin colours seem obvious – from all we can determine, Gothos was closer to their central star than our Earth is to Sol. The dark pigmentation would have offered significant protection from ultraviolet radiation damage and all the subsequent pathologies that arise from that exposure. For the sake of simplicity, I will call the aliens who settled Baylock the Blacks and those who tried to colonize Zar the Browns.

"We think the Blacks may have been successful in colonising Baylock, but we have no direct knowledge of the Blacks at this point. The history we have discovered from the data cubes on Mars was written by the Browns. We have learned that the Browns initially landed a small group to establish a colony on Baylock, but the bulk of the Browns continued on to establish settlements on Zar. Conceivably, the aliens thought that settling two planets would double the chances of survival and better assure the continuation of the species. Regrettably, there are many indications that the Blacks and Browns simply could not live peacefully together on any home planet. I freely admit that we – I – may be projecting our own hopes, our own fears into all of this interpretation.

"Do we have any numbers? Through deduction, we believe hundreds-to-a-few-thousand were left on both Baylock and Zar. The Browns indicate they landed at most a few hundred of their family members on Baylock, but that none of the Blacks family attempted to settle on Zar. The Browns spent several years on Zar – we can find no exact length of time recorded so far. The Zar conditions were just too harsh. Many Browns died there, and the remaining ones decided they had to go to Baylock. We lose the story from there and, at this point, have no idea if any Browns were successful in travelling back to Baylock. At this point, the history contained in the cubes ends with the small group of Browns on Zar.

"I do have two final slides to show here, and we will then follow the same procedure all these interplanetary press conferences do and take questions submitted to us by the randomly selected journalists."

Arya's next photo flashed onto the big screen. "This is an

orbital image of Baylock." The image was of Earth, the radiant, blue and green ball so familiar to them all. There could be no coincidence, no mistake here... All the familiar continents were easily recognisable, save for a few small shoreline variations. North America was connected from Alaska to Siberia across the Bering Sea and the Great Lakes were noticeably missing, but it all looked strikingly familiar. His final picture showed Earth-Moon from close enough in that Luna showed all the familiar craters. There could be little doubt any longer that the Earth-Moon system was quite obviously the same as Baylock.

* * *

Misha's face filled the screen. "That concludes our prepared presentation. All that we currently have processed will be available on Skynet 4 after this press conference. As has been the precedent in previous interplanetary press conferences, we will now take questions that have been submitted to us in the past few hours by a randomly selected group of journalists from around the world. Please preface your question by identifying yourself and your affiliation."

"Thank you for that incredible presentation. I am Luz Alvarez of the *Havana Periódico*. I realise there has been far too little time to learn the alien history in any detail, but when we see the orbital image of Baylock, it seems apparent that Baylock and Earth are one and the same. Is there any supporting evidence at all that the aliens were on Earth somewhere during this time?

"Thank you for that excellent question, Ms Alvarez, and I will attempt to answer as best as I can. Thanks also for recognising how little time Arya or any of us have had to extract information, let alone to somehow interpret it. I have no doubt the five data cubes will be explored for decades if not more by scientists and historians across Earth. I also have no doubt that what is learned of the alien history from the cubes will point archaeologists in the right direction to find the evidence you mention, should it exist. It is so early at this stage to draw any conclusions. The purpose of this presentation has been to inform all of humanity about this discovery, but it is also a call for help. As a species, we need to learn as much as we can about the aliens as is possible. I will leave this there right now, but your question will no doubt need a generation or more to be answered to even a minimum of our satisfaction."

"Good evening, Dr Romanov. I am Ling Chin from the CCHV, that's *China Central Holovision.* You began your presentation by saying the first discovery was made on 1 September. Can you explain to us why it took four weeks to release this news to the public? Though the news a few weeks ago concerning simple life found on Mars seemed to be the biggest story of all time, that pales compared to finding intelligent life in our solar system. By looking at the dates given, you people on Mars must have known about the news of intelligent aliens at the press conference announcing the microorganisms. Why did it take four weeks to reveal this?"

"Thank you for your question, Ling Chin. When the discovery was first made, we were very uncertain as to exactly what it was that we actually found. True enough, it seemed to be an artifact created by an intelligent life form, but there were so many questions that we just didn't know what to report. Because of that, we increased the pace of our surface explorations in the hope of finding more supporting evidence. Fortunately, this led to so many more finds. Frankly Ms Chin, we barely had time to bring our discoveries in from the surface and make the most incomplete analysis of what we actually had here. I apologise if it seems as though we waited a long time to pass on this incredible finding to you. We moved on it as quickly as we could, and yet deliberately enough that we could give a fuller report on just what we had found. Our intention was never to hide anything from all of you back on Earth."

"Hello to our Martian scientists. I am Jabulani Chetty, and I report for the SABC, the *South African Broadcasting Corporation*. Have you been able to draw any connection between the microorganisms discovered near Alpha Colony on 22 August and the intelligent alien life that produced the artifacts first discovered on 2 September near Gale Crater?"

"I will speak to that." Misha leaned forward as the camera focused on her face. "There is no direct or indirect relationship between the two discoveries, Mr Chetty. Humans have wondered about other life in the universe for as far back as we could even conceive of the feasibility of other worlds away from Earth. Over all of that time, we have questioned the prospect of the existence of other living creatures. As amazing as it seems that these two separate discoveries of life were made less than two weeks apart, it is one hundred per cent an incredible coincidence. The two discoveries are totally unrelated.

"I might add though that at this point, we have a high degree of confidence that the Alpha Colony microorganisms are indeed Martian life. We have no confidence at all that the intelligent aliens are Martians though. As far as we can ascertain, the intelligent aliens that are the subject of this presentation were NOT from Mars, rather they were from the planet of Gothos that Arya told you about earlier. Now as to whether or not the aliens evolved on Gothos or settled there from somewhere else originally, we have no way of telling at this time."

Nigella spoke up. "I'm sorry Misha, are you done with your answer?"

She nodded yes to her. "I am."

"Please let me excuse myself and say something before the next question. Obviously, because of the time delay between Mars and Earth, we are all aware of the fact that journalists are not able to ask follow-up questions. For that reason, I will answer a follow-up question I am certain the previous journalist, Mr Chetty from South Africa, would have asked if the laws of physics had permitted." Nigella smiled. "Mr Chetty, I am sure you wanted to follow up by asking just what the initial origin of the intelligent alien life could have been? As Misha just said, we are unanimous in thinking the evidence of intelligence we have found did not evolve on Mars. For that matter, we don't believe intelligent life COULD have evolved on Mars. I want to also reiterate her conjecture that at this time, we have no idea what the origin of the intelligent aliens might be.

"In all honesty, we are operating with a lack of data here. We are all agreed that there is zero indication that Mars had even the remotest conditions hospitable to life for the billions of years we have had on Earth. Realistically, it is incomprehensible that intelligent life could have evolved here on Mars from the simple microorganisms you asked about.

"I reiterate, we here are all in agreement that our aliens are NOT from Mars. We are fairly certain that they travelled from Gothos or, most likely, Venus in our terminology. We can NOT say with any degree of confidence that if Gothos is Venus, or that they evolved there. For all we know, they could have evolved on a planetary system that could be light-years away from us. We are hopeful we have the information within the data cubes needed to make that determination, but that research is yet to be done. So there is no confusion, I want to emphasise that at this point, we can NOT state unequivocally that the aliens evolved on Gothos, only that they inhabited that planet for some unknown time before it met with an extinction event."

"Thanks." Misha nodded to Nigella before the next questioner was spliced in.

"Hello, Dr Romanov. My name is Oliver Bartlett with *The New Zealand Herald*. From what you have presented to us here, we must accept the fact that Gothos is our own solar system's Venus, Zar is Mars, and then, of course, Baylock must be Earth. Are we to accept the fact that astrophysicists may have had it wrong for such a long time in leading us to believe that Venus was never hospitable to life, let alone hospitable long enough for intelligent life to evolve there?"

"I'll take that, please." The camera panned to Lochie. "I'm sorry to be repetitive, but we have data stored on the cubes left by the aliens that would fill millions of books, and I mean that quite literally. None of us pretends to be able to answer all of your questions, so I certainly echo Misha in calling on the scientific community of all of the Earth to help investigate these discoveries. We can say this much, however. As a species, humanity has learned so very much, but please never mistake that accomplishment by confusing 'learning much' to 'knowing everything.' There is so much that we do NOT know. This recognition of our incomplete knowledge must be included in any conjecture on our part.

"What does all that mean? Well, we base our modelling on physical principles, on gravitationally calculations, on Earth-based biochemistry and other natural laws in which we have strong confidence. That does not mean our understanding is perfect. As for Venus, I repeat what my colleague, Nigella Dougan, just told you. Though we are not certain that Gothos and Venus are one and the same planet, there is reason to believe that just might be the case.

"Now then, was our understanding of Venus so wrong? Let me try speaking to that by first telling you that I am a geologist, not an astronomer or cosmologist. I am sure those who dedicate their lives to studying these disciplines will be more than anxious to pour through these data. As for our understanding or misunderstanding about Venus and the origins of our solar system, you must realise our knowledge has limits. Possibly we overestimated the energy output of our sun throughout the past several billion years. In the case of Venus, it is possible that modelling of its early atmosphere was incorrect. We always thought there were bodies of water on the Venusian surface early in its history, but not to the extent we see in these images. There is so much we just don't know.

"Remember Mr Bartlett, as of today, the total surface exploration of Venus is limited to a half-dozen or so *Venera* landings conducted by the Russians some 75 years ago. The aggregate time they spent gathering data in total is less than a day or two for the simple reason that the Venusian heat and atmospheric pressure destroyed the probes within minutes or – at best – hours. No one has successfully landed a craft there since *Venera*. This paucity of data samples from Venus makes speculation very difficult. Naturally, this could lead to all sorts of errors resulting in what may be large discrepancies of surface temperatures from our current calculations. Add to this the whole *Ghia* hypothesis that argues life itself has various feedback loops in ecosystems, and it's pretty obvious that Venus absolutely could have been hospitable to life and evolution at some time in the past. For that matter, if Gothos and Venus are the same planet, then our human understanding of this part of our solar system has been incredibly incorrect for a hundred-and-fifty or two-hundred years."

"Liam Fairchild, *The Guardian*. Can you tell us any more about the lead up to the global war on Gothos? Do we have any idea how that happened?

"Arya, would you take this one?" Misha nodded towards him.

"It became apparent at some time before the final conflict broke out on Gothos that environmental degradation had passed the point of no return. This is such a familiar story to us today because quite regrettably, we are experiencing a very similar degradation on Earth. In short, there seemed to be no agreement amongst the aliens that any of them, Brown or Black, willingly admitted any responsibility for their technological impact on the ecosystems of Gothos."

Arya paused, took a deep breath and ran his open hand over his mouth. "Frankly sir, I have had only two or three days to study this, and I admit that the narrative I have given here has shaken me quite personally. I apologise if my emotions catch up with me." He exhaled noticeably. "The aliens paralleled us in their use of fossil fuels, of dumping incredible amounts of carbon dioxide into the atmosphere, of sea levels and temperatures going up and of the global temperatures skyrocketing. It's very difficult to put times on these events. When you consider that the entire life of our solar system is 4.5 or 4.6 billion years, a few hundred thousand years here or there is practically nothing. That said, *Homo sapiens* only appeared on our planet some 165,000 or 175,000 years ago. That is very much less than an error bar in graphs we look at regarding many astrophysical events.

"One thing we can say about Gothos with a high degree of certainty: the alien residents there undoubtedly experienced what we refer to as ecoanxiety, as solastalgia. In the short time we have had to explore even the bare minimum of the history contained in the data cubes, there is a reference to explosive population growth, to excess resource exploitation, to global competition among 'families' which again, we interpret as nations. Part of the historical summary text refers to the aliens losing place, losing a sense of belonging, losing involvement with the planet's ecosystem. Somehow, it seems the population became separated from the ecosystem in which it lived.

"Frankly, it seems one of the most remarkable discoveries I have had so far concerning the aliens is just how much they seem to behave like humans, think like humans, feel as we humans feel... The ambivalence of their leaders, the alienation of their youth, the crumbling of their social and political institutions... Unnerving as it is, the aliens were not strangers to violence against one another in the form of war, or to violence against self in the form of suicide. In the end, the aliens expressed this anger and aggression to the extreme in the form of military hostilities. Sadly enough, Gothos reached a point where it was on a glide path to destruction one way or the other. If the aliens hadn't destroyed their planet overtly by using nuclear weapons, they had already set in place the inevitable destruction of their planet's ecosystems by social and environmental neglect."

"Leyla González, *Telemundo News*. In hearing Dr Nigella Dougan speak about the early DNA analysis of the alien burial medallions or from the transparent disks, you seem to indicate that the aliens had a very high content of what appears to be human DNA or vice versa... it was unclear in your presentation. Does this mean that the alien DNA is different at all from *Homo sapiens*? And if I may, what does this say about whether aliens are mostly human, or humans are mostly alien?"

"Thank you for your question, Ms González." Nigella looked right into the camera. "I apologise Ms González. I have not been unclear because of any reprehensible plot to withhold information from you. I am unclear because I am not a geneticist and freely admit I need a great deal of help from the experts to make sense of all these data. Surely you will understand that after nearly twenty years of scientific study on Mars, no one ever thought it imperative to include a team of geneticists or even molecular biologists out here. We are fortunate to have an array of analytical tools at our disposal, but we need to communicate the data to colleagues back on

Earth to maximise the investigation of this information. Until today as we share these discoveries with the entire world, this has not been possible. From my point of view, I hope that one of the most significant outcomes from this presentation will be our call to you for help. As Misha, Arya, Lochie... all of my colleagues have previously mentioned, we need the input of the entire science community.

"I do know this, though; we share DNA with other species in our *Hominidae* family, and we most certainly share a great deal of DNA with others in our *Homo* genus. I am making no great revelation today when I say we have known for the better part of a century that *Homo sapiens* did interbreed with other hominins including *Neanderthals*, *Denisovans*, and *Homo heidelbergensis*.

"As to what degree aliens and *Homo sapiens* are related, I am not in any position to answer. This is a complicated question since short of evolving within the same environment, there must be zero chance we would be related to the aliens. But the genomic evidence is perplexing and beyond my understanding.

"For that matter, it seems a moot point right now pinpointing any dates for the alien samples, so I can't speak at all as to whether we predated the aliens or vice versa. I can say this though, it seems apparent that there is a substantial level of overlap in our *Homo sapiens* genetic makeup with our alien relatives, possibly more than what we know of our overlap with *Neanderthal* and *Denisovan* genes. Frankly, Ms González, I am reporting what we have found and at the same time telling you it appears to be impossible. I must leave this to the scientific community back on Earth to try to decipher.

"I don't mean to be trite, Ms González, but I find it amazing that for thousands of years back to biblical days we humans have dreamed of encounters with aliens. In the most unexpected twist in the millennia-long quest to find aliens, I believe we have finally found them. Amazingly, the aliens seem to be us!"

There was silence in the staff room at Gale Crater Outpost. There was silence in the Xianghui Auditorium at Fudan University. It was quite probable that most of planet Earth was silent for a full minute or more. Finally, Misha stepped back into the picture. "That was very profound, Nigella... Along with everyone else, I am sure I need time to digest the implications of your hypothesis. I do think we need to complete our press conference and conclude with the last question scheduled here."

"Good day. I am Reggie Cooper from the *Los Angeles Times*. I direct this question at any and all of you willing to take it on. There has been much talk here on Earth over the past several decades concerning the plight of our own planet in terms of the potential for another great mass extinction event. We have just been through the trauma of the *Thánatos* impact and the global danger that it still represents to us if the Clathrate Gun Hypothesis proves to be true. In light of this possibility and your discoveries up there, can we Earthlings take away anything from our understanding of what the aliens' faced? Do you believe we can somehow learn from their experience to help us avoid the Sixth Great Dying event – I believe it has been referred to as the Anthropocene Extinction – that many predict for Earth in the very near future?"

Lochie raised his hand, indicating that he'd like to answer the question. "That's an exceptional question, Mr Cooper, though I fear you may not like my answer. I imagine you all know what he is asking here, but quickly, let me say that Earth has gone through at least five periods of great dying or global mass extinction events. Palaeontologists have found much supporting evidence for these events in the fossil record. These dying events do not occur at any set frequency, and the exact times cannot be marked in any precise way because of the difficulty in dating events accurately.

"The first identifiable event was about 450 million years ago, and, in total, there are five recognised periods in which high percentages – between 70% and 90% – of all the species on Earth at that time simply disappeared. The causes of these great dyings have been speculated on and may include catastrophic events such as multiple volcanic eruptions, cosmic rays, solar energy variations, ice ages and asteroid impacts.

"The most recent of these disasters was the one you are possibly familiar with, the so-call the K-T mass extinction. This is so named because it happened timewise at the boundary between the Cretaceous – K – and the Tertiary – T – geological periods. Lest you are curious, the 'K' comes from the German word for Cretaceous, *Kreide*. That extinction occurred about 66 million years ago and was directly related to a giant asteroid impact that slammed into the Earth at Chicxulub on Mexico's Yucatán Peninsula. That asteroid made *Thánatos* look small since it was 10 or 15 kilometres in diameter and weighed possibly a thousand times more than *Thánatos*. Over 75% of the species on Earth died out during that Fifth Great Extinction. That event wiped out nearly all of the dinosaurs, save for early crocodilians, turtles and the flying ancestors from which our modern-day birds have evolved.

"Many present-day geologists talk of any 'Sixth Great Dying' being designated as the Anthropocene Extinction Event after the name given twenty-some years ago to our current geological epoch. The Anthropocene received that name because so much global atmospheric, oceanographic, geologic and ecologic change is now predominantly marked by human intervention. You may be aware of the fact that the root word for Anthropocene is *anthrop*, the Greek word for human.

"Mr Cooper, in response to your question, I certainly hope our species can learn from the aliens. For that matter, should the aliens prove to definitively be our ancestors at any level, it will be fair to say we would need to update our numbers. Considering the Earth's five previous extinctions, the Venusian extinction and the disappearance of intelligent aliens from Mars, the Anthropocene Extinction would not equate to the Sixth Great Dying. In fact, should all that we have found prove true, our current planetwide plight might just be the Great Dying Event number eight."

ABOUT THE AUTHOR

Born in Pottstown, Pennsylvania, Dan earnt his bachelor's degrees in Illinois and Hawaii, master's in Rhode Island and PhD at Curtin University in Perth, Australia.

While looking around each corner to see what beckons next, Dan and his wife Karen have embraced each move from the big city to remote community living. In his books, Dan leads you on a journey where critical thinking explores current scientific questions with attention to the physical environment in which his characters inhabit. *EIGHT* is his fourth published novel, dealing with the relationship and impact of the environment on ordinary people.

Having spent a career as a university lecturer and a high school teacher, Dan believes that a good educator must be a good storyteller. The constructivist educational theory asserts that new knowledge must be built upon the learner's existing constructs, and storytelling enhances this process. With a formal background in the sciences and academic research, the reader can be assured that his fictional writing is firmly based on a foundation of scientific reality.

Dan's previous novels include *DREAMS, FEVER, PROOF!* and *Back to Paradise*, all available from Amazon.com.

Dan and Karen live with pups Bomber and Rocky in Perth, Western Australia, always with a keen eye for what is around the next bend.

Check Dan's website at www.churach.com

Made in the USA
Middletown, DE
07 June 2020

96379373R00281